ANGEL OF THE NORTH

Nurse Marie Larsen has grown used to the challenges of keeping Hull Royal Infirmary running during the Germans' attacks on her city. Amidst the sudden power cuts and blown out windows, and with wounded civilians pouring into the hospital at each new attack, she always thanks her lucky stars that the latest bomb didn't have her name on it. But when a fresh wave of bombings tears Hull apart, tragedy strikes close to home. With her mother now critically ill in hospital, and her father missing, Marie will have some tough decisions to make if she is to keep her younger brother and sister safe.

ANGEL OF THE NORTH

ANGEL OF THE NORTH

by

Annie Wilkinson

Magna Large Print Books
Long Preston, North Yorkshire,
BD23 4ND, England.

British Library Cataloguing in Publication Data.

Wilkinson, Annie
Angel of the north.

A catalogue record of this book is
available from the British Library

ISBN 978-0-7505-3929-6

First published in Great Britain by Simon & Schuster, 2013

Cover illustration © Collaboration JS by arrangement with
Arcangel Images

Published in Large Print 2014 by arrangement with
Simon & Schuster UK Ltd.

Magna Large Print is an imprint of Library Magna Books Ltd.

Printed and bound in Great Britain by
T.J. (International) Ltd., Cornwall, PL28 8RW

This book is dedicated to the firemen, engineers, rescue workers and medical and nursing staff of Wartime Hull.

Acknowledgements

I am indebted to:

Emma Lowth, my editor,
Judith Murdoch, my agent,

Authors:
T. Geraghty, *A North East Coast Town*
Rev. Philip Graystone, *The Blitz on Hull*
Esther Baker, *A City in Flames* – A firewoman's recollections of the Hull Blitz, which I highly recommend.
Dr Barry C. Hovell, *The Hull Royal Infirmary 1782–1982*
Dan Billany, *The Trap* – a novel, also highly recommended.

Rex Needle, writer, researcher and photographer of Bourne, Lincolnshire, for his impressive website and CD. The people of Bourne housed 900 evacuees during the Second World War, keeping them safe from the bombing in Hull. Most of the children remained until the war ended and many made lifelong friendships. The infamous Mortons of my story are complete fictions, and bear no resemblance whatsoever to anyone in Bourne.

Brian Pears of Gateshead, for permission to use information from his very informative website, North-East Diary, Bridget Renwick, Alumni Relations Administrator of Hymers College, for unstinting help with the wartime history of Hymers.

Jean, of Keel Road, for sharing her memories.

All the volunteers at the Carnegie Heritage Centre in Hull.

The staff of Hull History Centre.

Chapter 1

31 March–1 April 1941

At the sound of the bombers Marie Larsen froze. The ominous thrum-thrumming of their engines was rapidly followed by the rattle of anti-aircraft guns. The doctor glanced up from cutting down through layers of fat in search of a suitable vein in his patient's well-covered ankle.

'You stay where you are, Nurse,' he said. 'We might just have enough time to get this job finished.'

Typical of Dr Steele, Marie thought. She lifted her vivid blue eyes to his face. Just managing to keep the tremor out of her voice, she said: 'I wasn't going anywhere, Doctor,' and turning to her patient gave him what she hoped was a look of reassurance that she was sorely in need of herself.

'Soon be done,' she told him. 'A couple of pints of blood and you'll feel like a new man.'

The words were barely out of her mouth when the night sky was lit by the eerie white light of chandelier flares. Next, incendiaries would come clattering down and bursting into flames. High explosives and parachute mines would surely follow. With a mounting sense of dread, and praying that none of the bombs would hit the infirmary, Marie concentrated on holding the retractors steady.

She had to live. All her fondest hopes, her most

glorious visions of becoming Charles's wife, of presenting him with his firstborn child, of becoming the mother of a large and happy family, had to be fulfilled. Now every time she heard the hum of a plane she thought of Margaret, killed stone dead in James Reckitt Avenue during just such a raid as this.

Killed! It was the first time anyone really close to Marie had died, and the shock of it had knocked her sideways. She still couldn't believe it – except that she surely did, because it had robbed her forever of that 'it can't happen to me' sort of confidence. If it could happen to Margaret it could happen to Marie herself and now, as soon as the sky began to vibrate with the thrum, thrum, thrum of German aircraft, she trembled.

The patient was not reassured by her words of encouragement. His fleshy cheeks were pale, and his eyes rolled skywards. Sweat stood in large beads on his forehead and upper lip. 'How much longer?' he moaned.

'Not much,' she said, forcing a show of confidence and raising her voice above the noise of planes and guns. 'We'll be all right. Only the good die young.'

Through a gap in the screens she saw those patients who could, taking shelter under their beds, the other two nurses in the ward along with them. The impulse to do the same was nearly irresistible.

The doctor gave her a sardonic smile. 'I take it you're not good, then, Nurse?'

'Not too good to live, I hope,' she said, steadying herself to hold the incision open, now with the rattle of incendiaries and the ack! ack! ack! of anti-aircraft guns sounding in her ears.

The doctor had a vein. As he inserted the cannula the screech of a bomb preceded an earth-shattering blast, shaking the floor beneath their feet.

'Keep calm,' Dr Steele insisted. 'I want this job out of the way. I don't want to have to do this again.'

Marie glanced up at his lined old face, its expression quite impassive. Dr Steele? Dr Nerves-of-steel, rather. Either he was very brave, or completely lacking in imagination. He had no bedside manner, there was not much sympathy to be had from him, but he was a good man to be with in a crisis. He left you very little time to think of the people being bombed, or to worry about any of your friends or family being among them; no time to think about ruined houses, or wonder whether your own home was still standing. But very soon they might all be dead and then his retirement would be permanent. This might be the last time he'd ever have to do a cut-down to find a vein suitable for a transfusion; but he'd finish it.

Marie ran the blood through the tubing as fast as it would go and hung the bottle on the drip-stand. The doctor attached the end of the tube to the cannula, and started to suture the incision.

The noise of the first wave of aircraft receded. Now from the south came the drone of an approaching second wave, followed by a whistling scream and then the deafening crump of a bomb, shaking the hospital to its foundations, ripping off the blackout blinds, shattering all the win-

17

dows and hurling lethal glass shards inwards with the speed of bullets.

'Ouch!' Marie almost jumped out of her skin when she felt a stinging in her left forearm, and saw that one of the smaller splinters had buried itself in her flesh.

With a palpitating heart she pulled it out, gritting her teeth against the pain. A deep gash about half an inch long gushed blood onto the sheet.

With his customary coolness the doctor took hold of her wrist and peered at the wound through his half-moon lenses. 'That needs a stitch,' he said, taking a lump of gauze from the trolley beside him and slapping it on the wound. 'Hold that on it for now, and go and see who else is hurt.'

Half a dozen bedfast patients were calling for attention, and the two other nurses on duty were hastening towards them. Pressing the gauze over her own cut, Marie went to make a swift inspection of their injuries. On passing the broken windows she hesitated for a moment, seeing searchlights crisscrossing the sky. Some of the buildings – mostly business premises – on the other side of Prospect Street were on fire. By the time she hurried back to report, the doctor had threaded another needle with black suture.

'You manage to keep pretty calm,' she said, shivering.

'I'm a fatalist,' he said. '"If your name's on it..." as people never stop repeating. And I'm an old man. I'll soon be dead anyway. I might as well go out with a bang as a whimper. All right, Nurse, sit down and calm down. I'll start with you, since you'll be needed to help evacuate the patients.'

'No local?'

'No time. Unless I'm much mistaken, the house governor will soon cut the juice off, and we'll have no lights. Be a brave girl. This won't hurt a bit.'

Marie looked him in the eye. 'Won't hurt you, you mean.'

'That's right.'

A bit of a sadist, Dr Steele, everybody said so. Marie hissed, drawing in her breath at the sting of the suture needle, the pain magnified by her keyed-up state. This seemed to afford him a rare amusement, and he chuckled.

'You must have been in your element when you were newly qualified, sawing people's legs off with only a glass of rum for an anaesthetic,' she said, after a minute or two of his excruciating needlework.

His weary old eyes suddenly glinted up at her from under their bushy grey eyebrows. 'But not as much as when I was giving my cheeky young assistant a good dose of the cat.'

At that moment, the place was plunged into darkness, except for the lurid red light thrown by the flames that were consuming nearby shops and houses.

'There, what did I tell you? Lucky I got your stitch in,' the doctor said, covering the gash with a dressing by the light of the flames. He taped it in place. 'Now get up and get on with it, Nurse. There's plenty to be done.'

Marie got on with it as best she could in the devastated ward, calming the patients and preparing them for the transfer to the lower floor, to another ward at best, or a place in a corridor, if the wards were crammed full. A porter rushed onto the ward with a trolley full of hurricane lamps and torches, and soon afterwards the night sister swept in to give them their marching orders.

'It's a miracle no one was killed,' Marie remarked to Nurse Nancy Harding, as she kicked the brakes off the cut-down patient's bed and began to push him in the direction of the corridor.

Nancy walked alongside, holding the blood bottle in one hand and a hurricane lamp in the other. 'Who's the idiot?' she asked, her face ashen. 'Is it me that's missing something, or is it the house governor? Shutting the lights off! What for? To me, it's bloody stupid. We've got to maintain the blackout, in case they spot where we are? Hasn't he noticed they've just been raining bloody bombs on us? They obviously know where we are! And I should think they could tell by their incendiaries now, if they didn't know already with their flares. I bet they can see us from Berlin. Can you see any sense in it?'

There it was again, that distant drone coming ever louder and nearer, a third wave of fire and blast borne on German wings.

The hair rose on the back of Marie's neck, and her suppressed tension escaped in a trill of near-hysterical laughter. 'Nobody's allowed to think these days, Nurse Harding. There's a war on! You just do as you're told,' she said. 'But maybe it's not just the blackout. The windows have blown out, and we'll soon have water coming in from the fire-hoses. Water and electricity, Nance? They don't mix very well, now do they?'

'Oh,' Nancy said, with a shiver. 'Anyhow, it doesn't make our job any easier, does it? All these patients to move; all these beds to shift in the dark, with all this bloody glass and rubble in the way. And the dust! It's enough to choke you. I don't see what there is to laugh at.'

'We're still alive. That's what there is to laugh at,' said Marie, working off her nervous energy by rushing the bed along as if they were in a race. 'Isn't that right, Mr Pattison?'

The patient grunted, evidently not trusting himself to speak.

'Not like Margaret, poor lass,' Nancy went on. 'It's hard to believe it's only two months since she died, and only twenty-five. It's cruel, isn't it? Bloody Germans, I hate them all.'

They came to a halt outside the lifts, and Marie pressed the button, wondering for a moment whether they would be working. They were. The hospital governor might have cut the power to everything else, but the lifts were vital, at least until they got all these patients to the lower floors.

'I know,' said Marie. 'I miss her like hell. But I seem to have lived a lifetime since then. Have you seen her husband since the funeral?'

'Only once, in one of the fire engines just as I was leaving the hospital. Funny, I never thought Margaret would be the first of us to be married. I thought you'd be first. You were always leader of the pack.'

Marie gave a little shake of her head. 'Well, she was a couple of years older than us, so she had a right to take precedence. And I'm glad she was

21

first, the way it turned out. I'm glad she had her six months of married bliss before she died. It's not much to ask, is it? I'm not going to pip you to the altar either, by the look of it. Now you're engaged, you're sure to be next.'

'Maybe I will,' Nancy said, and Marie knew that had her hands been free Nancy would have pulled the engagement ring out from its hiding place on the chain round her neck and she would have had to admire it, yet again. Marie inwardly congratulated herself on the startling success of her one and only attempt at matchmaking. She and George Maltby had almost been brought up together, their parents were such good friends. Contrary to all expectations, quiet, self-effacing George had done rather well for himself. He would make her best friend a good husband. Nancy would be well provided for.

''Course you'll be next!' Marie said. 'Chas needs a squib up his backside. I know he loves me, but he's taking so long over popping the question, I'll probably die an old maid. I suspect his mother might have something to do with that. I don't think she considers me top-drawer enough to be admitted into the Elsworth family.'

'You'll never be an old maid, and he's a fool if he lets his mother stop him marrying you,' Nancy said, as they steered the bed through the open lift doors.

'You never know; families have a lot of influence,' Marie said, smacking the button to take them down to the ground floor. 'But I hope I shan't be like Margaret: no sooner in my wedding dress than in my shroud. Oh, poor lass! I got the shock of my life when that happened. It's never been the same since, without her.' She paused, remembering the good times they'd shared with Margaret. 'Do you remember how, when the three of us went dancing, she'd have half the hall watching her? And to watch her dance with Terry! What a team they were, like Rogers and Astaire. I thought of going to see him after the funeral, but – you know...'

'I know. For one thing you don't know what to say; you're scared he might start crying or something, and what can you do, anyway?'

'He's got loads of friends at Central Fire Station, thank goodness.'

'I know. There'll be plenty of shoulders for him to cry on. Thank goodness.'

Chapter 2

Charles Elsworth's mother pushed her spade into the soil, pulled herself up to her full five foot eight inches and fixed Marie with a severe stare. 'His name,' she said, 'is Charles.'

With her patrician features and her haughty manners, Mrs Elsworth was a doughty opponent. So, here was the challenge. Marie had seen little of the Elsworths in the eight months that she and Charles had been going out together. But his parents knew after this time that marriage might be on the cards and Marie saw that the pecking order was being established, right here and now.

There had to be a winner and a loser and Marie did not intend to lose.

She pushed her garden fork into the ground and accepted the challenge. 'Hear that, Chas? Your name's Charles,' she said, with a sneaking suspicion that he enjoyed being the object of their rivalry.

'Humph,' he grunted, sweeping back a shock of wavy brown hair. His mouth, which almost always looked ready to break into a broad grin, was determinedly straight now, and his hazel eyes fixed themselves on some point in the middle distance. He was doing his best to ignore both women, remaining neutral as far as he could, keeping himself out of trouble. Then he seemed to rethink that strategy, and a second later pulled Marie close into him, lifting her off her feet, pressing his lips against hers in a smacking kiss. 'I'll be Chas if you like, or Sam, or Bill, or Ebenezer,' he laughed, drawing back, 'if you'll ask me back to Clumber Street for a nightcap.'

His mother frowned. 'You're not Chas. You weren't christened Chas, and you never will be Chas.'

Marie grinned up at him, showing a row of perfect white teeth. He'd been Chas when they'd been in the same class in infant school, and Chas he would remain, as far as she was concerned. But confident of her victory, she said no more.

Charles's father looked up from his place outside the shed, where he was screwing together the last frame for the raised beds that now disfigured their large and once beautiful lawn and deep flower borders. A slow smile spread over his face.

'I think you've met your match there, Marjorie.'

'Put her down, Charles,' Mrs Elsworth snapped. 'It's embarrassing.'

Charles put Marie down.

'Her mum and dad are out of the way at her aunt Clara's, that's why he's dying to get round to their house,' Charles's 15-year-old brother piped up. 'That means we won't be seeing him until after breakfast.'

Mr Elsworth gave him a warning look. 'That's enough, Danny.'

Marie's eyes widened. 'Cheeky pup! It doesn't mean anything of the sort.'

''Course it does,' Danny persisted. 'Mum found one of your hairclips in his bed when she stripped it after his last leave.'

Marie felt Mrs Elsworth's eyes appraising her, watching her reaction, and a deep flush rose to her cheeks. 'What? *My* hairclips? That's not possible, you cheeky monkey! You'd better watch out, or I'll have you up for slander.'

Charles gave Danny a cuff round the ear. 'You little liar. Mum found nothing of the sort. Now apologize.'

'Ow, Charles! I'm not a liar, and I'm not apologizing.'

'You are. And you will end up in court, if you carry on,' Charles insisted.

Danny rubbed his ear. 'Get lost! Anyway,' he said, turning to Marie, 'if I do, that'll be two of us. Dad's got a summons for driving without due care and attention. He forgot to put the brake on when the car in front stopped.'

Charles gave him another clout.

'Ouch!'

'And you're making your mouth go without due care and attention. Time you put a brake on that.'

'Leave him alone, Charles.' His mother's voice was very quiet, but there was an edge to it that made Charles stop. He looked about to say something, then caught his mother's eye.

'Stop squabbling and give me a hand to get this frame in place,' Mr Elsworth said, putting an end to the dispute. 'Then we can start filling it with topsoil. We should just manage to get the kale planted and watered before it gets dark.'

Her hairgrips in Charles's bed? That was just young Danny's idea of a joke; he loved trying to embarrass her. But Mr Elsworth, driving without due care and attention? Marie couldn't believe it. His face was giving nothing away, and although she would have loved to know how that had come about, when he'd driven for years with not so much as a scratch, she decided to change the subject to spare his feelings.

'We planted some kale last year,' she said. 'We're not bothering this year, though. None of us liked it.'

'Don't you want to know what happened?' Danny insisted.

'Get hold of the end of this, and make yourself useful for a change,' his father said, 'instead of telling tales. Let's see if you can make up with brawn what you lack in brains.'

They carried the frame to the end of the lawn and placed it a couple of feet beyond the last raised bed, leaving enough room to kneel in between them. Charles, his mother and Marie began filling it with topsoil while Mr Elsworth went back to the shed to get the plants.

Danny stood watching them. 'Don't you want to know, then?'

Marie could see he was dying to tell her, but she gave him no encouragement.

None was needed. 'We were driving up Beverley Road, and I spotted some looters pulling the board of one of the bombed shops loose, and pointed them out to Dad. They had a quick look round, then one of them got inside and started passing stuff out to the other one. They hadn't seen the copper walking along the side street to-wards them, and from where he was, he couldn't see them, either. We just knew what was coming when he got to the corner, like something out of a Charlie Chaplin film. We both started laughing, and that was when Dad smacked into the car in front.'

'Don't say "copper", Danny, it's vulgar. Say "policeman". And that's when it stopped being funny for your father,' Mrs Elsworth said, and for Marie's benefit added: 'Leonard offered to repair the other man's car, but he was very aggressive. Some people just won't listen to reason.'

'The biggest laugh was that the policeman saw the crash, and came running straight over to us; he didn't even see the looters.' Danny grinned. 'But as soon as they saw him, they beat it. And then he started chasing them, with the other driver yelling at him to come back and look at his car. Yeah, it was just like something off Charlie Chaplin. Hilarious.'

Mr Elsworth was back with the plants. 'I never liked Charlie Chaplin; too silly for words. Go and fill those watering cans, Danny, instead of standing yapping.'

'Oh, Dad! I think I'm the only one in this house who's got a sense of humour!' Danny picked up the can and went, a look of disgust on his face.

'Clown! He's got more chatter than a cage full of monkeys,' Mr Elsworth said, carefully lowering himself to the ground to begin the planting.

Charles hunkered down on the opposite side of the bed. 'Empty vessels make most noise. You let him get away with far too much, and you're wasting your money, sending him to Hymers.'

Mrs Elsworth kneeled beside her husband. 'You went to Hymers. It got you into university, and we can't do less for Danny. We let you both get away with far too much. And I don't regret it, either, now. If the war lasts much longer he'll be called up, and then who knows what might happen to him? They were sending 16-year-olds to the front line in the last one.'

'He'll never get into university; he's too fond of playing the fool. The Forces would do him good. Make a man of him. He gets away with murder at home.'

Marie quietly took her place beside Charles and worked quickly, pushing the plants in.

Mr Elsworth began to cough, and pulled a handkerchief out of his pocket. 'You should have stayed out of it, never mind trying to get Danny in. You should have taken that job in Kemp's solicitors, and worked for your articles. I've never been right since the last lot. And don't say I didn't warn you.'

'How could I stay out of it? Everybody at university was joining up. Anyway, I didn't want to stay out of it.'

Mr Elsworth raised his eyebrows, and gave a snort of contempt. 'You fool! You think you're going into some sort of adventure straight out of the *Boy's Own Paper*. That's the young, you can't tell them anything. But you'll know what war's all about before you've finished. I only hope you'll live long enough to profit by it.'

He pushed his handkerchief back into his trouser pocket, and they worked on in silence. The kale was in the ground before Danny came back with the watering cans.

When they'd finished, Marie turned to survey the garden. 'Potatoes, onions, runner beans, beetroot, cabbage, carrots. A good bit of stuff in there. Not a bad day's work.'

'My lovely lawn and my beautiful borders,' Mrs Elsworth lamented. 'Ruined.'

'We kept them as long as we could, but you can't eat grass or flowers, Marjorie. This will be more use, especially at the rate we're losing shipping. The civilian death toll's nowhere near our shipping losses, in my opinion. If it goes on at this rate, we'll have neither ships nor men to bring any food in.'

'That's defeatist talk, Dad,' said Charles.

'It's facts. How many times do you hear of ships and men who'll never come home again, and read nothing of it in the papers? So, we'll grow our own, and rely on ourselves as much as we can, and then we'll have a bit of a chance if some of those convoys don't get through. That's not defeatist, is it? We might even get a pig.'

'We might not!' Mrs Elsworth protested. 'I've let you ruin my flower garden, but I draw the line at pigs.'

'You'll get your share, as well, Marie, for all the help you've given us,' Mr Elsworth said, ignoring the protest.

'I didn't do it for that. We've got plenty growing on Dad's allotment. Everything – veg, apples and pears, rhubarb, soft fruits, the lot. We hardly ever have to buy vegetables, or fruit.'

'It was very good of you to spare the time to help us, especially after the terrible time you've had at the hospital lately,' Mrs Elsworth condescended.

'Yes, it was high jinks at the infirmary, the night before April Fools' Day!' Marie pulled up her sleeve to display her newly healed scar. 'Glass splinters shooting into the ward like bullets, and then we were dragging beds around with only hurricane lamps and torches for light. But we were lucky, there was none of us badly hurt, not like people in the buildings round about.' She pulled her sleeve down again. 'It put the Victoria wing out of action, though – three wards lost. We're about 160 beds fewer because of it, but I was more upset by the damage to the Metropole Hall on West Street than anywhere else.' She sighed heavily. 'It had the best dance floor in Hull. I'll really miss that place; I learned to do the Lambeth Walk there.'

That earned her a disapproving frown from Mrs Elsworth. 'There are more important places to worry about than dance halls, my girl.'

Mr Elsworth, who was in the civil defence, backed his wife up. 'Control HQ, for example,' he said. 'When that land mine fell outside the Shell Mex building on Ferensway we hardly knew what had hit us. People blown in all directions, ceilings and walls caving in, furniture and filing cabinets picked up and dropped anyhow, and fires breaking out all over the place. People dead, people wounded, and a lot of those who weren't were shocked rigid and useless for anything. A few of us were trying to put the fires out, and give the layout of the building to the rescue services, but it was a complete bloody shambles.' He gave a hollow laugh. 'I was glad I'd lent the Wolseley to you, Charles, or that would have gone up, too. All the official cars outside were blown sky high. And nothing left of the policeman but bits of his uniform.'

'I know that poor man's wife,' said Mrs Elsworth. Her eyes were so reproachful Marie felt as guilty as if she'd dropped the bomb on the Shell Mex building herself.

'I know, it was awful, but I wasn't talking about what got hit the worst, just what I'll miss the most.'

'Doing the Lambeth Walk, evidently. Poor Dr Diamond killed as well, and only the day after we'd seen him when we went to give blood. Charles came home early that night, didn't you, Charles? They had to clear the dance hall to make room for homeless families.'

Charles looked as if he'd have liked to cuff his mother round the ear.

Marie's jaw dropped. 'Dance hall? You never

31

told me you'd been to a dance hall!'

'Hang it all, you were at work, and it was my first night on leave. It won't last for ever. I've got to make the most of it. Live life to the full, while I can,' he protested.

The heat rose to Marie's cheeks. 'So it seems,' she said. 'I'm helping to move a hundred and odd patients, imagining you out of the shelter and safely tucked up in bed, and you're swanning off to dance halls – without a word to me!'

Charles reddened. 'It's pretty obvious you go dancing without *me*, if you miss the Metropole Hall so much,' he retorted. 'We've hardly ever been there. I suppose you dance with a lot of foreign servicemen.'

Unable to deny the charge, Marie was silent for a moment, now on the defensive. 'Well, there was never any harm in it! I went with Nancy, or Margaret – when she was alive – even after she got married, if her husband was working. And we always left by ourselves.'

'Well so did I!' Charles protested, with a glance in his mother's direction, 'and I didn't get the chance to tell you; I went on the spur of the moment. So while you were moving your patients about, the place was closing, and not long after that I *was* tucked up in bed. It hardly seemed worth mentioning.'

So why had his mother mentioned it, Marie wondered, catching that grim expression on Mrs Elsworth's face. Probably because she wanted to put a spanner in the works. Probably because she didn't want any girl who'd left school at fourteen, whose parents could barely afford the rent on their house on Clumber Street, getting her hooks into her privately educated darling Charles. She frowned.

'More old edge than a ragman's saw,' Marie's father had once said, of Mrs Elsworth, and her father was pretty good at sizing people up, she thought.

Marie had every intention of getting her hooks into Charles, in spite of his mother. They'd been good friends as children until the parting of the ways on the day they left St Vincent's for secondary school – Charles to fee-paying Hymers College, Marie to St Mary's. After that the crown prince of the Elsworth clan had associated with friends suitable to his private school, and Marie had barely seen him, until the war came. They met again at a dance at Beverley Road Baths, when he cut in on her partner during an 'excuse me'. Before she knew what was happening she found herself gliding swiftly over the floor in his arms, leaving her former partner standing. Charles had propelled her expertly round, while reminiscing about the funnier incidents and high points of their infant days in a voice that had become thrillingly deep.

'I think I've been in love with you since we were five years old, when I used to dream about the fairy princess with the piercing blue eyes and the flaxen plaits. I see you've chopped them off,' he joked, his eyes full of laughter as he appraised her now much shorter hair.

'I'd look a bit silly with plaits, at twenty-three,' she said.

'Perhaps, and now I shall pick up that outsized torch I used to carry for you, and love you just as much with a flaxen bob.'

'Idiot,' she laughed, but she was inclined to believe him. At school, he'd always sat as near to her as he could get in class and at dinner, and he'd fought her battles in the school playground. At the womanly age of five, she had known that Charles Elsworth was seriously smitten with her, and that she could wind him round her little finger.

'You've managed all right without me for long enough,' she said. 'We've hardly exchanged half a dozen words since you went to Hymers.'

His expression became serious. 'Till now, I've loved you from afar – rather like Dante loved Beatrice. He didn't have to see her all the time to make her his ideal, and write reams of poetry about her.'

Marie raised her eyebrows. 'I wasn't afar,' she said. 'I was only half a dozen streets away. So how many poems have you written about me?'

'Well, to tell the truth–' he hesitated and broke into a grin – 'poetry's not really my strong point.'

She laughed at that. Charles's hazel eyes still danced as they looked into hers, and his sense of humour was the same, regardless of the polish he'd gained. She warmed to him. Her own partner saw it, and abandoned the field.

Now, every time they crossed the road on the walk from his parents' grand house, with its vast rear gardens on wide, tree-lined Park Avenue, to her parents very modest home in narrower, close-packed and treeless Clumber Street, he moved smoothly to the kerbside, and offered her his arm.

She pretended to despise all the old-fashioned courtesies and attentions he showed her, but deep down she loved them. Charles made her feel as if she counted for something.

The gardening finished, Marie and Charles walked to her parents' house. The milkman was standing on the doorstep, hands in his fingerless gloves, licking his indelible pencil.

'She's never in, your mam. She owes two weeks.'

'I haven't got it,' Marie told him, cheerfully. 'You'll have to come again, when she is in.'

Charles followed her through the wrought-iron gate, and handed him a ten-shilling note. 'Here you are, take what they owe you.'

The milkman counted the change into his hand. 'Yer ration's goin' to be cut, startin' next week.' The news seemed to give him some satisfaction.

'How much?'

'A seventh. Pint a week, for you,' he said, and was out of the paved front garden in two strides, slamming the gate behind him.

'Seems to have made your day, anyway,' Marie called after him.

'Less work, in't it?' he said, climbing back into his cart and taking up the reins. 'There's summat to do your roses good, though. Gee up!' The horse moved forward, and the cart rumbled away, leaving a heap of droppings steaming in the road.

Marie opened the door, and the strains of 'How High the Moon' drifted towards them. Her parents had left the radio on.

Charles followed her in, closed the door, then

pinned her to the wall in the tiny passageway. 'This is the first time we've had a house to ourselves. What games shall we mice play, while the cats are away?' he asked, brushing his lips against hers. Her spine tingled. Charles was a beautiful kisser. Not that horrible tongue-down-your-gullet style of kissing that made her want to go and gargle with carbolic, but real, lingering, sensuous kisses, that made her melt. Made her want to...

Not surrender! No, no no! Best put a stop to that, before it went any further. Her eyes snapped wide open. She ducked under his arm and picked up the black kitten her mother had taken in, and began to stroke it. 'Sorry to disappoint you, but the cat's back. Say hello to Smut.'

He let her go. 'Hello, Smut!'

She laughed and put the kitten down. 'Off you go, Smut.'

'It's nice to be on our own, anyhow, without any younger brothers about, giving a lot of lip to their elders and betters,' he said, helping her off with her coat and hanging it on the newel post. 'Horrible when they're younger, like yours, with their frogs, and their pet rats, and their marbles and cigarette cards, everlastingly pestering people to play battleships, and hanging around where they know they're not wanted. I bet you were glad when he was evacuated.'

'No I wasn't,' Marie protested. 'I like our Alfie. We work pretty long hours in nursing, anyhow, so I didn't see much of him before he was evacuated, and I never minded his cigarette cards and his marbles. I even played battleships with him sometimes.'

36

Charles threw his coat on top of hers and followed her into the front room. 'Oh, well, you might be singing a different tune when he gets older, and starts sticking his nose into everything you do.'

Marie moved the fireguard to stir the coal fire into life. 'Like the tune you sang, when Danny told that story about how your mother had found my hairclips in your bed?'

An indignant flush rose to Charles's cheeks, and he pulled at his tie. 'Quite. I hope you don't take any notice of him, little shit-stirrer.'

'I don't think he means any harm by it. It's just his heavy-handed idea of humour. You were a boy yourself once.'

'I was a different boy from him, then. I say, I'm starving, aren't you?'

She stood up and went to draw the curtains hanging at the long bay window. 'We should have stayed at your house for some of your mother's steak and kidney pudding, instead of having to faff about making something here.'

He caught her and held her close. 'So we could listen to Danny's tittle-tattle and attempts to be funny all night? No fear. I'd rather be here with you, just our two selves with no ghastly younger brothers around; that's enough company for me. We'll have a cosy evening in.'

'That's if the sirens don't go. We used to have some lovely cosy times here, before the war, with our Alfie on the carpet playing with his train set, and Mum and Dad teaching me and Pam how to play whist. She was only eleven then, but she soon learned to play a decent game, and she could shuffle like a cardsharp. It seems like a different world when I look back on it, it was so peaceful,' Marie said, and the thought struck her that of the two children it was Pam that she missed the least. Alfie might be a bit of a scallywag, but he was a real companion. Whatever was going on, he wanted to be in the thick of it. Pam was quieter, and more self-contained, a very stately little body, with a high opinion of herself – maybe because she'd always been their mother's favourite.

'With just you and me, it will be a lot more than cosy,' Chas said, holding onto her more determinedly this time, brushing his lips against hers.

A surge of dangerous desire made her take fright, and back off. A lot more than cosy might be a lot less than safe.

'Shall we find something to eat? You're not the only one that's starving.'

He held her at arm's length, and kept hold for a moment or two. 'I think you realize I'm starving for a lot more than food,' he said. 'But we'll go and forage first – if you insist.' He released her, led the way through the dining room into the kitchen and began opening cupboard doors.

'There's a dance on at the Baths,' she suggested. 'I wouldn't mind going for a jig.'

Chas turned from his foraging, and looked directly into her eyes. 'When we've got a house entirely to ourselves, for the first time ever? How long do you think it will be before this happens again? You are joking, I hope?'

'No. And the cupboards are bare, except for a few bread cakes and some potted meat Dad made. And a few jars of pickles and bottled pears from last year. I told you we should have eaten at your mother's.'

'Potted meat on bread cakes will do. I say, what's this?'

He pulled a couple of corked bottles out of the cupboard.

'Dad's wine, elderberry and parsnip. Be careful of that.'

'Your dad won't begrudge a drop to a service-man defending his country, will he?'

'You're not defending his country, you're standing about in his kitchen. But it's not that he'd begrudge it – it's just that it's a lot stronger than you'd think.'

'Oh, it won't be too strong for me. I can hold my drink all right. You make the sandwiches, and I'll pour the wine. Where are the glasses?'

'Oh, Chas, not with beef paste and pickled beet-root. A cup of tea will do for me, thanks. I might have a glass when I've done the washing-up.'

At half-past eight, Marie drew all the blackout curtains, and then joined Charles on the sofa in the front room. He poured her a glass of parsnip wine, and raised his own glass. 'Here's to us,' he said, and took a sip.

'Hey, this stuffs not bad. Not bad at all.'

'Glad you like it. Usually kept for high days and holidays, like Christmas and New Year. We popped a few corks for Mam and Dad's silver wedding last year as well.'

She relaxed against his shoulder, sipping her wine and gazing into the fire, the strains of the Glenn Miller Orchestra wafting peacefully over them. He gave her a gentle squeeze and nuzzled her ear. 'I'm certainly in the mood, Marie. Aren't you?'

She pushed him away, but not too far, and saw his eyes, dark with desire. He pressed towards her again until she felt his breath on her neck. 'Come here,' he persisted, and turning to kiss her he let his hand fall on her knee and began gently stroking her leg. 'You've got no stockings on. Oh, for the day when women start to wear nylons again. It's so exciting when you get to their suspenders, and a bare stretch of skin, and you know you've nearly reached the Promised Land.'

'The allotment's the only Promised Land I'll be going to, and I'm not likely to be wearing nylons to go there, am I? Or to help in your garden.'

'No, and you've still got dirty feet. Tell you what,' he murmured, 'I'll run you the regulation five-inch bath, and help you to undress...'

There was a faint scent of fresh sweat on him, warm, male, and wildly erotic. 'And just whose suspenders did your hands ever get to, Charles Elsworth?'

'None that matter, certainly,' he said, caressing that area of her thigh as he spoke. 'Yours are the only ones I care about.'

'If I had any on. Stop it, will you?' she murmured, tilting her head back as he kissed her throat and making no effort to hold him off.

'Stop it, why? Stop it because you like it? You do like it, don't you, sweetheart?'

'It's too dangerous.'

'That's why it's so exciting,' he murmured, kissing her briefly on the lips, while his hand moved ever higher, until his fingers were inside her knicker leg. 'I do love you, Marie.'

'I love you too,' she breathed, knowing she must be mad to let him carry on. She ought to stop him for both their sakes, but something primeval in her thrilled to his touch. She felt herself on the brink of something profound and powerful, some forbidden knowledge, deep and carnal, from which there could be no return, and despite her parent's oft-repeated warnings about 'not bringing any trouble to this door' running through her mind, she couldn't summon the will to resist. She let him push her onto her back. Oh, well, to hell with it, she thought. Let nature take its course...

The wail of the air-raid siren jolted her back to sanity. With her senses aflame and knees trembling, she pushed Charles away and got up unsteadily. Laughing with relief at her escape, she threw a bucket of slack on the fire and put the fireguard up.

'There's still some hot water in the kettle, Chas. Boil it again, will you, and chuck a couple of spoons of coffee in the Thermos flask? You'll find it in the cupboard nearest the outside door. I'll get us a blanket apiece.'

'Relax. It might be a false alarm.'

'Relax nothing!' she said, beginning to feel even more jittery than usual when anticipating a raid. 'It's coming, I tell you, and seeing I'm off duty I want to be in the shelter. Especially if it's as bad as the one we had a fortnight ago.'

'Bugger! Bugger! Buggeration!' Charles swore. 'Bloody Hitler, bloody Goering, bugger them all!'

Poor Chas! Nearly reached his promised land,

41

then foiled by the Luftwaffe. Her honour, saved by Herr Hitler! Marie exploded into laughter and ran upstairs for the blankets. Life, survival, first and foremost. And virginity keeps pretty well, she thought. She was beginning to think she'd kept hers almost too long, but maybe it wouldn't hurt to preserve it a bit longer, seeing that, for all his protestations of undying love, Chas had made no serious commitment as yet. And going by all that talk about bare thighs and suspenders she wasn't his first. 'Who runs for a bus they've already caught?' she'd once heard said, and Chas had caught one or two, by the sound of it. No, if he was a very good boy, he could have her honour at a more convenient time – maybe *after* he'd given her that engagement ring – and she wanted one just as good as Nancy's. 'Do you good to wait, my lad,' she murmured. 'Nobody values anything they get too easily.'

On her return downstairs she threw the blankets down by the front door and then put on her coat and went into the kitchen to lock the back door and toss the first-aid kit, a torch and a bottle of brandy into a bag. Charles was still waiting for the kettle to boil.

'Just like a nurse,' he said, looking at the first-aid kit, and then at the brandy. 'Are we going to get sozzled?'

'Medicinal purposes,' Marie answered, listening to the fearsome rising and falling of the sirens. 'I wish that kettle would hurry up. You get your coat on while I wait for it.'

'We could go without the flask.'

'You've changed your tune. I thought you didn't

want to go at all. Better hang on till it's boiled. It might be hours before the all clear. We might be glad of a hot drink. Where's Smut?'

Charles went to get his coat, and find the kitten. Marie was just filling the flask when she heard a howl of pain followed by a string of curses. He returned to the kitchen holding Smut by his scruff.

'I guessed you'd found him,' she grinned.

'Vicious little beast,' he said. 'He's scratched my hands to ribbons. Here, you can have him. I'll carry everything else.'

Marie followed him out, flicking off the lights as she went.

Chapter 3

It was ten o'clock by the time they left the house and joined a group of neighbours trooping to the communal shelter. Feeling even more jittery than usual during a raid, Marie looked skyward at a moon that was a week past full.

One of the neighbours gave a sardonic laugh. 'Aye, a lovely bomber's moon that, lass! I wonder what they've got in store for us this time.'

'At least Pam and Alfie are safe,' she said. 'Thank God Mam saw sense in the end, and got them evacuated.'

Edith Maltby, known to Marie since childhood as Aunt Edie, was clinging on to her son, George's, arm. Her poor eyesight made her very cautious outside, though she managed well enough in her own home. Her late husband had been in France with Marie's father during the Great War, and the two men and their wives had been neighbours and the closest of friends until his death. 'Your mam got the bairns out of the way just in time,' she said. 'I've hardly had two nights' sleep this past three months. It's been terrible.'

'She didn't do it willingly,' Marie said, linking Aunt Edie's other arm, 'especially after so many bairns went off at the start of the war, and then came back home because nothing was happening.'

'Where is she? Are they following us, your mam and dad?'

'No. They've gone to East Hull, to my aunt Clara's. They'll be going to the shelter on Ellis Street.' Marie shivered, as the feeling that 'someone had walked over her grave' swept through her: 'I hope they'll be safe,' she said.

'I hope we'll all be safe. Have you packed nursing in, then, Marie?' George asked.

'No. Just got a couple of days off, before Chas's leave ends. I'll go to the infirmary as soon as the all clear sounds, see what the damage is. I'm working in casualty now; there'll be plenty to do there when the raid's over, I've no doubt.'

'You must wish you'd gone in for being a shorthand typist. They're crying out for them as well as for nurses.'

'I couldn't sit still for long enough.'

'Funny, after all the time we spent together as kids, I never pictured you as a nurse. Always imagined you'd faint at the sight of blood.'

'I never pictured you as a civil engineer, come

44

to that. But it's surprising how soon you get used to the sight of blood. One of our doctors keeps telling us: other men's pains are easy to bear – and when you've seen enough of them, they are! Isn't that shocking?'

'No, it's as it should be. Otherwise nobody would be able to do the job, would they? Seen anything of Nancy?'

'Just about every day. I've seen the engagement ring,' Marie said, with a telling glance up at Charles. 'I did her a big favour, introducing her to you. You've done her proud, George.'

He gave her a satisfied smile. 'Be a while before we can get married, though. She wants to pass her finals first, and I want to get a bit of money together so we can set up home in style. What about you two?'

Lieutenant Charles Elsworth gave George a frosty stare. He didn't approve of men who failed to enlist. Reserved occupations, cowards and conscientious objectors, they were all the same to him, and Marie was embarrassed to see that he took no trouble to hide his contempt for her childhood companion.

She answered George for both of them. 'Oh, well, I have to get my finals as well. We don't want to rush into anything, do we, Chas?'

'Some of us might not survive the war,' Charles said. 'Men who are at the front, fighting for their country.'

'Any one of us might not survive the war,' George commented. 'So far there have been more deaths among civilians than soldiers. Our firemen have got more chance of being killed than them,

45

not to mention the engineers. My mother's got as much chance of being killed as anybody at the front.'

Charles did not deign to answer, and knowing George as she did, Marie expected him to drop the argument. To her surprise, he persisted. This was a very different George from the kid she'd grown up with.

'Imagine if every able-bodied man joined up – who'd keep the city functioning after the raids?' he demanded. 'Repair the gas mains? The water supply? The electricity? Everything that's vital to the life of the city? What about the roads, bridges, houses? What would happen to the people? How would the port function – what about the shipping? We can't leave it all to women and old men.'

'George is an assistant to Mr Morris, the City Engineer.' Aunt Edie said, her voice so full of pride and awe that she might have been speaking of some sort of deity. And she had good grounds for her pride in her son, Marie thought. Throughout his childhood George had been the sort of quiet lad that nobody took any notice of. He'd never distinguished himself at school, and he'd had a long spell of unemployment after losing his delivery job. But to everyone's surprise it had been the making of him. He'd used the time to go to night classes and study, and everybody had been staggered when he'd won a scholarship to university, none more so than George himself.

'When every raid is over there's plenty of hard work for us,' he went on. 'Day and night.'

'Don't the military take on rescue work? Don't

46

they carry out demolitions?' Charles demanded. 'I seem to remember seeing some of our chaps doing that. I've even read about it in the papers. In fact, I know some of the chaps who've done it, and there are long, hard days of work for them, as well as for the civilians. The military don't shirk anything.'

'And we're very glad of the help. But they're not ultimately responsible for getting everything back in working order, we are. And they help when they happen to be around, and they aren't, always.'

'Really!' Charles bristled, and left it at that, since they had arrived at the shelter and George, ever careful of his mother, was helping her down into it.

'I wonder how long we'll be here this time?' she said, groping her way along. 'I hope them Londoners realize how lucky they are with their Underground. They're a lot safer than we are, with our three sides and a concrete top, and only one step down.'

'It's the water table, Mam,' George said.

'Well it's a poor lookout for us, lad, whatever it is.'

'I'm off to Control Headquarters,' he said, when his mother was settled. 'We're a double act, you and me, Marie.'

'How's that?' she smiled.

'You bind the wounds of the people, but the city is our patient. We bind the wounds of the city. We can both look forward to plenty of hard work, I reckon.' George glanced in Charles's direction. 'Will you see Mam back home?'

'We'll see her all right, lad,' another neighbour

piped up. 'No fears on that score.'

'Jumped-up delivery boy,' Charles muttered, glaring at George's retreating back, 'Binding the wounds of the city! Pompous ass! Who does he think he is?'

'Shut up, Chas!' Marie hissed, and glanced towards Aunt Edie, who showed no sign of having heard. 'You must be very proud of George,' Marie spoke up. 'He's done well.'

'I am.' A look of anxiety clouded her face. 'I only wish his work wasn't so dangerous. If anything happens to him, it'll be a bad job for me.'

'He'll be all right,' Marie reassured her, and then thought how stupid her words were. How could she or anyone else know whether he'd be all right or not? It was just one of those things people said that sounded kind, but was really meant to shut other people up, and make them keep their worries to themselves. She wrapped herself in her blanket and leaned on Charles's shoulder, listening to Aunt Edie regaling her neighbours about George and his achievements, and how highly the other gods in the city engineering department thought of him...

Marie had dozed off before the first bomb jolted her awake at half-past three. At five o'clock the all clear sounded.

'I'm going down to the hospital,' she said when they left the shelter, to breathe the smoke and smell the bombed city. 'I might as well go now. I'll take Smut home and shut him in, and then I'm off. I'll only feel worse if I try to snatch an hour's sleep. I'm on an early shift anyway.'

'If you'll wait another half an hour until the

blackout ends, I'll bring Dad's car round, and drop you off. If we can get through the streets, that is,' Charles said.

'No. It'll be quicker to walk straight there than walk to your house and then drive.'

'Not for me. I'll have to walk back.'

'I'm not forcing you to come, Chas! Go home! I'll be there before the blackout finishes.'

'No. I'll walk with you,' he said. 'Come on, let's be off.'

Chapter 4

The infirmary was heaving with injured people, many completely stupefied by their nightmare ordeal, others weeping and distraught, and a couple screaming uncontrollably.

'Nurse!' one of the Casualty sisters called. 'Take that to the incinerator. Quickly.'

Marie felt the bottom drop out of her stomach as a severed limb was thrust into her hands – a woman's blackened leg, blown off at the knee.

'Go. Go on,' Sister urged, 'and get back here double quick.'

Marie ran as fast as she could with the sickening object, and was never so glad as when she got it out of her hands.

Dr Steele spotted her in the throng as soon as she returned.

'You there!' he shouted, over the hubbub. 'Yes, you there, that nurse with the blonde hair! What's-your-name! Nurse Larsen! My colleague says you can suture. Come and put a couple of stitches in this chap's hand.'

But as she started towards him, Marie was stopped by two women ambulance drivers with a stretcher case. The patient they were bringing in looked as if someone had set about her head with an axe. Half her scalp was torn away and hanging over her face, and her hair was matted with a mixture of drying blood and thick dust, which also caked her chest. Her clothing and stockings were torn, and her shoes missing.

'Anybody with her?' she asked, instinctively curling her fingers round the woman's wrist to feel for a pulse. 'Any family? Have we got a clue who she is?'

'No, sorry.'

'What happened?'

'Parachute mine,' one of the drivers said. 'Shelter on Ellis Street took a direct hit; they reckon there must be dozens killed. Lucky for her she hadn't reached it. Scores of people injured round there as well; the nearer first-aid stations are chock-a-block.' She nodded towards the woman on the stretcher. 'She was buried under a pile of rubble. If it hadn't been for a dog yapping its head off, the rescue workers wouldn't have found her so quickly. She'll be lucky if she's still got a home to go to. Ellis Street's completely wiped out.'

Ellis Street! A terrible apprehension seized Marie. She looked wildly round. 'Sister! Sister!' she called, still trying vainly to feel a pulse. The ring on the woman's pallid left hand looked ex-

50

actly like her own mother's wedding ring. Marie froze, too terrified to move the hair and see who it was beneath that filthy, blood-caked mess.

Sister was soon beside her, lifting back the hair herself, revealing the bloodless face beneath. 'Get her into a cubicle, and stay with this one, Larsen. We'll get plasma up as fast as we can, and we'd better send blood for cross-matching. She's going to need a surgeon. She'll have a stinking head-ache when she comes round – if she ever does.'

'You there!' Dr Steele again. 'Nurse Larsen! Come and attend to this patient – at once!'

Marie's face had turned ashen.

'What's the matter, Larsen?'

'It's my mother,' she whispered.

This was the horror that Marie had deliberately pushed out of her mind since the start of the war – the chance that someone she loved would come through those doors badly injured, or even dying. She clung onto the stretcher as the madhouse around her began to recede, struggling with her whole being against this nightmare that could not be happening and must not be happening.

'What's the matter with the girl? Has she gone deaf?' Dr Steele's muffled words reached Marie as though through a fog as Sister got her to a chair and thrust her head between her knees.

The sound of screaming was the first thing she was aware of as the blackness ebbed away. She lifted her eyelids to find herself gazing into eyes like brown pebbles behind a pair of horn-rimmed spectacles, and recognized the junior houseman who had taught her to suture.

'All right? It's not like Nurse Larsen to turn

squeamish. Take a few deep breaths.'

'I knew it,' she said, struggling to her feet and looking around her. 'I just knew.' Her mother was nowhere to be seen.

'Knew what?'

'The woman the ambulance just brought in; it's my mother. Where's she gone?'

'I'm sorry,' he said, his face full of concern. 'No one told me, or if they did I didn't hear for the racket in here. The doctors are with her now, then she'll be sent to one of the wards. It'll be better if you don't see her for a while, until they get her tidied up.'

Tidied up. So that's what you do with a woman whose scalp is ripped away and pulled over her face, Marie thought, you tidy her up. She had an insane urge to laugh at the strange choice of words. 'No. I've got to see her now,' she said. 'God, can't anybody stop that woman screaming?'

'I doubt it. She's just watched her husband roast to death, trapped between two burning rafters.'

'Oh, my God,' Marie shuddered.

'Listen, there's nothing you can do that's not being done already,' the junior houseman insisted, 'and if I know Dr Steele, he won't have you there. The WVS canteen's outside. Get a cup of tea; hot and sweet. And then pull yourself together and come straight back here. We need every pair of hands we can get.'

No doubt Dr Steele wouldn't want her there, Marie thought as she leaned against the wall sipping tea in the crowded waiting room, away from the busy treatment areas. His tolerance level for any display of emotion was practically nil. Emotional display had never been the Larsen way, either. It had never been needed; the ties of love were deep and loyalty a given, making display superfluous. But seeing her mother's injuries, Marie doubted that she could have kept her distress in check. Tears stung her eyes at the thought of her mother and she bent nearer to the cup to hide her face, inhaling the steam, trying to calm herself.

If her mother was as badly injured as that, what about her father? She hoped to God he hadn't reached the shelter either, and was safe somewhere. But if he hadn't been in the shelter, he would have been with her mother at the hospital. Since he'd been invalided out of the army after the Great War, they'd been like a pair of bookends, hardly ever more than a few yards apart, unless they'd been at work.

If he were alive and well, he'd come in search of his wife. If she didn't see him soon, it could only be because he was either dead or lying badly injured somewhere. It was hard to know which was worse but she was helpless either way; she had no hope of finding him, miles away on the other side of the bridge. She would have to wait, and pin her hopes on the rescue services. The only useful thing Marie Larsen could do was to pull herself together and get on with whatever needed to be done here and now, to throw herself into work, and treat these injured people as she'd want her dad to be treated, if he arrived at any of the other hospitals or first-aid stations.

She gulped down the last of her tea and went

back to work, trying not to think of her own concerns until the staff on the late shift reported for duty. Then she went to the ward, where she found her mother still unconscious, but clean and very nicely 'tidied up'. Her breathing was shallow and rapid and she looked bloodless, almost as white as the bandages that bound her head, and the pillow she rested on.

'She's in a critical condition; the doctor's been in to see her every quarter of an hour. She's had three pints transfused but,' the ward sister grimaced and said, with a slight but significant shake of her head, 'it's touch and go – no point telling you anything else.'

Marie knew that, and she dreaded to think what the outcome might be, even if her mother survived. Her external injuries, the ones they could see, were bad enough. But what was happening on the inside? What about brain damage? Even if she survived, she might never be able to work again. She might need to be looked after for the rest of her life.

Well? Well then, she would have to do it. Marie took the work-worn hand that rested on top of the blankets, and held it to her lips. It felt cold. Someone had removed her mother's false teeth and her mouth was hanging open, making her look much older than her years and terribly vulnerable. Marie had never felt more helpless in her life.

Sleep had always come easily to her. Before the air raids she would fall asleep as soon as her head touched the pillow and hardly stir until she awoke the following morning, bright and eager for the challenges of the day, with enough energy and stamina to keep her going for sixteen hours at a stretch.

Not so this night. Marie lay in bed in the Nurses' Home and closed eyes that were swollen with crying. She had nothing to disturb her but the monotonous tick-tock of the alarm clock and the beating of her own heart, yet sleep evaded her. After a long day of horror piled upon horror, she was tired in a way she had never known before, not only the tiredness of sheer physical exhaustion, but also the tiredness of anxiety and apprehension, of dread – dread of the future and what it might bring. She felt like a traitor for abandoning her mother to the pain and fear she would feel when she came round and found herself in a strange place, with none of her family near. Her mother, the mainstay of the family – always rushing off to work or rushing home, and at home forever busy, always doing – now lying completely still, and looking as if she might never get up again. The fact that her mother was in good hands and that Marie herself could be there in two minutes if needed was small consolation. And where was her father? Was he dead, or trapped and in pain under a mass of broken bricks and concrete? She felt crushed at the mere thought of it.

And then there were Pam and Alfie. Tomorrow she would have to find out about travel arrangements to Bourne, to go and tell them what had happened. They were overdue a visit anyway. No one had been to see them since they'd been evacuated in February. The journey to the south of Lincolnshire was a long one, and time and money were short. So the days had slid into weeks and the realization that it was now the middle of April came as a bit of a shock.

Marie made up her mind. She couldn't write such terrible news to them; she'd have to tell them face to face, and it wouldn't be easy. Telling Pam would be the worst, and Marie dreaded the floods of tears and near hysteria that would be her reaction to the news. Pam had always been their mother's shadow.

It wouldn't be quite such an ordeal telling Alfie, Marie predicted. Nothing seemed to make an impression on him for long; trouble seemed to slide off him like water off a duck. He'd be upset, but nothing like Pam. It was to be hoped that Mam would be much better before she went, and Dad would have been found alive and well.

Chapter 5

At the crack of dawn on the Saturday, six days after the bombing of the shelter, Marie stood alone in the kitchen making sandwiches. Her mother was showing feeble signs of recovering, but Marie had still heard nothing about her father. The rescue services could tell her nothing, and there was no one else to ask.

She had been to see Ellis Street for herself, and her heart had plummeted when she saw the devastation. Broken walls stood like jagged teeth above piles of rubble. It was impossible to tell whose houses they'd been. Whether he'd been in the shelter or in Ellis Street, Marie was hard put to hang on to any hope of seeing her father alive again.

Fighting back a rising wave of tears, Marie opened the loaf of Mother's Pride she'd bought on the way home from the hospital the day before, imagining what her parents would have thought of it. Bought bread! The waste of it! The sheer, near-criminal laziness of women who bought shop bread! Her mam and dad would have been shocked. But with so many poorly patients after the raids Marie's life had been all work and worry, and sleep – when complete exhaustion forced it – so that the Larsen family rule book had been thrown overboard.

As she scraped off the last of the potted beef clinging to the sides of the bowl she saw her dad making it as clearly as if he were beside her, carefully covering the top with clarified butter the way he always did and putting it in a paper bag, and then in the cupboard away from dust and flies. Unless there were a miracle this would be the last of her dad's potted meat she'd ever taste. She had reported him missing, but she knew that if he were alive, she'd have heard from him by now. Unless he were trapped, and hurt...

She shuddered, fought down the unbearable thought, and concentrated on wrapping the sandwiches in greaseproof paper and putting them in her bag. She wouldn't take a flask. They were heavy to carry when full, and a nuisance when you had to lug them back home empty. Surely one of the families would offer her a cup of tea. She'd given them warning she was coming, after all.

Charles drove her down to Corporation Pier in time for the 7.30 ferry to New Holland. 'I hope you don't get stuck there, miss the bus, or anything. I'd like us to have a final evening together before I go.' He drew out his wallet, and held out a five-pound note. 'Just in case you need it.'

She hesitated, and took it. 'I'll pay you back.'

He shrugged. 'It's not necessary. I'll be waiting for you when you get back.'

She gave him a quick kiss, and followed the other passengers up the ramp.

On the ferry Marie stood and watched him out of sight, breathing in the mud and salt-laden smell of the River Humber on the fresh moist April air – a tonic after hours spent indoors at the hospital and at home. She stayed on deck for a while, looking at the rippling water, listening to the crying of the gulls, as they wheeled round the sky, completely free. Free of care.

A smartly dressed woman with beautifully cut hair came to stand near her. 'Nice day, isn't it? Nice to get away from Hull for a change.'

Marie guessed she must be in her late thirties, and she was obviously very well off. 'Lovely,' she agreed.

'I'm going to see my little boy,' the woman volunteered. 'He's ten. He's staying with my sister and her husband in Sleaford; they've got no children. I try to go at least once a week, if I can, although it's quite expensive. I'm glad he's there, though. Hull's been such a hellhole this year, what with the air raids. If it's only a false alarm, it still puts your nerves on edge. Even if there's no raid, you're sleeping with one eye open, just waiting to have to jump out of bed, get dressed again and go down to a freezing cold shelter. I don't think I've had a decent night's sleep for weeks; it wears you out. You can hardly blame people for chancing it, and staying in bed.'

'They might as well, for what use the public shelters are,' Marie said bitterly. 'A whole lot of people were killed in the shelter on Ellis Street a few nights ago. My mother hadn't quite got there, so she escaped, but her injuries are terrible. My dad went into the shelter, and we haven't seen hide nor hair of him since. I'm praying he'll turn up, but there's not much hope. It took a direct hit from a one-ton bomb. The whole street was completely flattened. They reckon about fifty people were killed, and there were scores badly injured.'

'How awful. We've had no tragedies like that so far in my family, but you hear of such horrible things happening, you wonder how long you can get away with it. And even if nothing terrible happens, it's so disruptive to business. We had to evacuate the office six times in one day not long ago. And this new air-raid insurance the government's making people get! Forcing you, whether you want to have it or not. In one way, you feel safer having it, but then it's another expense on top of everything else. They always seem to be dreaming up some new way of getting money off us, as if they didn't take enough already. And then the cost of this trip every week! And it's a lot dearer if there isn't an excursion running.'

'Why do you do it,' Marie asked, 'if you know he's safe, and in good hands?'

'I don't want him to think we've forgotten him. And I don't want him to end up thinking more, about them than he does about me.'

'I'm sure he won't,' Marie said, and wondered fleetingly if there were any danger of Pam and Alfie forgetting their own parents. From what her mother had said about the tears Pam had shed when they were evacuated, there was certainly none in her case. Alfie had taken it all in his stride, but his loyalty lay with his own family, Marie was sure of it. There might be some danger of their new families getting too attached to them, though. They were both attractive children and although he was a scamp, Alfie had some very winning ways.

The other woman frowned. 'I'm not. They spoil him rotten.'

'Why not go to Sleaford and stay with him then? Quite a few women have evacuated with their children.'

'I've thought about it, but it's not so easy for a grown woman to live in someone else's home, is it? And then, I've got to think of my husband. There are far too many easy women about.'

'Don't you trust him?'

'I don't trust *them!* Especially the young ones whose husbands are away in the Forces. Some of them, well, if their own man isn't there to give them what they want, they've no scruples about getting it from someone else's, have they?'

'I suppose,' said Marie, finding it hard to believe that any woman whose husband was fighting for his country would do such a foul thing.

'How old are your children?'

'I'm not married. I'm going to give my brother and sister the bad news about my mam and dad. They're in Bourne, at different addresses. I hope they're not very far apart. I hope I can manage to spend a bit of time with them before I have to get the bus back.'

'How awful. I don't envy you a bit.'

'I'm dreading it, especially telling my sister. And I'm dreading having to leave her afterwards, to get back to Hull. But I work at the hospital. I'm on an early shift tomorrow, and I can't miss it, we're so short staffed.'

'No, I suppose the hospitals are packed. Here we are!' the woman said, as the ferry slowed for the approach to New Holland pier, where the coaches were waiting.

How different from the bombed streets of Hull, Marie thought, as the coach travelled through the quiet countryside south of Lincoln and dropped her on the edge of Bourne. Some people lived charmed lives; they escaped everything.

She was amazed at the size of the house where Pam was staying, all gable ends and creepers up the walls, and a front garden full of spring flowers with neat, pruned roses just coming into bud. The sight of it made her glad she'd dressed carefully. She'd thought long and hard before taking her last remaining pair of block-heeled

61

nylons out of their Cellophane packet, but had finally put them on with her smart new navy costume. It was a good decision: this was no place for the slacks and old checked jacket she'd have been far more comfortable wearing.

A plump lady in late middle age, with grey hair and rosy cheeks, answered the door and gave a restrained smile as she extended her hand in welcome. Marie shook it.

'You must be tired after your journey. Hungry, too, I shouldn't wonder. I'm Morag Stewart.'

Marie followed her into the largest drawing room she'd ever seen. A grand piano stood in one corner, with a fringed silk shawl draped over it. Morag led her to a leather wing-backed chair by the bow window.

'Sit here while I find Pamela, and then I'll leave you together for a while.'

Pamela. She was just 'our Pam' at home. After about five minutes, Pamela appeared alone, dressed in unfamiliar clothes, looking every inch a child of the upper-middle classes. Marie got up and threw her arms round her, clasping her tightly. Pam's response was more restrained.

'Come and sit down,' Marie said, releasing her and drawing her towards a chair. 'I've got something to tell you.'

Pamela sat with her hands folded, bewildered, but quite composed.

'Our mam's in hospital. She was caught in an air raid and badly hurt. She was unconscious for a day or two, and she's still very, very poorly, and...' Marie blurted it all out like a dam bursting, and ended by dissolving into tears. Pam stood beside her chair, patting her shoulder and murmuring words of comfort, while Marie mopped her floods of tears with her embroidered handkerchief, conscious while she did it that this was the exact opposite of the scene she had imagined.

'What about Dad?' Pam asked, when Marie's sobs had abated.

'He's dead, Pam! He must be, short of a miracle. He went into the shelter on Ellis Street, and it got a direct hit. Everybody inside it was killed, and some of the bodies they've found couldn't be identified. He hasn't been seen since. I can't see how he can have escaped, Pam.' Marie delivered the last with a strangled sob, her tears flowing copiously again.

Amazingly cool and collected, Pam said: 'I'll go and get you some clean handkerchiefs, and I'll ask Aunt Morag to bring the coffee in.'

A little later, with her make-up ruined and face blotchy, but with some of her self-possession restored, Marie sat by the bay window with Pam and Mr and Mrs Stewart, looking out at the beautiful spring flowers. The coffee was all milk, she noticed, and the scones thickly buttered. There seemed to be no shortage of anything here, and nobody mentioned coupons. The fertile fields of Lincolnshire evidently didn't stint the people who lived beside them.

After a string of platitudes followed by a long silence, Mr Stewart said: 'Why don't you play your sister something on the piano, Pamela? I'm sure she'd like to hear you.'

Pamela turned towards him, and with absolute

assurance said: 'I won't if you don't mind, Uncle Alec. I think I'll go to my room now.'

He gave her hand a squeeze. 'All right, dear. We realize how terribly upsetting this is for you.'

Marie watched her sister's retreating back and thought: we've lost her. At the door Pam turned, and Marie was struck by her fair hair, long and loose, and falling in waves to her shoulders, how like a pale rose petal her skin was, and how perfect her features, her blue eyes and lithe little figure, just beginning to take on a woman's shape. Funny how she'd barely noticed these things when Pam was at home.

'Do you realize,' Pam said, 'that if we hadn't been evacuated, Alfie and I would have been in that shelter with Dad?'

Alfie and I. It would have been 'me and our Alfie' two short months ago. Pamela hadn't forgotten her grammar in her grief, and she hadn't been slow to realize that she might also have been killed, had she stayed in Hull. Marie finished her coffee and took leave of the Stewarts, and then walked rapidly towards the address she'd been given for Alfie. Pam – *Pamela* – was evidently so well settled in her new home with her new, doting auntie and uncle that except for her Hull accent – already far less pronounced – no one would guess she'd ever lived anywhere else, or known any other background. She'd always been their mother's pet, and now she was the pet of a couple of retired teachers with no children of their own, who gave her music lessons and sent her to dancing classes, and generally treated her like a princess. They were friendly with other teachers and lecturers, the sort of people who have friends round for musical soirées on the piano and the violin. The cultured sort, devoted to music, literature and painting, and everything that makes life civilized. Even the Elsworths looked like barbarians beside them. Marie had left the Stewarts' house feeling that if Pam hadn't already forgotten them all she probably intended to. And what a beautiful new knitted jumper she'd had on, in blue Robin Pearl with a lacy feather stitch. Marie recognised the pattern; she'd seen one of the nurses on nights knitting a similar one. Pam seemed to belong more to the Stewarts than to her own family now. And since she was taking it upon herself to provide Pamela with clothing perhaps Auntie Morag had better start knitting her something in black, Marie thought, grimly.

An overfed and malevolent-looking grey cat sat in the front window of a modest little end terrace house on Hereward Street, staring at Marie as she raised her hand to knock on the green gloss-painted front door. It was opened before her knuckles made contact with the wood by a tall, sour-looking woman, her dark, greying hair tied severely back.

'Go round the back, will you?'

Marie went round the back. No creepers here, all was unrelieved brick and concrete. At the back, mangle, mop bucket and zinc washtub took the place of roses and spring bulbs.

'You're half an hour late. You'd better come in.'

'Sorry. You must be Mrs Morton,' Marie said,

stepping into a beautifully clean but cheerless kitchen. There was no fire in the grate; but Marie noted the Calvinist motto worked in cross-stitch prominent over the mantelpiece: 'Thou God seest me.' Very cheering. Marie had a feeling that Mrs Morton's god might be the spiritual equivalent of the boss of the Gestapo.

Mrs Morton looked aggrieved. 'You're late,' she repeated. 'It would have been a bad job if I'd had to go out, wouldn't it?'

'I'm sorry. I had a bit of trouble finding you,' said Marie.

'Can't think why. It's easy enough. There aren't that many streets in Bourne. Not like Hull.'

Alfie was sitting unnaturally still on an old chaise longue under the window, beside an older boy. He was scrubbed to a shine but he looked pale, and skinnier than when Marie had last seen him. She was struck by the dark circles under his eyes.

'Hello, Alfie,' she said.

'Hello, Marie.'

'He's clean, for once. It's nearly killed him, having to sit there for half a day and keep clean. He's forever bringing mud into the house on his boots, and getting his clothes dirty, aren't you, Alfred? This is my son, Ernest,' Mrs Morton said, nodding towards the older boy.

'Hello, Ernest.'

'Hello, Marie.'

Marie didn't like the uninvited familiarity from a youngster. 'Don't you like to go out with your friends, Ernest?' she asked.

Ernest assumed a virtuous expression. 'Not

66

when we've got visitors, Marie.'

'I'll boil the kettle again, then. Stop picking your nose, Alfie,' Mrs Morton said, and then directed her accusing gaze at Marie. 'If there's one thing I can't abide, it's having to stand in my own kitchen, watching him picking his nose.'

'And he wets the bed,' Ernest sniggered.

The picking stopped. Alfie looked browbeaten.

'Be quiet, Ernest. Don't embarrass the poor lad in front of his sister,' Mrs Morton said, and in an undertone to Marie she added, with a sniff. 'Makes no end of washing, though, and him eleven years old! But we've all got to make sacrifices in wartime, I suppose, and I won't have it said I've done less than anybody else.'

'Very good of you, I'm sure,' said Marie, far from enchanted to be on the receiving end of such goodness – even if only second-hand.

'And he roams about till all hours at night, till I'm worried sick and Ernie has to go out looking for him. I want you to give him a good talking-to about that.'

'I will,' Marie said.

Ernie sat there looking smug and long-suffering, reinforcing her aversion to him. He reminded her of a sly kid she'd gone to school with, whose chief pleasure lay in inciting other children into mischief, then sitting back to enjoy the show when they got caught and punished. 'Are you eating properly, Alfie? she asked.

He shot a wary glance in Mrs Morton's direction before saying: 'Yes.'

That sniff again. 'He certainly is. He eats us out of house and home.'

'Oh dear,' Marie said.

It was apparent that Mrs Morton was not going to leave her alone with Alfie so that she could tell him the awful news in private, and she would have to tell him before she left to get the bus back. Marie took a deep breath. 'Well, Alfie, I'd better tell you why I've come... Marie's dam of pent-up misery had burst at the Stewarts', and now she managed to tell her brother about the disaster without a tear.

He howled. Marie handed him a couple of the handkerchiefs Pam had given her.

'Oh dear,' Mrs Morton said, with great politeness but no discernible sympathy, 'oh dear. That *is* unfortunate.'

'Never mind about the tea,' Marie said, in a manner decided enough to deter opposition. 'I'll take him outside for a few minutes.' She ushered Alfie to the door, with Mrs Morton so close behind that for a moment Marie thought she was going to follow them out into the street.

'I'm coming home with you,' Alfie said, as soon as they were out of earshot.

'It's impossible, Alfie. Mum's in hospital, and it'll take her a long time to get better. And I have to work. There's no one to look after you. And the air raids are terrible. A lot of people have been killed in Hull. If you'd been there the other night,' she said, repeating Pam's instant realization, 'you'd have been in the shelter with Dad. You'd have been killed as well.'

'I don't care. I want to come home. She's horrible, and Ernie's a dirty, nasty bugger. She gives him my sweet ration.'

Her heart sank. He might be exaggerating, but even if he wasn't he was better off here than in Hull. 'There's worse things than having your sweet ration pinched,' she said, 'and if you'd been in Casualty when they brought our mam in, you'd know that. And don't swear. What's the school like?'

'Lousy.'

'Pam likes her school. The people she's with say she's doing well there.'

'She sucks up to everybody.'

'It would be better all round if you did the same, Alfie,' Marie said. 'Why the hell can't you behave yourself? Get on Mrs Morton's good side; give her less to complain about.'

'Can't stand her, and she hasn't got a good side. Or Ernie, either; rotten bully. Take me with you. I want to see our mam.'

She tried to impress on him the sheer impossibility of taking him with her as they walked back to the house. When they reached the gate it was evident he'd heard nothing she had said. 'Take me with you,' he repeated, in a very subdued voice.

'I can't, Alfie,' she said, despairing and exasperated with him. 'You know very well I can't. I have to work at the hospital. Our mam's so badly wounded she won't be home for ages, and there's nobody else to look after you now. We're fighting a war, remember? We're all in it, and you'll have to be brave and do your bit, like the rest of us. Anyway, the bus is full, there isn't a seat.'

Alfie started to weep. 'I'll sit on your knee!'

'Come on, buck up.' Marie pulled a lace hankie

out and wiped his tears. You'll have to make the best of it for a bit, Alfie. I've got to work. There's a lot of wounded people need looking after. And apart from everything else, we need the money.'

'If you're so sure Dad's dead, we ought to be having a funeral. I want to come to the funeral.'

'I'm not sure what's happening yet, Alfie.' Marie said, not yet ready to give up all hope. 'I'll write to you as soon as I find out.'

She took his hands in hers, and noticed his fingernails chewed down to the quick. That was something new. He'd never been a fingernail biter before, and he'd never wet the bed, either. She threw her arms round him for a last hug. 'I'll come and see you again as soon as I can, Alfie,' she said, and fled for the bus.

She boarded it with a bad conscience. In no mood for conversation, she sat down beside a woman who was gazing out of the window, wrapped in her own thoughts. To Marie's relief she proved equally unsociable, and they travelled in blessed silence all the way to New Holland and the ferry. By the time they got there, the force of circumstances had helped Marie to talk herself out of her misgivings about Alfie. Almost.

Charles was waiting for her on Corporation Pier, his hazel eyes full of sympathy. 'Your ordeal's over, poor girl. How was it?'

'Bad enough.'

'How did they take it?'

'Not as I'd expected. Still, it's over now.' She held out the money he had given her. 'Here's your fiver. I didn't need it.'

70

He tucked it into his inside pocket. 'Are they all right?'

'Our Pam is. She's got a very good place,' Marie said, taking his arm and walking with him towards the car. 'Trust Pamela to land with her bum in the butter. I expected her to be beside herself with grief, but you'd have thought I was talking about people she hardly knew.'

'Maybe she hasn't had time for it to sink in.'

'Well, it certainly sank in with Alfie. He cried his eyes out; I couldn't console him. And he's with a real sour-faced widow and her horrible son.'

'Perhaps he gives her plenty to be sour about,' Charles said. 'Most of Alfie's troubles are of his own making, if you ask me. Remember the day he thought it would be a good joke to stick a spud up the exhaust of Dad's car? If I hadn't caught him it would have ruined the engine. That would make anybody sour. And when he carved his initials into your piano with that Swiss army knife some idiot gave him?'

That brought a smile to her lips. How could she forget? Her mother and father had gone to the allotment to gather in the last of the vegetables, Pam was with a friend down the street, and she and Charles had sent Alfie out to play so they could take this golden opportunity to have an hour or two to themselves on the front-room sofa. They'd been in a Hollywood-style embrace when Charles had suddenly frozen, staring at the window. Marie had turned to see Alfie making hideous faces at them, his features distorted and whitened by the pressure of the glass. It was then that Charles had given Alfie the knife as a bribe

71

to 'hop it'.

'That idiot was you, Chas,' she said.

'And I've never regretted anything as much in my life,' he said. 'And I got the blame from your mother, not him, the little rotter. Still, I'll forgive and forget, things being what they are.'

'You're all heart,' she laughed.

Chapter 6

Charles was waiting outside the hospital when she finished her early shift the following day. He jumped out of the car and opened the passenger door for her. 'I'd have liked to take you dancing on my last night of freedom, but I thought you'd be too tired, so I got us two tickets for Hull New Theatre,' he said. 'All you have to do there is sit and relax. They're doing *Rebecca*. It got a rattling good write-up in the paper.'

'That's nice,' said Marie, although she was not in the mood for either dancing or playgoing. 'I wonder if I'm ever going to get to know something definite about Dad. Alfie asked about a funeral. If he's dead, I'll have to organize one.' She sniffed back sudden tears.

Charles put a comforting arm around her. 'Does your mother realize he's missing yet?'

'Well, she knows he's not with her because the nurses say she keeps asking for him, but I don't think she realizes he's missing in the sense of "presumed dead". I've tried to tell her but it's hard to know whether you're getting through, because she doesn't hear half of what you say, and she forgets the rest. God, what a mess. She wouldn't be fit to go to any funeral anyway. It's Pam and Alfie I'm worried about. Alfie would definitely want to come, and I wonder if I should send for them both. What do you think?'

'Oh, I don't know,' said Charles with a frown. 'Pretty gruelling for anybody, I should think. Maybe Pam's old enough to stand it, but it might be too much for young Alfie. I'd have thought so, anyway. But you know them better than I do.'

'I ought to let them know – give them the choice.'

'Cross that bridge when you come to it. Until you know something definite; there's nothing you can do. I'll run you home, we'll get something to eat, and then you get your glad rags on. Let's try to take your mind off it all for our last evening together, at least.'

Marie put on the brightest face she could manage and went to the theatre with him, determined not to spoil what Charles called his last night of freedom. Driving through the centre of Hull for the first time in weeks, she saw the wrecked streets, with half-demolished buildings, craters and broken masonry everywhere, but Hull New Theatre had been lucky enough to survive the bombing. She took her seat, determined to forget her troubles for a while and immerse herself in the play, but her mind kept flitting to thoughts of her missing father, her injured mother, Alfie's misery, Pam's apparent indifference, and the awful responsibility of having all of it dropped squarely on

73

her shoulders. During the interval she pretended enjoyment, smiled, nodded and agreed with the people who were raving about the performance, and when they left the theatre she couldn't have told anybody what the play had been about.

'Lucky you're on a late tomorrow,' Charles said, as they drove home.

She agreed, her thoughts elsewhere. The journey continued with Charles making conversation, and Marie replying in monosyllables until he brought the car to a halt outside her front door. They sat for a while, idly watching a couple approaching from the far end of the street, the man with his arm round the woman's waist.

'Are you going to ask me in for a cup of tea?'

Marie appeared not to have heard. 'You know, I think I'm going to have to bring Alfie home. I can't get him out of my mind. There's something wrong there.'

'Are you insane? You said yourself that if they hadn't been evacuated, they'd almost certainly be dead. And at least half of what's wrong there is Alfie, if you ask me. Your mother was summoned to school to hear complaints about him twice, to my knowledge, and we hadn't been courting ten months before they went to Bourne. If you want my opinion, the happiest day of your parents' lives was the day they waved him off.'

'It was not. How can you say such a thing! Alfie's a bit impish, but he's not a bad lad at heart.'

'A bit impish? Always up to no good, you mean, always playing some stupid prank on somebody. And even if he were the best lad in the world, how can you manage with him at home, with no one to look after him?'

'He's eleven. He should be able to look after himself.'

Charles gave a wry smile, and shook his head. 'There might be some 11-year-olds you'd dare trust in the house on their own, but I wouldn't take a chance on Alfie. Just don't do anything hasty, Marie. My mother gave in to Danny and brought him home, and now she's got even more reason to be terrified during the bombing, and he's got her on a string, the crafty little twerp. Don't let Alfie pull the wool over your eyes. Give it a bit longer, see how things go. It'll probably do him the world of good to be somewhere where he's not coddled. Toughen him up a bit.'

'He might not survive being toughened up by a lad twice his size; Ernie strikes me as a nasty piece of work. And his mother's face would turn the milk sour. They haven't a good word for our Alfie, either of them.'

'Well, just let's forget about Alfie for a bit. Are you going to ask me in?'

She nudged him and nodded towards the couple who were approaching, linked arm in arm.

'That's Hannah, that woman who cleans for your mother, isn't it?' Marie said. 'I thought her husband was on the convoys.'

'He is.'

'That's not him, then. He's in an army uniform.'

Charles eyebrows shot up, and his eyes widened. 'So he is!'

'Mam! Mam!' A little girl dashed out of a gate and ran to greet her. As soon as she was within striking distance Hannah landed a slap on her face that sent her reeling off the pavement and into the road.

Marie jumped out of the car and bounded down the street, reaching them just as Hannah was inserting the key into her front door.

'Just hold on,' she shouted, 'just hold on a bit. I saw that.'

'Saw what?'

'I saw what you just did to that bairn. I saw the crack you gave her. You ought to be ashamed of yourself.'

Hannah looked her up and down. 'You get away and mind your own business. It's no concern of yours how I look after my own daughter.'

Marie exploded. 'I've just watched you walk down this street, and this bairn's been sitting on the doorstep, waiting for you. How old is she? About six? You leave her roaming the streets on her own till this time of night and you call that "looking after"?'

Hannah flung the door open. 'Jenny! Get in that house.'

With her nose and eyes streaming and stifling her sobs, the little girl pulled her cardigan round her skinny frame, and with a wary eye on Hannah, dodged quickly under her arm and went inside. Three strides brought Hannah to the gate, where she tried to stare Marie down – while addressing her comments to Charles, who was just approaching them. 'Can't you control your young woman, Charles?'

'I'm sorry, Hannah, you'll have to excuse her. She's got a lot on her mind. Come on, Marie.

Come away,' Charles urged.

'That's right, you get her away, tell her to mind her own bloody business, before she gets a piece of my mind. It's nothing to do with her if I give my own bairn a tap.'

Marie couldn't believe her ears. 'I'm sorry, Hannah? That wasn't just a tap!' She turned to Charles, outraged. 'She nearly knocked the bairn's head off her shoulders. You saw it yourself! And who's that she's with, while her husband's away risking his life on the convoys? Standing there watching her knock the poor man's bairn about?'

Charles grabbed her shoulders, pulling her away. 'Come on, Marie. Come away, it really is nothing to do with us.'

The soldier with Hannah shrugged and gave Charles a wink before following Jenny into the house.

Marie shook Charles off, and advanced on Hannah. 'I saw what you did, and if I see any more of it, I'll have the law on you. Don't think I won't.'

Hannah went in and slammed the door.

'Marie, let's go,' Charles begged. 'It's really none of your business.'

She gave him a blistering look. 'What's wrong? Are you scared of falling out with her? She's your mother's charwoman – it's her that should be scared of falling out with you! Are you worried your mother might have to scrub her own bloody floors for a change?'

'Marie, you're not being rational.'

'Rational! Is it rational to leave a bairn her age roaming the streets on her own till this time?

Anything could have happened to her. What if there'd been a raid?'

'She'd have known to go to the shelter.'

'A 6-year-old? What if she'd been hurt?'

'Come off it, Marie. She'd have been among neighbours. People pouring out of their houses, neighbours who knew her. Somebody would have helped her.'

'At times like that, people might be too busy looking after themselves and their own. And it's her own mother that should be the one helping her.'

'Yes, of course she should, but you can't impose your standards on other people. And how do you know she's six?'

'She can't be more. I've seen her going to school, and she's not been going that long.'

Marie could barely speak to Charles when they got back to the house.

'You're tired,' he said, trying to placate her, 'and overwrought. With good reason, I know.'

'Yes, I am.'

'Too tired to invite me in for a cup of tea?'

'Yes, I am.'

'Don't I even get a kiss? I'll be off tomorrow.'

She kissed him on the cheek with as much grace as she could muster.

He held her waist in two strong hands, and gazed deep into her eyes. 'Will you come and see me off?'

'I'll come and see you tomorrow morning before you go,' she said, turning her face away to evade a kiss. 'I'll just have time before I start work.'

She watched him get back in the car and

managed to wave him off fairly civilly as he dro
away, then went in and closed the door, not bes
pleased with Charles for taking Hannah's side
when she was so clearly in the wrong.

Within half an hour she was in bed, desperate
to get enough sleep to see her through her next
shift at the hospital. Again sleep eluded her.
There was nothing she could think of with an
easy mind; nowhere she could rest her thoughts
and feel tranquil. Her mother had been transferred to the hospital in Beverley, and was out of
danger, but still gravely ill. As soon as she was a
bit better the hospital would want to discharge
her, and who was there to care for her but her
daughter? She would have to leave work, and
then what would they do for money? No, she
couldn't leave work, she'd bring Pam back from
the Stewarts to help, but that might not be easy.
Pam had her feet well under the table there, and
it was a better spread table than anything Marie
could provide. Pam seemed to belong more to
the Stewarts now than to her own family. Never
mind! If Pam was needed at home, she'd have to
come home, and that was the end of it.

And that bloody woman Hannah, having men
round while her husband was risking his life on
the convoys. He might already be dead; hadn't
Mr Elsworth said that 700,000 tons of shipping
had gone to the bottom already? And God knows
how many men. But that obviously didn't bother
Hannah. And poor little Jenny – left out all
evening and then nearly getting her head
knocked off. Poor little scrap – somebody had to
stick up for bairns like that.

But what rankled most was Charles. He'd been a dead loss, not only failing to back her up, but apologizing to that slut! 'I'm sorry, Hannah, you'll have to excuse her,' he'd said. Outrageous! Talking about her as if she were deranged! Her thoughts flitted back to Alfie then, crying and pleading to come home, and she pictured herself as hard and cruel as Hannah, fobbing him off instead of comforting him, and then waltzing off and leaving him to the tender mercies of the widow and her son. Alfie wanted to come to the funeral, and it might be soon – something else to face.

She got up and wrote a letter to Pam but left it unsealed. She'd finish it and send it as soon as she knew something definite. That done, she went back to bed to toss and turn, sleep little and fitfully, and wake from time to time in the middle of dreams of attacks on defenceless children who changed from Jenny into Alfie and then back again, until they were one and the same. She awoke at dawn to the awful realization that she truly was on her own. There was no one else to shoulder any of the responsibility for them all. Everything that had to be done would have to be done by her, and her alone.

Hannah opened the door of the Elsworths' house the following morning, and gave Marie one long, silent, hard-faced stare, but she had misjudged her opponent.

Marie stared straight back, boring right into her eyes, and Hannah was the first to look away. Then she turned her back and sauntered up the stairs.

Marie stepped inside and closed the door after herself.

'Hello?' she called.

'In the kitchen!' Mrs Elsworth answered.

Marie walked along the hallway past the telephone on the polished table, and found her by the Rayburn, pouring steaming coffee into four cups.

'You see, you were expected,' she said. 'We'll just have time to drink this before Charles has to leave.'

Marie went and stood beside her. 'I thought Hannah might have had her orders to register for employment in some government work by now,' she commented.

'If she has, she hasn't mentioned it to me.'

'Have you ever seen her daughter?'

Mrs Elsworth's manner became guarded. 'Once or twice.'

'Did Charles tell you about last night?'

'He mentioned something, very briefly.'

Marie gave her version, also briefly, and as dispassionately as she could.

'I'm afraid I agree with Charles,' Mrs Elsworth said. 'I never get involved in other people's family affairs. Hannah's worked here for three years, and she's been very reliable. I really prefer not to know about her private life. It's not my concern.'

Marie felt she'd been properly put in her place, and resolved to say no more – not here, at any rate. What would be the point? It was clear that she would receive no back-up from this quarter.

Charles and his father provided a welcome interruption.

'I'm glad you've come.' Charles gave her a wide

81

smile and pulled out a chair for her.

'Thanks, Chas,' she smiled back, using the nickname more as one in the eye for Mrs Elsworth than because she felt much friendlier towards him. He dropped a kiss on the back of her neck as she sat down. His father carried two of the coffee cups to the table, and pulled a chair out for his wife. Mrs Elsworth brought the other two, and put one down in front of Marie, her lips compressed into that increasingly familiar thin line of disapproval.

When the coffee was finished Mrs Elsworth took the cups to the sink. Charles got up, and putting his arms round his mother, gave her a squeeze.

Marie saw the tears start to her eyes. 'Come back safe,' she whispered. 'I won't come to the station. I'll say goodbye here, and here's where I pray I'll see you again.'

She followed them to the door, brushing tears away with a lawn handkerchief and Marie regretted her childish insistence on her pet name for Charles. She was just about to say so when Hannah came downstairs with her yellow duster and thrust herself into the gathering.

'So long, Charles,' she said, with a knowing wink. 'When you're at that camp, and they bring a lorry load of Land Army girls in for you to dance with, don't do anything I wouldn't do!'

Marie's jaw dropped at the cheek of her, and Charles gave Hannah an unfathomable look. 'I certainly won't,' he said.

Mrs Elsworth stopped crying in an instant, her face taut and her manner icy. 'You'll find some washing-up in the kitchen, Hannah, and the floor needs mopping,' she snapped.

Nothing daunted, Hannah sashayed down the hallway singing a snatch from an Andrews Sisters number about a boogie woogie bugle boy. 'Da daah – da da – daah da!' she bawled. 'Da daah – da da – daah da!'

'We'd better be off,' Mr Elsworth said.

He tactfully said his own goodbyes when he dropped Charles and Marie at the station.

Beneath her all-sweetness-and-light exterior Marie was still smouldering about Charles's failure to back her up with Hannah, but now was not the time to bring it up and spoil their last few moments together.

He was happily oblivious, or pretending to be. 'I'm sorry I have to go and leave you to deal with this mess with your parents on your own, Marie,' he said, and the hazel eyes gazing into hers had a truly troubled look. 'If I had any choice in the matter, I'd stay and help, but I haven't, so I'll have to do it by proxy. Dad's promised to run you up to Beverley whenever you want to visit your mother, as long as the petrol ration stretches to it.'

'I should think his petrol ration will stretch a lot further with you away,' she said.

'Ha ha. Anyway, keep him to it. I was thinking that if we got married on my next leave, you could get the allowance. At least it would help towards paying the rent and other expenses. Until then you might be able to get some help from the government. Dad will look into that for you, as well.'

She looked up, startled. 'Is that a proposal? We're not even engaged!'

Charles pulled a tiny box out of his inside pocket. 'That's your fault. We might have been engaged yesterday, if you'd asked me in. What do you say, Marie? Shall we make a go of it?' He placed the little box in her hand.

She flipped the lid open. On a cushion of deep blue velvet lay a beautiful gold ring. Three bright diamonds twinkled up at her.

'Oh, Charles, I'm sorry.'

His face fell.

'I mean, I'm sorry about last night,' she said. 'But why on earth didn't you back me up with Hannah?'

'Let's forget last night; it's water under the bridge. Does that mean yes? Do you like the ring?'

She slipped it onto her ring finger. 'It's a dead fit. I like it better than Nancy's. It looks real nice, doesn't it?'

'Does that mean yes?'

She looked up and laughed. 'Go on, then.'

'Don't go overboard, will you?' he grinned and, pulling her towards him, gave her a long, lingering kiss before releasing her and looking deep into her eyes. 'I've got some plans for us, my beauty, when the war's over. Wider skies, and broader horizons. We're going to spread our wings and fly.'

'Hull's got pretty wide skies and broad horizons,' she said. 'The countryside's flat for miles around.'

'You know what I mean.'

'I do, but I'm needed here.'

'I know. I understand what a terrible time you're going through, Marie,' he said earnestly, 'but it won't last forever. I wish I could be with you but I can't, so I'll help in the only way I can.'

He put two five-pound notes into her pocket. 'Keep them, just in case. I don't want you to be stuck for money.'

'I'll take it, but I won't spend it unless I absolutely have to. I'll hand it back when I see you again, if I can.'

He pulled her close and kissed her, then said: 'You know, I'd trust you with my life, never mind ten pounds. It's there for you to spend, if you get stuck. You're the most honest, decent, unselfish girl I've ever met, but don't let that brother of yours con you into having him home. He can't look after himself, and you'll find you've made a rod for your own back. When your mother comes out of hospital get Pam back instead, and let her make herself useful. She's old enough to do her share. It shouldn't all land on your shoulders.'

'I'll have no choice if I want to carry on working, but I don't think she'll come willingly.'

'Then make her come however it has to be. I do love you, old thing. Did I ever tell you that?'

'Once or twice.' He looked expectantly into her eyes, and she softened enough to say the words she knew he was waiting for: 'I love you too.'

And it was the truth. She did love Charles. She watched him go, certain they would marry and longing for the day when the war was over and she was settled with him, with a couple of miniature Charleses clinging to her skirts, but she'd lied when she'd said she was sorry about last night. She wasn't sorry at all, either about having a go at Hannah, or sending Charles home after he'd failed to back her up. He'd let her down, and he deserved to be made to feel it.

85

Chapter 7

'What did you think to the play?' Nancy asked.

'All right,' Marie said, suppressing a yawn and longing for the end of her shift so that she could collapse into bed.

'Only all right? I thought it was real good. So did George.'

'George? I wouldn't have thought he was the play-going type.'

'He's not really, but a couple of the actors are lodging at my mother's, and they said it's the best production they've ever been in, so I got him to take me. Thank goodness we didn't have an air raid to ruin it for us.'

'How much does she charge them – the actors?' asked Marie. 'If I have to leave work to look after my mother, taking a couple of lodgers might help with the housekeeping.'

'Never asked,' Nancy shrugged, 'and Mam wouldn't tell me anyway. But actors are ideal, she says. They never stay too long. One of them's gorgeous, though. He's been offered a job in the films.' Nancy tilted her head back and gave a self-conscious, tinkling little laugh. 'He says the only thing stopping him from taking it is he'd never see me again.'

'He's got it bad, then,' Marie said sardonically.

Nancy looked ecstatic. 'He has,' she replied, oblivious to the sarcasm. 'He says he'll only take the job if I promise to move down south with him.'

'You're not serious?' Marie said, suddenly wide awake.

'I'm thinking about it.'

'You're telling me you're going to chuck a man like George – who you're *engaged* to, by the way – for a slick-talking fly-by-night you've known about half an hour? Yes, Nancy, if I were in your shoes I'd certainly think about that, long and hard. I'd think about it until I'd thought myself back into some sense. George is a good lad. He's a qualified engineer, and he's dead keen on his job. He's got good prospects, Nance.'

'Well, you're not in my shoes, and prospects don't set anyone's pulses racing.'

'And the actor chap does, I suppose?'

'Yes, he does! And how do you know Monty hasn't got good prospects?'

'Monty!'

Nancy blushed. 'Yes, Monty. His real name's Montgomery Holmes.'

'I bet that's not his real name, Nance. Don't let him kid you.'

'It's his professional name, then. And it's a very good name for a film star, if you ask me. And he's good company. He took me to a restaurant on my day off, treated me like a queen. He thinks I ought to have drama lessons. He says Hull's got the best-looking women in England, and I'm the best-looking woman in Hull. He says I'm pretty enough to be in the films.'

'He's got a hell of a lot to say, by the sound of it. What's he after – or has he already got it?'

Nancy tossed her head, very miffed. 'What a

rotten thing to say! He's not after anything – and he hasn't got anything, either. Can't anybody pay anybody a compliment, without being after something? You're in a nasty mood today, Marie.'

'No, I'm not. You're talking about doing the dirty on George, and I'm being honest, telling you it's ten to one you'll regret it if you do. I can't help it if you don't like the truth.'

'I could tell you some truths, if I wanted to, that you wouldn't like,' Nancy flared. 'Are you sure you know Charles as well as you think? There might be a lot about him that you don't know.'

'What do you mean by that?'

'Nothing.'

'You don't say something like that, and then say "nothing". What are you talking about? What is it about Charles I don't know?'

'Nothing, I said. But maybe none of us knows what's round the corner, until it falls on top of us. Or what we might do when we're put to it.'

'I don't know you as well as I thought I did,' said Marie, 'but I know this, Nance. You're a lot too deep for me.'

Nancy abruptly turned her back and flounced off down the ward.

What was she talking about? Marie watched her go, liking her no better for her treachery to George, and determined to get to the bottom of that last comment as soon as she got the opportunity. Her thoughts flashed back to George on the night he'd taken his mother to the shelter, how happy he'd been to tell her about their engagement, the poor fool. And here was Nancy, shamelessly talking about going off with some poncy actor.

'Montgomery what?' she muttered to the patient, who was too ill to care. 'I don't remember seeing that name on the playbill. And what's the use of plays anyhow, when there's more drama going on around us than they could show on a stage in a million years?'

Nancy was soon coming down the ward again, making directly for her. Marie gave her a disapproving look, but Nancy didn't respond in kind.

'Sister sent me to tell you there's someone in the office wants to speak to you,' she said, her voice subdued, then added: 'Marie, it's the police.'

Marie flew the length of the ward, moving as fast as she could without actually running. Sister answered her knock on the office door.

'Come in and sit down, Nurse Larsen, I'll leave you alone for a minute.'

A burly policeman stood up as she entered. 'Sit down, lass.'

Marie sat, and waited.

He took an identity disc out of his pocket and placed it on the desk in front of her. 'Do you recognize that?'

It was what her dad had called his dead meat disc, a leftover from the Great War. She picked it up. 'You've found him, then.'

He nodded. 'The rescue services have. We went to your house. One of the neighbours said you'd be here.'

'Dead, I suppose?' she said, tears suddenly welling into her eyes.

He nodded. 'I'm sorry, lass.'

89

Marie was silent for a few moments. Nothing else could have kept him from her mother's side. She'd known from the outset that it must be so but still, a little flame of hope had burned deep within her, until this moment. 'I had an idea,' she said. 'As soon as I saw my mother without him, I knew he'd be dead. It's a relief to know for sure, all the same. At least we can stop worrying about him lying injured somewhere. He was in that Ellis Street shelter then?'

The policeman nodded. 'His remains are at Albert Avenue Baths, badly mangled, I'm afraid, but enough to identify. Somebody will have to go and do that, and get a death certificate. Then see the undertakers. You should go through his papers. If he was in a Friendly Society you might get help towards the cost of the funeral...'

The advice went on. Marie was back on the ward as soon as he'd gone. She found Sister helping Nancy to put a patient back into bed. They finished the task, and then Sister took her aside.

'Are you all right?'

'They've found my dad's body,' Marie said.

'I'm sorry, Nurse. I'd let you go now, but we're so short-staffed.'

Nancy was hovering nearby. Sister gave her a look, warning her off.

'It's all right,' Marie said. 'Nancy and I have known each other for years. The news is a shock, but I've been expecting it to come. Going off duty won't make it any better. In fact, I'll be better working; I don't want to think about it too much just now.'

Sister gave Marie's hand a gentle squeeze.

'Take Nurse into the kitchen, and make her a cup of tea,' she told Nancy. 'It's not much, but at least we can do that for her.'

Nancy put a comforting arm round her, to lead her away.

Marie had been steeled against everything but sympathy. She shook her head. 'I'll be better working. Deep down, I've known ever since he went missing that he was...' Sudden tears blurred her deep blue eyes and glistened on the pale lashes beneath. A painful lump rose to her throat making it hard to get the words out. '...that he was dead,' she managed to say. Then, struggling hard to regain her composure, she added, 'But tomorrow I'll have to go and tell my mother the bad news, and see the funeral director, and send invitations to all the relatives, and let the war pension people know, and...'

'Isn't there anybody but you to do any of these things?' Sister asked, her eyes full of sympathy.

'No.'

'Then we'll have to manage without you. I'll change the duty rota. Somebody else will have to work your shift.'

'I'll do it,' Nancy volunteered. 'It was my day off tomorrow, but Nurse Larsen can have it.'

'Thanks, Nancy, you're a pal,' Marie said, her eyes filling with tears of gratitude. A friend in need is a friend indeed, as the old saying went, and whatever was happening between her and George, Nancy had been a good friend since the day they'd first started nursing.

Chapter 8

'Marjorie's gone to do her bit for the WVS. There's only me in the house, and I'll have to get back to the shop soon,' Mr Elsworth said, putting a cup of watery tea on the kitchen table in front of Marie. 'It should be all right; it hasn't been made all that long. Unfortunately, there's no milk or sugar, thanks to Danny. He hasn't quite got the hang of rationing yet, but we live in hope. If you'd come any earlier I'd still have been out. I've only just got back from the police courts.'

'What happened?'

'Fined thirty shillings, and licence endorsed. I haven't paid it yet. My God, Jerry has made a mess of the city centre.'

'Pity they didn't drop one of their incendiaries on the police courts and send all the records up in smoke,' she said. 'You'd be thirty bob better off.'

He smiled. 'I could almost like them if they'd done that. But they've a nasty habit of dropping them in the wrong places.'

'Like on top of people huddled in air-raid shelters. Dad *is* dead. It's official. A policeman came yesterday to tell me he's been found and give me his identity disc. I was rooting all over the house last night to find the papers for the funeral club he's paid into for years, and I had to go and identify him at the mortuary this morning.'

Mr Elsworth looked aghast. 'You mean you

went on your own? You shouldn't have done that. I'd have gone with you, or Marjorie.'

'I wish Charles were here. I wouldn't have minded having him beside me.'

'I think Charles told you he'd deputized us to look after you while he was away.'

'He did, but I can't pester you with my troubles; you've got your repair shop to run, as well as everything else. So I just got on with it. Anyway, you couldn't have helped, you had your court case, remember? I've been to see the undertaker, as well. "We can squeeze you in on Friday," he said. "Two o'clock. If not, it'll have to be next week." So I decided to let them squeeze Dad in on Friday. I've written to most of our relatives, and if they can't come, it's a bad job, but the sooner it's all over the better, as far as I'm concerned.'

'I'm sorry, Marie.'

'You sometimes hear people say: "Oh, they looked real peaceful," after somebody's died. My dad didn't look peaceful. He looked absolutely terrible, as if he died in agony. It was awful.'

'That doesn't surprise me. My views on the glories of war are well known, so I'll say no more, except – please accept my condolences, and if I can do anything to help, you only have to ask. I just wish I could have given you a better cup of tea; that would have been more use.'

'This'll do. At least it's warm and wet. I'd like you to come to the funeral, if you will.'

'I will, but if the invitation includes Marjorie, I can tell you she'll refuse. I've never yet been able to persuade her to set foot in a Catholic church.'

'Just you, then. My mother doesn't even know

he's been found yet. Charles said you wouldn't mind driving me up to the hospital.'

'Of course not. I'll get my coat.'

'There's another thing, Mr Elsworth,' Marie said, encouraged by his offer of help. 'I sent Pam a letter with a postal order for the fares for her and Alfie, and then I remembered the people she's with have a telephone. I wonder if you'd mind if I rang them from here? Only I don't know the number.'

'If you have their name and address you'll get them all right, as long as the lines aren't damaged. But won't Pam be at school?'

'Yes, I suppose she will. Well, I'll see my mother first, and come back this evening to talk to Pam, if you're sure you don't mind.'

Her mother's bloodshot eyes peered out from under the bandages. 'Who is it?' she croaked. 'Marie. Oh, my bairn, I am glad to see you. Where's your dad?' Her voice was slow and it seemed an effort for her to force the words out.

Marie's eyes brimmed with tears. 'Oh, Mam, Dad's dead! He died in the shelter.'

'I can't hear you; I can't tell what you're saying. My ears ache real bad, Marie, and my head's bursting.'

Marie sank down on the chair beside the bed, feeling utterly helpless. That her mother, a vigorous, capable woman, should be reduced to this. What harm had she ever done? None, and yet her life had been deliberately destroyed. Marie held her mother's hand and, raising her voice as much as she could, she said: 'The police came yester-

94

day, Mam. To tell me Dad's body's been found. I've sent a letter to our Pam and Alfie, and I'm going to ring our Pam this afternoon. I've arranged his funeral for Friday.'

Her mother's face was a picture of fear and bewilderment. 'What? What?' she asked, in a quavering voice. 'A funeral? Your dad?'

'You were right then, he is dead.' Pam's voice sounded flat when Marie telephoned her from the Elsworths' that evening.

'No doubt about it, I'm sorry to tell you. There's no chance our mam will be able to go to the funeral, either. She can't even get out of bed. Her head still aches and the explosion was so near it's nearly deafened her. It took me ages to make her understand what's happened. I sent you a letter today, with a postal order in it. I want you to cash it and use the money for the fares for you and Alfie, and maybe a bite to eat on the way. You can show him the letter. It's Monday today, and the funeral's on Friday, so you'll have to be here by Thursday at the latest. Better come on Wednesday to be on the safe side.'

'I don't want to come,' Pam said. 'I'm not coming. Hull's too dangerous. That's why Mum and Dad sent us away.'

'Don't you think you should be at your own father's funeral, Pam?'

'What's the use? He won't know whether anyone's there or not, and neither will Mum, if she's not going – unless you tell her. Anyway, he wouldn't want me to. I know he wouldn't want me to be anywhere so dangerous.'

95

'Mam would like to see you.'

'She's too ill for anything, and she can't hear. You just said.'

'Alfie does want to come, Pam.'

'Then I'll give him the postal order, and he can come on his own.'

'He's too young.'

'No he's not. All he has to do is get the bus to Lincoln, and then to New Holland, and then get the ferry over, and he's there.'

'You think he can do that? Sort his fares out, and get the connections? He's only eleven. I can't believe how selfish you're being, Pam.'

There was no response to that. Marie hesitated, wondering if she dare allow Alfie to travel on his own. 'All right, then, Pam. Cash the postal order, pay Alfie's fare to Lincoln, and see him onto the bus. He'll have to come on his own if you won't bring him. Is Mrs Stewart there?'

'No, but Uncle Alec is.'

'He's not your uncle, Pam. Your uncles live in Hull.'

'He's better than a lot of uncles. None of the ones in Hull would do half as much for me as he does.'

'I'll have a word with him, please.'

'It won't make any difference. He won't make me come.'

'Just get him, will you?'

No doubt he wouldn't make her come, Marie thought, while she waited for him. Pamela seemed to be able to twist 'Uncle' Alec round her little finger.

When he answered Marie explained the situation again, and got a promise from him that either he or Pamela would personally see Alfie onto the bus on Wednesday, and pay his fare with the money from the postal order, and give him the rest for the fare to New Holland and the ferry to Hull. If Pamela wasn't coming, Alfie could bring the balance of the money back with him. Marie banged the receiver down. Pam would not be keeping the rest of that money, even if she thought she might.

She went into the sitting room, and found Mrs Elsworth on the settee with her feet up, still in her immaculately pressed green uniform, apart from the matching hat, which sat on the sideboard proclaiming 'WVS' in embroidered letters.

'You might have gathered that Pam's not coming, but Alfie specifically told me he wanted to be at Dad's funeral. But letting a hare-brained 11-year-old come all that way on his own...' Marie paused, then said: 'I wonder if I've done the right thing? I've a good mind to ring again and tell them not to send him. But he really wants to come.'

'He'll be all right,' said Danny, his eyes shining. 'It'll be an adventure, coming on his own. I wish it was me.'

'"*Were* me", Danny,' Mrs Elsworth corrected him. '"I wish it were me."'

'Let him come,' Mr Elsworth said. 'Most lads are capable of a lot more than you imagine, when they're really up against it. But I'll go and fetch him myself, if you're so concerned.'

'What about your petrol ration?'

'I'll go by train, or bus.'

97

'But if you didn't get there and back in the day, you'd have to find somewhere to stay for the night,' said Marie. 'I'd go myself, but we're not exactly overstaffed and I'm not flush with money. I couldn't get the time off even if I were. Injured people can't look after themselves. Anyway, I don't want to put you to any more trouble or expense. You've run round enough as it is.'

'Trust him, then,' Mrs Elsworth said. 'He might surprise you.'

'I suppose I'll have to. I'd better go. I've still got to take some funeral invitations to Dad's friends, just round where we live, you know. I've already posted the ones to people I can't get to on foot, and if I get it all done before I go to bed it'll be one less thing to worry about.'

She came away from the Elsworths feeling almost part of the family. Mrs Elsworth had admired the ring, and had told her that they'd congratulated Charles when he'd telephoned. It seemed that her mother-in-law-to-be had resigned herself to the inevitable. But by the time she got home Marie had a violent headache. Smut came trotting to welcome her, crying and mewing after being left alone so long. She bent to stroke him. 'How long is it since you got fed, Smutty? You'll have to go a-hunting and fend for yourself, like we all do, now. Catch your own or starve, you lazy tomcat.' She gave him a saucer of leftover porridge, and then boiled the kettle. She would blitz her headache with aspirin. She took four, washing them down with a beaker of Horlicks so thick she could almost stand the spoon up in it.

Dr Steele's fatalism had a lot to be said for it, she concluded, draining the thick, warming liquid to the last drop. If there were an air raid, she'd take her chances. There would be no getting out of bed to run and sit in a cold shelter this night. For all the protection they gave she might as well stay warm and cosy in her bed, unless the Nazis blasted her out of it.

With Smut curled up at her feet and purring like an engine, she slept soundly all night and reported for duty the following morning feeling better than she had for days. A couple of anti-aircraft shells had done some damage around George Street, but Marie had never heard a thing.

On Wednesday afternoon Sister called her into the office. 'There's a telephone call for you, Nurse. Something to do with your brother. But you know the hospital telephones are not for staff use, so just this once, Nurse, and make it quick.'

It was Pam. 'You're not supposed to ring me here,' Marie told her. 'You'll get me into trouble. You'll have to ring the Elsworths, and leave a message, in future.'

'I did ring the Elsworths, and he told me to ring you at the hospital. Alfie wasn't in school yesterday, so I couldn't tell him about the funeral. We – Uncle Alec and I, I mean we went to Mrs Morton's after tea, and she told us she'd sent him to school, and if he didn't go, it wasn't her fault.'

'What did Alfie say?'

'He didn't say anything, because he was out. So we told her we'd come for him today to put him on the bus for home, and she told us it wasn't a minute too soon. She was going to get the authorities to take him away. He's a thoroughly bad boy, she said, he ought to be in that approved school–'

'What's she talking about?' Marie interrupted. 'How is he a thoroughly bad boy?'

'She said he'd tied a can to her cat's tail, and nearly tormented it to death. She said it was tied so tight the end of its tail will probably come off, and it's been ill ever since, and she wouldn't be surprised if it dies of the shock. And he won't do anything he's told, he's got filthy habits, and a filthy mouth. She said: "You should have heard him when Ernest chastised him for tormenting the cat, and he tried to throw the blame on Ernest! And some of the names he called me! Disgusting! We'll be glad to see the back of him." That's exactly what she said.' Pam's voice was becoming ever more shrill. 'Can you imagine how I felt, hearing all that about my own brother, and Uncle Alec standing there, listening to every word?'

'Chastised him? What does she mean by "chastised"? And why was Ernie doing the chastising, and not her?'

'How do I know? All I know is I just wished a hole would open in the ground and swallow me up! I felt so ashamed!'

'Never mind your bloody feelings, Pam. What about Alfie?'

'What about Alfie? Well, he wasn't there this morning either, when Uncle Alec went to collect him for the bus. Mrs Morton said he'd sneaked out, and Ernest said he was always having to go out looking for him, and he was sick of it! So Uncle Alec asked where he'd be likely to be, and Ernest said St Peter's pool, or the woods. But Uncle Alec couldn't find him anywhere, and I'm ringing to save you the trouble of going to the ferry for him, Marie, even though you don't care about me or my feelings!'

'She's lying,' said Marie. 'Alfie would have been ready and waiting, bag and baggage, if he'd known someone was coming to put him on the bus home, and he'd have been on that bus like a shot.'

'Well, he did know, because she told him, and he wasn't there.'

That made no sense. It was obvious the woman was lying, but why would she, if she was set on getting rid of him? Marie was at a loss. 'Well, you go again tomorrow, and you get him on that bus,' she said.

'I can't go. Have you forgotten, Marie? I have to go to school. So Uncle Alec will have to go.'

Our Pam, Marie thought, a great help in a crisis. She drew a deep breath, and paused to get her tongue under control before she spoke. 'This is your brother we're talking about, Pam. He's eleven years old, and nobody seems to know where he is. That's more important than missing a couple of hours of school. Is Mr Stewart there?'

'No.' Pam sounded sullen. 'They've gone out. They've both gone to get some shopping.'

'Well, tell them I'll ring tomorrow morning, after someone's been to the Mortons'. And if Mr Stewart doesn't want to go, you go, Pamela. Alfie's your brother; you're the only family he's got nearby, so it's your responsibility. And if Alfie isn't there this time, I'll be ringing the billeting officer and the police.'

Marie replaced the receiver, feeling as if she'd lost her stomach. The Alfie she knew would never torture an animal. When her mother had taken Smut in, Alfie had doted on him. If Alfie had changed into a little demon the Mortons had made him like that, but she didn't believe it, and she didn't believe the Mortons' story that he'd run away knowing someone was coming to put him on the bus home. Some very dark suspicions of the Mortons loomed into her mind.

Sister was back in the office. 'Are you all right, Nurse?'

'No, Sister, I'm not. I'm really not,' Marie said. 'But it's my own trouble, nobody else can do anything about it, and it won't stop me looking after the patients.'

Sister let her off early on Thursday to make preparations for the funeral. Marie rang Mr Stewart from the public telephone in the hospital foyer before she went home.

'Yes. I went to collect Alfie for the second time this morning,' he said. 'He wasn't there, and Mrs Morton told me he hadn't been in all night. Ernest went out to look for him on Wednesday evening, and Alfie attacked him.'

'Attacked him?' Marie exclaimed. 'How could he? Ernest's twice Alfie's size.'

Mr Stewart sounded mildly offended. 'The fact remains, Miss Larsen, that's what happened. He was searching for Alfie around St Peter's pool, and he said Alfie jumped at him and headed him under the chin. Ernest fell down, and then Alfie gave him a thrashing with a willow stick. I'm afraid it's true. I saw the marks.'

'Listen, Mr Stewart,' said Marie, 'the likelihood that my brother would be avoiding someone who was coming to put him on the bus back home is somewhere between nil and zero, or even less. Something's going on there that I don't understand. All I know is, nobody but the Mortons seem to have seen him all week.'

'No ... but Mrs Morton's a very respectable lady; she attends the church. I can't think of any reason why she would lie. And I did see the weals on her boy. I also went to the school. Alfie hasn't been in since Monday and I'm sorry to have to tell you that he hasn't got a shining reputation there, either. Apparently he's quite an unruly pupil.' There was a note of deep disapproval in Mr Stewart's voice.

'Pam said you went yesterday to look in all the places Ernest said he might be.'

'I did, and having had no success yesterday I saw no point in repeating the performance today, especially as it's impossible to get him home in time for the funeral now.'

Evidently the man was tired of running around on wild-goose chases in pursuit of other people's children. Marie could hardly blame him for that, but it should have been Pam doing the searching, not him.

'Well, thank you for everything you've done, Mr Stewart,' she said. 'I'm sorry to have troubled you, but my 11-year-old brother hasn't been seen since yesterday evening, and I can't just leave it at that. Do you happen to have the number of the nearest police station?'

Chapter 9

Holding the funeral at two o'clock at least meant there was enough time for all the friends and relatives to get to the church and for Marie to make the final preparations. She was up at dawn to make a mountain of sandwiches with Mother's Pride and baked ham – bought with Charles's money from somebody at the hospital who knew somebody who knew somebody else who could get such things with no names, no coupons and no questions asked. When she came to the end of the baked ham, she looked dubiously at the pile, wondering how many people would actually turn up. There might be enough, but to be sure she'd better open those tins of salmon her mother had been saving, and get another loaf as soon as the shops opened. The postman came while she was mixing scones. Rubbing her floury hands on her apron she went to the door to pick up a letter from Charles and sat at the bottom of the staircase to scan it.

'Sorry you're having such a rotten time of it,' he wrote, '...sorry I can't be there to help ... Dad's promised to do everything he can ... don't be too soft with Pam and Alfie, whatever you do ... if he comes to the funeral, send him back as soon as it's over, for his own good, and get her back to look after your mother...'

The letter took on a much brighter tone as he came to news of his own, as if he couldn't conceal his excitement at his forthcoming adventure. His fellow officers were a good bunch, and he was discovering he could play a decent hand of bridge. The men were a decent bunch as well, except for one, who so far had been a bloody nuisance, and showed every sign of continuing to be one. He would have to be squashed, in short order. They might be shipped off somewhere very soon, or so rumour had it. He'd let her know as soon as he could, and write to her as often as possible.

Marie folded the letter with a grim smile, and put it in her apron pocket. Her dad was going to be shipped off too – off to four clay walls about six feet deep, and there she'd have to leave him. He wouldn't be making the return trip, and he wouldn't be writing.

'He's bound to turn up soon,' George said, from the back of Mr Elsworth's car where he sat beside his mother as they followed the hearse up Princes Avenue towards St Vincent's Church.

Marie turned to him, her face even paler than usual, and drawn with the strain of the past few days. 'Preferably alive and well,' she said.

She had telephoned Bourne that morning and the news was the same from Alfie's school and the Stewarts. Neither hide nor hair of Alfie had been seen by anyone.

'Well, he can't have dropped off the face of the

earth. He must be somewhere,' George said, stating the blindingly obvious.

'He's been missing for two nights now.'

Both Pam and Mr Stewart had mentioned St Peter's pool and an image of the place loomed into Marie's mind. Was that where Alfie was? Drowned?

After a few moments' silence, George tried again. 'Well, maybe it's not such a bad thing if he misses the funeral. My dad died when I was about Alfie's age, and you took me to his funeral, didn't you, Mum? I'll never forget looking down at the coffin in that awful hole, and then that horrible sound of the earth, landing on top of him. I dreamed about it for years afterwards.'

'George!' There was a warning note in that one word from his mother.

'Oh, yes. Sorry, Marie.'

'It's all right, George,' she said, 'Nothing you can say can make things any worse than they are already.'

'Don't say that. Alfie'll turn up soon. Sure to,' Mr Elsworth said.

'I hope you're right. I'm not looking forward to telling my mother her baby's missing, on top of everything else. That would be the end of her.'

The hearse stopped, Mr Elsworth slowed his car to a halt behind it, and they got out. Marie heard a voice she recognized.

'Hello, Mr Elsworth!' Hannah hailed him. At the sight of Marie she pulled her face into an expression of sympathy. 'Oh, Marie!' she said, with her mouth turning up at the corners and eyes dancing with malice. 'I heard. It's your father, isn't it? And your mother's not very well, either. What a shame. I am sorry. Some people have no luck, have they?'

Marie gave her a dour look. 'Save your sympathy for Jenny, Hannah, and your husband, risking his life somewhere in the Atlantic. You must be frantic with worry about him.'

Hannah's repressed little smirk burst into a full-blown grin. 'Funnily enough, I'm not,' she said. 'Lucky Larry, that's what they call my husband. And he is lucky, like me.'

'I'm pleased to hear it, for Jenny's sake as well as his,' Marie said, and turned to walk into the church on Mr Elsworth's arm. Gloat while you can, Hannah, she thought – and watch your step with that little lass, or you'll be laughing on the other side of your face.

The church held an amazing number of people, given the short notice they'd had. Her father had been a kindly, sociable soul, with time for everyone. This turn-out was the result. It was a real comfort to Marie, but those two tins of salmon would definitely have to be opened if everyone here came back to the house.

'Charles will telephone tomorrow evening, if he gets the chance,' Mr Elsworth told her, before leaving them at Northern Cemetery. 'Come and spend the day with us, if you're not working.'

Marie promised she would, and shortly afterwards walked home with the rest of the funeral party and put her key in the lock. The door was already open.

'That's funny,' she said, standing back to let George and his mother in first. 'I must have forgotten to lock it.'

'I'm not surprised. You've had a lot on your plate this past month, lass,' George's mother sympathized.

The crowd of mourners followed Marie into the house. The front room was packed to suffocation with ten people, and the middle room was the same. People began spilling over into the kitchen and sitting on the staircase, so there was no room for all their coats and baggage.

'If you'll take your coats and everything upstairs and put them on the bed in the front bedroom, they'll be out of the way,' she said. 'We'll have a bit of room to manoeuvre.'

Uncle Alfred handed his coat to his wife, Dorothy – Auntie Dot – and edged his way into the front room to stir the fire into life, warm his backside, and start his familiar style of genial pontificating, a habit Marie well remembered from her childhood. This time the pontificating was about the war. She left him to it and went through to the kitchen to put three kettles on the stove, two of them borrowed from neighbours. They had also swelled the supply of crockery sufficiently to go round, but the piles of sandwiches didn't look quite as high as Marie had thought. She opened the salmon and started making more, until a neighbour relieved her of the task so that she could join her guests. The family had congregated in the front room with Aunt Edie and George, the rest of the neighbours occupied the dining room. By the time Marie joined the party in the front room Uncle Alfred had given them the solution to the problem of Adolf Hitler.

108

'I'm going to write to the War Office people and tell them to put you in charge, Uncle,' she teased. 'We'll have the war done and dusted in a fortnight.'

'That's just what your dad would have said. Our Alf, setting the world to rights again,' Uncle Alfred said. The recollection brought a tear to the corner of his eye, which he surreptitiously brushed away with the back of his hand before pulling a handkerchief out of his pocket, to give his nose a good blow. 'Aye, but we've had some fun in this house in the old days, lass. I'll never forget the parties your mam and dad used to have on New Year's Eve. You remember some of the games we played? I've laughed till my sides ached, in this house. Poor old Bert. Poor old lad.'

'He was a great practical joker,' Auntie Ellen said, after a moment or two of solemn silence. 'Do you remember that game where he used to have us blindfolded, feeling things, and guessing what they were? Do you remember when he put that raw sausage and some warm water in the chamber pot, and made me put my hand in it and tell everybody what it was? My God! I nearly died!'

'We all nearly died – of laughing,' Uncle Alf said, as the whole room erupted into mirth. 'It's a pity we don't get together more often. We've always got on.'

'If you thought that, why'd you move out to Dunswell?' demanded Aunt Lucy, who had lived in Anlaby for the past ten years with her husband and family.

'You know why. We wanted the smallholding,'

Alfred said. 'Same as you wanted that little shop you got in Anlaby.'

Auntie Dot looked up. 'Pity we had to get together at all for something like this. I got the shock of my life when we got Marie's letter,' she said.

'Our Bert. I still can't believe it,' said Aunt Lucy. 'My baby brother, gone.'

Marie had been wondering how to drop her bombshell about Alfie, and here was the perfect opening. 'My baby brother gone, as well,' she said. 'We sent him away to keep him safe from the bombing, and now he's gone missing. I can hardly believe that, either.'

All eyes turned towards her. Auntie Dot gaped. 'What, our Alfie?'

'What do you mean?' Auntie Ellen demanded. 'Gone where? Not killed, surely!'

'I certainly hope not killed. Only our Alfie wasn't happy where he was, and now he's just vanished. Nobody seems to have seen him for the past two days. I told the police yesterday, and I rang them again this morning. They're going to contact me when they've "had time to look into the matter."'

'Oh, that's good of 'em!' Ellen's husband, Jack, exclaimed. 'And when might they manage to find the time, do they think? Do they need a squib up their arses? They'll get one if they don't sharpen up.'

'He'll be trying to make his way home. Bet you,' said Alfred. 'Bet you anything you like.'

'He'll turn up, I'm sure. Leave it at least a week before you start worrying, Marie,' George soothed her. 'He's probably hiding out with some school friend or other in Bourne. You know what lads are like, always up to some prank. He'll be somewhere. He'll be all right. Don't fret.'

'That's the kettle,' Marie said, and took refuge in the kitchen.

Ellen followed her. 'My old neighbour's just flitted down to Lincoln. We've known each other years, and I was sorry to lose her. Her new husband's in the police there. As soon as we get back, I'll write to her, and see if he can get things moving.'

Marie stood sloshing milk into china cups, feeling her nerves beginning to crack. She paused. 'Thanks, Aunt Ellen. I know it sounds far-fetched, and I'm probably imagining things, but I've got a real bad feeling about the people our Alfie's been staying with. I wouldn't trust them as far as I could spit; the story they're telling just doesn't add up. When I looked at my dad's coffin in the church, I really wondered whether they've seen our Alfie off to the same place. You know, the next world.'

'You don't really think that, do you? I mean, not really.'

'I'm beginning to wonder. Will you take some of this food in? I'll bring the tea.'

'I'll write to my friend in Lincoln the minute I get home,' Ellen promised.

'Keep your eye on the time, Harry,' Aunt Lucy said, draining her cup. 'We don't want to miss the last bus back to Anlaby.'

'You could keep your own eye on the time if you wanted to. Why do you always leave everything to me?'

111

'I don't leave everything to you.'

'Don't worry about the bus,' said Marie. 'There's plenty of beds here. I'm the only one left, now.'

'I don't know as I'd want to stay here, and risk being caught in an air raid,' Aunt Lucy said. 'What a to-do. Your dad dead, your mother in hospital, and now Alfie missing. I never heard of a family having such bad luck.'

'You hear of plenty of them round here. We get them at the hospital all the time.'

'He was a wonderful feller, your dad,' Aunt Edie said. 'He could turn his hand to anything. Any mortal thing. My husband thought the world of him. He used to say he was the best little bloke in the world.'

Uncle Alfred swallowed a mouthful of tea. 'He used to be a dab hand at wine making. Some o' them parties him and your mam used to have... I don't suppose there's any handy?'

'What – parties?'

'Wine, you daft ha'porth.'

Marie rolled her eyes and tilted her chin in the direction of her neighbours in the dining room. 'Not enough to go round,' she said.

'Meaning there will be enough when the company thins out a bit?'

'If it thins out enough before you have to go for the bus, there will.'

All the coats had gone from the double bed with the exception of Alfred and Dot's. Having opted to risk an air raid rather than curtail the wine-tasting they went tipsily up the stairs, to sleep in the front bedroom. A couple of minutes later Marie heard a blood-curdling shriek, and dashed out of the kitchen in time to see Auntie Dot come tumbling down the stairs, white as a sheet and suddenly sober.

'Oh dear,' she said, clutching at her heart as she fell into Marie's arms. 'Oh dear me! There's something there.'

'Something where?'

'Little bedroom,' Auntie Dot shuddered. 'I didn't like to go poking about in your mother's wardrobe so I went to lay our clothes on the bed in there, and something moved ... ugh, ugh, ugh!' She shook herself from head to foot.

'Well, I'll be...' she heard Uncle Alfred exclaim. With no trace of horror in his voice he called, 'Marie, come up here.'

She found him in the smallest bedroom. There in the bed, filthy, fully dressed, and sound asleep with a half-eaten baked ham sandwich in his grimy hand, lay Alfie.

Uncle Alfred began to laugh. Alfie didn't stir.

'What are you laughing at?' Auntie Dot called.

'Come and see, Dottie.'

Marie greeted her with a broad smile. 'There's your "something".'

'Oh, my goodness! Well, thank heaven for that.'

'He'll cop it tomorrow, the little so-and-so. I'll skin him for what he's put me through,' Marie said, and went downstairs with a lighter heart to finish tidying up and lock the doors.

So ended the day she buried her father. He was gone, and all the talk about 'just like old times' only served to underline the fact that the old times were gone with him. Nothing would ever be the same. There would be no more of his practical jokes on New Year's Eve, no more of his allotment veg, his potted meats and pressed tongues, no more rabbit stew, no more home-made wine, no more Dad. The last he'd used to cobble their boots and shoes on stood propping the dining-room door open. The Great War had taken his leg and ruined his lungs, this second war had taken his life, and now her father's troubles were over.

But Alfie was home and safe, and Marie could feel nothing but overwhelming relief.

'I never touched her cat,' Alfie told them the following morning, as they breakfasted on toast and jam, and weak tea. 'I never laid a finger on it. It was Ernie tied that tin can to its tail, and he was laughing when it was jumping round the yard, going mad trying to shake it off. He thought it was real funny, then as soon as he sees his mother coming back from the shops, he stops laughing, and he says: "You're in trouble, boy, for doing that to our Smoky," loud enough so she could hear him and she'd think it was me. So I says I never touched your cat, it was you that did it, loud enough so she heard that as well. Then he says: "Don't lie. You'll never get to Heaven if you tell lies." So I told him: "You'll never get to Heaven at all, you rotten lying swine."

'So then she takes the shopping in and shouts us both into the house, and when we get in there she tells Ernie to get a stick from the yard, and beat me with it. So he did, real hard, and they both start laughing their heads off while I'm struggling and

114

trying to get away. Then she gets hold of one of my ears, nipping it to keep me still.'

'He's not fibbing,' Uncle Alfred said, pointing to big blue bruises on the top parts of Alfie's left ear.

'She ought to be reported,' Auntie Dot said. 'You ought to report her to the police, Marie.'

Marie nodded, looking at Alfie. 'Then what happened?'

'I told them, "I'm telling on you!" so Ernie says: "Who're you going to tell? Your dad's dead, you moron! You going to tell your mother? She's in hospital, she i'n't going to help you."

'So I said I was telling on them both. "As soon as I get in that school, I'm telling the teacher and all the other kids, and I'm showing them what you've done. And I'm telling our Marie," I said. Then she says: "You get upstairs to bed, you nasty little guttersnipe. You won't be telling anybody anything, and nobody will believe you if you do."'

'Let's have a look where Ernie hit you,' Marie said.

Alfie took off his shirt. There were small round fingermark bruises on his upper arms, and larger bruises all over him.

'Then they shut me in the bedroom and bolted the door so I couldn't get out and they kept me there for two days,' he went on. 'Then I thought I aren't sticking this a minute longer, I'm getting out of here if it kills me.'

'How did you get out?' Uncle Alfred asked.

'There were some horrible old women's stockings and two scarves in one of the drawers, so I tied them together to make a rope and tied it round the bedstead and let it out of the window and climbed out. It wasn't long enough, and I had to drop the rest of the way into the yard.'

'And he did come looking for you, I suppose.' Marie said, drily.

Alfie nodded. 'I picked a willow stick up by the Wellhead as soon as I saw him, a real whippy one. And I let him get real close, and then I thought: right, you've asked for this; it's your turn to get some stick, now. So I got my head down and jumped up and chinned him, then before he could get up I gave it him, tit for tat.' Alfie snorted with laughter, and added, 'I told him: "It's your turn now, you moron!" I don't think he knew what was happening.'

'But how did you get back home?' Auntie Dot asked. 'You can't have walked it.'

'I slept in the waiting room in the train station, and the next morning, I just got on the train with some other people, and stayed on it, and when I saw the ticket collector I locked myself in the lav, then I got off and walked a bit, and then I got a lift on a lorry that was going to New Holland. Then I got on the ferry, and told the man what had happened, and showed him my bruises, and he brought me over for nothing. I got on a bus on Corporation Pier, and when the conductor came, I told him the same.'

'Did you call Mrs Morton any names?' Marie asked.

Alfie nodded again. 'I called her a nasty old witch, and she is. And I'm never going back there.'

'Obviously not. They wouldn't have you, for one thing, even if I wanted to send you, which I

116

don't. But what do you think I'm going to do with you? How am I going to go to work, with you to look after? Answer me that,' Marie said, directing her question at Alfie, but hoping his godfather and namesake would take the hint and step into the breach.

Uncle Alfred didn't fail her. 'He can come and live with us on the smallholding, can't he, Dot? There's loads of room now our three have flown the coop. It's not far out of Hull, but it's a lot safer than where you are.'

'Well, I don't know,' Auntie Dot wavered. 'I think I'm a bit too old to be taking any youngsters on.'

'I'm not going anywhere,' Alfie cut in. 'I'm staying here. Don't worry about me, I can look after myself'

'You change your mind, and you can come and stay with us,' Uncle Alf told him before they left to catch the bus to Dunswell.

Marie stood at the gate with Alfie, and watched them go.

'Where's my dad buried?' Alfie demanded, when they were out of sight. 'I want to see his grave.'

Marie took care not to let it show, but she was proud of her baby brother. Alfie had guts and initiative. He'd proved it by thrashing Ernest, and by finding his own way home. I can look after myself, he'd told her, and she thought he probably could. So now she'd better telephone the police in Bourne and tell them to call off the search for Alfie – not that they'd been looking very hard.

It would have been the perfect solution if she

could have sent him to Dunswell, but Auntie Dot had brought her own children up, and obviously wasn't keen on taking on any more. So Marie decided to give him a fair chance to prove himself before she tried any more experiments with evacuation.

'I'm sorry you missed the funeral, Alfie. I sent the money for your fare, and Pam and Mr Stewart took it down to Mrs Morton's for you on Tuesday afternoon, and again on Wednesday,' she told him, as they stood beside the freshly dug earth of their father's grave later that morning.

He looked swiftly up at her. 'I never heard her. They had me locked up in the back bedroom. Why didn't she come to Dad's funeral herself?'

'She didn't want to.'

Alfie looked down at the grave again. 'Poor old Dad.' His voice was full of compassion, but there were no tears this time.

'Well, it's like she said, he wouldn't know whether she was there or not. He wouldn't know anything about it, would he?'

'If he's in heaven, he knows everything. But because she's with posh folk, our Pam thinks she's posh an' all. We're not good enough for her now. I'm not, anyway. She didn't want to be seen with me, in Bourne.'

'She'll have to forget about being posh before very long. Mam will be coming home soon, and I'll need our Pam to come and look after her while I'm at work.'

'I'll look after her.'

'You can't. You'll have to go to school, and there might be things to do that Mam wouldn't like to

118

have a boy doing. But I've been thinking, Alfie. I'll give you a week's trial. If you shape up, you can stay at home. If not, you'll have to go to Uncle Alfred's, or be evacuated again.'

'I'm not going back to Mrs Morton.'

'Do what I tell you, then. For a start, you'll have to get up and get yourself off to school every day, and behave yourself when you get there. And make sure you do get there – no twagging. Aunt Edie hardly ever goes out, so I'll ask her to keep a key for you, so you can let yourself in when you come home.' A thought suddenly struck her. 'By the way, how did you get in the house? I was sure I'd locked that door before I went to the funeral.'

'Got the spare set of keys out of the outside lav.'

'Oh, yes! I'd forgotten they were there. All right then, you've told me you can look after yourself; and you'll have to. You had plenty of complaints about Mrs Morton and Ernie, and they had a few about you as well. The main one was you roaming the streets till all hours at night. Well, here, you're undressed and in bed for eight o'clock, and make sure you lock the door and take the key out of it, and close all the blackout curtains before you go. Any trouble, and I'll be packing you off again, so be warned. And if there's an air raid, you get down to the shelter.'

'I won't cause any trouble, Marie. I'll help. You'll wonder how you ever managed without me.'

'I doubt that,' she smiled. 'Now get your coat. We're going up to Mr and Mrs Elsworth's. I'll ask him if he minds taking us up to Beverley Westwood. Mam will be glad to see you, anyway.'

Her mother would be more than glad to see Alfie, Marie thought. Thank God she'd been spared the task of telling her that he was missing.

'Good Heavens,' Mr Elsworth exclaimed. 'How did you get here?'

Alfie took the question literally, and treated him to a blow-by-blow account of the whole escapade.

Danny hung on his every word, his eyes round with admiration. 'Good for you, Alfie! I'm glad you gave that stinker a good thrashing. That's just what I should have done.'

Alfie grinned, basking in glory and not shy of giving himself even more credit. 'One of the other lads at the school tried to get back to Hull before, but the police picked him up and billeted him with a different family. Well, I wasn't going to let them collar me. No fear.'

To Marie's surprise, Mrs Elsworth's smile stretched from ear to ear. She seemed unable to take her eyes off Alfie. 'Oh, no fear! No, indeed!' she laughed.

'Sounds like something out of the *Boy's Own Paper*,' Mr Elsworth said. 'It shows initiative, anyway, Alfie. It's a pity you're not old enough to help us at the ARP post. We're going to need runners, if Jerry puts the telephone lines out of action.'

'I'll be a runner,' Alfie volunteered. 'I don't mind.'

'You're too young. It's dangerous work. It must be quite a relief to your sister to have you back safe, and she'll want to keep you safe. So will your mother.'

'I'll volunteer then,' Danny said. 'I'm fifteen. I can do it as well as anyone else.'

'You'll do no such thing,' Mrs Elsworth told him. 'Most of the runners are eighteen, from what I hear.'

'That doesn't matter. I can do it.'

'No,' she insisted, dismissing the subject. 'Have you told the people in Bourne that Alfie's here, Marie? They must have been quite worried, as well.'

'No, I haven't.' Marie had been reluctant to mention it, in case the Elsworths thought she was angling to use their telephone again.

'I'd let you phone now, but I'm waiting for Charles to ring. He said he would if he got the opportunity, sometime between now and bedtime.'

'It's all right,' said Marie. After all, none of the people in Bourne had shown all that much concern about Alfie, not even Pam. They could wait, especially the Mortons.

The phone rang. Mr Elsworth lifted the receiver, and mouthed, 'Charles!' He exchanged a few words, and then said, 'Guess who I've got with me. Marie – yes. And Alfie. I'll put her on.' He handed Marie the receiver.

'Alfie got to the funeral in the end, then. Did Pam come?' Charles said.

The sound of his deep voice made her spine tingle. 'No. Says she's frightened to come to Hull, because of the raids. She's got a point.'

'It would have been better if they'd both stayed away. A funeral's no place for a kid. But I'm sorry I couldn't be there, old thing. Was it awful?'

121

'Yes, but Alfie didn't get here in time for the funeral. He came later, under his own steam.'

'What, you mean he absconded? Went absent without leave?'

'You could put it like that.'

'You'll send him straight back, of course.'

'No. I'm going to give him a week's trial.'

There was a long pause, and Marie imagined Charles counting to ten on the other end of the line. 'You'll regret it,' he said, at last.

'No I won't. If he doesn't shape up, he'll have to go and live with Uncle Alfred in Dunswell. He's offered to have him. He's not going back to Bourne, or if he does, they'll have to find him another billet. He's not going back to those bloody Mortons.'

Another long pause followed that. 'You're going to be lumbered; I know it. How do you think you're going to manage to work?'

'He's old enough to look after himself.'

Charles sighed heavily, obviously trying to keep his patience. 'We've discussed this before, no point going over it all again. I wish I were there, though. I'd make you see sense. Any news of your mother?'

'Your dad's taking us to see her.'

'She'll probably be discharged soon, and then you'll have something else to contend with. Drop Alfie off at your uncle's on the way back, and get Pam home. I love you, Marie, and I don't want it all falling on you.'

'I love you, too.'

'Well, remember what I've said.'

'I will.'

'Bye, then, sweetheart. Is Mum there?'

'I'll drive you to the hospital,' Mr Elsworth said, as his wife took the receiver.

'Don't you dare say anything about what happened in Bourne while we're there, Alfie,' Marie warned him. 'Mam's too poorly to be worried about all that.'

'What do you take me for?' Alfie demanded. 'I'm not silly.'

'Alfie, it's Sunday tomorrow. Come round, and we'll go and have a look round Hull together,' Danny said.

'All right.'

'Hold on.' Mrs Elsworth put her hand over the receiver, and smiled at Alfie. 'In that case, since Marie will be at work, you'd better come to lunch here, Alfie.'

Marie smiled her thanks. There was a turn-up, but all to the good as far as cementing family relationships went. Mrs Elsworth obviously didn't believe Alfie was as black as he'd been painted, or she wouldn't have invited him.

Alfie cocked his head on one side and gave her a thoughtful look. 'Are you a good cook?' he asked.

Their mother seemed much clearer mentally than the last time Marie had seen her. Marie didn't go into the details of why Alfie was at home, but let her mother believe he'd only come back for the funeral.

Mrs Larsen kissed him, and cried over him, and then said: 'Our Pam didn't come, then?'

'No. She was frightened of the air raids,' Marie said, voice raised.

'She was always nervous, our Pam,' their mother said. 'She should stay away.'

'Uncle Alfred's offered Alfie a home for the duration,' Marie said, after her mother had heard all about the funeral.

'Dunswell's not far enough away. I want you right out of it, Alfie.' She tore her eyes away from Alfie to look at Marie. 'They're sending me home soon. Poor lass, everything dropping on you. But don't worry, I'll look after myself.'

'You can't possibly look after yourself, Mrs Larsen,' a staff nurse cut in as she passed the bed. 'You might be able to wash and dress yourself and do a bit of dusting and peel a few vegetables, but you'll be surprised how tired you'll get just doing that.'

Their mother looked directly at Marie. 'Don't you worry, Marie. I won't be a trouble. I don't intend to be a burden on anybody.'

'You heard what she said, Mam. You'll be tired even waving a duster about. You'll have to take it easy at first.'

The nurse caught up with Marie as she and Alfie were leaving the ward and out of their mother's hearing. 'Have you got anyone to help you look after your mother? You're going to have to leave work if not.'

'When will you be sending her home?'

'In a week or so, all being well.'

'Well, it's a bit sooner than I thought,' said Marie.

'Go and see the Lady Almoner. She might know of some help you can get.'

'I will, but we'll manage. My sister will have to

124

come home.'

The words conjured a vision in Marie's mind of Pam in her pretty Robin Pearl jumper, leaving beautiful Bourne and her piano playing to come back to bombed-out Hull and slave over the stove and the wash-tub.

Chapter 10

'Alfie arrived home yesterday, Mr Stewart,' Marie said, speaking from the Elsworths' house with Alfie beside her. 'We found him after Dad's funeral, much too late for me to telephone you. He was in the Mortons' house both times you went, as it turns out. They kept him off school because they'd given him such a thrashing he was covered in bruises, and they didn't want anyone to see him. Anyway, I'd just like to say thank you for everything you did.'

'You're very welcome, but I'm surprised at what you say about the Mortons. No, that's an understatement. I'm shocked.'

Marie had the feeling that Mr Stewart doubted what she was telling him. She repeated the news to Pam, when Mr Stewart had recovered enough from his shock to hand her the receiver.

'Shall I go and tell Mrs Morton he's come home?' Pam asked.

'If you like. And while you're at it, you can tell her I'm having him examined by the school doctor, and she'll most likely get a summons for

125

child cruelty, depending on what he says about Alfie's bruises. And another thing: I'm just going to the hospital to see Mam, and I'm expecting them to tell me when she can come home. I'm sorry, Pam, but your days in Bourne are numbered. You'll have to come home and help look after her. I can't do everything.'

She cut Pam's protests off with a curt 'Goodbye'.

'Stay for tea,' Mrs Elsworth invited them, still in her WVS uniform. 'Come and see us on your way home from St Vincent's sometimes, if you like, Alfie,' she said, much to Marie's surprise. 'It's not very far out of your way.'

Marie got home from the hospital to find a letter from Charles on the mantelpiece the following Tuesday, along with a summons of her own, to attend the police court for breaching the blackout. Alfie was already in bed. She went up to him.

'What? What are they talking about?' she exclaimed. 'I've never done anything of the sort. I've never breached the blackout. There must be some mistake.'

He looked at the summons, and then at her, with guilt written all over him.

'You know something about this, don't you?'

'Sorry, Marie. The ARP warden came knocking at the door on Sunday night. He said a woman down the street had reported us, and when I switched the light off for him he said it was all right. I didn't think they were going to send you a summons. It was only the bathroom.'

'Only the bathroom? Only a day wasted going

126

to court, and a fine THAT WE CAN'T AF-FORD! You'll have me wishing I'd never let you stay at home, if you go on like this. And you–'

Alfie went pale. 'It wasn't me. It was a friend, and it was a mistake. I'll be careful in future. I'm sorry, all right?'

'A friend? Who was the friend? I told you not to have anyone in the house when I'm not here.'

'Not really a friend. Just that nipper from down the street. She was outside, waiting for her mother to come home, and she came to talk to us when the other little uns had gone in. I felt sorry for her, on her own, so when my pals had gone home as well I let her come in for an hour before I went to bed and gave her some pickled beetroot in a sandwich.'

'Has this kid you let in got a name?'

'Jenny. I'm sorry, Marie.'

'Not half as sorry as I'll be when I'm standing in front of that magistrate,' Marie said, her expression grim. She had a summons, and Jenny was the one who had managed to get it for her. Hannah would be crowing, if she knew. Maybe she did know... She was probably the one who reported them, Marie thought. One up to Hannah, if that was the case.

Charles's letter made depressing reading when she got back downstairs. It was full of dire warnings about 'getting lumbered' with 'that little so-and-so of a brother of yours' and included the line: 'If you want my opinion, he probably richly deserved the thrashing he got.'

She folded it and put it back on the mantel-piece, thinking of her coming court appearance.

'If only you knew,' she murmured.

'You'll have to leave school. You're nearly fourteen so you'd be leaving for good in a month, anyway. You won't be missing much,' Marie said, standing with her back to the window in the Stewarts' beautiful drawing room at eleven o'clock on the first Sunday in May.

Not trusting Pam to come back to Hull on her own, Marie had told the Elsworths she was going to Bourne on the next available evacuation excursion to collect Pam, with all her things. Mr Elsworth had insisted on driving her and was now sitting waiting in his car, just outside the house.

'If Pamela were to stay, we would keep her in school,' Mr Stewart said. 'Perhaps send her to music college.'

Marie felt strong disapproval emanating from the Stewarts. 'I have to work,' she insisted. 'They've been very good at the hospital, about letting me have time off to deal with everything I've had to deal with since Dad was killed, but they can't do it for ever. Mother's due for discharge tomorrow, but it'll be a long time before she's properly better. Someone will have to look after her, and the only person who's free to do it is Pam.'

'Is there absolutely no other way?' Mrs Stewart asked.

'If there were, I wouldn't be here. Pam's first duty is to her mother.'

That was the argument to cap all other arguments. After that, all opposition ceased.

Throughout the conversation Pam had been

silently running her fingers over the French-polished piano. She looked at 'Auntie' Morag and 'Uncle' Alec, and burst into tears. The Stewarts looked just as upset.

With her shoulders stooped, and looking a picture of dejection, she picked up her battered old suitcase, and a new one Mrs Stewart had given her, and followed Marie to the door. There Marie waited while Pam and the Stewarts exchanged kisses, said anguished goodbyes, and made fervent promises to keep in touch. She barely answered Mr Elsworth when he greeted her. They drove for miles, with only an occasional stifled sob to break the silence. Marie felt like a criminal.

At last, red-eyed and with a face full of resentment, Pam said: 'I'd have loved to go to college to study music, and Auntie Morag and Uncle Alec would have sent me. I might as well be dead now. I might as well be blown up as well as Dad.'

'Don't you dare say that near Mam,' Marie warned. 'You say anything like that, and it might be the end of her. She'd just give up and die.'

'No, she wouldn't. She's as tough as old boots.'

'Was tough,' Marie stressed. 'She's not tough any more, so let me hear you've said anything to upset her, and you won't need any music college because you won't be playing any more pianos. I'll chop your bloody fingers off.'

'That's rather extreme,' Mr Elsworth protested.

'It's not extreme enough,' Marie said, wishing she'd avoided getting into a dispute with Pam in front of him.

'Why can't Alfie look after her?' Pam demanded.

'He's there anyway.'

Marie's jaw dropped. She was astounded at the very idea of a boy doing that. Impossible. An idea so ludicrous, it didn't merit consideration. 'Anybody but you, I suppose, Pam,' she said. 'Fine daughter you've turned out to be.'

'Oh, it's so nice to be home,' their mother kept repeating, when they brought her back. 'Home, sweet home.'

She was home, but it was a different mother from the one they had known. Her pleasure at being among her own familiar things was heart-breakingly childlike. An ugly, deep purple gash scarred her forehead and it was plain that Pam could hardly bear to look at her. Marie's hope that her mother's mind had stopped its wanderings was soon dashed. She had to be told three times that Dad was dead, and then: 'Ah, yes. I'd forgotten,' she said, with the same look of desolation and perplexity. She suddenly seemed so old. It all made Marie very apprehensive about going back to work.

'Put that landing light out, Bert,' her mother called, an hour after she and Pam had helped her to bed.

The sisters looked at each other. Pam's resentment seemed to have burned itself out, or turned into despair. 'This is a sad house, now,' she said.

Never in her life had Marie imagined that she would ever have to undergo the excruciating embarrassment of asking for time off to answer a summons to court. Matron had granted it very disapprovingly, with the proviso that she report back on duty as soon as her case had been dealt with. So here Marie sat, down at the Guildhall, feeling like a criminal fish out of water, clueless about what was going to happen and very anxious.

A man she often saw around her own neighbourhood came out of the courtroom just before she was due to go in. 'You're Bert Larsen's lass, aren't you?' he croaked, through a rattling smoker's cough. 'I was sorry to hear about your dad. And your mam's in hospital, isn't she?'

'Not any more. She came home yesterday.'

'How is she?'

'You know what they always say – "as well as can be expected". Truth is, it's knocked the stuffing out of her. She's got a terrible scar running right across her forehead. You'd hardly recognize her now.'

He grimaced. 'Bloody shame. She was a real good-looking woman, your mother. Bloody Germans. So what are you here for, a good lass like you? You've not turned into one of these young looters who burgle people's houses as soon as they've gone down to the shelter, are you?'

'Don't be daft. I'm carrying the can for our Alfie,' Marie said. 'He let a light show through our bathroom window, and the ARP warden copped him.'

'Showing a light. Same as me. These bastards treat people like bloody criminals. I got fined two pounds five shillings.'

The shock must have shown on Marie's face.

'The five bob was for foul language, though,' he reassured her. 'I gave them a right bloody

131

mouthful. They knew what their bloody mothers were before I came out of there. But you be polite, and you'll get off with less.' He gave her a hint of a smile.

Marie was appalled. Using strong language to a magistrate was something that would never have occurred to her, but even without the language, Alfie's escapade might still cost her two pounds! She'd never be able to hand Charles his ten pounds back at this rate. Not that he'd begrudged it, but it was a question of pride. She prided herself on her independence and would have liked to be able to say: 'Look, here's your money. It was nice to have it to fall back on, but I managed all right. Thanks anyway.' The chances of that nice little daydream becoming a reality was fast disappearing. What was worse, she might not even be able to keep her head above water. She might have to spend more of Charles's money, and if it ran out...

'Miss Marie Larsen,' the usher called.

She went in, with her heart in her mouth. High in their seats of judgement and reeking of authority, with an imposing coat of arms at the back of them, the three magistrates looked down on her, their faces like granite. When the preliminaries of name and address and guilty plea were over, the one in the middle fixed her with an unfriendly stare and began: 'There are still far too many of these incidents and they deserve to be very severely dealt with. Since you choose to be irresponsible, and endanger the lives of all your fellow citizens...' Marie listened in fear and trepidation. When asked what she had to say for herself she could hardly separate her tongue from the roof of her mouth, it was so dry. She did not protest that she was not the culprit, in case they started asking awkward questions about Alfie's being in the house unsupervised. That might have resulted in proceedings against her for some other horrible crime, like child neglect, for example. The thought scared her witless. She managed to croak out her apologies, and must have looked sufficiently contrite and terrified even for these grim judges.

'Very well,' the chief magistrate said, looking slightly mollified. 'Take more care in future, young woman, and see that you do not appear before us again, or we shall have to deal with you very severely.'

She got off with thirty shillings, and came out thinking herself quite lucky.

Marie walked home from the hospital under a brilliant bomber's moon, humming a quickstep to keep her weary legs moving along, anxious to know how her mother was, and how Pam had coped in her absence. She heard the piano being played in the front room as she got to the door, the first time she'd heard Pam play since she'd gone to the Stewarts. And it had to be said, she was good.

'This piano needs tuning,' Pam told her, when she popped her head round the door.

The place was a shambles, with dirty cups and saucers dotted about, clothes dropped, shoes kicked off, books, magazines and sheet music strewn all over. It looked as if Pam had dragged as much stuff as she could out of the cupboards to throw it all over the room.

'We've got a lot more to worry about here than tuning the piano,' Marie rasped. 'I really don't give a tinker's cuss about the piano. What does Mam need? That's more to the point. Has she had anything to eat?'

'She didn't want much.'

'I don't suppose she would, if she knew she'd have to disturb your piano playing to ask you to get it for her. Where is she?'

'In bed,' said Pam, idly fingering the keys. 'She said she was tired.'

'I know how she feels,' Marie said, and went through to the kitchen to put the kettle on. Every surface was littered with things that should either have been put back in the cupboard, or washed up. The floor was half mopped, and the mop bucket stood in the middle of the kitchen floor, full of dirty water.

Too tired to be angry, Marie went back into the front room and swept the hearth, then began picking things up. A wave of despair engulfed her.

Pam slammed the piano lid down with a mighty crash. 'There's no need to sulk. You only had to ask.'

Marie's tired eyes widened. 'Have I got to ask for every plate and cup to be tidied away, every surface to be dusted, to ask every time the hearth needs to be swept? I've been on my feet for twelve solid hours. Can't you see for yourself things need doing, Pam?'

'Don't look at me like that. I have been doing things, only every time I start, someone comes to

134

the door, or Alfie wants something, or Mother. It's impossible to get on with anything without constant interruptions. Anyway, I shouldn't have to do this! You're the nurse, not me.'

'Nobody's asked you to be a nurse. Mam doesn't need nursing now; she looks after herself. You've been asked to wash, and make a meal every day, and do enough to keep the place clean, because there's nobody else in the family to do it. Mum needs help, and you're the only one that's free to give it.'

'I'm not free! I'm only thirteen. I should be at school. I'm not a washerwoman, or a cleaner, and I don't want to be one. I can't do it.'

'You're nearly fourteen, and your trouble is that you see everything through Mr and Mrs Stewart's eyes now. You really think you've joined the upper classes, and you look down on your own family. Well they're not your uncle Alec and auntie Morag, Pam; they're not related to you at all. They're the people you were billeted with for the duration, and they get ten and six a week for having you. We're your family, this is where you belong, and this is where your loyalties should lie.'

Had the piano lid not already been slammed down, Marie was certain it would have been then. Pamela jumped off the stool, her cheeks pink and eyes blazing, and walked towards her, trembling with anger, arms rigid by her sides and fists clenched. 'Oh, shut up, Marie! I'm sick of you, sticking your nose into everything and taking over. Who do you think you are? You're not my mother! You can't tell me what to do! I'm going to bed.'

Lowering her voice to prevent her mother from hearing, Marie said bitterly: 'You always said you loved Mam! This is your idea of love, then. Just think about this. Your mother's loved you all your life, and now she needs some help from you. You shouldn't begrudge it...'

But Pam was halfway up the stairs. Now equally angry and energized by fury, Marie finished tidying the living room and started a vigorous mopping of the kitchen floor. After that, she dragged out the ironing board, and put the radio on. One of the big bands was playing a quickstep. Her mother had been almost deafened by the blast on the shelter on Ellis Street, and Alfie would be too fast asleep to be disturbed by it, so she turned it up a fraction, and took her temper out on a pile of ironing until a week's worth of neatly finished laundry was draped over the clothes horse, airing by the dying embers of the fire. It's amazing the amount of work you can get through in next to no time when you feel like strangling someone, she thought.

There was only one thing for it, Marie decided, as she put the ironing board away. She hated having to do it, but she would have to go to Matron and ask for a leave of absence, at least until Pamela was doing things properly, and the running of the house got back onto an even keel.

The warning sounded at quarter past eleven, just as she was undressing for bed. Marie threw on her old checked dressing gown, and went in to her mother.

'The siren's sounding, Mam!' she shouted.

'What?' her mother croaked.

'An air raid, Mam. We should go to the shelter.'

'I'm not going to any shelter. They're not shelters; they're deathtraps.'

'We ought to go to the shelter. There's going to be a raid.'

'I'm not going!' her mother screamed.

Pam came out onto the landing, her face sheet white. Alfie soon joined them.

'You two get dressed fast as you can, and get down to the shelter,' Marie said. 'I'll stay here with Mam. She's refusing to go.'

'It doesn't seem to make much difference whether you're in a shelter or not. You've got a good chance of being killed either way,' Pam said, looking askance at her mother. 'Anyway, I'd rather be dead than scarred.'

'Be quiet.'

'Why? She can't hear me.'

And it was evident from the puzzled expression on Mam's face that she could make nothing of what they were saying.

'Me and Danny were all over Hull the last two Sundays, and you know what we noticed?' Alfie said. 'When you look at the houses that have been bombed, the staircase is always there, all the ones we've seen, anyway. Even if the front of the house is blasted out, and all the tiles are off one side of the roof, the staircase is still there. I reckon we might be as safe under the stairs as in a shelter.'

It was a common observation. Marie wavered, then: 'All right,' she said. 'We'll be cramped, but at least we can dodge out between waves of bombers and put the kettle on. Go on then, bring your pillows down. Bring Mam's, as well.'

Within a minute Marie was dragging mop and bucket, sweeping brushes, ironing board, and everything else out of the kitchen cupboard, and stacking it by the kitchen door while her mother stood helplessly by. Pam was soon down with her pillow, followed by Alfie.

'Where's Smut?' he demanded. 'Anybody seen Smut?'

'Still upstairs, on Mum's bed.'

Pam clutched her chest. 'Can you hear my heart beating?' she gasped. 'It's so loud, I think everybody must be able to hear it.'

'No, but I can hear mine,' Marie said, 'and I suppose everybody else can hear theirs.'

'What? What are you saying?' their mother said, looking at Pam with an apologetic half-smile for making her repeat herself. Pam said it all again, at treble the volume.

Her mother's expression was a mix of pity and guilt. 'Oh, my poor bairn. I'm sorry you had to come back.'

'It's not your fault, Mam,' said Pam, the first time she'd called her mother by the old name since her return home. 'It wasn't your idea.' She went into the cupboard, studiously avoiding Marie's eyes, and sat on her pillow. Mam went in, and sat opposite to her. Marie waited by the door until Alfie returned with Smut, then followed them in with the torch.

'How long will the battery last?' Mam asked.

'I don't know, Mam. An hour or two, maybe. I'll turn it off, as soon as we're settled.'

'How can anybody be settled in here? Squashed in like this, among dust and spiders' webs?' Pam whined, averting her eyes from the scar across her mother's face, which looked even more lurid in the beam of the torch.

Mother was looking at Pam's averted face, with a pleading in her eyes that wrenched Marie's heartstrings.

'First job for you tomorrow, then,' Marie snapped. 'Scrub the cupboard out, and then you won't have to put up with dust and spiders next time. You look tired out, Mam. Let's hope it's no more than a bomb or two dropped near the docks, and then the all clear. We could all do with a decent night's sleep.'

'I'm all right,' said Alfie, stroking the cat.

'Right. I'll put the torch off, then.'

Night wore on, the family cramped and weary. Sleep lay heavy on Marie's eyelids. It was nearing half-past twelve, just as she was lapsing into an uncomfortable doze that she heard the drone of the first wave of bombers. She flicked on the torch. The others were gazing upward, all wide-eyed with apprehension. The drone increased in volume until the air vibrated with the noise. Smut began mewing and clawing at the cupboard door, frantic to get out. A series of piercing shrieks rent the air as the planes released their cargo. Then the dull thud, thud, thud of their landing signalled that the bombs were falling some distance away. Marie took Pam's hand to calm her.

'It's all right,' she said. 'It's probably the docks.'

With that came the crash of closer explosions,

some of them shaking the house. Smut yowled horribly and scratched ever more frantically at the door.

Mam looked like death. 'I bet the roof's gone,' she croaked.

'I wish we'd gone to the shelter,' Pam said, her teeth chattering.

Marie was frightened for her mother. 'I'll get Mam something to lie down on, then I'll sit outside, to make more room.'

'I'll get her something.' Alfie was at the door before Marie could stop him, and Smut shot out before him. After what seemed an age, Alfie came back with a quilt, looking awestruck. 'Hull's afire,' he announced.

'What, *all* of it?'

He nodded, his eyes wide with wonder. 'All of it! I had a look out of the bedroom windows. It's blazing! Everywhere you look, everything alight! Everything must be gone, telephones, the lot. They must need runners now.'

He thrust the bedding into Marie's arms and was out of the back door before she even noticed he was carrying his coat.

She went after him. 'Hey! Come back! Come back here this minute! Where the hell do you think you're going?'

He was already on his bike, with the back-yard gate wide open. 'ARP post!'

Even standing at the door, Marie was breathing smoke. The air was thick with the haze and the stench of it. 'No fear! You're too young. Come back here this minute! You'll get yourself killed!'

'No fear! Old No-balls can't kill me! You'll see.'

Alfie was gone.

Their mother gave a cry of anguish. 'Stop him, stop him, Marie! Where's he going?'

'It's too late, Mam,' Marie shouted. 'He's gone to the ARP post. Don't worry, as soon as Mr Elsworth sees him, he'll put him somewhere safe.'

Except that Mr Elsworth would undoubtedly be fully occupied elsewhere – and haring off to volunteer his services as a runner would never have entered Alfie's head had it not been for Mr Elsworth. Thanks a lot, Leonard, Marie thought, angry at him and fearful for her little brother, and at the same time feeling put to shame by him. For a moment she thought of going to the hospital, but after one look at her mother and Pam she knew it was hopeless. She couldn't leave them.

Chapter 11

The all clear sounded at ten past five. Marie wearily got dressed and left the house to cycle to work. Outside, acrid smoke filled her nostrils and her lungs. The air was like fog. She rode down Princes Avenue, turned onto Spring Bank and froze, stunned at the devastation. The street was shining with broken glass; it was everywhere, absolutely impossible to avoid. It seemed impossible that so much glass could exist in the world, and it would have cut her tyres to ribbons. After a minute or two, when she'd regained the power of thought and movement, she turned for home.

She'd leave the bike there, where it would be safe, and go to the hospital on foot. Back on Spring Bank broken glass crunched under her feet as she walked. She moved on, now clambering over rubble or striding over places where the pavement was split and lifted as if by an earthquake. People she passed looked as dazed as she felt. Tangles of firehose lay across the roads in all directions as firemen whose faces were grey with fatigue and besmirched with soot trained jets of water on buildings still crackling with flames. The spray from the jets swirled with ash and embers on the warm air. A breeze sent piles of charred paper from a bombed offices fluttering along the road. She jumped when a wall collapsed a hair's breadth away from her with a crash louder than a thunderclap, throwing up sparks from smouldering beams. With her heart racing, Marie walked round the rubble wondering how she'd escaped with her life.

Lamp posts were bent or broken. The trolley bus wires were down and lying on the smouldering debris like a cat's cradle tossed aside by some giant's child. There seemed to be nothing left to destroy. Turning down Prospect Street, she saw the once lovely church roofless and still smouldering, and half the street in ruins. Gone was beautiful Thornton-Varley's, where as a toddler she'd thrown a massive tantrum, and had been shocked and stunned when her mother had walked off and left her threshing on the floor. Another pile of rubble had once been Powolney's restaurant, where she'd been to a wonderful dinner-dance. And the top floor` of Hammonds had

142

been blasted away, its superb dance floor gone with it. Everything she loved, the scenes of all her happiest times had been wiped out in one night. At the end of the street, the tower of the Prudential Assurance building was listing like some punch-drunk lighthouse in a sea of devastation, a battered beacon in a haze of smoke and dust.

To Marie's relief, the Infirmary was still standing, its four fluted stone pillars with Corinthian capitals and the pediment they supported still solid, apparently aloof from destruction. Throughout her journey, she had been hoping to meet Alfie on his way home. Instead she met Margaret's husband just coming out of the hospital, looking the archetypal tall, intrepid fireman. Sheer exhaustion now bent his shoulders and etched its lines in his blackened face, but his sense of humour was intact. He gave Marie a fleeting smile of recognition and the snatch of a song – 'It's a Lovely Day Tomorrow' – and then, encompassing the devastation with a sweep of his arm, he added: 'But not today, is it? There must be hundreds died or injured last night, and thousands homeless.'

'Oh, Terry, it's worse ... worse than I could ever have imagined. My 11-year-old brother went out last night to volunteer as a runner; I'm worried sick about him. I just hope he gets back safe. What are you doing here?'

'Just came in the ambulance with one of our lads. We've had more fires than you can count, and all of them major. There were hundreds of incendiaries dropped on the warehouses near the dockside, so some of us climbed onto the roofs to

143

get them off, and the quickest way was to go along the eaves, and kick them off. Some unlucky lads got burned.'

She looked into his eyes, reddened from the smoke. 'I thought it must be something like that.'

'He's real bad. Probably had it.'

'Oh, I hope not. We'll do our best for him. He might pull through.'

'I think he's gone past that stage.'

'No harm in trying, though. Never say die.'

'See the Prudential building?' he asked. 'Or rather, you can't. Everything's gone but the tower, the rest's nothing but rubble. There's no hope for any of the people trapped under that. If they escaped burning, they must have drowned by now in the water from the burst main. There was nothing we could do to help them.'

'Oh,' she shuddered. 'Oh, I wish you hadn't told me that!'

'Sorry. Aye, well, I'll get back to the flat while I can still stand, and get some sleep. There won't be as many of us to man the pumps come the next onslaught.'

She watched him go for a moment or two, shoulders bent, trudging wearily along towards George Street and his empty flat near Central Fire Station, as if he could barely summon the energy to put one foot in front of the other. Poor man: no Margaret to look after him when he got there, only silence, and fending for himself. Marie wished that there'd been the time, or that she'd had the courage, to say something kind, something about Margaret: to tell him how much she and Nancy missed her, that their lives would

144

never be the same.

Well, he already knew that, better than any-body. And after tonight, life would never be the same for hundreds of people, either maimed or grieving over their injured and dead. She went into the hospital still sick at the thought of those people trapped under the Prudential Building. Maybe a few of them were still alive, even after fire and flood, she thought, and felt an enormous and irrational guilt at her powerlessness to help them. She'd certainly picked her moment to tell Matron she had to beg off nursing, just when there was so much to be done. But what alter-native had she? Needed at the hospital, and needed at home, she felt torn in two. Until she learned the trick of being in two places at once the choice had to be made, and her own mother had the strongest claim. And Alfie was still miss-ing. She wouldn't be able to settle to anything until she knew he was safe.

She went into the hospital and onto the ward, stopping at the office to ask for permission to go and see Matron sometime during the morning. Inside the ward one of the nurses was pulling the screens round a patient's bed and Marie went to speak to her. The patient was still in his fireman's uniform, probably the lad brought in by Mar-garet's husband. His cheeks were almost burned off, exposing grinning teeth and his red, lidless eyes stared unmoving at the ceiling. The nurse looked at Marie and, mouthing the word 'gone', pulled the sheet over his head.

Never say die, had she said? Marie was glad he had died. Die a thousand times and be at peace,

145

rather than face the torment, the lifetime of pain and misery that would follow injuries like that. Die rather than face the comments and the stares, or the politely averted eyes of more sensitive souls. The way Pam looked at her mother's injury was bad enough, but to have to face the world as disfigured as the man now hidden under that starched white sheet could only have been a constant torture. There was someone whose future had been wiped out as well as his past. Completely wiped out, wiped off the face of the earth. And she was glad that he was dead, and out of it.

But there were so many others who weren't out of it, and so much that needed doing here. Maybe she would put off speaking to Matron and have a real heart-to-heart talk to Pam instead, then give her another day or two and see how things went.

Marie trudged home through the wreckage of the city, weary, and hardly able to take it in. Everything but the infirmary and the Prudential tower had been demolished. Poor Thornton-Varley's, she could have wept over it, that and the dance halls. Roads ruined, bomb craters all over the city centre, water seeping up from broken mains, hardly one stone standing on another, it was destruction beyond anything she could have imagined. There was more than enough work here for a thousand engineers. Their once beautiful town centre looked broken beyond repair.

'What's it like in the city?' her mother asked, when she got home. There was no confusion there, Marie thought. Her mother seemed a lot more coherent, and Marie guessed that Alfie must be all right. Had it been otherwise, his name would have been the first word out of her mother's mouth.

Marie threw up her hands and shrugged, words failing her. 'Ruined,' she said. 'It's got to be seen to be believed. I reckon our Alfie's back, then?'

'He's at the Elsworths'. In bed.'

Marie breathed a sigh of relief 'Thank God for that. Where's our Pam?'

'Gone.'

Marie's jaw dropped. 'Gone? Gone where?'

'Back to Bourne, if she can get there. She was crying after you'd gone, and she said: "Mam, I love you, but I can't stay here; I can't go through another air raid." So I gave her all the money I had in my purse, then she packed her case, and she went. She said she'd ring Mr and Mrs Stewart as soon as she could get to a telephone, and if they were willing to have her back, she'd get the ferry over to New Holland, and bus it to Lincoln. "It was like being cast out of heaven having to come back to Hull," she said. "This place is hell on earth."'

Marie saw her mother's lip tremble. Silent tears filled her eyes and spilled onto her cheeks. Perhaps she was beginning to realize what Marie had known deep down since her first visit to Bourne. They'd lost Pam. The air raid had been a bad one, but it wasn't the only reason Pam had gone back to Bourne, or even the main one. As far as Marie was concerned, the main reason was that Pam had learned to look down on them, with their lives of constant penny-pinching and making do, and pianos that nobody bothered to get tuned. She had an altogether superior life with the Stewarts and was adapting herself to it as fast as she could, picking up their middle-class vowels and manners and even their expectations, and fast discarding her own. Marie had a feeling that Pam meant to fasten herself onto the Stewarts for the rest of her life if she could, and she didn't mean to let her own family get in the way.

She sat down and put an arm round her mother's shoulders. 'Buck up, Mam. The war can't last for ever.'

Her mother sniffed hard, and wiped the tears off her cheeks with the back of her hand. 'Take no notice of me. I'm just being stupid. I *want* her out of the way of the raids. I wish our Alfie would go back as well. It's just ... I wonder if I'll ever see her again.' She gave a heavy sigh and patted Marie's knee.

'You will; don't worry. I meant to go and see Matron this morning, to get leave of absence for a few days until our Pam started to shape up, but there were so many people so badly injured, I couldn't do it. I've seen some terrible sights today. But there, *Pamela*'s hopped it back to Bourne, so now the die's cast. I'll have to put my notice in, and that's all there is to it.'

'Poor Marie, everything drops on you. But Pam's frightened of the air raids, that's all.'

Marie didn't argue. Now that the decision she'd agonized over had been made for her, she jumped to her feet with a sudden surge of energy. 'Well, we're not going to sit here staring at each other with long faces, making each other miserable either. I've had enough of misery today, so I'll

148

make us a cup of tea and a sandwich and then I'll go up to the Elsworths for our Alfie. I'll ring the Stewarts in Bourne while I'm there, make sure she's got back safe, although what I can do about it if she hasn't, I don't know. And when I get back, we'll all listen to the wireless for a bit. We must be due a broadcast from Lord Haw-Haw soon. "Germany calling! Germany calling!" I could do with a good laugh, and he's the best comedy show of the lot.'

While making the tea, Marie was struck by how rational her mother had suddenly become, not confused at all. Well, long may that last. She carried the meal into the front room, so that they could sit in the armchairs and listen to the programme in comfort. But she managed to eat only half a sandwich and to hear about five minutes of the programme before that second wind of energy was gone, and she fell into an exhausted sleep.

'We were out as soon as the all clear sounded with the mobile canteen, dishing tea and snacks to the rescue parties,' Mrs Elsworth said, when Marie went to collect Alfie later that evening. 'I've only just got back, and after what I've seen today, I feel very, very lucky to have a home to come back to. Thousands haven't, after last night. All those houses destroyed, and so many poor people still trapped, children terrified out of their wits – it's been a nightmare beyond your worst nightmare. What am I saying? It still is a nightmare for a lot of families, and it will continue to be for months to come. And the city centre beggars description.

Absolute havoc, but you must have seen it for yourself, Marie.'

'Havoc's an understatement,' Marie nodded, 'but let's look on the bright side. We're still alive, and the Nazis have done such a good job on us it's hardly worth their effort to come back and bomb us again tonight. There's nothing left to destroy. They might leave us alone for a bit after this.'

'I hope you're right, but I wouldn't bank on it.'

'Is Alfie still here?'

'He's upstairs with Danny. They've been asleep most of the day, I think. Danny put him in Charles's bed when they got back from the ARP post.'

Marie laughed. 'Charles will appreciate that, I'm sure.'

Mrs Elsworth cracked a rare smile. 'He really wouldn't mind, you know, but he won't find out unless you tell him. Those boys get on famously. I think they're going to be great friends, which is nice, if we're going to be related.'

'I've worried about Alfie all day, ever since he cycled off to do his bit. In my imagination I've had him bombed, falling into craters, fried by incendiaries, buried under rubble, everything you can think of.'

'Instead of which he was safe in the ARP post with Danny all night, playing billiards, apparently. Their services as runners weren't taken up. Brave boys, though, to volunteer.'

'Not brave,' Marie frowned, 'foolhardy. They think it's all a lark. They don't see the dangers, or they think nothing can happen to them. The trouble with boys his age is they think they're immortal.'

'I know, and with some boys, the feeling lasts until they're into their twenties.'

'You're talking about Charles. Have you heard from him?'

'He'll telephone this evening, if he can.'

'Do you mind if I wait, and have a word with him? I was going to ask you if you'd mind me ringing Bourne again, as well. Pam went back there this morning.'

'Your mother thinks Alfie's a brave boy,' Marie told Charles when he rang. 'He went up to the ARP post and volunteered to do his bit as a runner last night.'

'Well, did he?'

'What?'

'Do his bit! What did he actually do?'

'No messages were necessary, Chas. The telephones were all right at our end.'

'Well, what did he do then?'

A great one for probing into things, Charles, Marie thought, feeling as if she were being cross-examined. 'Played billiards,' she admitted.

'And I suppose he missed school today.'

'Well...'

'Well, of course he'll volunteer to play billiards all night! And since it got him off school all day, I've no doubt he'll volunteer again. And that's contrary to treaty, isn't it? I thought you warned him he had to go to school, if he wanted to stay at home?'

'Well, yes, but–'

151

'But nothing, Marie! You let yourself be hood-winked by that little horror. He runs rings round you.'

'I don't think you realize how bad last night's raid was. There are hundreds dead and injured, umpteen people homeless, the town centre just about demolished. Hardly one stone standing on another.'

'You're exaggerating.'

'I'm not! Ask your mother, if you don't believe me.'

'All right, you're not,' he said, sounding a little subdued. 'Well, I'm glad you're all right. But take my advice and keep Alfie with you tonight, and out of harm's way. And tomorrow, make him go to school. You don't want an illiterate on your hands. How's your mother?'

'All right.'

'Pam looking after her properly?'

'Pam's gone back to Bourne.'

There was complete silence on the other end of the line.

'I'll have to give up work for a while, and look after her myself,' Marie said.

'Of course you will. Everything drops on you, as always.'

'That's exactly what Mam said.'

'And she's right. And that's your salary gone, not that it amounted to much. Ask Mum to steer you round some of these assistance people, see if you can get any help from anywhere. I'll chip in as much as I can and we'll stick to our plan to get married on my next leave, so you can get the allowance. I'll see about getting a special licence.'

'Chas, you're so romantic.'

'Ha! Don't think I don't detect the irony. I'm more the naked lust type than the romantic, as we both well know. If I had you here, I'd show you what I mean.'

Marie laughed. 'Me Tarzan, you Jane?'

She could hear the smile in his voice. 'Something along those lines. Not much more refined than that, anyway.'

'I think I'd better say goodbye. Your mum's here.'

'Maybe you should, before the conversation gets completely out of hand.'

'Yes, Pamela's here, poor child. She was in tears when I met her in Lincoln.'

'I see. You met her in Lincoln. I'm sorry you've had to go to all that trouble and expense, Mr Stewart. If you'll let me know the cost of the petrol, I'll send a postal order,' Marie said, banking on his refusing her offer, considering her chronic lack of funds.

He did refuse. 'Pamela said the air raid was nothing short of terrifying,' he went on, 'but we already knew that. My niece knows some of our pilots. They told her they could see Hull blazing from the coast of Denmark last night.'

For a fleeting second Marie wondered what our pilots were doing on the coast of Denmark. Going to bomb hapless Germans while they lay in their beds, presumably.

'Of course,' Mr Stewart conceded, 'you were concerned about your mother, and your work at the hospital, but I must say, it's a great pity no other solution could be found than to take Pamela back to such a terribly dangerous place as Hull.'

In spite of his magnanimity about the petrol money, the strong note of reproach in his voice got Marie's back up. 'You're right,' she said, 'Hull is a terribly dangerous place at the moment. I walked through it twice today on my way to and from the hospital, and the damage is beyond belief. And they could see it blazing from Denmark, did you say?'

'That's right, yes; they could see it quite clearly. It's terrible for the people who have to be there, but really, everybody else should be evacuated. It's certainly no place for any child. They should all be sent into the country, and kept away until the end of the war.'

He'd taken her bait. Now to make him squirm. 'Well, after last night's raid, I have to agree with you, and now I'm quite frightened for Alfie. Would it be too much to ask, I mean, could you see your way to taking him for the duration, as well as Pamela? It's so much better when brothers and sisters are kept together, don't you think?'

The silence was so long Marie almost began to think Mr Stewart had collapsed and died at the other end. 'I'm sorry,' he said eventually, 'but we haven't really got the facilities for two children. My wife is used to a very ordered life; she couldn't possibly cope with a boy, and a boy like Alfie would be too much of a handful for her. Even the school found him a handful, and perhaps Mrs Morton wasn't entirely unjustified in...'

Marie held her breath at that, and counted to

ten, while Mr Stewart went on with his criticism of Alfie and his feeble excuses for not having him. But Marie didn't push her request so far that it might have spoiled Pamela's little idyll with the Stewarts, despite her annoyance with both 'Uncle' Alec and Pam.

'That's an awful pity. It would have been nice for them to be together. But you're right, and it's very good of you to keep Pamela out of harm's way. We do appreciate everything you're doing,' she added, although it nearly choked her.

They hadn't the facilities for two children – in that palatial house? Marie didn't believe it, or that Morag Stewart couldn't have coped with Alfie, had she wanted to. The top and bottom of it was that decorative and devious young girls who could forget their own families and adapt themselves like chameleons to their more luxurious new homes deserved protection from German bombs, but straightforward boys who had the temerity to be loyal to their own people and stick up for themselves in the face of bullying hypocrites did not, as far as Mr Stewart was concerned.

Marie hung up. Mr Stewart had been quite safe from a one-boy marauding party, had he but known it. Wild horses couldn't drag Alfie away from home again. She tried to imagine him doing his piano practice in the Stewarts' plush drawing room in Bourne, and liking it. No, it was impossible. Much easier to picture him playing billiards with another evacuation-dodger in an ARP post in Hull.

That business over, her mind turned to the next

task on her list and the one she had the least relish for: giving notice at the hospital. It had to be done, and the sooner the better. She glanced at the lovely ormolu clock on the Elsworths' mantelpiece. Half-past eight. Far too late to go back and ask to see Matron today. It would have to keep until tomorrow.

'Would you mind calling Alfie, Mrs Elsworth?' she asked. 'I'm dead tired. I just hope the Luftwaffe will leave Hull alone tonight.'

'Amen,' she said.

Alfie protested he wasn't tired when they got home, not surprising since he'd been in bed all day at the Elsworths'. Their mother was easily persuaded to let him stay up and listen to the radio, more than happy to keep him with her, and Marie was cajoled into playing battleships with him. Dad and Pam were missing, but the evening was as near to old times as it was ever likely to be again. They pulled the curtains and went to bed an hour before the blackout started, and in spite of her apprehension about another raid, Marie felt strangely light of heart. Charles had telephoned, and she hadn't had to beg or plead, or even ask him for a thing. He'd taken it for granted that he should 'chip in as much as I can' and offered his help freely, even to the point of marriage. And Mrs Elsworth wasn't as bad as Marie had previously thought. She'd been out with the WVS doing what she could for people, and she actually liked Alfie, which was a great point in her favour. Better for knowing, was Marie's verdict on Mrs Elsworth, and the future showed every sign of being good – if they could just live long enough to see it.

The sirens wailed their first warning at five minutes past midnight. Marie groaned and rolled out of bed, feeling half dead. Alfie was up and dressed before she was fully conscious.

'Where do you think you're going?'

'To the ARP post.'

'Not tonight, my lad. You're staying here with us.'

'I'm not,' Alfie said, and before she could get hold of him he ran downstairs, unlocked the kitchen door, and was out and off on his bike.

'Where's our Alfie?' her mother demanded, after Marie had helped her to get up and dressed, and brought her downstairs.

'Gone to the ARP post, again.'

Her mother's face fell.

Marie put the kettle on to boil. 'Don't worry, he'll be as safe there as he would be here, or in the shelter,' she said, with more confidence than she felt. 'He told you, all he did last night was play billiards with Danny Elsworth. If it's the same again tonight, he'll be just as safe there as anywhere else.'

'And what if it's not the same?'

'Well, it can't be any worse, can it? But if the phone lines come down, well, everybody knows he's only eleven. Don't worry, Mam, nobody's going to send a kid so young with any messages. Look, I'll go and get the chair cushions and put them in the cupboard so you can lie down if you want to; we might be here a while.'

Marie had just managed to fill the flask and get the usual bag of comforts ready when the second siren went. She stooped to get into the under-stairs cupboard beside her mother, prepared for another long night of terror with the air filled with the screaming and crashing of bombs.

'Look on the bright side, Mam,' she said. 'We've a lot more leg room than last night. We can nearly lie straight,' she said, struggling to keep the bitter-ness out of her voice at the thought of Pamela in bomb-free Bourne, safe and very comfortable in the Stewarts' mansion. She knew which side her bread was buttered, that one. She certainly knew how to look after herself.

At five to six, after six hours of relentless bom-bardment, the all clear sounded. Marie opened the door to Alfie and Danny shortly afterwards and gave her brother an accusing stare. 'Where the hell have you been? We've both been worried sick about you.'

Danny sprang to his defence. 'He's been with me; we've been running with messages for the rescue services. And if it hadn't been for me and Alfie, Constable Kilkenny would have been a gonner. He was blinded by a blast from a high explosive, and we had to lead him through some blazing incendiaries and then all the way to the first-aid post. I reckon he'd have burned to death if it hadn't been for us, groping about like he was, wouldn't he, Alfie?'

Alfie gave a modest half-smile. 'We did all right, I suppose.'

'Then we started roving the streets with a bin

158

lid apiece, snuffing incendiaries out.' Danny went on. 'That was Alfie's idea. Great fun, though. I bagged about nine.'

'You mean you lidded them,' Alfie said.

Marie went cold with horror at the thought of it. 'Come in, both of you. Alfie shouldn't have been roving the streets to drag anyone out of anywhere, or to lid anything. He's only a bairn.'

'I'm not. If you're big enough, you're old enough.'

She rewarded him for that with a clip round the ear. 'Well, you're not big enough, and you're not old enough, either. Don't you dare run off again when there's a raid on, or I'll have you, if the bombs don't.'

'Who's there, Marie?' Their mother's cracked voice came from inside the house.

'It's Alfie with Danny Elsworth, Mam,' Marie said, leading the boys into the dining room where Mam sat at the table. 'They've been a pair of heroes, rescuing blind policemen from burning, apparently. Sit down, Danny. I was just making some tea for Mam. We'll all have a cup, and you can tell us all about it, but speak up, so you don't have to keep repeating yourself for Mam. And you make the most of it, Alfie, because you won't be going again. Good luck to that policeman, and I'm glad you helped him, but there'll be no more heroics for you, my lad. You'll be staying where you're safe, if I have to chain you to the floor.'

'There's nowhere safe in Hull,' Danny shouted, for the doubtful benefit of Mrs Larsen. 'All the rescue people we saw were saying the same.'

'There isn't a place of safety in the whole city,' Alfie bellowed. 'Nowhere.'

'Thank God our Pam's gone back to Bourne,' Mrs Larsen croaked. 'You're going to have to go as well, Alfie; you'll have to. I can't rest with you here. You'll have to be evacuated again.'

'You're right, Mam,' said Marie, looking severely at Alfie. 'I blame myself. I should never have agreed to let him stay at home. Chas warned me what it would be like, and he was right.'

When she arrived at the infirmary, she found that the hospital hadn't been quite so lucky this time. The Wilson Wing was still burning after last night's raid. Marie picked her way over rubble to get to the offices at the back. To her relief Matron was there. She could get her business over with.

'Yes, it was a terrible tragedy, that parachute mine on the shelter in Ellis Street,' Matron said, when Marie had briefly explained her circumstances. 'Really terrible. Well, it can't be helped, Nurse. We're sorry to lose you, but if there's no one else to care for your mother, then of course, you must leave. And really, there's so much bomb damage here we'll be left with just two wards, as well as Out Patients and the Orthopaedic department.'

'I feel awful,' Marie said, 'like a rat abandoning a sinking ship.'

'It can't be helped. Put your notice in writing, will you? And if your circumstances change, you'll always be welcome to come back to us and carry on with your training. And now, I'm afraid I'm very busy...'

'Of course.'

Looking at the devastation as she left, Marie wondered whether they'd ever be able to get the place running again.

Chapter 12

George looked haggard.

'Have you seen Nancy?' he asked Marie when she met him coming along Clumber Street.

'No, not for a day or two. I've just been to the infirmary to give my notice in. It's still burning! They say the fire started when an incendiary fell on the Wilson Wing.'

George spread his hands in a gesture of helplessness. 'No water, couldn't put the fire out. The pressure's too low, with all the incendiaries, and bomb damage to the mains. It's going to take some work to repair all that, after the past two nights. If there's another raid like that tonight, I don't know how we're going to manage. It might finish us.'

'Well, there won't be many patients treated at the infirmary for a while. There's hardly anything left of it, everything's being moved out and all the patients are being transferred to other hospitals. Our beautiful infirmary; I could weep. Even the kiosk's gone, where I got my goodies, and Nance used to get her cigs. It's enough to break your heart.'

'It'll break mine, if anything's happened to her.'

161

'Oh, George, you don't really think it has, do you?'

'I don't know,' he said. 'I thought she was at the hospital but I can't find her anywhere, and nobody seems to have seen her. That's why I'm here, asking you. I nearly copped it myself, down near Ranks flour mill on the riverside. There was a blaze and a half there. I was standing watching it, absolutely mesmerized, until I saw the factory wall start coming down towards me, and picking up speed on the way. I ran like the clappers, and I just managed to get behind a lorry before the whole bloody brick façade crashed down on top of it. I've had some near misses, but that...' He blew the air expressively out of his lungs and, shaking his head, added, 'I thought my time had come.'

'Oh,' said Marie, with a shudder. 'Oh, George, I don't know. I haven't seen her for a few days, what with Dad's funeral, and Mam coming out of hospital, and having to get Pam back from Bourne. I didn't–' The thought suddenly struck her that Nancy might have been working on the Wilson Wing.

'Didn't what?'

'Didn't even know what shift she was on. I hope nothing's happened to her. I've got to go to Thoresby Street, to see about getting our Alfie evacuated again just now, but I'll ask my mam to send her down to your house if she turns up while I'm out.'

'They've opened Albert Avenue Baths up as a temporary morgue. Just so long as she's not there, that's all.'

'Oh, George, she's not, surely! You've been to

162

see her mother, I suppose?'

He nodded. 'She said just the same as you, but with her having lodgers Nance stays in the Nurses' Home most of the time. Have there been any casualties there, do you know?'

Marie shook her head. 'There might have been, but I don't know anything. Ask at the hospital again. It's chaos but there are still people there; they're open as a first-aid post.'

'I know, and that's my next port of call. And then I'll have to snatch a couple of hours' sleep. I'm dead on my feet.'

Poor George, Marie thought, as she closed the door on him, praying to God that Nancy would soon be found, because if she'd been on the Wilson Wing... Well, Marie just couldn't bear to think about it.

'I'm not going,' Alfie said later on, when Marie demanded he accompany her to Thoresby Street school to see the evacuation officers. 'If I've got to go out of Hull, I'll go to Uncle Alf's.'

'You'll have to go a lot further than that,' their mother said. 'If we send you to Alfred and Dot, you'll just keep coming back.'

'I'll just keep coming back wherever you send me. I've already proved that, haven't I?'

'You're getting far too cheeky, my lad; you'll go where you're sent,' Marie told him.

Alfie gave her a defiant stare, arms folded. 'No, I shan't. I aren't going back with that dirty bugger Ernie, or his rotten old mother, or anywhere else like that. You've never had to go away from home. You don't know what it's like.'

'I'll wash your mouth out with carbolic if you keep swearing like that, and I did have to go away from home. I went to the Nurses' Home, remember?'

'That's not away. You could still walk home if you wanted to, and anyway, you came home more times than enough even when you weren't supposed to, and always on your days off.'

They were well into the argument, with Marie threatening and their mother cajoling when George knocked and came in, looking like a broken man.

'There was nobody killed at the hospital, as far as they know, but Nancy's nowhere,' he said. 'I've asked everybody I can find who knows her; I've looked everywhere she could possibly have gone, and ... nothing. I've even been down to Albert Avenue. It's just indescribable; some of the bodies there, you can't tell who they are; I don't think even their mothers would know them. You can't even tell by the clothes, if they're burned. And the stink!'

Marie's legs started to shake so badly she had to hold onto the table to prevent herself from falling. She'd vowed not to be miserable, had kept herself determinedly cheerful, kept telling herself to look on the bright side. But now even that prop was kicked from under her. Nancy wouldn't have disappeared unless something drastic had happened to her, any more than Marie's father would have. With her dad, she'd kept that little bit of hope alive, in the teeth of all the evidence. She couldn't do it again. It was odds on that Nancy had gone the same way as Margaret and her dad; she'd better face it first as last, instead of clinging on to vain hopes. There was no bright side to this, but she couldn't say that to George; it would crush him.

'It's early days yet. She might turn up. There might be a simple explanation,' she told him, offering her crumb of comfort with as much conviction as she could summon.

The sirens went just before midnight, signalling five hours of strain and anxiety before the all clear sounded, but George's fears about another devastating raid were mercifully not fulfilled.

Each morning, with a heart like lead, Marie went to see Nancy's mother after settling her own mother for a sleep. There was no good news, and Nancy's mother looked more haggard with every passing day. Marie valiantly tried to encourage optimism but it was uphill work, since she herself was convinced that this was a repetition of what had happened to her father. She couldn't believe that the outcome would be any different with Nancy. In the evenings she went to Aunt Edie's to see George and ask whether he had heard anything, but the answer was always the same – nothing.

After three harrowing days, on a fine May evening they were in Northern Cemetery, at a mass funeral. Mourners stood four deep beside a moss-lined trench, which held a long line of earth mounds. From where she stood Marie could just see her own father's grave in the distance.

Nancy's mother looked ready to collapse, and George put a supporting arm around her. He

165

looked as devastated as Marie felt, and so did everybody else she could see in that huge crowd. People of all ages and all walks of life were there, including soldiers and airmen in uniform. Almost all these relatives and friends of the dead carried flowers, from simple posies to elaborate wreaths. The tiny children's coffins were the most heart-wrenching of all.

On the other side of the trench stood Hull's civic leaders, resplendent in their chains of office, along with the Anglican bishop and clergy, the Catholic clergy, the priest from St Vincent's, rabbis, and the leaders of all the nonconformist denominations. The service was short: a hymn, a psalm, and then a message of sympathy and an address from the bishop. Some people were sobbing so sorely that others, who otherwise might have managed to keep a stiff upper lip, began weeping with them. The whole vast crowd seemed to be drowning in an ocean of grief. Marie's gaze was fixed on the pale face of a little girl, no more than three. Her tiny hand was held by a grey-haired old man, probably her grandfather. Perhaps that baby's mother was being buried today; it was very probable. Mrs Harding had lost a daughter, and in all likelihood this little mite had lost a mother – just as bad, if not worse. Definitely worse, Marie thought, looking at that bleak-faced old man. How could he soothe a baby's fears, or kiss her hurts better with as much devotion as her own mother?

When it was over and the officials were moving off, Mrs Harding stood holding her wreath with its simple little message: 'God love my Nancy'.

She scanned the line of mounds in total be-wilderment. 'Where am I supposed to lay this?' she asked. 'I don't even know where she is.'

'Wherever she is, it's not here,' an airman beside them told her. 'The remains might be here, but that's all. The people are gone.'

'Let's find a grave that's got no flowers, Mrs Harding,' Marie said. 'We'll put ours on that one.'

'I never thought to see my own daughter buried before me, and like this – not even a coffin with her name on it.'

George surveyed the graves, awestruck. 'Four hundred people. Four hundred people dead, and thirty-six not identified,' he said. 'In two nights. It's cruel. Poor Nancy, our poor lass. Takes some believing, doesn't it?'

'My poor bairn. You spend years bringing them up, and it's all destroyed, your whole life's work, all your hopes for them gone in one night. Poor little lass. She never did any harm to anyone. I had my differences with her dad, but I'm glad he's been spared this; she was the apple of his eye. Lucky for him he died before he saw this day.'

'What was that bloody idiot bishop on about?' George demanded when they were back in Duesbury Street with Nancy's friends and relations, all sharing a modest cup of tea and a piece of funeral cake. 'The loss we have suffered will be a gain to the whole world! How does he make that out? What's the whole world got to gain by people who never did any harm being killed in air raids?'

'Nothing that I can see, but they've got to say something, I suppose,' one of the neighbours said.

'Everybody liked Nancy, poor lass,' one of her old school friends said, not much to the point.

'I can't stand these parsons, and the claptrap they spout,' George said.

One of the uncles nodded agreement. 'Weddings, christenings and funerals. That's always been enough church for our family, hasn't it, Betty?'

Mrs Harding nodded. 'That's about as often as we ever went. And after having a baby. You went then, to get churched.'

George's mouth was turned down in an expression of utter disgust. 'And the mayor and corporation, dressed up like Christmas trees. They make it look like a bloody pantomime. Then at the end, he says we should dedicate ourselves with "smiles, and gladness and hope"? People have lost husbands, wives, children, mothers, fathers, fiancées, everything they lived for, their lives completely buggered. Thirty-six people couldn't even be identified, and he wants people going about with "smiles, and gladness and hope"! It's obvious to me he's never lost anybody he cares about, or he'd know better than to say a stupid thing like that. I hope he gets a good dose of what we're suffering. See how he feels about smiles and gladness then.'

'You should never wish ill on people,' an auntie said. 'It only comes back on you.'

'How am I wishing him ill?' George demanded. 'I'm just wishing him a good reason for plenty of the smiles and gladness he's talking about. Maybe his wife or his kids will cop it, to be a gain to the whole world. That should give him enough to smile about. If they all go, he can laugh his socks off.'

'There's no point being bitter,' the aunt commented.

'Oh, right. I won't, then.' George said, staring into his teacup. 'Nancy's dead, and the happy years we should have had together have gone for a Burton, but I'll just swallow this down, the cup that cheers, and then I'll be as right as rain, smiling and glad enough to please the bishop.' He lapsed into silence, not far, Marie suspected, from tears.

After an awkward pause the conversation resumed with reminiscences of Nancy at various stages of her life. One of the cousins asked to see the photograph album, and Mrs Harding dragged it out of the sideboard, to be passed round the little groups of people, all asking each other – 'Do you remember when...?' about the half-forgotten times the snaps brought back to mind. Marie thought of all the people buried in that awful mass grave, and imagined hundreds of similar funeral teas held in similar houses to this, and thousands of mourners poring over photos of people who smiled into the cameras with the sun at their backs, mercifully unsuspecting of the brutal and untimely end awaiting them.

Nancy's mother seemed comforted by all the reminiscing. 'It's nice to think she was so well liked,' she said, reverently stroking the album.

'You've got no lodgers at the moment, then,

Mrs Harding? someone asked when the album was back in the cupboard.

'I have, but I told them to make themselves scarce for the evening. This is a private family do; I don't want any strangers about.'

'I don't blame you; neither would I,' one of the neighbours said. 'You're too soft on them, Betty, you let them have the run of the place. You ought to be like the landladies at Blackpool, chuck the boarders out at ten, and don't let them back in before five.'

'I can't do that. They're theatricals.'

'I'm going to have to do something to earn a few bob myself before long, now I've had to give up the hospital,' Marie mused. 'I've been thinking I could maybe fit a couple of lodgers in the middle bedroom, but I'm a bit dubious. I mean, you never know what type of person you might be letting into your house, do you?'

'If you don't like the look of them, you don't take them in. It's all right if you're careful, though the ones you'd want, the ones you'd pick yourself, the real charmers – they're the ones you've got to watch, sometimes. That last pair I had – "Ah, you're looking blooming today, Mrs Harding,"' she said, mimicking a charming Home Counties accent. '"If you weren't wearing a wedding ring, I wouldn't know which was the mother and which was the daughter!" one of them keeps telling me. And he seemed so genuine I fell for it, as if I were fifteen instead of nearly fifty. I gave him the best of everything, and now the bugger's run off without paying his rent. It serves me right, for being a silly old woman.'

'You're not silly, and you're not old either,' Marie said, gazing into Mrs Harding's pretty face, so like Nancy's except for the crow's feet around her eyes, and the white hairs almost imperceptible amongst the blonde.

'What a rotten trick,' George said, 'He ought to be birched. I can't stand con men.'

'Con men and parsons, then,' observed the uncle.

'Much of a muchness, if you ask me,' George said.

'Six months, with hard labour – that's what I'd give him – after I'd made him pay his dues,' a cousin said, grimly.

'Not arf!'

'I'll string him from a bloody lamp post, if he ever shows his face in Hull again,' Mrs Harding's brother promised, and a couple of the other men offered to help him.

'If you take any actors for lodgers, Marie, make sure you get the money off them well before the end of the run,' Mrs Harding said, when the outrage died away. 'Either that, or get hold of something of theirs as security.'

'Yes, well, I don't know how my mother will take to the idea – she's not well at the moment, as you know – but we'll have to do something to bring a bit of money in before long,' Marie said, making her mother the excuse. In reality she had no relish for the idea of taking strangers in. It would be the very last resort, but she wasn't going to say that to Mrs Harding.

Chapter 13

'Marie, that window's all over smears! You never seem to be able to clean a window without leaving smears!'

Her mother's plaintive cry brought Marie back into the front room with the bucket of vinegar and water. She stood it in front of the window and wrung out the wash-leather. 'Where?'

Her mother pointed. 'Can't you see? There! And there!'

Marie went over the window again, wishing that the nets were ready to hang up to hide any smears she might leave after this second attempt, but they were in the kitchen, waiting to be washed and put out to dry. She shouted loud enough for her mother to hear: 'There, it's done again. Will that satisfy you?'

Her mother looked petulant. 'If a job's worth doing, it's worth doing right. And there's no need to shout at me. I'm not as deaf as all that.'

There seemed to be no escape for Marie from the drudgery and privation and strain of looking after the house, and the cantankerous invalid her mother had become, on top of the constant dread of air raids or of struggling with their horrible consequences. For the first couple of years of the war the raids had been few and relatively mild, and day-to-day contact with people at the hospital had provided interest. She had a vital job of work to do and it had even been uplifting, the feeling that they were all in it together, working for a greater good. Her job, and regular outings to dances and the pictures with Margaret and Nancy or her current admirer, had added a sparkle to her life. Meeting Charles again put the icing on her cake. Her future had been settled, and it looked rosy. Sirens and bombs might scare her for the moment, but they couldn't squash her zest for life. She had leaped out of bed every morning with an unquenchable optimism and absolute faith that they would all come through unscathed.

Margaret's death had shown her how misplaced such blind faith was, and her father's death and her mother's devastating injury drove the lesson home. Now Nancy was dead, as well. For Marie, the companionship of her friends and the cheering visits to dance halls and the pictures were over, and with Charles away with the army all the joy had leached out of her life. For her mother's benefit, Marie kept up a façade of determined cheerfulness, but faith and optimism were at a low ebb.

The wireless was her sole remaining pleasure and saver of sanity, and she played it all day long. She was standing in the kitchen with her hands in the sink, squeezing suds through the net curtains, half listening to *Forces Favourites*, broadcasting requests from servicemen. She was singing along to some of the music when her heart turned over at the sound of a familiar, cheerful voice.

'Hello, Marie! This is Charles!'

Her hands became still. As she listened intently

173

to the words she felt that Charles was almost in the room beside her.

'You accused me of not being romantic, but just now I'm as romantic as anyone you can name, from my East Yorks cap to my size ten army boots,' he said. 'I'm sending you all my love, so keep it safe, all right? You're always in my thoughts, and I can't wait to see you again. I hope you'll like the song. I mean every word.'

A male vocalist started singing 'It Had to Be You'. She would have given everything to have Charles there in reality, to take her in his arms and listen, while she poured out every fond thought in her mind. 'For all your faults, I love you still,' the singer crooned. Tears welled into her eyes and rolled down her cheeks at the tenderness of it, for their hopes of a future together, and the sadness of separation. His next leave was probably a long way off, but that he was alive and she would see him, and hold him in her arms, and love him were the sweetest feelings of that bitter-sweet moment. The bitterness came with the thought of poor George and also Margaret's husband, Terry, so that the programme, intended as a morale-booster, filled her with a sorrow so overwhelming she opened the back door and sat on the kitchen step well out of sight and hearing of her mother, with her heart bursting and eyes streaming.

Alfie came crashing through the door of the yard with his bike, home from school. He leaned it against the wall, then crouched down beside her and put a comforting hand on her shoulder, round-eyed with concern. 'What's up, Marie?

What's up? Is it Nancy?'

She dabbed her eyes on her frilly apron, her voice thick. 'It's everything.'

'You'll be all right, don't worry. Anyway, she might be all right. One of the assistants at the Co-op when I went for my sweet ration said she doesn't think Nancy's dead. She says she could have sworn she saw Nancy in the station before the hospital got bombed, getting on a train.'

Marie shook her head. 'She'd got nothing to get on any trains for,' she said, 'and even if she had, she'd never have gone without a word to any of us. Your assistant must have seen somebody who looked like her, that's all.'

'No, I don't suppose she would,' Alfie said, after a moment's consideration. 'Oh, well, we're alive, and we've got to soldier on, till we beat old No-balls. So come on, buck up.'

She laughed through her tears at this child who was sometimes so like a man. 'I'll be all right in a minute, Alfie. I'm in a funny mood, that's all. Don't tell Mam. I'll pull myself together, then we'll have a cup of tea and a lump of vinegar cake, all right?'

'Right-o. And what about a game of battle-ships?'

'Maybe.' She heaved herself up and put the kettle on, then rinsed the curtains and pegged them out before making a pot of weak tea, sparing the rations.

'Have you been crying?' her mother asked when she took it through to the front room. 'You haven't been crying just because I told you the windows were smeared, have you?'

'No, Mam,' Marie said, delving into the sideboard drawer for writing materials. 'I'm going to write to Charles.'

'Pass me a couple of sheets of paper, will you? I'll write to our Pam while you're doing that. You should write as well, and so should you, Alfie.'

'What for?' he demanded. 'She never writes to me.'

'She would if you wrote to her.'

'No, she wouldn't. She thinks I'm not good enough for her, now.'

Marie handed him a sheet of paper and said, softly: 'Just write, will you? Not to upset your mam. Just put: "Write to your mother, will you, Pam? She looks for a letter every day." You don't have to say anything else, if you don't want to.'

Alfie glanced at his mother, and sat down, seeming more than happy to send this reproach to his sister. Marie started a long letter to Charles telling him all the news, ending with things she would never have said on the phone at his parents' house.

She sealed it, feeling much better. A good cry and an hour's peace and quiet had made her ready to look on the bright side again. If her mother was well enough to be constantly picking and fault finding she might soon be well enough to be left while Marie went back to nursing, and work a lot more rewarding than cleaning windows to her mother's exacting standards.

There was a knock on the door. 'Is your Alfie in?' Jenny asked. 'Me dad's come home. They've sent me out to play for a bit.'

'Come in,' Marie said. 'He can show you his

shrapnel collection, and teach you how to play battleships while I go and peel the spuds.'

'Did you manage to get Alfie off with the evacuees?' George asked, a week later.

'Not a hope in hell. When it was time to go, I searched high and low for him, but he was nowhere to be seen. Later on Danny Elsworth came round to tell us they'd had a phone call from my uncle Alfred saying he'd landed at their place. Uncle Alfred's not objecting and we're obviously fighting a losing battle trying to make him go anywhere else, so we've left him there.'

'He's a wilful little blighter, isn't he? Well, the reason I've come is, I've had a bit of an upsetment,' George said with a perplexed frown on his face. 'I'd been meaning to do it all week, and today I finally managed to get to the bank to draw Nancy's share of our savings out, to give them to her mother. Nance never made a will, and I thought: her mother's not well off, and I've got a decent job, so she's got more right to the money than me, seeing me and Nance weren't married. Well, I couldn't find the book, and when they looked into it at the bank, it turns out that Nancy drew all our money out the day before she died, all bar the shilling that you have to leave in to keep the account open. I just don't know why she'd do that, or where the money's gone. We'd no plans to buy anything. I can't understand it, and I wondered if you knew anything about it.'

Marie felt her face drop.

'What's the matter?' George asked. His wounded grey eyes searched her face intensely and a sudden heat flooded Marie's neck and cheeks. Out of the corner of her eye she caught her reflection in the mirror over the mantelpiece, and saw that she had turned brick-red. But to open her mouth about the awful idea that had struck her was impossible. After all, she might be wrong.

'Look, George, I don't *know* anything,' she said, 'so I can't tell you anything. If I were you, I'd go round to see her mother, and tell her what you were going to do.'

A cloud of suspicion settled on George's transparent face. 'You know something, don't you?' he said.

Marie felt like a butterfly on a pin: no escape whichever way she squirmed. 'Oh, George, I don't *know* anything,' she repeated, her voice betraying her anxiety. 'Go and see her mother, and tell her what you were going to do. Just see what she says.'

'She might think I'm lying. She might think I decided to keep all the money, and I'm trying to throw the blame on a poor lass who can't defend herself.'

He had a point. It would seem like that to anyone who didn't really know him. Poor George, he looked like a wounded puppy. Marie wavered for a moment, and then much against her better judgement said: 'She won't if I go with you. I will, if you want me to.'

'Has she written to you?' Nancy's mother demanded, as soon as they were inside.

George's jaw dropped. 'Written to me? How can she? We buried her last week.'

'Ha!' Mrs Harding's eyes flashed, and her mouth turned down in an expression of contempt. 'She hasn't written to you then. I never would have believed a daughter of mine would carry on like she has.'

George sat down on the settee, blank bewilderment on his face.

'We buried nothing, George! Our Nancy's cavorting about down South somewhere, with that bloody actor! The one I was telling you about, who needed a wedding ring to tell which one was the mother, and which was the daughter. He seems to have worked it out now.' Mrs Harding stared at him, waiting for his reaction.

Then Alfie flashed into Marie's mind, with his tale of the assistant at the Co-op having seen Nancy at the station. She sank down onto the seat beside George, and watched his face turn drip-white. He was speechless.

Mrs Harding leaned towards them, her eyes popping with indignation. 'That same bloody tripe-hound that was sweet-talking me, that's who she's gone off with. He's spinning her a yarn about taking her to see some important friends of his at some film studios; they're going to give her elocution lessons and turn her into a film star, or so she thinks! They've put me through hell, thinking she was dead, torturing myself. Then I got that letter, and after I got over the shock, I could have gone and strangled her, and him as well. The bloody rotten trick she's played, letting us all think she'd been killed.'

Marie rallied from the shock enough to put in a word in Nancy's defence. 'No, I can't believe

179

she'd do that, not deliberatcly,' she said. 'She can't have known about the raids; they don't report Hull in the papers.'

'Everybody round here knows that "a northeast coast town" means Hull!' Mrs Harding said, 'and well she knows it.'

'Then she hasn't seen the papers,' Marie said. It had just been thoughtlessness. Nancy was so infatuated with the 'tripe-hound' there had been room for nothing else in her mind. It was on the tip of her tongue to say so, and then she saw George's stricken face, and held her peace.

'Hmm. Maybe.' Mrs Harding contemplated George for a moment or two, and her anger subsided. She bit her lip, and slowly shook her head. 'Just look at him – poleaxed! I've known for two days, and I still haven't got over the shock. I should have come to see you, George, but, honestly, it's taken me all this time to pull myself round. It's not a very nice trick she's done, or a very pleasant task she's left me with.'

'She's drawn everything we've saved out of the bank,' George whispered.

'You can kiss that goodbye. You've about as much chance of getting that back as I've got of getting my rent,' Mrs Harding said. 'And that's about as much chance as she's got of being made into a film star.'

'Everything. She's taken everything,' George repeated.

'You knew, Marie,' he accused, as they walked back to Clumber Street. There was an expression of absolute disgust on his face.

'I knew one of her mother's lodgers had been sweet-talking her,' Marie said, 'but I'd no idea she was going to run off with him. It never entered my mind until you said your savings were gone, and even then I wasn't sure until we heard it from her mother.'

'Weren't you?'

He said it in such a queer tone that Marie felt offended. 'You don't think I was in on it, do you?' she demanded.

'Weren't you?' There it came again, tone and all.

Marie drew herself up to her full height, and gave him a look of disdain. 'I thought you knew me better than that, George. I'm not the sort for tricks like that. I'm engaged myself, and an engagement means something to me. And even if it didn't, do you seriously think I'd have gone to a funeral with you and her mother, and all her friends and relations and watched everybody sobbing into their handkerchiefs without saying anything, if I'd had the faintest idea she was still alive?'

He didn't answer. Marie parted from him outside her door in Clumber Street sensing that George was more than hurt. He was angry too, and he was tarring her with Nancy's wrongdoing. Well, if that's his attitude, she thought, let him stew in it. Trying to help people – 'meddling in other people's business', as Charles called it – was a mug's game. How she missed him, and the good sense he talked. She would certainly take a lot more notice of him in future. George had been injured, no doubt about it, but he had no reason to be disgusted with her. Marie couldn't help resenting the injustice. The whole episode and her part in it left a nasty taste in her mouth.

It preyed on her mind after she went to bed that night. Added to the everlasting fear of air raids it kept her awake for what seemed hours. Eventually she succeeded in putting George out of her mind by determinedly thinking of Chas, and fell into an uneasy sleep. In her dreams she and Chas, light on their feet, were dancing on air under a beautiful chandelier flare, gazing fondly into each other's eyes and smiling, heedless of the bombs shrieking downward to explode on the tormented city far below them, engulfing it in flames.

Chapter 14

Auntie Dot had a pan of mash for the hens bubbling on her Yorkshire range. 'They've even put restrictions on how many you can have now,' she said, 'or as good as. You can't get the feed for more than thirteen, so Alf killed a couple of the old boilers yesterday. I've had one of them in a low oven for hours, so it should be nice and tender.'

'You can take the other one home, Marie, stretch your meat ration out a bit,' Uncle Alfred said.

It struck Marie hard, the way he addressed his remark to her, unconsciously recognizing her as the responsible one, and relegating her mother into the place of a dependant, someone it was unnecessary to consult.

'I've never plucked and drawn a hen before,' she said. 'You always did all that sort of thing, didn't you, Mam?'

'There's a first time for everything, lass,' Alf said. 'You can do it while we're having a cup of tea. Spread a bit of newspaper round for her to drop the innards and feathers on, Dot.'

'Ugh!' Marie pulled a face.

Uncle Alfred grinned. 'Just think yourself lucky you didn't have to wring its neck.'

'I'd like to see this,' Mr Elsworth said, as Dot spread the newspapers. 'I've been thinking about getting a couple of hens myself. They make a mess of flowerbeds, I know, but we haven't many flowers this year. You can't eat flowers, can you?'

'Keep them in a cage, and keep shifting it about like I do. They're good for keeping slugs and other pests down, and the manure's good for the land.'

'It must cost you a bit in fuel, boiling that stuff up for them,' Marie's mother commented, nodding towards the stove.

Dot nodded. 'It does, but we've got plenty of logs, and it's handy to have the eggs. It'll be handy to be able to swap them with neighbours for butter and sugar if eggs go on ration. There's a rumour that they will, before long.'

'I might get some,' Mr Elsworth said. 'I'm getting quite keen on this digging for victory; I feel better for the fresh air and exercise. Of course nothing's actually ready to eat yet, but so far so good, everything seems to be doing all right. I wish we'd taken a house outside Hull, except it was convenient for my boy going to school, and

183

my business is in Hull, as well.'

'Convenient for Hitler's bombs, as well, eh?' Uncle Alfred said.

'Much *too* convenient for them. Have you seen the city centre since they flattened it? I could hardly believe my eyes when I saw it. They seem to be laying off us a bit, though, since they started on Greece. It's just as well for Marjorie. It's enough for her to look after the house now Hannah's husband's at home, without putting in extra hours with the WVS.' Dot and Alfred looked at him, evidently wondering who Hannah was. He paused, Marie guessed feeling a bit embarrassed at displaying his middle-class affluence before the less well-off. 'Our daily help. Her husband's on the convoys. He's home on leave so, naturally, she's given herself a holiday to be with him.'

Uncle Alfred gave a dirty laugh. 'When a bloke's been away at sea for months, he's got a lot of catching up to do,' he said.

'Don't be so coarse, Alfred.' Auntie Dot shot a meaningful glance towards Danny and Alfie and gave her husband a warning look before handing Marie a dead hen.

Mr Elsworth's lips twitched. 'He deserves his catching up, after being on the convoys. We can't begrudge him, but Marjorie's certainly missing Hannah. Housework's never been her favourite occupation.'

'What am I supposed to do with this?' Marie asked.

'Rip all its feathers out, to begin with.'

'You've seen me do it before today,' her mother said.

'Yeah, but I've never done it.' Marie began to pull, and found it a tougher task than she'd imagined. She dropped the feathers on the paper, and was arrested by one of the leading articles.

'There's that story about Hitler's right hand man, Rudolf Hess, and his mad parachute drop into Scotland,' she said. 'What do you make of it?'

Mr Elsworth shrugged. 'He wanted to see the Duke of Hamilton, by all accounts. He's come with an offer of peace, or so he says, but it seems an extraordinary way to do it, especially after the Nazis dropped a bomb on the House of Commons. The government's evidently quite agitated about his antics; closed sessions in Parliament, and all that.'

Auntie Dot fixed her gaze on the scar on her sister-in-law's face. 'I wonder how he dares, after they've been across here, flattening our cities, murdering us,' she said. 'I wonder he hasn't been lynched.'

'We haven't had any peace from Germany since the Kaiser decided he wanted an empire as big as King George's,' Uncle Alf said.

Mr Elsworth gave him a wry smile. 'Well, we haven't had a raid since the thirteenth, you know. That's nearly two weeks of peace – for Hull, at any rate.'

'Look on the bright side. Like you said, we might have seen the worst of it, now they've started on the Greeks,' Marie said.

Uncle Alf nodded. 'You might be right. They can't be everywhere, can they? Not even Germans can do that.'

'I should have been there on the thirteenth, at

185

the ARP post,' said Alfie.

'It wasn't much of a raid, and anyway, there was nothing for us to do. The telephones were working,' Danny said.

'I could have given you a game of billiards,' Alfie grinned.

'And I'd have beaten you, like last time.'

'One of these days you won't. Do you want to come and see the pig? He loves it if you scratch his back.'

'I'll come as well, if nobody minds,' Mr Elsworth said. 'I'd like to see the hens and their wire cage, as well.'

'I've neglected Dad's allotment,' Marie said, still yanking feathers after both men had gone out with the boys. 'I'd better go and see what needs doing there as well, now I've got more time. You can come with me, Mam, sit in a deck chair with your sun-hat on.'

'Me and Alfie'll come down on the bikes, and give you a hand,' Auntie Dot said.

'I wouldn't say no, but you're doing enough, looking after Alfie,' Marie said. 'We've still got to straighten up with you for that.'

'Have you got any money?'

'Well, I got my last pay packet on Friday, and there's the bit that my dad had saved.'

'You'd better hang on to that; you don't know how long you're going to be off work. The bed's there, whether there's anybody sleeping in it or not, and he doesn't cost much to feed, being as we grow a lot of our own stuff. It's like old times, with the clockwork train set out all over the floor and marbles rolling about under every chair. The

186

only thing that's different from when my lads were at home is hearing: "D'you wanna play battleships?" every two minutes. But it brings the place to life. Alfie's not a bad lad, and it's as good as a tonic for us to see things through young eyes again. He's no trouble at all, young Alfie.'

Mr Elsworth changed up a gear, and for Marie's mother's benefit raised his voice well above the hum of the engine. 'What a healthy life it is! Fresh air and the space to breathe it in, always busy, and nearly self-sufficient. It's much better for Alfie, even aside from keeping him safe from the bombing. He's learning a lot about country ways, as well. And he was telling me he's settled well in that nice little school.'

She heaved a sigh. 'I miss him. I miss them both. I don't think things will ever be the same now they've had to live away from their own home.'

'If you miss him so much, why not go and stay with them, Mam? You'd be a lot safer in Dunswell, and I'm sure they'd make you welcome,' Marie said. 'I could go back to nursing then. They're always crying out for nurses.'

'No.'

No apathy there. The answer was too decided to encourage any further argument. Apart from the purr of the engine, the rest of the journey back to Hull passed in almost unbroken silence.

'No,' her mother repeated when Marie broached the subject again back at home. 'It would drive me crackers. I'm a bit too particular for Dot. And to pluck and draw that bird in the kitchen – all its guts all over the floor. I'd have had that outside.'

'It was too windy, Mam. There'd have been feathers all over the place,' Marie said.

Her mother continued as if she hadn't heard. 'And did you see her kitchen floor? Alf walks straight in from the garden, never bothers to take his boots off, and she never says a word to him. And did you see that towel by the kitchen sink he wiped his hands on? Black bright. I wouldn't have used it for a floor cloth. And that sticky American cloth on the table, looked as if it hadn't been wiped for a week. It's a wonder they haven't all got a fever. I felt really ashamed, in front of Mr Elsworth. I don't know what he must have thought.'

Marie was very thankful she hadn't pursued the discussion in the car. Mr Elsworth was such a gentleman she'd have felt really ashamed for him to hear her mother's opinion of the couple who had opened their hearts and their home to Alfie and were looking after him as if he were one of their own, who had brushed aside the offer of payment and evidently wanted none, unless they could make the government cough up the billeting allowance.

'Well, none of them has ever had a fever as far as I know,' she said, 'and you'd be a lot safer there, Mam. Uncle Alfred and Auntie Dot would make you welcome, and you'd be with Alfie, so why worry about a bit of muck on the kitchen floor?'

Her mother's face became a frozen mask. 'I'm sorry to be a burden to you, Marie,' she said, stiffly, 'but I'm not going to Dunswell, and that's flat. I couldn't live in any other woman's house,

188

and especially not with potty Dottie. We'd drive each other mad. You go back to nursing, if that's what you want. I don't want to stand in your way. I'll manage somehow.'

Marie saw it was useless. 'You're probably right, Mam,' she said. 'It was just a thought, and you'll never be a burden to me, all right? You're my mam, and I love you.'

'I sometimes wonder,' her mother said. 'I sometimes wonder if anybody does, now your dad's gone.'

The postman managed to put a smile on her mother's face the following morning, when he handed her an envelope addressed in Pam's handwriting. 'I knew she'd write. I knew our Pam would never forget her mam,' she said, ripping the envelope open in a more animated fashion than Marie had seen her do anything for days. As she devoured the contents eagerly, the smile froze on her lips. She handed Marie the letter.

'She's doing well, there, Marie,' she said, a little too brightly.

'Dear Mother', it began – the familiar, working-class 'Mam', and the middle-class 'Mummy' both neatly avoided, Marie noted. She read on:

Bourne is really, really beautiful at this time of year. I'm doing very well with my lessons and the teacher is very pleased with me. Mr and Mrs Stewart say if you're agreeable they'll keep me at school until I'm sixteen, or even eighteen if the war lasts that long. I might even be able to get a scholarship to go to college if I stay on.

I'm doing so well with my piano lessons I won't need to take the first examination. I take the second one next month, and Mr and Mrs Stewart say I'm sure to pass. They think I'll make a very accomplished pianist. I might even have a future as a concert pianist, if I work hard. What I really want is to go to music college.

I hope you are all as well as we are here. The last couple of raids haven't been as bad as when I was there, have they, thank goodness.

Your loving daughter,
Pamela

She writes, Marie thought, as if to a stranger. No warmth or intimacy in the letter, not a word about Alfie, or even real concern for her mother. No hint that she was missing any of her own family – there was no feeling there at all, just me, me, me. And then that 'Pamela' again at the end, when she'd always been plain Pam at home. Marie handed it back to her mother, thankful at least that Pam had written 'Mr and Mrs Stewart' rather than 'Auntie Morag and Uncle Alec'. That might spare her mother's feelings a bit.

'They're certainly filling her head full of a lot of big ideas there, aren't they?' she said. 'Are you going to let her stay on?'

A brief struggle played itself out on her mother's face. 'Of course' she said in the end. 'Of course she can stay on. She's a clever girl, and I won't stand in her way. She's got to have her chance.'

'Do you want to talk it over with her? Shall I ask the Elsworths if you can phone her from there? You can sit down and do it in comfort from their house.'

'No. I wouldn't phone her from there anyway, for them to hear everything we're saying. If I wanted to phone her, I'd go to the phone box.'

'They wouldn't listen to what you were saying. The phone's in the hall. They'd leave you alone to talk.'

'I don't want to be any more beholden to them than I already am. Anyway, I'd rather write.'

'I'll get the dinner on, then.'

Marie left some yeast to ferment and then she put the boiling fowl in the stew pot with a couple of onions, and a few old carrots a long way past their best, and set it in a low oven. After that she worked off her irritation with Pam by kneading a couple of pounds of flour into dough, which she covered with a cloth and left in the kitchen away from the fire, so it wouldn't rise too quickly.

Her mother was sitting listlessly in the front room, her letter still unwritten.

'I'm just going to nip out to the allotment, Mam, see if I can rescue some of the stuff Dad planted. It's a shame to let it spoil,' Marie told her, and escaped with a jumper and the key to the shed.

The soil was dry and full of weeds between the rows of potatoes and vegetables, giving her a job of hoeing and hand weeding and earthing-up and watering that seemed to last for hours, but work in the fresh air and the banter from other allotment holders made a pleasant change. When she got back home her mother's letter to Pam was written and sealed.

'Take it to the post box for me, will you?' she asked.

Marie took it to the post, then knocked the dough back and shaped it into two loaves. She left them before the fire to rise, then set the table for a very late dinner.

The old hen was just about edible. Well fed and pleasantly tired after all the exercise and fresh air, Marie relaxed as they listened to *It's That Man Again*, telling herself to be thankful for small mercies. The trick seemed to be to expect very little, then anything more was a bonus.

Her mother hardly seemed to hear the programme. She was quiet all evening, gazing into the void. 'They've stolen my bairn,' she said, at last. 'That's what they've done. Stolen her.'

'I thought you said there wouldn't be as many raids now the Germans are moving east,' Marie's mother accused her later that week, as they sat face to face again in the cramped little cupboard under the stairs listening to bombs being dropped.

'I didn't say it for a fact. I just didn't think they'd have the men.'

'I'm sick of this,' her mother said, as if Marie herself were to blame for the raid. 'Absolutely sick. Next time the sirens go, I'm staying in bed. They can all do what they want.'

They sat the raid out in the cupboard and went back to bed safe and unharmed after the all clear. But the next time the sirens blared Marie's mother refused to get out of bed in spite of all Marie's pleas, entreaties, and dire warnings. With her nerves tightly strung after losing her exasperating battle of wills with the stubborn woman Marie drew aside the bedroom curtain, to gaze

192

anxiously at the half-moon. When the all clear sounded at five minutes to midnight without a bomb having been dropped, she felt as if a death sentence had been lifted and let out her pent-up breath in a long sigh of relief.

'Thank God for that,' she said, 'We've got away with it, this time. But next time, you're coming down into that cupboard with me, even if I have to drag you there.'

'You go into that cupboard on your own, there's nothing to stop you,' her mother shouted. 'There was nothing to stop you tonight.'

'There was you to stop me. Not wanting to leave you here on your own is what stopped me.'

'Well, you can go to bed now, or go downstairs and make a cup of tea, if you want to do something useful.'

Marie went downstairs and put a scant two cups of water into the kettle. When she was half-way upstairs with two cups of tea she heard the drone of bombers, and the hair stood up on the back of her neck. Somebody had made a terrible mistake in sounding that all clear. She'd only just made it back to her mother's bedroom when the familiar, screeching whistle came and the house shook as a bomb landed with an almighty crump. Smut streaked past her and ran yowling downstairs.

'That was a near one,' Marie gasped, her shaking hands spilling tea into the saucers. Sick with dread, she put the cups down on the dressing table, and drew aside the curtain to look through the window. The glare of another bursting bomb lit up the room. The floor shook.

'Come on! Come on! Get out of bed! We're going under the stairs.'

Her mother was stiff with fear. Her teeth were chattering and she clung on to the brass bed rails with hands like claws, resisting all Marie's attempts to pull her away and down to the safest place in the house.

After another long and terrible screech and a mighty crash the floor heaved up beneath her feet. Marie lost her hold on her mother as she was blasted into the air, the whole of the clean and dainty bedroom thrown up with her – walls, ceiling, bed and burr walnut bedroom suite all in the air for seconds, as if they were weightless. Then she felt herself falling, and crashed down to earth, stunned and winded, with rubble battering her, blow after blow until she was buried alive under the weight of it all. She struggled to blow dust out of her nostrils and spit soot and dust and grit and blood out of her mouth, to get some air. Air!

'Mam! Mam!' she called, in a shrill, tinny voice nothing like her own. She struggled with all her strength to get loose, and more debris fell, small stones and gravel cascading through the spaces of bricks and plaster. She could just see the half-moon shining brightly in a sky still humming with enemy bombers. The weight on her chest pressed down so that she could barely breathe.

The first feeble shafts of dawn light were penetrating gaps in the rubble when she came to. 'Mam, Mam,' she gasped again.

'There's somebody alive under there! Hello! Hello, can you hear me?' a man's voice shouted.

Marie almost wept with relief and, trying to shout, managed a feeble little croak. 'Yes, yes. Can you see my hand?'

'Where? Where?'

She moved her hand, then the man said something she couldn't make out. 'I can't hear you,' she said.

'Yes, we can see. We've got you, lass. Your mother's under there as well, is she?'

It was George. Now the tears began. 'I think she's dead.'

'It's all right, Marie. The rescue party's here. We'll soon have you out, and then we'll see what the damage is.'

'Get my mam out first. She'll be worse than me.'

'We'll start with you, we know where you are. Then we'll get your mam out, don't worry.'

They were soon moving debris in earnest, working so close to her she was terrified they might stand on rubble she was lying under and dislodge bricks or lintels or shards of glass to crush her or cut her to ribbons. She was already in agony. Her chest hurt like hell.

'Don't worry, Marie, not long now. We'll soon get you out.'

'I'm in my pyjamas,' she said, and thought, how ridiculous to worry about that, when she might have died. All the same, thank God! If she'd worn her nightie, both rescuers and sightseers might have had a good view, but her mother only had a nightie on. If she were alive and conscious she'd be mortified. Her mother might think death preferable.

George must have read her mind. 'Not too

many sightseers, Marie. Most of the Hull people are in bed, and not many trippers in yet. Might not be any. They might be getting bored with it by now, this being our fiftieth raid. And don't worry about these lads, they've seen it all. They've seen people in less than pyjamas. They've seen people with every stitch blown clean off.'

'Not me, they haven't,' she managed to gasp.

After what seemed an age George's face was near hers, grimy and running with sweat but reassuring.

'I've never been so glad to see anyone,' she told him.

'Can you move?' he asked, when she was finally free.

She could. Her arms, legs and shoulders were stiff, but she could move them.

'Easy, lass,' another rescuer said, then she felt their strong, competent hands lifting her onto a stretcher. She winced with the pain of her shoulders and back, but stronger than the pain was an overwhelming feeling of relief, and gratitude to these men who had worked so long and so hard to free her. Her heart was full of it, towards George above all.

'You've saved my life,' she told him. 'I'll never be out of your debt.'

Dr Steele scribbled as he talked, his head bent over the notes on the table at the end of her bed in the infirmary. 'I strongly suspect you've got a couple of cracked ribs, but they're not displaced, so no point sending you for X-ray. You'll find breathing painful for three or four weeks.'

She gave him an apologetic smile and leaned forward, carefully guarding her ribs and turning an ear towards him. 'Pardon?'

He looked towards her and, raising his voice considerably, he repeated himself. 'We could put some strapping round your chest to relieve the pain, but it would restrict your breathing, so better not. Just put up with it. Take painkillers, if you have to. Now, tell me what I've said.'

Marie repeated his words.

'Well, you're not completely deaf; just some sensorineural damage because of the explosion. You'll miss the high-frequency sounds, but your hearing should improve, given time. Get people to speak up, and learn to lip-read. You seem to have had one of those rare hair's-breadth escapes. You're a very lucky young woman. If I were a religious man, I'd call it a miracle.'

'Have you seen my mother?'

He nodded. 'Mrs Larsen; she's still unconscious. I remember her well, from the last time. Hardly healed from the first injuries, and now a broken ankle, dislocated shoulder, and a heart that needs careful watching. "Lucky" is not a word we'd apply to her, is it? But it might have been worse. She might recover with good nursing, but you won't be fit to take it on. You need nursing yourself – your ribs and ears will be painful and you'll feel very tired for quite a while. We're sending your mother to Beverley. We'll keep you here overnight. We should be able to discharge you tomorrow. I used to say "send you home", in those happy days when we could take it for granted that people had homes.'

'It's gone,' Marie croaked. 'Flattened.'

There was an unnaturally sympathetic expression on Dr Steele's face that Marie had rarely seen. 'Better get the Red Cross lady to come and see you then, unless there's a relative or neighbour you can go to,' he said. 'And come back and see me at once if you suspect anything wrong. At once, do you hear me?'

She heard him, but only just.

Chapter 15

When George came down the ward the following day Marie was sitting by her bed waiting for the ambulance, clutching a paper carrier bag containing her pyjamas. She saw him looking at the strange assortment of clothes she was wearing: an old cotton dress two sizes too big and a shrunken cardigan of yellow wool, whose sleeves ended half-way up her forearms. On her feet were a pair of old blue peep-toed sandals, also too large.

'Red Cross,' she explained. 'They offered to find me somewhere to live as well.'

He gazed pointedly at her clothes. 'Going by the rigout, I wonder what that would be like – probably somebody's chicken-coop. But you've got somewhere to live while my mother's got a house and a bed. She's already told me you're staying with us, and your mother as well, when she gets better. We haven't been friends for donkey's years for you to be sent to some homeless dumping ground when you're in a fix.'

The donkey's years friendship had been between their parents, to be precise. She and George had mostly gone their separate ways in recent years, but Marie let that pass. George was offering the olive branch after that business with Nancy, and she accepted it. He had more than earned the right to call himself her friend, but she wasn't going to impose on his partially sighted mother.

'No, George. I can't put your mother to all that trouble. She's not fit to be looking after invalids.'

'Rubbish. She's as strong as an ox.'

'I'll go to stay with my aunt and uncle in Dunswell,' she said. 'I feel bad enough having to bother anybody, but they're family, so theirs is the first door I ought to be knocking on.'

'Do they know you've been bombed out? You haven't had time to let them know, have you?'

'Not yet,' she admitted.

'Better hang on a bit, then, until they're prepared. My mother's already got the room ready for you,' he insisted. 'So you're coming to us, all right? For now, at least. She'll be upset if you go anywhere else.'

A nurse came to the bed. 'Ambulance waiting for you, Marie. Have you got everything?'

Marie waved her bag. 'All my worldly goods,' she said. 'They don't half fill a carrier, now.'

'Have you heard anything from Nancy?' George asked that evening, while they were sitting at the table waiting for his mother to bring the food in.

199

Much against her better judgement, Marie had let George talk her into staying with them. It was hard to resist someone she felt so deeply indebted to, and now she was confronted with the situation she would have given a great deal to avoid.

'No.'

'Neither have I. She's made a right old fool of me, hasn't she?'

Marie said nothing. There was nothing she could say, and even if there had been, she hadn't the strength, after the torture of being jolted around in the ambulance for an hour on roads raised in some parts and pitted in others by bombing and patchy repairs.

'I always knew she didn't think as much about me as I did about her, but I'd never have believed she'd have done a trick like she has done,' George went on.

'I can hardly hear you, George. My ears ache like hell, and it's painful to breathe,' she almost wept, as his mother put the food on the table.

When Auntie Edie had asked her whether she liked herrings, Marie had said yes, imagining the skinned and boned dry fillets her father used to fry in butter, not this waterlogged object complete with head, tail, bones and skin that Aunt Edie now proudly lifted onto her plate. It gazed dull-eyed up at her, floating limp and lifeless in its pool of cooking water.

'Help yourself to bread and marg,' Aunt Edie smiled.

Marie helped herself, and picked at the fish, searching for some part of the watery flesh that she could force down without gagging.

'I was just telling Marie, I'd never have believed Nancy would do a trick like she has,' George said.

'Nobody would. She's a bad un, that lass, and she'll come to a bad end,' Aunt Edie said. 'Think yourself lucky she showed herself in her true colours before you got married. You might have been saddled with her for life. You've had a lucky escape, George. You used to be a friend of hers, didn't you, Marie?'

Used to be? Marie thought. She and Nancy were still friends, as far as she knew.

'No appetite, Marie?' George asked.

She shook her head. 'Not really. Sorry.'

'Pass it here then,' he said, taking her plate and sliding the contents onto his own. 'Waste not, want not.'

Aunt Edie forgave the snub to her cooking, and lavished sympathy on her. 'Not surprising, after what you've been through. And your poor mam, first injured in that hit on the shelter, and your dad killed, and now this. Now they've smashed her home to bits as well as putting her in hospital, bloody Germans. All her poor bits of furniture, fit for nothing but firewood.'

'It's that man again!' said George.

'That man again! I know what I'd do with that man. I'd Hitler him. I'd Hitler him where it hurts.'

'Don't be ridiculous, Mother,' he laughed. 'By the way, Marie, I managed to salvage a bit of stuff from your house – mostly the stuff that was in the garden shed. Your dad's gardening tools. The only thing I got from the house was the last he used to mend our shoes on. I saw a pile of plates

201

that looked perfect, but when I tried to lift them up they fell through my hands, in smithereens.'

His mother smiled fondly at him. 'I'm not ridiculous,' she said, and turned to Marie. 'Cup of tea, then, love?'

What an uncanny sensation of travelling back in time Marie had on entering the bedroom. Nothing seemed to have changed in the twelve years or so since she last stood on that very spot. Everything was familiar to her from her childhood days, when she and George were sent to play upstairs while downstairs their parents played whist for halfpennies if they were flush, or matches if they were hard up. The same curtains and lamp, the same cast-iron bedstead stood there, with the same beautiful thick eiderdown covered in a silky gold material. She put her carrier bag down on a rickety old dining chair lavished with polish, which had been there as long as she could remember, and undressed slowly and painfully, hanging her charity clothes over the chair back. Pyjamas on, Marie eased herself between sheets that were snow white and beautifully ironed, wondering how Aunt Edie, with her poor eyesight, managed to keep it all so clean. The bed might have been comfortable had she not been tormented by her cracked ribs, multiple bruises and jangling nerves. As it was, she could find no ease anywhere.

It was still light outside, and through the open window the faint smell of explosives drifted in on the breeze. Marie lay still and silent, her thoughts in turmoil. The main worry was her mother.

Would she survive, and where would they live if she did? Where was the house that they would be able to afford? They couldn't stay with neighbours for ever; even the most easy-going people get sick of permanent visitors. Alfie would have to be told, but Pam, well, no urgency there. Pam could wait. For all Pam cared, it hardly mattered when she found out, if at all. And Chas, what would he say? Marie prayed the night would pass without another visit from the Luftwaffe. If the sirens went, she couldn't go and crouch in a stinking public shelter with forty or fifty other people pressing against her, she just could not. She couldn't stay in the house either, not after the night before last. Utter ruin surrounded her on every side. There was not one aspect of her life that she could rest her thoughts on without a rising panic – except for Alfie. She closed her eyes and tried to breathe without jarring painful ribs, praying the bombers would stay away, and thanking God that Alfie was all right.

Chapter 16

The following morning George poked his head round the bedroom door, dressed and ready for work. 'I've been knocking, but you can't have heard,' he shouted. 'Then I thought I'd just see whether you were still asleep. I've brought you a cup of tea.'

Nothing could have been more welcome. Marie

was parched. 'Come in,' she said, pulling the quilt up to her neck. 'Thanks for this, George, but you shouldn't have. I don't want to make you late for work.'

'I won't be late. I bring Mam her cuppa every morning before I set off. It's no trouble to make an extra one. I'll tell you what,' he said, looking at the pathetic rags Marie had hung on the chair, 'you're about Nancy's size. I'll go round to her mother and ask if she's left any decent clothes. She can offset them against some of the money she owes me.'

'No, thanks. I don't want Nancy's clothes.'

'No, I should think you don't,' he said, his expression grim. 'I should think you wouldn't be seen dead in them.'

That wasn't what she'd meant. Nancy's clothes were Nancy's clothes, and Marie still regarded her as a friend, even if a selfish and thoughtless friend. She had no intention of taking any of her things, but she was in no condition to think of a tactful way of explaining that to George.

'He thought the world of her, you know. She was everything to him. He said if he hadn't had me to think about, he'd have done away with himself,' Aunt Edie told Marie, later that day. 'He's talked about nothing else since he found out. He said: "Just think, Mam. There must have been times when she was with me and thinking about him. Kissing me, even, knowing all the time that she intended going off with him, and saying nothing about it, just stringing me along." Well, he's right, isn't he? You don't just up and off with somebody unless there's been plenty between you before-hand. And for her to pinch all his savings into the bargain, well, it knocked the stuffing out of him.'

'I'm certain he blames me as well,' Marie said, 'because she's my friend. But I had nothing to do with it. I couldn't stop her telling me that actor was sweet-talking her, but I gave her no encouragement, and she certainly never said she intended running off with him.'

Aunt Edie smiled. 'He's been thinking every-body's against him, laughing at him behind his back, poor lad, so I'll tell him that. He'll be glad to know.'

He knows; I've already told him, Marie thought, but her chest hurt too much and she was too weary of it all to repeat it. But there was something she really had to say.

'It's real good of you to take me in, but me being here, it's all George's doing. All the money we had was in the house. If it's not under the rubble it's been burned, or some looter has made off with it. I can't pay my way, and I'm making extra work for you and I shan't be able to pull my weight with the work for weeks. I don't want to be a nuisance. You shouldn't have to be bothered with it. I'll go and stay with Uncle Alfred and Auntie Dot as soon as I can get Mr Elsworth to take me.'

'Be bothered with it?' Aunt Edie exclaimed. 'You can put that idea right out of your head. It's not a bother, it's a pleasure to be able to help old friends! This was your second home when you and George were little; you used to run in and out of here as easy as your own house. Your mam's coming here as well, if she pulls through.'

205

'I'm worried sick about her,' Marie said, 'especially after the last episode. Especially after Dr Steele saying she's got a weak heart, as well as everything else.'

'Well, we'll do everything we can. We're all in this together. Don't you worry about me, I might not be able to see very well, but I can get round my own house all right, and cooking for three people's not much more trouble than cooking for two. You'll be able to peel veg. You can do that sitting at the table, if you feel up to it. And rub a bit of pastry up, or a few scones. And you'll soon get another ration card.'

'There's the washing. Not that I've got much to wash.'

'You won't make much. And anyway, they've got mobile laundries on the go now, I've heard. I don't know how they work, but you could maybe get your stuff done at one of them. And it seems to have perked George up a bit, having you here. Gives him something else to think about.'

A warning bell rang in Marie's brain, muted, but insistent.

'You look done in,' Aunt Edie said. 'Why don't you go upstairs and have a lie-down? Maybe have a sleep?'

'If only I could.'

Aunt Edie gave her a thoughtful look. 'Tell you what,' she said. 'My husband used to keep a bottle of rum under the bed and have a swig at that when his wound was bothering him. They started him on it in the army, when they used to get them half soused before sending them over the top, and he drank it for the rest of his life.

There's a bottle left, never been touched since he died, and how many years ago is that, now? Lucky it keeps. I'll make you a cup of tea and slosh some in it, see if that does you any good.'

'I'll give it a try,' said Marie. 'I'd try anything, for an hour's sleep.'

She must have slept, because it was late afternoon when she walked ever so carefully downstairs. George had just come through the door, home from work. His mother was there to greet him.

'I've just let Marie's young man's mam and dad in. You've got some visitors, Marie.'

Mr Elsworth jumped to his feet as she entered the front room, and taking her hands in his, began to speak.

She looked at him, straining to hear, trying to read his lips, and failing. 'Pardon?' she said.

Mrs Elsworth spoke up. 'It's the explosion, Leonard. She's deafened because of the explosion. Come and sit down beside me, Marie.'

Marie sat down.

'We went to spend a couple of days with my sister in Malton,' Mrs Elsworth explained. 'We came back today to see that the house two doors down from us had been bombed flat, so as soon as we'd had something to eat, we came to see if you and your mother were all right. We've seen your house, or what's left of it. The neighbours told us you were here, so we've come to offer you a home. It's what Charles would expect, and it's what we want. You're more than welcome to stay as long as you like, and your mother, as well.'

George looked steadily into Mrs Elsworth's face. 'We've arranged for her to stay here,' he said. 'My mother's known her since she was a baby. Marie and I were just about brought up together. Our fathers went through the last war together. We've been friends all our lives. My mother's only too pleased to be able to look after her.'

The Elsworths gave Marie querying looks, and she looked back, groping for the right words to contradict George without seeming ungrateful for everything he'd done for her.

'Has Marie anything to say about it?' Mr Elsworth asked, after a long pause.

Nothing came to mind. Everything George had said was the perfect truth, and her brain was too dulled to find words to explain. 'I thought it would be too much for Aunt Edie, looking after me, but she says not,' she finally said.

Mrs Elsworth nodded. 'Aunt Edie's blind, isn't she? Surely it would be easier for her if you came to us?'

'My mother's not blind,' George said. 'She's partially sighted. It's a different thing altogether.'

'But surely, even from a financial point of view—'

George's resentment showed on his face. 'Well, we're obviously not as well off as you, but we can certainly manage to help our friends.'

'We must all do as much as we can to help our friends,' Mrs Elsworth said carefully. 'Clothing's going on ration, and you must have lost most of your things in the raid, Marie.'

'I've got a pair of pyjamas of my own, and a dress and cardigan and some underwear I got from the Red Cross.'

'I know someone who works in the Relief Office. I'll get him to fetch me all the forms you need to apply for assistance,' George said. 'You don't want to have to go down there yourself if you can help it. They're always packed out with people. You'd be waiting for hours, and you're in no fit state, Marie, so I'll bring the forms, and I'll help you fill them in.'

'Thanks, George,' Marie said. 'I went down there a couple of times after Dad died, to see if I could claim anything for my mother, and I waited for hours to get the right form. But then they wanted copies of my dad's death certificate, and a doctor's certificate for my mam's injuries, and with having to make arrangements for the funeral and going to Bourne to see Pam and Alfie, and then Alfie going missing, and what with work and everything, I had too much else to think about, so I missed the boat. We've been living on what I earned, mainly, and eking it out with Dad's savings.'

'Don't worry. I'll see about getting them. And I'll help you to fill them out, the sooner the better. These things take ages.'

'Well, you seem to be in good hands, Marie,' Mr Elsworth said, when they parted at the door. 'We'll send a telegram to Charles, to let him know what's happened, and we'll ring the people in Bourne if you like – that's if they don't already know, of course. If there's anything else we can do, let us know.'

'Please, take me up to Beverley to see Mam, and call in at Uncle Alfred's on the way back, so I can see Alfie,' she pleaded.

'Of course he will, as soon as we get enough petrol,' Mrs Elsworth said. 'But the trip to Malton's used the ration up for this week, I'm afraid.'

'Don't you worry about that, Marie, love,' George called from the passage. 'I'll take you up on the motorbike.'

Mr Elsworth looked at his wife and raised his eyebrows, then turned again to Marie. 'If we can do anything to help, you just let us know.'

'I've been talking to a chap in the Legal Department,' George said, after the table had been cleared and his mother was in the kitchen, washing the tea things. 'He says if I can find Nancy's address, I can get a solicitor and make a claim against her for the money she took. I don't suppose you might have it, being as you were her best friend?'

Marie shook her head. 'I haven't heard from her since before...'

'The funeral? Or the mock funeral, rather.'

'Yes. I mean no. I don't know where she is,' said Marie, very glad not to know.

'Never mind. I dare say there's ways and means of finding out,' he said, replacing his empty cup in the saucer. 'We'll go up and see how your mam's doing now, if you like.'

'Do you mind if we don't, George?' she said. 'I wouldn't dare. I don't think I'm up to a spin on a motorbike just yet. It's painful to breathe, and I have to be careful how I walk.'

'Oh, yes,' he said. 'I was forgetting – although I don't know how I could, seeing I was the one who dug you out. Lucky I heard you, though, wasn't it?'

Lucky for her, Marie thought, wondering how anyone could forget saving someone's life.

George brought the forms the following day, and Marie sat down with them after tea, completely flummoxed at some of the questions. 'They're asking me what my dad's income was during a representative working year,' she said. 'How do I know? He never talked about money, and now he's dead, the house is flattened, Mam's in hospital, and I can't get there to see her.' She read on. What other earnings went into the house, what pensions had they? Well, there was her dad's war pension, but she wasn't sure whether that had stopped when he died. Her mother would know, but she wasn't fit to be worried with questions. And what scholarships? None yet, but Pam might get one before long. Did she still count as a member of their household, seeing that the Stewarts seemed to have taken her over, and she might never come back home at all? Not that there was a home to come back to, unless Marie could find somewhere affordable to rent, where she could look after Pam and Alfie, and her mother – if her mother pulled through. Nothing was settled. Everything was an 'if,' and what was true today might not be true tomorrow. There were endless questions enquiring into the minutest details of their lives, demanding to know things she didn't know herself, and that her mother had probably forgotten. At the end of it all came the demand for a medical certificate to be attached to the form, which would mean trailing back to the hospital and waiting hours until Dr Steele could see her.

'I can't fill this in, George,' she said. 'Apart from telling them what our names are, and what the address was, I can't answer any of these questions.'

'Just guess,' he said, 'and write a note at the end, explaining. That's what other people do. One of the chaps at the Relief Office says he thinks some people make it up as they go along, and claim for all sorts of stuff they never had in the first place.'

'And then I suppose they end up in court for trying to defraud the government.'

'I've yet to hear of one.'

Marie looked again at the form, unconvinced. But she'd have to make a stab at it; living off George and his mother was something she couldn't contemplate. She began to write down her guesses, picturing herself sitting in a gaol cell if they turned out to be wrong.

George suddenly jumped up and went into the passage, reappearing with his jacket half on. 'Right! I've decided! I'm going to go and see Nancy's mother and get her address,' he said 'I shan't tell her I'm starting court proceedings; better let her think I want Nance back, for now, although I definitely don't. She's made a complete laughing stock of me, and she's going to pay me everything she owes me, or else. Including giving back that engagement ring. I haven't forgotten that, either.'

'Why not just let it go, George?' she said. 'It's eating you away.'

That was not what George wanted to hear. 'It's obvious nobody's ever done the dirty on you, or you wouldn't talk like that,' he snapped. 'She's a Judas, Marie. A Judas!'

She heard the slamming of the front door as he left; she would have had to be stone deaf not to. Let him go then, the idiot! She had enough troubles of her own without listening to him, harping on all the time. She was beginning to see why Nancy had gone. If only she'd insisted on going to Dunswell in that ambulance, instead of letting him persuade her to come here, so he could din his complaints about Nancy into her aching ears every minute of the day.

When that reaction subsided she felt a spasm of guilt at harbouring such uncharitable thoughts about the man who'd saved her life. George had been very good to her, and she ought to re-member it. She turned her attention back to her forms, to struggle with them unaided – not that he could have helped, anyway. If she couldn't answer the questions, what hope had he, for all his promises? She put the form aside. She'd write to Pam, instead. That would be a pleasanter occupation than form-filling, if only by the nar-rowest margin.

'You'll be happy to know we're still alive, if you can remember who we are, now you've got your new relations, who aren't related to us,' she began. Her mam was at death's door, she was injured, the house was blown to smithereens, and they hadn't seen Smut since the bombing, she continued, and ended with: 'Hope you're having a lovely time in Bourne and doing well with your piano lessons.'

213

Aunt Edie emerged from the kitchen with three beakers of tea as she put the finished letter aside.

'Where's George?'

'Gone to see Nancy's mother.'

'What for?'

'To get her address.'

'I hope he hasn't decided he wants her back. She's not worth it. He won't touch her with tongs again, if he's got any sense...'

Aunt Edie drank the extra beaker of tea herself, intermittently slaking her throat throughout her excoriations of Nancy and 'sluts like that'.

After she'd returned to the kitchen Marie read through her letter to Pam, and tore it up. Her father was dead, and her mother might not be long for this world. It looked as though they'd lost Pam, so what good could such nastiness do? And really, was it fair to blame a girl of thirteen for wanting to be safe, and get the best from life?

George was back an hour later, very pleased at his own cleverness in getting Nancy's address by playing the broken-hearted lover. 'Well, that was a good ruse,' he laughed, 'and Nancy's mum fell for it, hook, line and sinker. I even got tea and sympathy! "Poor George," she said, but you wait: it'll be "poor Nancy" by the time I've finished with her.'

Marie was appalled. 'But you lied, George!' she said.

'Of course I lied! She wouldn't have given it to me if I'd told her I was going to drag her daughter through the courts, would she? When you're dealing with liars, you play by their rules, or you lose! Nancy started it, and I'll finish it – by being a better damned liar than she is.'

'But did she ever actually tell you any lies, George?'

He gave her a look of fury. 'Of course she did!'

'When?'

His face flushed and twisted in anguish, and brimming tears glittered on his lower eyelids. 'When she told me she loved me!' he almost sobbed. 'She *lived* a lie!'

Marie looked away and there was a minute's painful silence. When she glanced at him again George's tears were gone, and in their stead she saw an icy composure.

'Do you want her address?' he asked. 'I'll copy it out for you. You can write to her yourself.'

'I'd better not. I wouldn't know what to say, and I've got too many other things on my mind just now.'

'Say the same as me. Give her the Scarborough Warning, like a true friend. Tell her: George is out for blood, so you'd better pay him what you owe him – or else! That's all she needs to know.'

In the privacy of her own room late that evening Marie did write – to Charles.

It hadn't crossed George's mind that if I did write to Nancy, I might have some news of my own – like being bombed out of my home and having my mother at death's door in hospital. It's the deliberate, malicious way he's going about it that turns me off. It wasn't like that with Nancy. She thought she was in love with fly-by-night Monty. She left George without a spiteful thought in her head...

On reading the letter through before sealing it, it struck Marie that Nancy had left without any thought for George at all. Malicious thoughts showed some feeling, at least. After years of devotion and planning for their future together George had been treated as if he counted for absolutely nothing. It must have struck like a dagger through his heart. The quiet, self-effacing lad of old, who'd never had much to say for himself, who had never attracted anybody's notice, was certainly intent on being noticed now. For Nancy's sake she hoped that 'Monty' – or whatever his name really was – turned out to be true to his promises.

The sole topic of conversation at the Maltbys' in the days that followed was Nancy. Hitler, Goering and the entire German armed forces couldn't match her for infamy, in the eyes of George and his mother. Nothing could deflect them from the subject. Marie's mind was full of her own disaster, but let her start talking about her own worries and by some convoluted path or other the discussion came back to Nancy. Everything came back to Nancy: Nancy's treachery, Nancy's lies, and Nancy's 'sticky fingers', and how Nancy was going to be made to pay back the money and suffer court proceedings if she didn't. The constant repetition of it all made Marie feel that the message was being purposely directed at her, as Nancy's friend.

The post brought her a letter from Chas early on Saturday morning, and she took it upstairs to read it in her bedroom. He was full of sympathy for the 'hellish time' she was having, and frustrated at being too far away to help. He'd always thought George an insipid sort of a chap, but he couldn't blame him for his attitude to Nancy. She should go to stay with his parents, then she wouldn't have to be bothered with it all. He couldn't get compassionate leave since she wasn't in danger, but he was desperately trying to get home, to swap leave with anyone he could. She should keep listening to the wireless, he would keep asking for songs to be played for her. 'You're always in my thoughts,' he ended, and signed off, 'With all my love, your own, Chas'.

'He can't get home,' she told them at the breakfast table, before George set off for work, disappointment written on her face and loaded in her voice. 'He says because I'm not at death's door, and we're not married, they won't give him any leave.'

'Well, at least he tried, and he's written to you; you've got to give him credit for that,' Aunt Edie sympathized. 'Nancy would have done a lot better if she'd had the decency to write to George, as well as her mother.'

'She'd have done even better if she'd had the guts to tell me what she intended *before* she buggered off, and she'd have done better still if she'd left my money alone,' George added, and took a vicious bite out of his toast, cut thick as a doorstep.

'She hadn't the guts. She's a coward, as well as a ... well, there's a word for women like her, who jilt decent young men and hop off with their mother's fly-by-night lodgers, but I'm not going

217

to soil my mouth on it,' Aunt Edie said, turning her wide, short-sighted eyes in Marie's direction.

It was too much. Marie's nerves were wrecked by her aching ears and painful ribs. Even taking a deep breath was agonizing. She was shattered by the bombing of her home and the loss of everything she had – every penny, everything she owned, except the pyjamas she'd been buried alive in. That was more than enough to deal with. George and his mother had been kind in their way, but the strain of being expected to take the opposing side in a war against Nancy, of being sucked into George's vendetta, was too much.

'I've got to go,' she said, more to herself than to George and his mother.

Aunt Edie's wide-open eyes were still on her. 'Go?' she asked. 'Go where?'

Chapter 17

Marie stepped carefully along Clumber Street in her too-large dress and her too-large blue sandals and her skimpy cardigan, inhaling the fresh air as deeply as she dared, trying to avoid an agonizing grating of her ribs. Through an open door she could hear a radio, and laughter. Probably *It's That Man Again*, or some other skit, she guessed. She stopped for a moment beside the skeleton that had once been their home. The front wall was almost gone, and the slates were off, but the staircase was intact. Paneless windows stared down at her like sightless eyes. She had a sudden vision of her mother, much younger, sitting on the sills to clean the outsides of those sash-windows, and the memory was so vivid she said: 'Mam.' The pavement sparkled with glass splinters that had had the benefit of her own smeary attempts at cleaning only a week or so ago. It hardly mattered now. All those days of hard work, washing and ironing curtains and running around trying to do everything to her mother's liking – it had all been labour in vain. If only she'd known.

The piano was smashed, its strings everywhere. It would take a bit of tuning now, she thought, and for some reason that struck her as funny. She chuckled, and quickly stopped, for the pain in her ribs. No, it wasn't likely they'd ever get another tune out of that, and they couldn't even use it for firewood, since the chimney was gone and the fireplace was hidden by rubble. That thought tickled her as well, almost to the point of hysteria, and stifling her laughter made her eyes water. Perhaps George could chop it up for his mother. She could tell him to imagine it was Nancy, and he'd have it reduced to matchwood in five minutes flat. Sheet music was spilling out of the broken piano stool, the top copy a sketch of a man's lovesick face and the caption above: 'It Had to Be You'. Her heart gave a painful little throb. Charles, she thought, why aren't you here?

She was about to walk on when Jenny's head appeared above the rubble, her mouth moving, saying words Marie couldn't make out.

'You'll have to shout, Jenny. Shout. I can't hear you.'

'I said why were you laughing? My mammy laughed as well, when she saw your house was bombed. Why is it funny?'

'It's not funny. What are you doing there?'

'I'm playing. It's my house now. I found Smut. He's dead.'

'Oh, my poor little cat! Where is he?'

Jenny disappeared for a moment and emerged holding Smut's body.

'Give him to me, Jenny, and don't touch any more dead animals. And don't play in that house. It's dangerous.'

Jenny clambered over the rubble and held Smut's lifeless little body out to her. He smelled.

The day was getting hot. Marie carefully took off her yellow cardigan with its too-short sleeves and wrapped Smut in it.

'I like playing here,' Jenny bawled. 'I used to like playing here before, when Alfie lived here.'

'Well, don't play here again. Why aren't you at school?'

'It's Saturday.'

'Oh... Go home then, to your mam.'

Marie got to the end of the street and walked up Princes Avenue with Smut in her arms. Everything was gone, even their kitten, so full of life a few short days ago. Nothing would ever be the same. The Larsens were finished as a family, their quiet, comfortable, unassuming little lives destroyed. There could be no going home ever again, and with that thought the true horror of homelessness was borne in upon Marie. If only Chas were here beside her she might be able to face it; things might not seem so bad, but he was beyond her reach, and she his, kept apart by this awful war.

'We'll bury him here,' Mrs Elsworth said, not forgetting to raise her voice.

Marie looked round the enclosed garden at the rear of the Elsworths' house. 'Thank you, I'd like that. I love it here. It's so lovely, and so peaceful.'

Mrs Elsworth smiled, quietly triumphant. 'Yes, as you can see, I couldn't forgo my flowers altogether, and I scattered a few California poppies and marigolds between the vegetables to cheer them up too. It doesn't seem to be doing them much harm. We'll have enough to feed you and your mother as well as us, and masses to spare, with a bit of luck. Autumn will be busy this year; we'll have a terrific glut to deal with unless the Luftwaffe drops a bomb on it all. Speaking of bombs, Leonard and Danny went round to Clumber Street as soon as we knew, with the last bit of petrol we had in the car to see if they could salvage anything, but there was nothing.'

'They shouldn't even have tried. They might have got hurt. It was Hannah's little girl that found Smut. I warned her off, but I doubt if she'll take any notice. She says it's her house now.'

Mrs Elsworth's brow creased in a frown, and her lips pursed. 'That child. She's like a feral kitten herself, by the sound of it. A good thing Hannah's a charwoman. You wouldn't want her as a nursemaid, would you? Your poor little cat. Shall we go and find a spot to bury it?'

'Him. He's a boy,' Marie said, and, looking down at his lifeless little body, she dissolved into tears, utterly distraught. 'Isn't it stu-stu-stupid to be so u-u-upset about a cat,' she gasped, when she could speak, 'after everything that's happened?'

'Not stupid,' Mrs Elsworth said, carefully taking the bundle from her. 'Just the last straw, after all the other disasters. The straw that finally breaks the camel's back. Come on, let's choose a nice bit of the garden for him.'

More composed after tea and half an hour of Mrs Elsworth's practical kindness, Marie sat down in one of the garden chairs, facing Smut's last resting place, a little mound drenched in sunlight. The sun felt warm on her face and arms, and every now and then a gentle breeze lifted her hair. Fat bees flew idly and silently to and fro around a clump of tall purple flowers that had also escaped the victory digging. She sat watching them until her eyelids began to feel heavy. Peace, perfect peace. Nobody would know such a thing as war existed here, in this garden. That sun was so warm her eyes began to close. What charmed lives the Elsworths seemed to live, she thought. Oh, to be married to Charles, and safe, and at peace with herself and the world.

The sun went in. She began to feel cold, and then she felt a shadow over her, and thought she heard a voice, very indistinct, and then another, a voice she recognized, though she could barely make out the words. Marie opened her eyes, and saw Mrs Elsworth, with Nancy. With a shock she sat bolt upright, straining to hear what Nancy was saying, watching her lips. She barely caught a word.

'We've been bombed out, Nance. Two of my ribs are broken, I'm as deaf as a post, and my mam's in hospital again.'

'Jesus, Marie, you look terrible,' Nancy shouted. 'I've seen your house; it's a miracle you're still alive. And what have you got on? You look like the Ragman's Revenge.'

Nancy dropped into a chair beside her, still talking. Mrs Elsworth excused herself and went into the house, leaving them to talk freely. Nancy would raise her voice for a while, and then it would drop again, forcing Marie to ask: 'Pardon? What? Eh? What did you say?' until embarrassed by having to keep on asking for things to be repeated, Marie gave up in despair and let Nancy talk on, without interruption. There had been no apology in any of the talk Marie *had* managed to hear and, judging from her expressions and gestures, the idea that an apology was due had never even entered Nancy's mind. She seemed to be completely oblivious to anyone's claims but her own, and watching her performance had the same effect on Marie as the sight of the broken piano. The sheer incongruity of it made her want to laugh.

'What do you think, then?' Nancy eventually asked, just loud enough to be heard.

'What about?'

'Monty and George, of course!'

'I don't think anything,' Marie said. 'I've hardly heard a word you've said.'

Nancy couldn't conceal her exasperation. 'Well, why didn't you tell me?'

'I did.'

223

'Look, I don't want to have to ring a bell and shout like the bloody town crier,' Nancy shouted. 'Come round to my mam's tomorrow. Come for your tea. We'll talk about it then.'

'I can't promise. Mr Elsworth's taking me to Beverley to see my mother, and then to see Alfie at Dunswell. I'll come if we get back in time. Does George know you're back in Hull?'

'How do I know? I haven't been hiding. He might have seen me. Or somebody else might have seen me and told him.'

'Do you want me to tell him, or not?'

'Please yourself,' Nancy shrugged. 'He'll know soon enough, anyway.'

After tea Danny was dispatched to the Maltbys to tell them that Marie wouldn't be back until late the following day. Marie's ears ached, her head ached and her ribs and shoulder hurt. Mrs Elsworth ran her an illegally full hot bath, and after that packed her off to bed in a pair of Charles's pyjamas, with a beaker of thick Horlicks and four aspirins. At the end of her emotional tether, too exhausted to resist even had she wanted to, Marie complied with all Mrs Elsworth's directions, and finally sank into Charles's comfortable bed and enjoyed the best few hours' sleep that she'd had since the bombing.

'She keeps telling us she's dying, the Germans have finished her, but she is better than she was. We have got concerns about her heart, though,' the houseman told Marie when she went to see her mother in the hospital. 'The shock has certainly had a bad effect on it. Not surprising, after two hair's-breadth escapes like she's had. She must have as many lives as a cat.'

Marie looked at her mother, lying pale, still and silent, her eyes closed. 'She's taken Smut's nine, all at once,' she said.

The houseman looked puzzled.

'Our little cat. He died in the raid that put my mother in here. How serious is it, the heart problem?'

'It's hard to say. It might get better, or she might go on for years with a weak heart, or...' he grimaced.

She heaved a sigh. 'Hope for the best and prepare for the worst, then. I thought I might have seen Dr Steele. I've got some forms I wanted to ask him about.'

'Dr Steele had a stroke.'

Marie was stunned. 'Where is he?'

'He's in the hospital mortuary. Worked himself to a standstill, I think.'

'Oh,' she said, more acutely sorry for the loss of the crusty old medic than she could have imagined. 'I'm very, very sorry.'

'So are we all. I think it got to him in the end. All the carnage, I mean.'

Dr Steele's dictum about other men's pains being easy to bear sprang into her mind. Apparently they hadn't been as easy as all that, even for him. And he'd worked himself to death for them all, never shirked, while she was idling about at the Elsworths', being waited on hand and foot. As soon as her ribs healed, as soon as she could hear properly again, as soon as she could get her mother settled, she would have to get back into

225

nursing. She wouldn't be a spectator any longer than she had to be. She had to make some contribution to the desperate struggle going on around her.

By the time she and Mr Elsworth had left her relations at Dunswell, Marie had reached the limits of her endurance. When they arrived back at Park Avenue she was fit for nothing but to creep upstairs to lie down and weep, crushed under the weight of it all, and completely forgetful of Nancy's invitation to tea.

She faced the ordeal of telling George of her decision to stay at Park Avenue later that evening. However she phrased it, Marie knew that he would take offence. She would just get it over with.

'You're not a burden at all. You're welcome to stay here as long as you like,' Aunt Edie said, after Marie's explanations.

George's eyes narrowed. 'Well, we've done everything we could to make you feel at home, but as you say, they've certainly got a lot more space, and she does have help with the work. There's no denying that, is there?'

George was offended, no doubt about it. Unwilling to set him off on another one of his diatribes, Marie decided against any mention of Nancy, and after profuse thanks for everything he'd done for her she collected her pyjamas, gathered up her government forms, and moved towards the door.

'You went to see your mam today, didn't you?' he asked, following her into the narrow passage.

226

'How's she getting on?'

'Not very well. She's got a weak heart, as well as everything else.'

'I'd go up and see her myself, but I wouldn't fancy going on the motorbike, and I don't know how the buses run to Beverley. Give her my love next time you see her,' his mother called from the front room.

'I will,' Marie promised, glad to get away.

Now that Nancy was back, staying with the Maltbys would have been absolutely impossible. But staying with the Elsworths was going to bring her into unwelcome contact with Hannah, who was probably crowing over her misfortunes this very minute. Marie wondered how she would manage to disguise the fact. Knowing Hannah, she probably wouldn't even try.

Chapter 18

'I've brought a couple of my frocks to lend you,' Nancy said the following morning, loud enough for all Newland to hear. 'Are you in on your own?'

Marie nodded. 'Mr Elsworth's out at his car repair shop. Mrs Elsworth's gone to the WVS. Danny's at school.'

'Good,' Nancy said, stepping inside. 'We've got the place to ourselves, then. Did you see George yesterday?' Marie nodded.

'Did you tell him I'm back?'

'No.'

'I wish you had. My mother says he still loves me. She said he said he was going to write, but if he did his letter must have arrived after I moved out of the flat, and that foul so-called friend of Monty's won't bother to send it on. And I don't think I even left my address for him, I was so upset. That's a thought. I'll write to Monty at the flat. He'll get the letter when he gets back.'

'Come through to the kitchen. There's still tea in the teapot. It'll be a bit stewed, but I'll water it down. I don't want to take any of the rations if I can help it. I haven't got another ration card yet – I just haven't had the time to go and get one.'

'Oh, well, as long as it's warm and wet...'

Nancy slumped on one of the kitchen chairs, and Marie put the tea in front of her. She'd hardly sat down before Nancy began, and it was altogether too evident that Monty was the man foremost in Nancy's thoughts.

'You'd better go back to the beginning,' Marie said. 'I didn't catch much of what you said before.'

'The beginning is, Monty's disappeared! I can't understand it. He was so nice to me – that first week we had together at his flat was wonderful. We've got everything in common. We both love dancing, and the pictures, and he took me up to Pinewood Studios, he was so sure he could get me a job there. But just going for walks in the park and holding hands was enough for me. We even like the same food, the same sort of people – we had the same tastes in everything. And he was such a laugh. He said: "Now I know why I've

228

never married; I was waiting for you. You're the one. You're the girl I want to spend the rest of my life with."'

'Pretty much the same things George must have said to you, when he gave you his ring,' Marie said drily.

'Oh, Marie! Monty isn't a bit like George! I can't even begin to explain it. I felt as if Monty really understood me, as if he was interested in me, and he was fun! And his kisses were...' Her eyes lit up, she gave a little smile, drew her shoulders in, and shivered. 'He was exciting! And to be honest, he didn't have a mother hanging onto him for grim death. And George is so dull and dour and dreary, you've no idea. All he thinks about is work, work, work, and save, save, save, and scrimp, scrimp, scrimp. You just wonder when you'll be allowed to start living. It's always jam tomorrow, and never jam today, with George.'

'You never said any of this before. You were happy enough to get engaged.'

'I was happy enough before I met Monty, and saw another side to life.'

'If it was all so jammy with Monty, why did he disappear?'

'I don't know! I can't understand it, except it started after his friend Miles was so horrible to me in those studios. Looked at me like a piece of dirt, and kept asking me when I was going back "oop to 'Ull", taking the mickey because of the way I talk and making me look stupid in front of everybody. I think he was just jealous of me and Monty. Then he started calling at the flat, even sleeping there, and Monty didn't want to make him leave. He said he depended on him for work and things.'

'What things?'

'I don't know! Just "things". Then he turned really nasty, and said if I didn't like his friends, I should eff-something off, out of his flat. That's what he said, Marie, and he actually used that horrible word – to me! I said I wasn't going anywhere, and when I woke up the following morning, he was gone. I asked his friend where he might be, and he said how should he know, he wasn't his keeper, probably on tour somewhere. So I told him that under the circumstances he should leave the flat. It wasn't decent for us to be there together, and he said not likely, the flat belonged to him! I couldn't believe it. Now I haven't a clue where Monty is. I waited a full week for him to come back, but by then I couldn't stand it any longer with this other chap there every evening. He wrote plays, or he pretended to, and he was there every single night. It was awful, Marie. I think something must have happened to Monty. I can't believe he could be so rotten as to walk out on me, just because of a few cross words.'

After he'd told you to eff-something off? And after you'd walked out on George, without a single word, let alone a cross one, Marie thought, now realizing the futility of trying to impress the enormity of her betrayal on Nancy, and too weary to attempt it. 'Haven't you any idea how to go about finding him? she asked. 'Has he got an agent?'

230

'I don't know. And they probably wouldn't tell me where he is anyway, even if I did. You know what these people are like. Well, I'll just wait a bit, and see.' Nancy held her beaker of tea against her cheek, and gazed into the garden for a long time. 'But if he's going to be like that,' she said finally, 'I'm better off with George.'

No doubt, but is George better off with you? Marie thought, and it must have shown on her face.

Nancy looked askance at her. 'You were living with them after you were bombed out, my mam said. So how's he taken it?'

'We had a funeral for you, Nancy; didn't your mother tell you? We thought you were dead! He was absolutely devastated.'

Nancy nodded, a spark of hope igniting in her eyes, but no sign of remorse.

'Then he found out you'd withdrawn all his savings, and after that, your mother told us she'd had your letter.'

'Yes, but how did he take it?' Nancy demanded. 'Mam said he'd told her he was desperate to get me back, but she wasn't sure whether to believe him.'

'He hasn't taken it very well, to be honest. He was on about taking you to court to get his money back.'

Nancy went pale, and paused for a moment. 'Oh, well, I'll talk him round.'

'I wouldn't bank on it, if I were you. After all, you walked out on him without a word, and stole his savings into the bargain.'

'I didn't steal them.'

'They're gone.'

'I didn't steal George's share of the money; I only borrowed it. Half of it was mine, anyway. I'd have thought you'd have been a bit more sympathetic.'

'Nancy, you'd been engaged to George for months. He bought you a beautiful engagement ring. He thought the sun shone out of your backside, but you left him in the lurch for a man you'd known about a week and you took his savings, whichever way you look at it. But I don't know why I'm having this conversation. What you do with Monty is nothing to do with me. Maybe we ought to christen him Minty, now he's got all your money.'

Nancy gave her an incredulous look. 'Very funny. And you're having this conversation because you're supposed to be a friend!'

'I *am* a friend, but that doesn't turn black into white.'

'Well, if I've been a bit naughty, I'm not the first, and I won't be the last.'

Marie's mouth fell open. 'I can't believe it's Nancy Harding talking like this. When we had that raid, and you were missing and he thought you'd been killed, he was running round everywhere, trying to find you. He went round all the hospitals, and then down to the mortuary they've set up in Albert Avenue Baths, and looked at a lot of corpses their own mothers couldn't have recognized. Just let that sink in for a bit, Nancy. And then we had a funeral, a mass funeral, believing you were one of those people who'd had to be gathered together in bits. It was harrowing. And then he found out you'd gone off with that actor. It completely knocked the bottom out of his world, Nance. It knocked me sideways as well, if you want to know. That's more than "a bit naughty".'

'Well, he'll have his world back soon. I've decided. I'm going back to him.'

'Good luck with that, then,' said Marie.

'You're not exactly oozing sympathy, are you?' Nancy snapped. 'But you watch. He'll be all right. I'll talk him round; I could always wind him round my little finger. A few tears, and that won't be hard; I've hardly stopped weeping since Monty left! George won't be able to withstand much of that. He'll give in, and then I'll make him happy, I swear I will. No more bloody lying, cheating actors for me.'

Nancy certainly had full confidence in her power over George, Marie thought, as she closed the door on her. She had certainly seen a side to Nancy that she would never have believed existed. But there was something to be said for listening to other people's troubles, even if you weren't exactly oozing sympathy. It took your mind off your own, for a little while.

'A visitor for you, Marie,' Danny said, ushering Margaret's husband into the drawing room later that evening.

'Another one!' Marie exclaimed, rising from her armchair to greet him. 'Goodness, Terry, I never expected to see you! How did you know I was here? Mr and Mrs Elsworth, this is Terry. He married the best friend I ever had. You remember

233

me telling you about Margaret?'

Terry was clean-shaven and very smartly dressed, but the effect was spoiled by the three carrier bags he was holding.

'I've just seen a ghost,' Terry said. 'I could have sworn I passed Nancy Harding when I was coming along Spring Bank on the motorbike. I heard she'd been killed when the hospital copped it.'

He was turned slightly away from her, and Marie didn't quite catch what he said. 'Pardon?' she said.

Terry was distracted from repeating himself by Mr Elsworth's enthusiastic welcome. 'Come in and sit down,' he said, drawing him to a chair beside the small fire, and shaking his hand enthusiastically as soon as he put the bags down. 'I remember you. We've worked alongside each other once or twice, although I never knew your name. This is a surprise. Come in. Will you have a cup of tea? Bring another cup and saucer, Danny. How are things at Central Fire Station?'

Terry's face fell, and he shook his head. 'Not good. There aren't so many of us as there were, after the blitzing we got last month. We've lost some good lads. Terrible for them, and terrible for their families, and nearly as bad for us. Bloody Nazis. And the worst of it is a lot of it could have been avoided. Like the lads at North Bridge, for instance. If there'd been a firewatcher with a key to the warehouse, they wouldn't have had to use the ladder, and they'd still be alive. But seeing as the Luftwaffe have given us a whole week's holiday, we're fit for action again, just about.'

'Yes, a whole week. They're busy with the Rus-

234

sians now, if you can believe what you read in the paper.'

The conversation became hard for Marie to follow as everybody threw themselves into it, and began talking nineteen to the dozen. She wasn't called on to say much, and sat watching them all, thankful they were managing without any effort from her. It was evident from the way they looked at him that the whole family liked Terry, and he certainly cut an impressive figure. Danny was hanging onto his every word, eyes wide and round with hero worship. Even Mrs Elsworth seemed susceptible, giving him a broad and approving smile as she handed him his tea.

Unable to hear most of what was being said, Marie's attention began to drift. It was coming up to midsummer, the nights were long and light, and through the open curtains she could just see over to the spot where Smut lay in the twilit garden. She started, imagining that she felt his furry paw against her ankle, and looked down to see that Mrs Elsworth's knitting had fallen off the side table full of family photographs, including one of Mr Elsworth and all the men in his car repair shop.

Mr Elsworth said something, and Terry began to laugh. His laugh was so infectious that the whole family started laughing. Laughing too, although she hadn't heard the joke, Marie looked at him in wonder. How long was it since Margaret had died? Six months. At the time, she'd thought he'd never laugh again and now here he was, enjoying a joke. When the laughter abated, and the flood of talk dwindled to a trickle Terry

235

turned to her, his face serious.

'I heard you'd been bombed out,' he said, 'and your mother's in hospital again.'

'That's right,' she nodded.

'Lost everything?'

'Everything but a pair of pyjamas and a nightie.'

Looking rather awkward, and with a faint blush rising to his cheeks he proffered his carrier bags. 'I don't want to offend – just say if you don't want them – but these might be some use to you. Sixty-six clothing coupons for a year aren't much for somebody who's been bombed out, not when you need fourteen for a mac, and seven for a decent frock. These aren't doing any good hanging in the wardrobe, and you were about the same size, you and Margaret.'

Inside one of the bags Marie found Margaret's best coat. In the other two she found blouses, skirts, a pair of slacks, three frocks and a couple of good cardigans together with underwear and two pairs of nylons, never worn.

She looked up at him and tears sprang to her eyes. 'It's a good job sometimes we don't know what's in front of us, isn't it? Who'd have thought when you got married that it would come to this?'

Chapter 19

'You're looking very smart. Haven't I seen them somewhere before?' Nancy said, when Marie joined her at the Elsworths' gate wearing a cotton dress and a cardigan.

'Terry came the other day and gave me a lot of Margaret's stuff.'

'How did he know where to find you?'

'I don't know. Word gets round, I suppose, and the firemen are everywhere, talking to everybody.'

'How's he getting on?'

'Quite well, I think. He was laughing and joking with Mr Elsworth, anyway.'

'Is he courting again?'

'I don't know, I didn't ask.'

'Hmm.' Nancy lapsed into a thoughtful silence for a while, then asked, 'Are you feeling any better?'

'A bit. My ribs aren't hurting quite so much and I'm not having so many headaches. My ears are a bit better as well,' Marie said.

They walked slowly to the end of Park Avenue, and crossed the road into Pearson Park. There was nobody about.

'Have you heard from Minty?' Marie jibed.

'Very funny. No, I haven't. Have you seen anything of George?'

'I saw him on Tuesday night, when I went

237

round to tell them how my mam was doing. Aunt Edie says Mam's to stay with them when she gets out of hospital, until we can find somewhere to rent.'

'The council will put you in a caravan, I expect. You can't get a house for love nor money, from what I've been told. What about George? Did you tell him I'm back?'

'Yes.'

'And?'

'He didn't say much. In fact, he didn't say anything. But he turned as white as a sheet.'

'Right.' Nancy took a minute or two to digest this information, then suggested: 'Let's walk through the park to Beverley Road, and then bus it down to Prospect Street, and see what they're dishing up at the so-called British Restaurant they've set up for the workers there. I'll treat you to a cup of tea and a sandwich. It'll save on the rations, anyway.'

Marie hesitated, very dubious about going into town, where they risked bumping into George. She certainly didn't want him to see her with Nancy. If it hadn't been for George she might have died, and he'd been good to her after her discharge from hospital. He'd see her friendliness towards Nancy as a poor return for his trouble, if not as outright treachery. But then, she thought, unless she was going to cut her best friend out of her life completely, he was bound to see them together some time. And she had her forms to take in to the Relief Office.

The centre of Hull was a burned-out shambles,

with shops and offices almost razed to the ground. The jagged and skewed remnants of once beautiful buildings showed in stark relief against the blue sky. Prospect Street was little more than a heap of rubble. The roofs were off many buildings, including the beautiful old church.

'It's enough to break your heart, isn't it?' Marie said. Everywhere she looked, the ruin of some once-loved building met her eye. The loss of her home was the worst thing, but with the destruction of her city she felt as if the whole of her past life had been wiped out. They stopped in front of what was left of the infirmary. Its impressive stone façade and massive Corinthian columns were still there, but not much else. 'What a sight! Just look at it! Open to the skies, and all the windows blown out.'

'I was stunned when I got back from London and saw it all. My God, I'm glad I wasn't there when that happened. That night at the end of March was terrifying enough.'

'It makes you want to weep. We had a good life there, before the war. Remember the tennis and fencing clubs? I might have got good at fencing, if they hadn't requisitioned our recreation hall for an air-raid shelter.'

'Ah well, the war soon put a stop to a lot of things. Remember drinking tea at the Kardomah Café on our afternoons off? There'll be no more of that, either.'

'We were in clover, if we had but known it. Now no home, and no hospital either. It's demoted to a first-aid station.' Marie said. 'What will you do,

Nance? Will you try to get your job back?'

Nancy pulled a face. 'I might. I can't say I'm looking forward to the interview with Matron, though; I don't think she'll be very impressed with me, upping and leaving without notice like I did. I keep trying to think of a good enough excuse, but it's not easy.'

'No, you'd need some imagination to dream anything up that could gloss over that. I doubt if "I lost my head over an out-and-out conman, Matron," would cut much ice after you'd left a ward full of patients with no one to nurse them – but it might work, especially since they're hard up for staff. Nothing ventured, nothing gained.'

'You're a right Job's comforter, you are. Well, I'd better find something, I suppose, before the government finds something for me. I might go in for typing. I'm always seeing advertisements for typists.'

'Except they usually want people who can type, and you can't. You'd better go and see Matron, make a clean breast of it, and get back into nursing and stick at it, this time. I'd love to go back myself, but it depends how my mother gets on.'

'But where would I end up working, now there's practically no infirmary? And why should you bother? You're marrying Chas on his next leave, aren't you?' Nancy asked, holding open the door of the restaurant for Marie to enter.

'So this is a British Restaurant,' Marie said, looking round the room echoing with the clatter of crockery and cutlery, the scraping of chairs and the chatter of people, and *Forces Favourites* playing in the background. 'Fancy title for a

240

glorified canteen, if you ask me.'

Nancy said, 'You should have seen the place Monty took me to in London. That was worth calling a restaurant.' Tears suddenly filled her eyes, and she pulled out a handkerchief to dab her reddening nose. 'I really loved him, Marie. I believed every word he told me, but I know now he was just stringing me along. I've looked for a letter every day since he walked out, both at the flat and since I came back home. He knows where my mother lives. There was nothing to stop him writing. I've hoped and prayed he'd get in touch, but now I know I'll never see him again. I've finally stopped kidding myself. And he's got all our savings – mine and George's – he's got my mother's rent, he's even got my engagement ring.'

'Oh, Nancy! You never gave him that as well?'

'I didn't give him it. He took it, and that was when he started being nasty to me – as soon as he'd got everything I had. What a mess.'

'Well, there's the rent he owes your mother to stop him writing to her address,' Marie said, very quietly. She could have added that Monty had been sweet-talking her mother as well, but Mrs Harding had probably already told her. If Nancy at last realized what a fool she'd been, there was no point rubbing it in.

They sat down to a cup of tea and a boiled egg sandwich, and had just begun a conversation with some ancillary workers from the infirmary when George walked through the door. He saw Nancy, and caught Marie's eye, and the look of reproach on his face made her wish she were a million miles away. Then he stopped in his tracks, and she watched him physically pull himself together and turn and walk out of the door. Nancy jumped up to follow him.

'Don't!' Marie grabbed her wrist, trying to hold her back.

'Why not?'

'Let him come to you, and he will come, Nancy. See him on your home ground, where it can't get too–'

But Nancy snatched her arm free, and went after George.

'Honestly, Nance...' Marie called after her, but a few people were already looking at them, and Nancy was too far away for any more warnings about how hurt George was, and how justifiably bitter.

Marie sat down again and drank her tea, glossing over the little scene as best she could for the benefit of the curious ancillary workers, who fortunately soon left to go back to work. She waited for half an hour after that, but Nancy didn't reappear, so in the end she gave her up and went to find the Relief Office, where she sat fretting about both Nancy and George. 'Don't get involved in other people's business,' Chas had told her, and it was good advice, but he hadn't told her how you can help it when the people themselves involve you, and one of them happens to be your best friend, and the other is someone you're indebted to for your very life. She had ample time to worry about everything else during that long and dreary wait, from her mother and the destruction of her home to what might be

242

happening to Chas, to guilt at being a burden and expense to the Elsworths. She sat there for hours beside a throng of other bombed-out, displaced people, all with similar stories and similar anxieties, all waiting to tell their tales of woe to the Relief Officer, and fill in the proper government forms, which demanded information that as often as not had gone up in smoke, in the ruins of their homes.

Chapter 20

'I really don't know what to do about Hannah,' Marie overheard Mrs Elsworth tell her husband as she descended the stairs the following morning. 'She's such a good worker it will be a pity to lose her but...'

The sitting-room door clicked shut, and the rest of the conversation was inaudible. Their discussion was evidently intended to be private, so Marie went through to the kitchen to get a drink of water, then out into the garden to sit in the sun. Considering what other people in the city were facing, Mrs Elsworth's servant problem got little sympathy from Marie. The house was massive, and cleaning it to Mrs Elsworth's exacting standards would be a full-time job for anyone, but doing your own housework wasn't the end of the world, even for women who spent hours of their time working with the WVS. Mrs Elsworth would just have to lower her standards and cut a few corners, like most people had to do these days, and as far as Marie was concerned, the less she saw of Hannah, the better she'd be pleased.

It wasn't many minutes before the Elsworths came out to join her in the garden.

Mr Elsworth took the hoe, and began slicing the tops of the few weeds between the vegetable rows.

Mrs Elsworth sat down beside Marie.

'I was just coming downstairs when you were talking about Hannah leaving. Don't worry. I'm getting better, and if she can't do it, I'll help,' Marie said. 'I'll help anyway. I'd rather pull my weight than sit around doing nothing.'

'Your hearing must be all right, if you heard that! Well, there's nothing really decided yet,' Mrs Elsworth hedged. 'And I'm not at all worried about the work. I've no doubt there are others who would be glad of a couple of hours every day if it came to that, and if not I'd do it myself.'

'What are you worried about, then?'

'Nothing,' Mrs Elsworth said, with a face that robbed her words of all conviction. 'I'm not worried about anything. But whatever happens, you won't be doing housework. You won't be fit for anything but the lightest jobs for quite some time.'

'I'm getting better every day.'

'Good. We want you to continue getting better; so that's all you've got to concentrate on for the moment. If you're fit enough to look after your mother when she gets out of hospital, that'll be enough. We'll move you into one of the larger bedrooms, so you can be together.'

'You mean you're saying she can stay here, Mrs Elsworth?'

'Of course she can stay here. We'll be in-laws soon. She's practically family. She'll want to be with her own daughter during her convalescence, and we're not short of space, are we?'

'Thank you. That's a weight off my mind. Some of the people who were in the Relief Office yesterday were saying you just can't get a house to rent. Half the houses in the city have been damaged. There's nothing. Not that I could afford the rent if there were.'

'Don't worry, Charles will help you with that. You should be able to get something, once you're married.'

On Sunday, the family were going to spend the day with Mr Elsworth's younger brother and his large and boisterous family in Hedon. Marie cried off, saying she didn't yet feel fit enough for such high-spirited company. She would stay behind, and write some letters, principally to Charles and Pam. After the family had gone, she went into the garden shed and helped herself to their hoe. She certainly did not want to go down to the Maltbys' and have to confront George to get her own. It would be two weeks tomorrow since that awful night they'd been bombed out, and she was beginning to feel a bit better – but better or not, she'd have to get up to that allotment or all the veg her dad had taken the trouble to plant would be choked with weeds, or dead for lack of water, and since the loss of their home it was all that she and her mother had left. She walked up Newland Avenue with the hoe resting on her shoulder, thankfully in the opposite direction to both Clumber Street and George, and Duesbury Street and Nancy.

She arrived to find George already there – busy with her hoe. She hesitated, but there was no hiding place in that flat, treeless landscape, with only the odd greenhouse or garden shed rising above the level of the strips of earth and the rutted pathways between them. He'd already seen her and stood facing her, awaiting her approach. As soon as she was near enough to hear, his words came in torrents.

'I haven't been able to sit still since I saw Nancy the other day. I was awake at four o'clock this morning, no chance of getting back to sleep again. I'm like a cat on hot bricks, jumping up and down all the time. My mother keeps asking me what on earth's the matter, and I daren't tell her. She'd throw a fit. In the end I thought I'd better get out of the way, so I came up here to try and work it off. The other allotment holders told me which was your patch.'

Marie looked along her father's strip: potatoes earthed up, and all the weeding done on the lazy beds that contained broad beans, runner beans, and peas. The pear tree was full of tiny fruit, and the raspberry canes promised a good harvest, she noticed.

'Goodness, George, you've done it all,' was all she managed to say.

'Do you know, Marie, she chased me all the way to the Guildhall, and she caught me just before I went in, and I've never seen so many tears. They

246

were rolling down her face; she was crying her eyes out, just about breaking her heart. People were looking at us so I couldn't just walk off and leave her. Besides, she might have followed me inside, and I didn't want her making a spectacle of us both in there, having everybody in the place talking about my private business.'

'I asked her not to follow you.'

'In a way, I'm glad she did. She told me she'd made a terrible mistake. She realized it as soon as she got to London, that it had just been a mad infatuation, because of him being an actor, and the glamour and all that. She soon realized she didn't love him at all. But she didn't know her way around London and she was nervous of the Underground and that, and she didn't know how the trains ran, or anything. And she'd left work without notice, so she was scared to come back.'

'It must have been terrible for her,' Marie said. She gazed into the middle distance, visualizing that star performance and thinking that the people at Pinewood Studios ought to be kicking themselves for the first-rate actress they'd lost in Nancy.

'Maybe I've been too hasty,' he said, looking at her for confirmation. 'Everybody deserves a second chance, I think. Do you?'

Looking at his tormented face Marie remembered Nancy's boast that he wouldn't be able to withstand her tears. How right she'd been, and how calculating. Nancy would hate her for it if she ever found out, but weighing her cold-blooded manoeuvring against his genuine feeling, Marie decided she couldn't really give a ringing endorsement to the idea of second chances in this instance, even disregarding her indebtedness to George. 'Well,' she said, 'if they really are truly sorry, and they're fully prepared to make amends, maybe. But you'd have to think about it very, very carefully, George.'

'That bloody actor's got all our money, you know. All our savings. She says she'd try to get it back from him, but she doesn't know where he is.'

'Surely there are ways of finding people,' Marie said. 'You sometimes hear of solicitors setting private detectives on, in divorce cases and suchlike. He'll have to work and make a living, I suppose, unless he's giving himself a holiday on your money. Even so, he'll have to go back to work sometime. They might be able to find him through theatrical agencies or actors' guilds, things like that.'

George nodded. 'I'll ask the lads in the Legal Department. I'll ask them what it costs. If we can find him, she can make amends by prosecuting *Monty*, and getting all our savings back. I can't stomach the thought that the blighter's got away with it. He's a thief. He's stolen everything I had, and not only the money.'

'There's Nancy's mother's rent, as well,' Marie said. 'She might be willing to share the cost of finding him, if it'll get her rent for her.'

'I doubt it. I don't think she'll want to throw good money after bad. And deep down, I don't really think we've got a cat in hell's chance of finding him.'

'To be honest, George, neither do I,' Marie said,

'but if it doesn't cost too much, it might be worth a try.'

George's face fell. 'And you know, Marie, even if we do get back together, I don't know whether I'll ever be able to trust her again. Nothing will ever be the same. Ever.'

Marie could think of nothing to say to that, except: 'I'll go and fill the watering cans.'

'No, I'll do that. You're not fit to carry them, with two cracked ribs. You go back, and have a rest till you're properly fit. I shouldn't really be pestering you with my troubles, after what you've been through. You've got enough of your own, I reckon. Oh, before I forget, this came for you yesterday.' He pulled a letter out of his pocket.

She took it. 'Thanks, George. Pull some of that rhubarb and take it for your mam, will you? There's loads of the stuff.'

Weeding and watering done, Marie tucked her letter in her pocket and carried the hoe back, feeling quite upset about George. At Park Avenue she had the house to herself, so she put the wireless on, then sat down and opened her letter. Charles was full of news about life in the army, which he seemed to be enjoying. He would keep trying to get leave, and was forever asking for radio requests, so she should keep listening to the wireless. He was glad she was going to live with his parents, and on his next leave they'd get married and get somewhere to rent, so at least her mother would have somewhere comfortable to be discharged to. As far as George went, he wrote:

He's as vindictive as he is precisely because Nancy

never gave him a thought. She seems to have acted as if he didn't exist. She did what she wanted to do, and his feelings didn't come into it. He was irrelevant. Nobody can stomach that, can they? However much they've idolized somebody. Unless they've got absolutely no self-respect. Or they have some other motive, like wanting to get their fingers on an heiress's fortune, and I don't think Nancy falls into that category. Leave them to it. Don't get involved. You'll get no thanks for it, from either party.

She poured her heart out in a letter back to him, confiding George's present dilemma and telling him how wise was his advice to keep out of other people's business – but how impossible it was to carry out at times.

Apart from occasional contact with Hannah, life at the Elsworths' was very comfortable, but with every passing day, Marie missed her own home more. Welcome though Mr and Mrs Elsworth made her, and comfortable though life in Park Avenue was, it lacked the deeper comfort of old, familiar possessions and old routines, and the time-honoured, taken-for-granted ways of doing things unique to the Larsen family. The closest she could get to that was to go again to the Maltbys', to familiar surroundings and links with her childhood, reminders of those happier times. Everything she knew seemed to be disappearing, making her want to cling on to old haunts and familiar habits as if to life itself. For now, at least, Aunt Edie and her house were still the same, and after seeing George at the allotment, she had dropped by a couple of times to give them the latest about her mother's progress. Mr Elsworth had picked Aunt Edie up to take her with them on their latest visit to the hospital, and Marie's mother accepted Aunt Edie's offer of a home after her discharge.

After dropping Aunt Edie off, Mr Elsworth left Marie at Park Avenue and went on to his car repair shop. She found Mrs Elsworth was standing at the kitchen table, putting a few flowers in a vase. 'The doctor says my mother should be ready for discharge in a week or two,' she announced.

'Does he, dear? That's good,' Mrs Elsworth said, with an abstracted air. Marie's eyes followed her gaze towards Hannah, who was kneeling on the draining board cleaning the kitchen windows, and stretching to get into the corners with the wash leather. Marie was suddenly struck by the broadening of her once-trim waistline. How unobservant she must have been not to have noticed it before.

'Thanks very much for your offer to have her here,' Marie went on, trying to break her mother's rejection of their invitation as tactfully as she could. 'I told her, but she said she wants to go and stay with Aunt Edie. They've been friends for years, you see. Their house is like a second home to her.'

'Did she, dear?'

The response was not exactly appropriate, but Marie was relieved that her news seemed to have given no offence. 'It's just that they've been friends for years,' she stressed. A moment later she

251

wondered if the news had penetrated at all.

Looking towards Hannah, Mrs Elsworth said, 'I would say you're about five months now, Hannah, at a guess.'

Hannah turned and stared at her, as if waiting for her to add something more.

'Are you sure you can still manage the work?' Mrs Elsworth asked, showing distinct signs of embarrassment under that unblinking stare.

'As long as I can manage to eat, I'll have to manage the work, Mrs Elsworth.'

Marie was surprised when, despite her own obvious discomfiture, Mrs Elsworth probed further: 'But surely you get support from your husband?'

'Well, whether I do or not, that's between me and my husband.'

'Of course. I only meant...'

Marie felt Mrs Elsworth's loss of composure so excruciating that she interjected with a sudden: 'How's Jenny? I haven't seen her for a while.'

Hannah's eyebrows arched upwards, and she gave a sardonic little smile. 'Very well, thank you, Marie. How's Alfie?'

'All right, thanks.'

'Good. Well, I'll just finish here, then I'll do the bedrooms, and then I'll be off, if that's all right by you, Mrs Elsworth? So I can be in for Jenny coming home from school, you know. Get on with it, and get off home, that's my motto.'

Five months? Marie thought. That put conception at the middle of January. But hadn't Hannah's husband been away at sea then? Maybe not. Marie couldn't really remember a lot of things since that awful night they'd been bombed out, although her memory of the bombing was sharp and clear. That, and being buried alive were the stuff of her recurring nightmares.

Chapter 21

On Sunday morning, after having spent an hour convincing the Elsworths that she really was well enough, Marie borrowed their hoe and walked straight up to the allotment. George was not there this time, but there was another crop of weeds. She began to hoe in between the broad beans.

One of her old neighbours came by on his way to his own patch, and stopped. 'All right, lass?'

She straightened up, and leaned on the hoe. 'Just about, thanks.'

'Bad job about your house. You're staying up at Mr Elsworth's now, aren't you? Aren't you going out with his eldest?'

She nodded.

'He's not a bad bloke, Elsworth. I used to work for him, years ago. Rum do about that Hannah, though, that goes up there to do their skivvying, ain't it?'

'What do you mean?' she asked, repelled by the knowing leer on his face.

'I should think it's obvious. I mean she's in the family way, and it's not her husband's, unless he managed to shoot it across the Atlantic.'

'Oh,' Marie said, turning to her work again. 'Well, I can't say I noticed. I've had a bit too much

253

on my plate lately.'

'You have that. I've seen the state of your house. You're lucky to be alive, I reckon. Don't you be struggling with watering cans. I'll do the watering for you.'

'Thanks. I won't refuse,' she said. 'Hasn't it been peaceful, lately? How long must it be since we had an air raid, do you reckon?'

'Well, since they did that bit of damage at St Andrew's Dock and Priory Sidings at the end of last month, it must be over three weeks. And that hardly counts. There were no fires blazing, and not much damage at all. One unexploded bomb, though, to keep the bomb disposal lads on their toes.'

Marie shuddered. 'I don't envy them their job. I'd rather keep a safe distance from bombs, thank you very much. Have the Nazis forgotten about us, do you think?'

'Doubt it. They're busy with the Russians now, by all accounts. Don't you read the papers? Don't you listen to the wireless?'

'Course I do. I live for the wireless. Not the news, though; it's usually too depressing, hearing about all the bombing in London and Coventry, although I like to hear Alvar Lidell telling us how many German bombers have been shot down. We never get a mention, though. It wouldn't be so bad if we ever got any credit for what we have to put up with, but we never do. I like programmes like *Music While You Work*, and *It's That Man Again*, something to brighten you up a bit. And we always tune into Radio Hamburg to listen to Lord Haw-Haw. He's hilarious. We always have a good laugh at him.'

He grinned at her, eyebrows arched and eyes twinkling. 'Germany calling! Germany calling!'

The expression on his face was so comical, and the intonation so exact that she burst out laughing, with no sharp twinge of pain in her ribs to stop her.

'Let's go and sit in the rose garden,' Marie said as she and Nancy walked across to Pearson Park later that afternoon. The sky was a brilliant blue, and the park full of people in their Sunday best, children on swings and slides, young lads with their shirtsleeves rolled up, playing football on stretches of green, older folk sitting on the benches, all out to make the best of a fine day.

'I'm fed up,' Nancy said, when they were finally seated on a bench, looking at a bed of roses. 'Absolutely stalled.'

'Minty hasn't been in touch, then,' Marie quipped. She quickly regretted it.

Nancy had dark rings around her eyes, as if she hadn't slept for a week. Her voice was thick with tears. 'His name's Monty, and no, he hasn't. George has set a private detective on to him, though. He says it shouldn't take long to find him, and then he wants me to take him to court.'

'That's good, surely,' Marie soothed her, keen to make amends. 'You might get some of your money back. You might get your ring back, if he hasn't already sold it.'

'I don't think we'll get anything back. And Monty might just put all the blame on me. And if it gets to court, my name will be mud, all over

Hull. George will hear a lot of things that will put him off me for the rest of his life. It'll be a disaster, and as far as the money's concerned, we'll get nowhere.'

Marie shook her head. 'What a hero your Monty is, Nance. You threw everything away for him, and that's how far you can trust him. But don't despair just yet. If he tries putting all the blame on you, he's lying. Your mother can testify to that; he waltzed off without paying his rent, remember.'

'There's something else,' Nancy said. 'I'm overdue. If I'm pregnant, I might just as well kill myself.'

'Here's half a dozen eggs for you,' Marie told Aunt Edie the following Friday, standing in her tiny backyard. 'Uncle Alf sent them. I borrowed Danny's bike to go and see Mam, and called there on the way back.'

George's eyes lit up. 'Boiled eggs for tea then. Make a nice change. Then a rhubarb pie tomorrow, maybe.'

'They've got a couple of elder trees; the clusters of flowers are as big as saucers, and I thought: I'll have a few of them, they're just ready to make some of that elder-flower champagne my mother used to do. Then I thought where will I get the sugar, now it's on ration, and where will I get the lemons? And then where will I get the time? So I've abandoned that idea.'

'How are they getting on with your Alfie? Has he settled all right?'

'Yeah, he's settled in the school there, but he'd

rather be in Hull. Uncle Alf nearly came a cropper the other day, skating on marbles he'd left on the kitchen floor. They found a mouse in a shoebox he'd punched full of air holes in his bedroom the other day; he told them he was keeping it for a pet. He didn't keep it long after Auntie Dot found it, though. And they can't sit down for two minutes before he's pestering them with, "Wanna play battleships?" She says it's as much a catch phrase there as "Mind my bike" and "Can I do yer now, sir?" are on the wireless.'

'Sounds as if he's driving them mad.'

'That's what they say, but underneath, I think they love it. Alf says he's brought the house to life. And I know what they mean. I really miss our Alfie; I used to get many a laugh out of his mischief. Lads are sometimes funny without meaning to be, aren't they?'

'I don't know,' Aunt Edie said. 'George was always a good boy. I never had any trouble with him at all. How's your mam?'

'She's a bit better. Sister says they might discharge her next week, if she keeps it up. But, you know, you can change your mind about having her here if you're not sure you can manage. The Elsworths will make her welcome.'

'No fear of that. I'm looking forward to having her. She'll be good company for me, somebody nearer my own age.'

'She might be too poorly to be good company, Aunt Edie, but I'll come and help you with the work: washing and ironing, and everything. And I'll go and fetch any shopping you want. I'll give

257

you her ration book, as well. As long as you're sure.'

'I'm certain, and I can manage most of the work, don't worry about that. You could do something for me, though, if you wanted.'

'What?'

'I wish you'd teach George to dance. He should be getting out, among people his own age, instead of sitting in the house with me.'

'Oh, now she's going to have your mother for company, she wants to push me out of my own home,' George joked.

Marie jumped up. 'On your feet, then,' she said. 'We'll start with a quickstep.'

But after half an hour of having her feet trampled on, Marie gave it up. 'You've got two left feet, George,' she said.

'He's never had the time for much going out, that's what it is, and the concrete's not a proper dance floor, it's not slippy enough,' Aunt Edie said. 'He'll never learn to dance on that. He'd do better on a proper dance floor. And there's no music. Why don't you take Marie to a dance hall, George, where she can teach you properly?'

George's eyes lit up. 'That's not a bad idea of yours, Mother. I fancy a decent night out, and I'm sure it would do you good, Marie. Forget your troubles for a bit. Have a bit of fun.'

Marie strongly suspected that if George went to any dance hall, Nancy would be invited as well. Marie had no relish for playing gooseberry, especially with things as dicey as they were between those two. 'I don't know what Charles would think to that,' she demurred. 'We're supposed to be getting married on his next leave.'

Aunt Edie's face was a picture of innocence. 'Well, you'd just be dancing partners. There's no harm in that, is there?'

'Come off it, Marie,' George scoffed. 'I've seen you out dancing without Charles before, and I've seen him without you. Come on, I want to learn. What do you say?'

'Well, if you've seen us, you obviously have been to dance halls, so why haven't you learned?'

'I didn't go often enough, and when I did I was always one of the chaps who stand at the bar, hoping to get the last waltz with some pretty girl and take her home. That's how I started courting Nancy.'

'Huh!' his mother snorted. 'Let that be a lesson to you then, and be a lot more careful who you get tangled up with in future. It's just a shame Marie's spoken for.'

'Come on, Marie, it would do you good, take you out of yourself. It's Saturday tomorrow. There'll be dances on at the Fulford, or Beverley Road Baths. And there's a charity dinner dance on at the City Hall, proceeds to the Lord Mayor's Homeless Fund. I'll take you to that, if you like. It'll do you good to get out.'

'That's hardly the place to teach anyone to dance, and the tickets will be too expensive,' she said. 'And I could do with getting something out of the homeless fund, never mind putting money I can't afford into it.'

'You wouldn't be putting money into it, I would.'

Marie's eyebrows lifted a fraction. No scrimping here. It sounded as if it really might be jam tomorrow, and that tomorrow might actually come. George had given a firm promise of jam, nothing vague about it.

'I haven't got anything to wear,' Marie protested, and then realized that she had. She had Margaret's dance dress. Not over-posh for a Lord Mayor's dinner dance, but it would pass muster. And to abandon her worries for the space of an evening of good food and toe-tapping music was too tempting to resist. The place would be packed with people out to enjoy themselves – not Charles, not the partner she would have chosen, but very passable substitutes in the shape of foreign servicemen, all themselves probably sorely missed by the sweethearts and wives back home: charming Poles; polite Canadians; tall, tanned Aussies; men dressed in unfamiliar uniforms, speaking with unfamiliar accents from every corner of the globe. She wouldn't lack for partners, and many of them would have fascinating stories to tell.

She would go. It would certainly take her mind off her troubles, if only for an evening.

The buzzing night life of the bomb-blasted city struck Marie as bizarre. Incredible, really. It had never ceased to amaze her, since the first really serious air raids had started. Hull wore both the comic and the tragic mask at the same time. Bombs rained down destroying everything in their path, razing people's homes to the ground, killing people, maiming people, destroying everything they owned but the clothes they stood up in and sometimes even them, and the city picked itself up and danced on. The dance halls were usually packed with young people. And now homelessness itself was the occasion for a grand dinner dance at the City Hall, so that the better-off could go out and have a lot of fun and get a glow of satisfaction at the thought of all the good that their enjoying themselves was doing for the bombed-out worse-off, who patently were not enjoying themselves – or hadn't been. Though bombed out herself, Marie had every intention of forgetting her troubles for an evening and enjoying herself as much as the next person. Amid all the grief, misery and devastation, people could dine and dance their feet off not only without conscience, but almost feeling it a duty, since they were doing it for the sake of the homeless. For the price of a ticket they could hobnob with the great and the good of the city, bask in their approval, and get their money's worth in sheer pleasure. 'Enjoy yourself while you can' seemed to be the general feeling, and most people were doing just that, for fear the next bomb might 'have their name on it'.

Marie sat at the table surrounded by the wreck of the dinner, drinking coffee and listening to the band, and watching the scene. Nancy was there, as Marie had known she would be, and she was not at all sorry to have left George to trample on Nancy's feet. They were just out of sight among the throng of couples when she felt a tap on her shoulder. 'Do you come here often?' a familiar voice behind her asked.

'Terry! Fancy seeing you here!' She turned, suddenly horribly conscious of the fact that she was wearing Margaret's dress.

He recognized it and smiled, but made no comment. 'Aye, just fancy. I didn't expect to see you out so soon.'

'Nor did I. I got knocked about a bit, didn't I? I'm still black and blue and sore in places, but I'd still be black and blue and sore if I'd stayed in the house, wouldn't I? So I might as well be out. And being out takes your mind off things.'

'Is your young man with you?'

'No, Chas is away with the East Yorkshires. I'm here with George Maltby.'

His eyes widened. 'George Maltby that was courting Nancy Harding?'

'That ghost you saw on Spring Bank? Yes, George Maltby that *is* courting Nancy Harding – just. She's here as well, and she didn't walk through the wall,' Marie said, and burst into laughter at the look on his face.

'She's...'

'Yes, she's alive. It's a long story. I'll tell you another time.'

'Let me take you for a dance, and tell me now.'

'What about your partner? Won't she mind?'

'I haven't got a partner. One of my mates and his wife came and dragged me out. They reckoned it would do me good.'

'What a coincidence. Well, then, you're on. Just be careful not to hold me too tight. My ribs won't stand it.'

'Mind my ribs. Is that a variation on "Mind my bike"?'

She laughed at that catchphrase from one of those comedy shows that lightened the dark days of war. Margaret's husband was refreshing company. He was every bit as good a dancer as Chas, and he had a sense of humour. As he whisked her round the dance floor, Marie gave him the gist of Nancy's tale, discreetly leaving out her latest bad news.

'He's not much of a dancer, is he?' he commented, as they passed George and Nancy on the dance floor.

'That's putting it mildly,' Marie grinned. 'Nancy had a job to drag him out dancing before, but since she came back he's taken it into his head he ought to learn. Maybe he's turning over a new leaf. Nancy hardly ever got to a dance at all unless she came with me and Margaret. Now his mother's egging him on as well; she had him trampling all over my feet yesterday.'

The music came to a stop, and they stood looking at each other, waiting for the band to strike up again with the next dance, and then Marie saw Nancy and George, back at their table.

'Shall we sit this one out? Go and join them?'

'If you like. I'll go and get us a drink.'

Marie pulled out a chair beside George and Nancy. 'How's the dancing going, you two?'

'He's definitely getting the hang of it, aren't you, George?' Nancy said, smiling adoringly up at him.

Marie just managed to keep a straight face. George's dancing was atrocious, and before her flight to London, Nancy would have made some crushing witticism at his expense, but crushing witticisms belonged to the pre-Monty era. Getting back into George's good books was her main objective now.

Terry was soon back with the drinks. The two men had been casual acquaintances for years. Although George's standing as a qualified engineer now put him on a higher social plane than Terry, he didn't put on any side with him. Since the start of the blitz, the firemen had had the status of gods in Hull.

'Not many women here without a male escort tonight, are there?' George commented. 'Although I suppose formal dinner dances are a different proposition to most hops. I used to be amazed at the number of women the few times I used to come, out dancing while their husbands were away in the Forces. I used to wonder what they would say if they could see them, cavorting with any Tom, Dick or Harry.'

'Or George, or Terry,' Terry laughed.

'Not this George,' George frowned. 'I don't believe in messing about with other men's women. That's not my style, at all.'

'It's not obligatory,' Terry said. 'Some people are just out with their friends for a bit of innocent fun, strange as it might seem.'

'And there's a fair proportion not just out with their friends for innocent fun,' George scoffed. 'They're out on the prowl, looking for men – Yanks, Poles, Canadians, anything that falls in their path. Dances are the best happy hunting ground ever invented.'

Terry laughed at that, then with a wink at Marie and Nancy said: 'Well, maybe you're right. If Margaret hadn't been out on the prowl with these two, I'd never have met her, and she gave me the happiest few months of my life.' His face lost its smile, and he added, quite seriously, 'I'll never find another Margaret, that is a certainty, but one day I might be lucky enough to bump into another gem, out on the prowl.'

'That's different,' George said.

Terry's smile returned. 'I'll take Nancy for a turn round the floor, then, shall I? If you don't mind taking Chas's woman.'

George stiffened. 'If you like.'

They watched them go, then George led Marie onto the dance floor. 'I'm sorry about his wife, and everything,' he said, 'but I can't stand people who twist everything you say. I wasn't talking about him and Margaret, I was talking about people who do the dirty on people. That *is* different.'

'I know. Don't take him seriously, he's only pulling your leg,' Marie said. After a turn round the floor she realized that her toes weren't being trodden on quite as often. 'You know, George, Nancy's right. I think you are beginning to get the hang of it.'

'Oh, I'm determined to learn,' he said. 'Absolutely determined. I'm going to book myself in for some private coaching.'

'Just try and relax a bit more, listen to the rhythm of the music, and let it flow through you.'

George took the advice to heart. With coaching from Marie and Nancy, and encouragement from Terry, he made steady progress, and the evening passed quite harmoniously.

'I don't suppose you'd fancy coming dancing with me now and again, Marie?' Terry asked as they left the hall. Glancing down at her engagement ring, he added: 'Strictly as pals, I mean. No prowling.'

'Well, as long as that's understood, I wouldn't mind,' she said. 'But it will be strictly as pals.'

Chapter 22

As he'd said himself, Charles was no poet, but he wasn't a bad correspondent. Since Marie and her mother had been bombed out, she'd had three or four letters from him for every one she'd sent. She reread his latest on Sunday, the day after the dinner dance. It was the usual cheery letter, full of news about life at base, observations on the men around him, and ended as always by telling her to listen to the wireless because he kept putting in requests for her, and how much he longed to get back to her. She sometimes wondered how that could be when he seemed to be having such a good time where he was. She wrote a long letter back, determined to make it as optimistic as his, and included a reassuring account of her outing to the City Hall.

…I'm a lot better now. I went out dancing yesterday, to a charity do for the homeless. Ironic, isn't it, me forking money out to help the homeless? But it wasn't my money. George paid for me and Nancy, and got his money's worth in dancing lessons. Nancy seems to be climbing back onto that pedestal he used to keep her on, but I'm not sure how long she'll manage to stay up

there. There might be more trouble on the horizon.

We met Terry, Margaret's husband. He's good company. Make the most of life, while you can, he says. He says he's stopped worrying about anything. If it happens, it happens. He wants to take me dancing again, strictly as pals, of course. He knows I'm engaged...

Marie travelled back from the hospital with her mother and helped to carry her into the Maltbys' front room on an ambulance chair. 'Her heart's quite weak, but we can't do any more for her, I'm afraid,' the doctor had warned. George arrived home from work just as the ambulance left. Marie elevated her mother's ankle, still in the plaster, and Auntie Edie fussed around arranging cushions to make her comfortable.

She sank gratefully back against them. 'Our Marie thinks I shouldn't trouble you. She says it'll be too much for you, you being nearly blind. I told her, you're not nearly blind.'

'We'll manage. We'll manage together, Lillian. I'm a bit short-sighted, but you'll be my eyes, when George is out.'

'Well, give it a trial,' Marie said, with no great hopes that they would manage, since apart from her heart condition, her mother looked as if she'd aged twenty years in the past month. 'If it's too much for you, we'll have to make other arrangements. Mrs Elsworth has offered us one of their big bedrooms.'

'I don't want to go to the Elsworths,' her mother said. 'I don't know them. I know Edie's ways, and she knows mine. I think you're the only woman on earth I could bear to share a house with, Edie. I'd rather stay here. This used to be your second home, Marie. Many's the night you've gone to bed here, while we've played cards until one o'clock in the morning, and we've carried you home in a blanket.'

Aunt Edie gave her a beaming smile. 'We'll be good company for each other when George is out.' Turning to Marie, she added, 'She'll be comfortable with me, more comfortable than anywhere else now her own home's gone.'

'That's the truth. Well, Edie, I've never had much, as you well know, but I'm a real pauper now. I haven't a stick of furniture left. I haven't a roof. I've no nest for my poor chicks. My husband's dead and gone. I just thank God I've still got a friend.'

Their eyes met, and two pairs of work-worn hands clasped and held each other for a moment. The look of gratitude on her mother's face, and the compassion on Edie's, brought a lump to Marie's throat and tears to her eyes. George had to look away.

'I'll come down every day, and do anything you want done, housework, shopping, and I'll come and help you get her up and put her to bed,' Marie said, 'I've been to see the hospital almoner, so there should be some money soon, and I'll stay off work as long as I can to help you. And some of the stuff at the allotment will be ready before long.'

'Well, I'll help get you up, before I go to work. We'll manage, don't you worry,' George assured Marie's mother. 'We don't turn our backs on our friends. Ever. We'll see you right. I'll have something to eat later, Mam. I'm going to get washed and changed, and then I'll be out. I've booked a dancing lesson.'

'All right, son.' Aunt Edie gave him a look that managed to convey pity and disgust in equal measure. It convinced Marie that she knew he was seeing Nancy again.

As soon as he'd gone Aunt Edie challenged her. 'He thinks I don't realize what's going on. Did you tell your mam the filthy trick she played on him?'

'What trick?' her mother asked, before Marie had a chance to answer.

'That Nancy Harding, your Marie's friend. She chucked him for an actor, and hopped it to London with him. Now he's chucked her. She put my lad through hell, and now she's back in Hull, hanging round his neck again.'

Marie escaped to the kitchen. When she returned with the tea tray Aunt Edie's tirade against Nancy had just come to an end.

'You ought to drop her as a friend, Marie,' her mother said. 'She's not our sort at all. We've never had much money, but we've always been respectable. She's not somebody you ought to know, unless you want to be tarred with the same brush.'

Marie was dropping her latest letter to Charles in the postbox when Hannah came out of the post office.

'Are you writing to Charles, by any chance?'

Marie's jaw dropped. 'What business is it of yours who I'm writing to?'

269

Hannah looked her up and down. 'Well, in your next to Charles, tell him he's going to be a daddy.'

Marie gave her a disdainful stare. 'He's going to be no such thing. Don't judge everybody else by your own standards.'

'I'm not judging *everybody* else by my standards,' Hannah said, returning both stare and disdain, 'only him. Just give him the message, will you?'

'What are you insinuating?' Marie demanded, but Hannah was already walking down Princes Avenue, and Marie had no intention of following her to bandy words in the street. Instead, she walked furiously in the opposite direction, towards Park Avenue.

Mrs Elsworth was in, and so was Danny. The two women went for a private talk in the kitchen.

'You know that baby of Hannah's isn't her husband's, don't you?' Marie began.

'Yes. I had realized that,' Mrs Elsworth said drily.

'Well, you know what she just said to me? "Tell Charles he's going to be a daddy," she said! Just like that. You know what she's insinuating? Unless I've got it all wrong, and I don't think I have, she's trying to pin that baby she's having on Charles.'

Mrs Elsworth sighed, and sat down. 'I should have sacked her the minute I suspected there was something going on, but I was so busy with the WVS and everything I kept putting it off, I'm afraid.'

Marie looked aghast. 'What? You're not telling me you believe her? She's lying! We've seen her out with other men – who knows who the father is? Charles could never be tempted by somebody like her!'

'I hope you're right.'

'Of course I'm right. She's lying, I tell you! She's lying! And you – his own mother – how can you believe her?'

Charles's mother maintained a discreet and ominous silence.

'Well? Do you believe her?' Marie insisted.

'You remember when I was questioning her the other day?' Mrs Elsworth said, looking Marie full in the face. 'I thought she might have told me then that it was Charles's baby. I dreaded hearing it, but I couldn't stop myself from quizzing her. Now I feel drained, as if I've had an enormous abscess that's burst at last.'

Danny pushed open the door and walked in. He stopped, looking from one to the other. 'Talk about an atmosphere you could cut with a knife!' he said. 'What's the matter?'

As Marie turned towards him a dim memory of his jokes about hairgrips in Charles's bed surfaced in her mind, along with a vision of Hannah's abundant auburn hair, always pinned up. Could it be true, then? Was she really having his baby? Her beautiful vision of herself, presenting Charles with his firstborn child, the first fruit of their marriage and supreme proof of her womanhood, was dashed to the ground. It had been her fondest hope, even more than taking her vows at the altar on their wedding day. Now it could never be, thanks to Hannah. Hannah had pipped her to the post.

The bottom dropped out of Marie's world.

Jenny was playing in the ruins of a house in Marlborough Avenue, when Marie passed on her way to Nancy's. It took nearly ten minutes to coax her out, and when she had, Marie decided to kill two birds with one stone. She would take Jenny back home, and have it out with Hannah, straight. But Hannah wasn't in, and a neighbour who called to her from across the street to tell her so got the full blast of Marie's anger about Jenny being left alone to get herself into danger.

'Hannah! She's not fit to have a child,' Marie ended.

'Her father's family live just off Hessle Road, Scarborough Street, number twelve,' the woman volunteered. 'Take her there if you're so concerned. She might stand a chance of being looked after there.'

'Right, then, come on, Jenny, we're going to see your grandma. If you see her mother, just tell her where she is, will you?'

'I certainly will,' the woman nodded.

Charles wouldn't approve of such interference, Marie thought, as she walked off holding Jenny's hand. Well, to hell with Charles. It was obvious now why he hadn't wanted to interfere in Hannah's business on the night she'd come home with that soldier, and smacked Jenny into the middle of the street. He hadn't wanted his own dirty little secret coming to light, and Hannah might just have trotted it out for all to hear. Marie glowed with anger. She was absolutely shameless, that woman. Absolutely without shame.

'You're walking too fast,' Jenny said, breath-lessly trying to keep up.

Marie slowed her pace as they walked along Spring Bank and down Albert Avenue. When they passed the baths, she thought of George, searching in there among a lot of battered corpses, trying to find Nancy. What a nightmare that must have been, poor lad, and how had Nancy treated him? Left him without a word. Without a thought, even, except she remembered to take all his savings with her.

'My dad brings me here,' Jenny said.

'What, to the baths?'

'Sometimes. But he brings me this way when we go to my nanna's.'

'Doesn't your mother ever bring you?'

'No.'

They walked in silence then until they came to Scarborough Street. Jenny left her side then and ran down the street, to hammer on her grand-mother's door. When it opened, Jenny flung her-self into a woman's arms, to be lifted and hugged – by a woman as fair as Jenny herself, who bore more resemblance to her than her mother did, and who had obviously been crying. Marie instinct-ively liked her.

'I found her playing in the ruins of a house on Marlborough Avenue. Those places aren't safe. There's so much rubble, you wouldn't even know if there was an unexploded bomb. It's not the first time, either. She'll end up breaking her neck, if somebody doesn't watch her. I tried taking her back home, but her mother was out.'

The woman showed not the slightest surprise.

'Well, just fancy that. Come in. You go into the kitchen, Jenny, love. Go and get a biscuit, while I talk to the lady.'

When Jenny was out of earshot, she closed the adjoining door and turned to Marie. 'We've had a terrible upsetment,' she said, with tears springing to her eyes. 'Her dad's been reported missing, presumed dead. The ship he was in copped a torpedo. Of course, Hannah got the letter the Ministry of War sent, but she didn't bother telling us. "Recorded as supposed drowned whilst on service with his ship," it said. 'His name's going on the roll of honour of men who gave their lives for their country, as if that's any consolation to me. We got the news third-hand, days after.'

'Jenny's dad? Your son?' Marie said, the wind completely taken out of her sails.

The woman nodded, and her face crumpled. She fished a damp handkerchief out of her apron pocket to dab her sore and swollen eyelids and blow her nose. 'We only heard a couple of days ago, and I've hardly stopped crying since. In his last letter, he told me, "Watch out for my Jenny," as if he'd had a premonition. And I've been trying to watch out for Jenny since he went away, I really have. But if I arrange to go and see her, Hannah makes sure she's out. And if I call unexpectedly, it's not convenient, because they're going out, or they're expecting company. There's always some excuse. That's the sort of game she plays. You're not a friend of hers, are you?'

'No, I am not. I live ... lived on the same street, that's all.'

'We don't get on, me and Hannah, as you might

have gathered. None of the family can stand her. None of us have any more to do with her than we have to, for our Larry's sake. I don't know how many blokes she's got off with, since the war started. She's a disgrace. She thinks I know nothing, but I get to know it all, from somebody I know who lives opposite her. Now she's expecting again. It can't be our Larry's, and I'm glad it's not. I shouldn't like to think she had another of his bairns, and him not there to look out for it.'

Despite the warmth of the day, a chill went through Marie. 'No, it's pretty certain it's not Larry's,' she said, grim-faced. 'What's your name?'

'Gertrude, really, but people call me Trudie.'

'Mine's Marie. I'll leave Jenny with you, then, shall I?'

The woman nodded. 'She might come looking for her in a day or two, if she bethinks herself.'

'I hope your son turns up safe, for all your sakes, Jenny's especially. It sometimes happens, doesn't it?'

Trudie gave her a look of bitter disbelief, and shook her head. 'The Atlantic's vast, and deep and cold. I've no great hopes of him turning up safe out of that.'

Marie walked away, grieved for both her and Jenny. She was too sickened by it all to call back at Hannah's. Jenny would be all right where she was, so leave it to the neighbour to tell Hannah where her daughter was, if she wanted to. If she didn't, Hannah would have to wonder for a while and then shift herself to go and find Jenny, if she cared enough. And a good fright might do her good, make her buck her ideas up and take better care of her daughter.

'Charles and Hannah?' Nancy said, when Marie finally got to the Hardings' house. 'It was on the tip of my tongue to say something many a time, especially that time you laid into me about Monty. Then the police came to see you about your dad, so I never.'

'Say what?'

'Say Charles might not be everything you think he is. Say quite a few people had seen them dancing together while you were at work, when he was at home in January, and again that night we were shifting beds after the bombing at the end of March.'

Marie flushed. 'It would have been nice if you'd told me as soon as you knew.'

'You're joking. Nobody does that. I didn't see them, so as far as I was concerned it was just a rumour, and you wouldn't have believed it anyway. People get themselves into a lot of trouble for gobbing off about things like that. Anyway, that's all there is to it. You know as much as me, now.'

Marie nodded. 'I meant to have an hour or two with you, but I got sidetracked, and now I'll have to go, to get my mam ready for bed. George has had to bring a bed downstairs for her.'

'He told me. Weak heart, he said.'

'He's been very good. There aren't many men would put up with somebody else's invalid mother.'

'He's been well trained. His mother's had him running after her ever since his dad died, cracking on she's nearly blind.'

'Well, she's certainly very short-sighted.'

'She can see what she wants to see.'

'Well, he doesn't seem to mind, anyhow,' Marie said, standing up to go.

Nancy's eyes narrowed, and her mouth compressed into a thin, hard line. 'He must be in his element now, with two old women to keep telling him how wonderful he is.'

'Hold on a minute, Nance,' Marie bristled. 'My mother's not fifty yet. That's not old. Do you call *your* mother an old woman?'

'Sorry. I wasn't really thinking about *your* mother.'

'Well, Aunt Edie's only a few years older, and she's been very kind to us, as it happens. Anyway, is he taking you out tonight?'

'He's coming round. We'll see what happens.'

The peculiar expression on Nancy's face gave Marie a very bad feeling. 'You're not going to try to land him with somebody else's baby, are you?' she demanded.

Nancy's cheeks and lips turned to flame. 'What? What are you talking about? I'm not having any baby,' she said, 'so don't you go spreading any rumours. There's nothing the matter with me.'

The front room at the Maltbys' was so crammed with furniture it was difficult to manoeuvre, but Aunt Edie seemed not to mind. The two women were sitting in armchairs opposite each other, seeming very happy in each other's company when Marie arrived to see to her mother, and help Aunt Edie with some of the rougher housework. George went out almost immediately, giving her a wink as he left, apparently oblivious of the fact that his mother knew that Nancy was 'round his neck again'.

'George says he's going to put the settee in the bedroom out of the way, as soon as he can get somebody to help him get it up the stairs,' Auntie Edie said, when he'd gone.

'I'd offer, but I think it'll need two strong men,' Marie said, picturing herself sleeping on that battered old settee, if the situation with Hannah made it necessary for her to leave the Elsworths. It looked like a back breaker, but it might be better to be on the spot for her mother. On the other hand, the situation with Nancy was very sticky, and not likely to get much better, all things considered, and she was determined to stay as far out of that as she could.

No, she decided. Between the Elsworths and the Maltbys she was between the devil and the deep blue sea. If she moved, it would have to be to Dunswell, however much of a nuisance the travelling would be.

When she got back to the Elsworths, she went straight to her room – Charles's room – and wrote him a very short letter.

Dear Charles,
Hannah's about five months pregnant, as you already know. Today she asked me to tell you you're going to be a daddy. In other words, she's accusing you of being the father. What have you got to say to that? Your mother's not exactly springing to your defence, by the way.

By one of those strange coincidences, Hannah's hus-
band has been reported lost at sea, although I'd never
have guessed it when I saw her this morning. She was
just as happy as Larry, who, come to think, is beyond
being happy now, or miserable, for that matter. Which
opens the way for you to make an honest woman of
her, and give the bairn a name. Which brings me to the
question – would you like your ring back, or shall I just
pass it on to her?

After signing it with a bare 'Marie' she hurried
downstairs to take it to the post box before going
to bed. There was a moment's awkwardness when
she bumped into Mr Elsworth in the hallway.

'I've heard all about it,' he grimaced. 'Marjorie
says she had a feeling there might be something
going on.'

'I've just written to him.'

'So have we. In case you had any thoughts about
moving, we'd like you to stay where you are, at
least until he gets some leave. And you needn't
worry about Hannah. Marjorie's given her a
month's wages, in lieu of notice, and she's found
her a place with our friends in Newland Park.
They haven't any adult sons – not that the damage
isn't already done.'

'That's very nice of you, Mr Elsworth,' she said.
'I appreciate it.'

And she did. They had been very kind to her,
and the way things had turned out, she might
regret parting with Mr and Mrs Elsworth more
than with Charles when – if – the break came.

Charles's reply arrived a couple of days later.

Dear Marie

I admit it. At least I admit it's possible. But it's also possible it's not. If it's true about her husband, I'm very sorry indeed, but Hannah is very liberal with her favours, and NOBODY COULD MAKE AN HONEST WOMAN OF HER. He couldn't, and I couldn't. That is simply not possible. I'm sorry I ever got tangled up with her. And no, I don't want my ring back. I want you to keep the ring, and I certainly don't want you to give it to Hannah. I care nothing for Hannah. You're the woman I want. We'll get married, and get you a house to rent so you can look after your mother in your own place. I'm trying desperately to get home, so that I can try and convince you that you're the woman I love, and I mean every word I've ever said to you.

All my love,
Forever yours, Chas

Marie read it over three times, and then put it aside, thinking of the air raid that killed her father. Had it not been for the siren, she and Charles would certainly have made love, and she remembered his comments about stocking tops and promised lands. Warning bells had rung in her mind at the time. Now she knew whose stocking tops he was talking about, and where that promised land was, and she imagined his hands on Hannah's thighs.

She blanked the thought out. It was too disgusting. Forgiveness for something so gross was too facile, too weak. She found some writing paper, and a pen.

'Well, Charles,' she murmured, 'I might be the woman you want, but I'm not sure you're the man for me, if you're tempted by a slut like her.'

Chapter 23

Terry came roaring up Princes Avenue on his motorbike, just as Marie was walking down towards Clumber Street on Friday evening. He stopped beside the kerb.

'You must have been busy last night,' Marie said. 'I was sitting in the Elsworths' air-raid shelter from one o'clock this morning with my teeth chattering, listening to the bombs going off, wondering if they had another one for me or my mother. It lasted for hours.'

'Aye, we had a lively time of it, and not only high explosives: they dropped loads of incendiaries as well. They were going for the railway, mostly. We put seventy-eight fires out all together; the worst one was Blundell Spence on Air Street. There's enough damage to keep the building trade going for a bit, I should think, as well as the doctors. About twenty people killed, and twice as many seriously injured. Anyway, it's earned me a couple of days off. I was just coming to see if you fancied coming to the dance at the Fulford tonight.'

'Tonight? Well, that's now, Terry! It's nearly eight o'clock.'

'I know. I slept a bit late after the high jinks last

night. What about it, then?'

'Oh, no! I haven't got time. It'll be ten o'clock before I get my mother settled and help Aunt Edie with the work.'

'Another time, then?'

'Yes, definitely. But give me more than a minute's notice, then I can get everything done in time. And I like to get dolled up a bit to go out.'

'What about tomorrow?'

'Yeah. You're on. I'll go to Auntie Edie's early, and get ready there. You can't miss it, it's two doors down from the one that got flattened. Come at about half-past eight. I can't be ready any sooner.'

She would get her glad rags on, Marie thought, and go out with him openly – flaunt him, even. No sneaking off, hole-in-corner stuff for her. Let people think what they liked about her going out with Terry. It was a pity he couldn't pick her up at the Elsworths', so they could get an eyeful, and report it all back to Charles. But going back there to get changed would be a waste of precious dancing time. Terry took her down to Auntie Edie's on the back of the bike. Marie spotted Jenny on Princes Avenue on the way there. Hannah must have been to collect her, then. Wonders would never cease, Marie thought.

George was still in when Terry dropped her off.

'Not out dancing tonight, George?' she asked, surprised to find him still at home.

He was quite morose. 'No, I don't feel like it.'

Marie suddenly remembered what they'd said about needing a strong man and dashed back into the street and, pressing two fingers over her curled tongue, sent a penetrating whistle after Terry. He stopped the bike and came back.

'Will you do us a favour?'

'Anything, for you.'

'Help George lug a settee upstairs?'

He switched off the ignition and came inside.

'And that will be that damned thing out of the way,' she said. 'At least we'll be able to move in the front room, then.'

Marie left her mother settled in bed, with Auntie Edie in the armchair yarning with her about old times, and went through to the kitchen, flicking the wireless on in the dining room as she passed. George folded up his paper and followed her, picking up a tea towel.

Marie turned the hot tap on, and waited for the sink to fill. 'What's up with you, George? You look as if you've lost a quid and found a tanner.'

'I've lost more than any quid,' he frowned. 'I've lost over a hundred and fifty – and that's not including Nancy's money. Another hundred and I could have bought us a nice little bungalow in Bilton, with a garage.'

'What a letdown.'

'I've finished with her,' he said quietly.

She turned the tap off, and began to wash the pots and put them on the draining board. 'Because of the money?'

'No. Because of some monkey business the other night. We were supposed to be going dancing, but she wasn't ready when I went round. Well, that was nothing new; I've always ended up waiting at least half an hour for her titivating herself. She takes

283

more getting ready than the Queen of Sheba. So she says, "The lodgers are out, and my mother's gone round to my nan's. We've got the house to ourselves."'

Marie paused in her task, and listened.

George gave a grim nod. 'Well, that was something new. Try as I might, I've never managed to get her on her own before; we've never got anywhere near the knickers-off stage. And quiet nights in aren't Nance's style; she likes to be out, enjoying herself. So she cosies up to me, and all of a sudden her mouth's clamped over mine like a bloody suction cup and she's groping inside my clothes. That's never been her style before, either – not with me, at any rate. So I said, "Get off! Somebody might come in." "No, they won't," she says. "Anyway, lock the door, if you're so bothered." And even if I'd been in the mood, which I wasn't, because it landed on me like a ton of bricks – there was something about it that … well, it would have put anybody off, even if they had been. So I got up as if I was going to lock the door, and I walked straight out of it. And it'll be a bloody long time before I go back.'

'Hmm,' Marie said.

'Hmm. Are you thinking what I'm thinking?'

'Tell me what you're thinking, and I'll tell you.'

'I'm thinking that Monty's left her with a little bun in her oven that she's trying to foist on me.'

Marie hesitated, then answered very carefully: 'Well, it's not beyond the bounds of possibility.'

'She can't think much of me, can she? Not a glamorous actor from London, just a single lad,

284

still living in Hull with his mam. She must think I was born yesterday.'

Marie made no comment, but continued with the washing-up.

'Has she said anything to you?' George demanded.

'Yeah. She's said there's nothing the matter with her.'

'Well, time will tell.'

'It usually does, I can vouch for that. Have you heard about Charles and Hannah? It's telling there, all right: five months.'

He nodded. 'Nancy had time to tell me that, before she started chewing my face off.' He paused, to put some of the dried crockery into the cupboard, then said, 'I wouldn't wish this sort of misery on my worst enemy, I really wouldn't. And you're a good friend. I'm sorry it's happened to you, Marie.'

'So am I. Don't tell my mother. I don't want her worrying.'

'I won't. But I'll have that bastard actor. You just watch.'

'I am watching. And you watch your language, George. Remember there's a lady present.'

The opening bars of a nonsensical old comic song began to play on the wireless. George looked grim-faced. Marie stole a glance at him, and began to sing along, to the words of 'The Spaniard That Blighted My Life'.

'That's not funny, Marie,' he said.

Marie thought it was, and went on with the song in the most comical way possible, singing lustily about a dirty dog of a bullfighter had stolen the victim's future wife when he'd gone out for some nuts and a programme during the interval of the bullfight.

A smile began to crease the corner of George's mouth. He twisted the tea towel into a rope, and tried smacking her with it.

Laughing, Marie fended it off and snatched it out of his hand, missing a few of the lyrics and picking up the next, swearing revenge, and threatening all sorts of dire retribution, tra la la!

Having lost the tussle, George gave in, and joined her in the chorus, promising to dislocate the wife-stealer's bally jaw.

'I bloody will, as well,' George ended. 'He won't know what hit him.'

Marie laughed and snatching up a pair of spoons to use as castanets she went on with the song. After it was over she was helpless with laughter. George laughed at her laughter.

Auntie Edie came through the door, and infected by it, laughed until she started coughing. 'I bet they can hear you at the end of the street,' she wheezed.

Marie's mother stood in her nightie, peering over Edie's shoulder. 'Whatever are you laughing at?' she asked, with a smile that stretched from ear to ear.

That provoked more laughter, until George and Marie had laughed themselves to tears. When the merriment died away George leaned against the draining board, wiping his flushed face with his fingers and flicking the tears away. 'I mean it, as well,' he nodded. 'I will have my revenge.'

Later, after he'd dropped her outside the Elsworths' and roared back down the avenue on his motorbike, Marie remembered her words to him the day he'd lied to Mrs Harding to get Nancy's address. *Why not just let it go, George? It's eating you away*. What a bloody stupid thing to say to someone who'd had all their trust betrayed, and their fondest hopes smashed. Through no fault of his own the beautiful future George had planned for himself and Nancy in his little dream bungalow had vanished like a mirage in front of his eyes. Letting something like that go was a sheer impossibility, and the chances of her saying anything so idiotic to anyone, ever again, were beyond remote. She knew exactly what it felt like, now.

Chapter 24

George was looking pretty down in the mouth when Terry called for Marie the following night.

'You don't mind if he comes with us, do you, Terry?' she asked, knowing that Terry could hardly object, since he'd agreed they were going as pals.

Terry's face fell, just slightly. He had been signalling a pretty strong attraction to her, and Marie was determined to keep things cool. A third party would be no bad thing – there was safety in numbers. She'd had another letter from Charles that morning, swearing undying love for her, and she wanted no other entanglements until she'd talked to him, and heard him out. But that hadn't stopped her from letting the Elsworths know she was going dancing with Terry, and she took considerable satisfaction in the thought of their telling Charles, and of his torturing himself about it.

George demurred.

'Come on, it'll do you good,' Marie insisted. 'You'll be better off out enjoying yourself than staying in, dwelling on stuff that makes you miserable.'

George was adamant. 'No, thanks. I'm not fit company for anybody. I'd only spoil your evening.'

'What's he got to make him miserable?' Terry asked, when they got outside.

'Woman trouble,' was Marie's terse reply.

Terry crooned the romantic words of 'Night and Day' in her ear to the music of the band, and Marie relaxed into his arms as they swung into a slow foxtrot.

'This is not a bad way to mend a broken heart,' she murmured, 'although mine's nothing near as bad as yours.'

'I didn't know your heart was broken.'

'Honestly? I thought the whole of Hull would have known by this time.'

A spark of interest ignited in his eyes. 'Not me. Has Charles broken your engagement?'

'No. But he's been doing his bit for the woman who cleans for his mother, while her husband's on the convoys. She told me to tell him he's going to be a daddy.'

'That is bad,' Terry said, after a long silence.

'Both for you and for her husband. It's worse than what happened to me, in a way.'

'I don't know how.'

'Well, it's awful going back to an empty flat, especially after having a good wife to make things comfortable, and Margaret was the best. But I don't really feel as if I ever lost her, in spirit. She was always mine, absolutely, solid as a rock. This will sound barmy, but I still hear her talking to me, in my head. The way I feel, she's mine still, even beyond the grave. I don't feel a bit like people do when they get the push from somebody else. There's really nothing left, then. In a way that's a more final separation than death. In a way ... well, I'm talking a lot of rubbish, so I'll shut up.'

'I don't think you're talking rubbish at all. I think you've hit the nail on the head. Margaret would never have left you, like Nancy left George. Charles didn't leave me, he just chose to muck about with Hannah as well. I don't know which is worse.'

She was struck by the blue of those eyes that gazed straight into hers. 'I don't think Mrs Elsworth's charwoman will be much competition for you, somehow,' their owner said.

Marie smiled at the compliment. 'There's something about her, though, something sort of primitive; I can't explain it, but I can understand how a man might be led on.'

'Like that duet,' Terry said. '"Will you come into my parlour? said the spider to the fly."'

She gave a bitter laugh. 'Yeah, exactly like that. And he might be trapped in her parlour for good,

289

if he's not careful. Her husband's been reported lost at sea.'

'He's past caring, then. The husband, I mean.'

'He must be, mustn't he?'

Terry dropped her at the Elsworths' house, after the best night out she'd had for months. He was a brilliant dancer, and they were absolutely on the same wave length. Being with Terry was deeply comforting; he was so easy to talk to. So easy that she'd almost talked too much. She'd almost told him of her crushing disappointment at being robbed of her right to present Charles with his firstborn child, and how obsessed she was with the thought of Hannah, and Hannah's baby. Would it be a boy, or a girl? And which would her own firstborn be?

It was well past twelve o'clock when she let herself in with a key Mr Elsworth had given her. The family were all in bed.

'We've heard,' Marie's mother told her the minute she stepped into the front room late the following afternoon. Auntie Edie was looking on from the other armchair.

Marie's heart sank. 'Heard what?'

'Heard about that Hannah. She's having a baby to Charles Elsworth.'

'How have you heard?'

'From the neighbours. She's been mouthing off to them about it. She evidently expects him to do right by her, now her husband's gone. So where does that leave you?' her mother demanded. She looked even more ill than usual, her face more pale and drawn.

290

'I really don't know where it leaves me. I'll be able to tell you that when I've seen him, and heard what he's got to say.'

'Has he admitted it?'

'He's admitted it might be.'

'My God. My poor lass.' What little colour there was in her mother's face drained, until she looked almost translucent, and Marie felt a stab of fear for her.

She sat on the bed and took hold of her hand, looking intently into her eyes. 'Don't worry about me, Mam. I'm a big girl now. I can look after myself.'

'You shouldn't have to,' Auntie Edie said. 'He should be looking after you, if you're engaged. But if that baby's his, she'll make him pay for it. She's not the sort to let him off scot-free. I'm just thankful George has finally seen the light about that Nancy. Finally.'

The two older women exchanged glances loaded with meaning, then her mother spoke up. 'It's a pity you and George can't get together. He'd never do a rotten trick like that on you. He'd look after you. I never liked *him*. I never liked Charles Elsworth. Been to Hymers, and university, and thinks it gives him the right to look down on everybody else. They're just full of themselves, that lot.'

'No, he doesn't,' Marie protested. 'Chas doesn't think he can look down on everybody, and his family have been all right to me. Anyway, can we drop the subject? I'll decide what I'm going to do when I've seen him.'

Marie went to see Nancy after she left Aunt

291

Edie's, fully expecting to have the door slammed in her face on account of her unavoidably close contact with George, but Nancy seemed glad to see her.

'My mother's out, so we can talk,' she said. 'How's George?'

'All right.'

'He hasn't been to see me since…'

'Since you scared him off when you told him to lock the door.'

Nancy's lip curled in scorn. 'Oh. He went tittle-tattling to you about that, then? I thought he might.'

'I wouldn't have known otherwise, would I?'

'No, you wouldn't. He'd make a better maiden aunt than a fiancé. And what did you say?'

'As little as possible.'

'Did he say whether he was coming back?'

'I don't think he will be coming back, Nance.'

'I can't believe it,' Nancy said. 'I can't believe he'd just chuck me like that, without a word.'

Marie couldn't prevent her eyebrows twitching upwards, but she managed to keep her face deadpan. 'Yeah, it is a bit hard to swallow, isn't it?'

Nancy failed to detect the irony. 'He's a rotter,' she said. 'They're all rotten. You can't trust any of them.'

'Well, I'm in no position to contradict you, am I? Considering what Chas has done. Have you heard anything from Monty?'

'No.'

'Try asking your mother's lodgers. One of them might know where to find him.'

'She's already asking them, on account of the

rent. Nobody knows him, or if they do, they're not telling. Anyway, I'm not sure I really want to find him.' She was silent for a moment, then said: 'I went to see Matron at the Western Infirmary, to see if I could carry on with my training. So she asked for references, and I daren't give her any, so she's given me a job as an auxiliary. An auxiliary, when I was nearly ready to take my finals! What a mess. What a bloody mess I've made of my life, Marie.'

Marie didn't ask her outright if she was pregnant. Nancy was denying it, but she would never have behaved like that with George unless she had been, and pretty desperate, too. Marie racked her brains to find a glimmer of hope somewhere in Nancy's situation so that she could offer her a few words of comfort, but glimmers were thin on the ground.

At around three o'clock that night Marie woke to a hammering at the door. Her first thought was that an ARP warden had seen a light somewhere. She dashed downstairs in the dark, holding on to the banister for safety.

It was George, on foot because of the blackout. 'Your mother's taken poorly, Marie, and she won't let us send for the doctor. She's that breathless, it's scaring the life out of my mam.'

'I'll come straight away,' Marie said, and bolted back up the stairs to get dressed.

Mrs Elsworth appeared at the top of the stairs, and called to George to come in and wait in the hallway.

'Dad would never pay the shilling a week to get

on a doctor's panel,' Marie said, as she passed her on the landing. 'That's why she won't send for one. She'll be scared of what it'll cost.'

'I'll send for Dr Thackeray. I'll phone him while you get dressed, and tell him to send the bill to us.'

'Thank you. Oh, thank you!' called Marie. She threw her clothes on as quickly as she could, and then went with George down to Clumber Street.

'If you don't want to take money from them, I'll pay the bill,' he offered, as they hurried along.

'I hate taking the money from anybody,' Marie said. 'I just wish Dad had paid to get us on some doctor's panel. But he lost all faith in doctors, and Mam just went along with most of his ideas. He reckoned if you got a good meal down you three times a day, a decent night's rest and plenty of fresh air, and a bit of fun now and then, you didn't need doctors.'

'I think your mother needs a bit more than that,' George said. 'She's wheezing like hell, and sweating like a bull. It's got my mother terrified – me as well, truth be known.'

When they got to Auntie Edie's, Marie found her mother every bit as bad as George had said. She could barely speak, and they had an anxious time of it, waiting for the doctor. George went to bed at around four o'clock, and Marie and Aunt Edie sat dozing in the dark in the armchairs, opposite each other.

'Can't do anything,' Marie heard her mother murmur, an hour or so later. 'My poor bairn ... Charles Elsworth.'

Marie was up and out of her chair in an instant,

and standing by her bed.

'What did you say, Mam?'

'I can't do anything,' her mother wheezed. 'Nothing to help you.'

Marie squeezed her hand. 'You just rest, Mam. I don't need any help. I can look after myself – I've told you that.'

'You can't. Marry George ... good lad ... look after you. Better than Charles. Tell her, Edie.'

But Aunt Edie was asleep. 'Don't talk,' Marie said, 'it's making you even more breathless. Close your eyes and rest. The doctor will be here soon.'

'I'm not going ... to hospital,' her mother gasped.

'We'll talk in the morning, when you're a bit better.' Marie wiped her mother's clammy forehead, and sat her forward to plump up the pillows, then left her to sleep, taking up her vigil in the armchair for the rest of that warm July night.

It was almost five o'clock before Dr Thackeray arrived, and Marie trusted him on sight. Middle height, middle-aged, solemn, calm, grey-haired and mild-mannered, here was a man they could have faith in. He took a brief history, and then did a thorough examination. Apart from gasping out an absolute refusal to go to hospital, Marie's mother was in no position to resist.

'Acute heart failure,' he said. 'People can recover from it, sometimes even without treatment. Keep her in bed. I see you've given her plenty of pillows. That's good; keep her sitting up. And give her these pills. They'll get rid of the fluid. These others are to strengthen her heartbeat. I've given you enough to last until you can get the pre-

295

scription from the chemist tomorrow. I'll look in to see her then.'

He saw Marie's expression, and gave her a few words of reassurance. 'It's not hopeless. She might recover, with careful nursing. It's amazing what people can survive, if they've got the will. Is she a fighter?'

'She always was,' Marie said, 'although I think a lot of the fight's been used up. How much she's got left, I wouldn't like to say. She's taken too many beatings lately, one way and another.'

Chapter 25

George was up at seven to go to Dunswell on his motorbike, to tell the family there before he started work. As soon as the shops opened Marie left Aunt Edie watching over her sleeping mother and went to the chemist to get the prescription and then to the nearest public telephone box. Mrs Elsworth answered the ring.

'Dr Thackeray's been,' Marie told her. 'What a nice man. He says it's not hopeless, but she's pretty bad. It could go either way. I'll be staying with her, until I know what the outcome's going to be. And thanks for recommending him, not to mention offering to pay his fee.'

'Don't mention it,' Mrs Elsworth said. 'And if there's anything else we can do, let us know at once. By the way, there's a letter from Charles in the post this morning.'

'For me?'

'Of course, for you. I'll send Danny down with it.'

Next Marie rang Bourne, and left a message for Pam. The very thought of Bourne and the Stewarts brought Alfie and the Mortons into sharp focus in her mind, but she made no mention of them, and neither did Mrs Stewart, who sounded very sympathetic and promised to tell Pam the news about her mother as soon as she got in from school.

When Marie approached the corner of Clumber Street she nearly bumped into Nancy's mother, coming out of the Co-op.

'There's less and less decent meat. All I could get was sausages. Links of mystery, I call them. I hope it's not horsemeat; I've heard they're passing that off on people now,' she said, and hesitated for a moment before adding: 'I've heard about Charles and that Hannah, by the way. I don't usually stick my nose into other people's business, and it might sound funny coming from me, with Nancy going off and everything, but I was tied to a bloke like that.' A light suddenly seemed to come on inside Mrs Harding's head. 'That must be where she gets it from! She takes after *him!*' she exclaimed, and nodding to herself she left Marie and walked on, without another word.

When Marie got back to Clumber Street Uncle Alfred and Auntie Dot had arrived, with Alfie.

'She's not going to die, is she?' Alfie demanded, the usual light of mischief absent from his eyes.

Marie put a warning finger to her lips. 'Ssh.

People can hear, even when they seem to be asleep sometimes.'

'Make them a cup of tea, Marie, and talk in the dining room. I'll stay in here with your mam,' Aunt Edie said.

'She's not going to die, is she?' Alfie repeated, the minute they were in the kitchen and out of earshot.

Marie stroked back his hair, and looked into his eyes. 'You're beginning to get some sense now, Alfie, so I'll give you it straight. Truth is, I'm no wiser than you. All I can say is the doctor's been, and he says if she's got any fight left in her, she might get better. And it's only a might.'

He stood back from her, and folded his arms. 'Well, I'm staying here, until she does.'

Marie shook her head. 'Oh no, you're not, my lad. For one thing, this isn't our house, and Aunt Edie's got enough to do with looking after Mam. I'll have to wake her to give her her pills soon, so you can stay and have a few words with her, and as soon as she's too tired to talk, you're going back with Uncle Alf and Auntie Dot.'

Uncle Alfred backed her up. 'That's right. If you want your mam to get better, the best thing you can do is leave her in peace, and not give her anything to worry about.'

'You all right, Alfie?' their mother smiled, as he squeezed her hand half an hour later.

Alfie nodded. 'Yeah, but I'm staying here until you get better.'

Alarm filled their mother's eyes. 'No. No. Go back to ... Dunswell ... safe there.' She gave him

298

a wan smile, the rest of her effort concentrated on getting her breath.

Marie ushered him out of the room. 'All you're doing is upsetting her,' she said. 'It'll make her worse, not better. You get back to Dunswell, like you've been told. I've got enough to worry about, without any of your nonsense.'

'Well, I'm coming every day after school, then. I'll come on my bike.'

'All right, and you go back well before it gets dark.'

There was a raid that night. The warning came at five to one, and George took Aunt Edie to the shelter, begging Marie to go with them. But taking her mother to the shelter, or even to the understairs cupboard was out of the question, and Marie insisted on staying with her. The bombs began their screeching descent at about ten to two, exploding so near that while trying to comfort her mother by holding her hand, Marie began to shake uncontrollably, unable to stop her teeth from chattering. Whether her mother felt any terror or not was hard to tell; if she did she was too ill to show any sign of it. When the all clear came at twenty minutes past three, Marie could have collapsed with relief.

'None of them had our names on it tonight, then, Mam,' she said, marvelling that they were still alive and whole.

'Thank God,' her mother whispered. 'Thank God. My poor lass.'

Thank God indeed, Marie thought, wondering if they'd be quite so fortunate next time there was an air raid.

George got home from work just as Marie was laying the table for tea.

'Sidmouth School copped it,' he told her, 'and some houses on Anlaby Road and North Hull Estate. A bit too close to home, that, wasn't it? Twenty-five people dead, and about thirty seriously injured. Plenty of clearing up for us to do, as usual. I'm starving.'

Half of those seriously injured would probably die before they were much older, just like her mother was threatening to do now, Marie thought. Half of the seriously injured might as well be counted among the dead from the outset. Some might not even last the day, like that burned fireman she'd seen in the infirmary. And Sidmouth School was right next to Dad's allotment, barely half a mile away. Thank God she'd insisted on Alfie going back to Dunswell. He'd probably have gone dashing off to the ARP station and maybe got himself killed otherwise.

Alfie emerged from the kitchen, where he'd put some eggs on to boil. 'Hello, George.'

'What are you doing here? I thought your mam told you to stay in Dunswell.'

'Don't be like that,' Alfie said. 'I *am* staying in Dunswell. I only came to see my mam and our Marie. And I've brought you six eggs for your tea.'

'Good. I'll be doing a bit of overtime after I've had something to eat, and you'll be going straight back to Dunswell.'

'I know. Our Marie's already told me.'

After the meal, when George and Alfie had

gone, Marie gave her mother another dose of the pills the doctor had prescribed. She collapsed back against her pillows, seeming exhausted by the effort of taking them. 'Our Pam lives in Bourne now,' she gasped. 'She'll be all right ... and Alfie's settled with Dot and Alf... There's just you, our Marie ... my poor lass. Who'll take care of you?'

'Don't worry your head about Marie, Lillian. We'll look after her. Me and George,' Aunt Edie piped up.

'Don't worry about anything, Mam. You're going to be all right. Your breathing's better already. Just you take your pills for a few more days, and you'll be as right as rain.'

Her mother shook her head. 'I doubt that, somehow,' she said.

When she'd gone to sleep, Marie sank into the armchair opposite Aunt Edie, looking forward to a comfortable hour or two listening to the wireless. But within a few minutes a frantic knocking at the front door disturbed her. She got up to answer it and was confronted by Danny Elsworth, red-faced and sweating.

'It's Alfie!' he gasped. 'Alfie's in hospital – going to hospital – in the ambulance. Charles, as well.'

'Alfie's in hospital?' Marie repeated. 'He should have been back in Dunswell. And Charles – what's he doing here?'

'He waited for you all day, Marie, and when you never arrived, he set off to come and find you.'

'Waited for me? I didn't even know he was at home.'

'I brought you his letter!' Danny protested. 'Didn't they give it to you?'

'I've had no letter,' Marie said.

Aunt Edie called from the doorway of the front room. 'Oh, sorry, Marie. With your mother being so poorly and everything, I forgot to mention it. It's still on the mantelpiece.'

'Well, he's home,' Danny said. 'And if he hadn't been, Alfie would probably be dead by now.'

Marie's knees turned to water. 'Oh, my God, come through to the kitchen, where we can talk without waking Mam. It might finish her off, if she hears.'

He shook his head, and backed away. 'I can't wait. I'll have to go and find Dad, and tell him about Charles.'

Marie stepped out of the house and closed the door, to prevent her mother from hearing anything.

'Wait, Danny. Calm down, and take two minutes to tell me what's happened.'

'I saw Alfie when he was on his way here. He said: "I'll go and see how my mam is, and then why don't we go and have that game of billiards before I bike it back to Dunswell? We could go up and see what damage they've done to Sidmouth Street and North Hull, as well." We agreed to meet on Marlborough Avenue after tea, so that's what we did. And then we saw Jenny. She was playing in the garden of that bombed house, the one that copped it on the same night as yours. We shouted to her to come away, and as soon as she saw Alfie her face lit up and she waved and came running towards us, and then – she just disappeared! We went to see what had happened, and where she'd been standing there was nothing but a hole, as deep as a grave, and it seemed to go into a tunnel. She started screaming, so we shouted to her and she answered, and then quick as lightning Alfie grabbed a length of washing line that was lying in the garden, and jumped down the hole to tie it to her for me to pull her up. And then I had a horrible thought that there might be an unexploded bomb down there, so I started shouting for help. And then both of them stopped talking. I knew then there was something really bad happening – they were both just sitting at the bottom of the hole...'

He paused for breath, his eyes flitting from side to side as he relived it all. 'Some people were coming out of their houses, rushing across to us to see what was up, and then I saw Charles. He just got into the hole really carefully and lifted Alfie out, and he told the people to call an ambulance, because it was gas, and Alfie was sick all over him, and then he passed out. So I started giving him artificial respiration, and Charles got Jenny up. She'd passed out, and she looked all red, so somebody started giving her artificial respiration. Charles was trying to take some deep breaths and then he just sat on the pavement with his feet in the gutter and his head in his hands. Then the ambulance came and Jenny started having a fit while they were lifting her into it. One of them said "My cat weighs more than this bairn. She's half-starved." Oh, it was terrible, just about the worst thing I've ever seen. I went straight home to tell Mum, but she must be at the WVS, so I'm going to find Dad now.'

'What about Hannah? Have you told her?'

As if to hide sudden tears, he turned quickly away and mounted his bike. 'Yes,' he choked, and sped off without another word.

'Which hospital, Danny?' Marie called after him.

He stopped, and shouted from halfway down the street, 'Children's, I suppose. And they said they'd take Charles to the Naval Hospital. He was still in his uniform.'

Marie went first to the Children's Hospital on Park Street. When the gabled red-brick building came into view, she thought she ought to be sick of the sight of hospitals but the façade looked solid and comforting. She hurried through the tall double doors and a sympathetic porter confirmed that the two children had been admitted. He let her in, and as she sped across the tiled floor she felt as if she were coming home. Here, as in Hull Royal, the patients' washbowls would be given out at six, then would come breakfast, and the making of beds. Temperatures, dressings, doctor's rounds, surgical lists – all would be done at the proper times and in the prescribed manner in an invariable routine that left you little time to worry about anything else. The predictability of it all was deeply reassuring. The gates of Hell could not prevail against hospital routine.

'He's very poorly,' Sister told her when she got to the ward. 'The doctor's only just left him. He put him on oxygen. You can see him for a minute or two, and come back tomorrow during visiting

304

hours. He should be a bit better by then. Second bed on the left.'

'How's Jenny?'

'Are you a relative?'

'Just a friend,' Marie replied, failing to add: to Jenny, but not to her mother. How she detested Hannah. If she had been anything like a mother, none of this would have happened. Why couldn't she have left Jenny with Trudie, if she couldn't be bothered to take care of her properly?

'Then I'm sorry, I can't give you any information. We need to speak to her mother. I've asked the police to contact her.'

'She's that bad, then?' Marie said. 'Well, her mother got the message before I did, so she's had as much time to get here as me.' With that, she went to find Alfie.

He looked unnaturally rosy under the mask that almost covered his face. His eyes were red and he looked so gone that her heart nearly stopped. Please, God, she prayed, don't let our Alfie die. I don't think I'll ever get over it if he dies. There'll be a sore spot on my heart until the day I follow him.

He gave her a wan smile.

'I think this is the first time you've ever kept still since you learned to crawl,' she said softly.

'My head aches,' he whispered, 'really bad, Marie. I think my brain's trying to burst out. And my eyes are really sore.'

He was suffering, but she nearly wept with relief to find him conscious, and rational. 'They'll only let me stay a minute. Try to go to sleep when I've gone, and I'll come and see you tomorrow.'

'Head hurts too much. Go and see Jenny.'

'They won't let me. I'm not a relative, and I can't see her on the ward, so I can't even sneak a minute with her.'

Chapter 26

Of course they'd need to speak to Hannah, Marie thought, as she left the hospital. Jenny must be in an even worse state than Alfie, having been trapped in that awful hole for longer. She probably hadn't regained consciousness. And where the hell was Hannah? There should be no need for the hospital authorities to send the police to find her; she'd had the news even before Marie herself. She'd had ample time to get to Park Street. It was barely a ten-minute walk from where she lived.

But thoughts of Hannah receded during the short walk past the bombed ruins of Clarendon Street, towards the Naval Hospital on Argyle Street. She was going to see Charles, to thank him for rescuing Alfie and Jenny, and that was all she cared about. What might have happened to them, but for him, was something she didn't dare to dwell on. Bursting with love and gratitude, and even ready to overlook his affair with Hannah, she entered the heavy oak doors of the hospital, and after a few brief words with the porter she found Charles's ward – and stopped in her tracks.

There he sat, with an oxygen mask clamped to his face, and *she* was with him – her chair right beside his! The face of it! With her luxuriant auburn hair done in the latest style she was dressed to the nines in black widow's weeds so cunningly cut that they managed to disguise her pregnancy. She looked like a fashion plate. No trouble or expense seemed to have been spared on this magnificent parade of her terrible grief. The outfit must have cost a packet, not to mention the clothing coupons. Marie's first instinct was to turn and march out of the ward, and then she stopped herself. She had a message to give.

She approached them, and gave it. 'They want to see you at the Children's Hospital, Hannah. Jenny's there.'

'Oh, she's in safe hands, then, isn't she?' Hannah smiled. 'She's a disobedient child, that girl. I've told her a million times not to play on bomb sites.' Hannah's eyes flickered over Marie's unmade-up face and workaday clothes so pointedly that she was glad she'd remembered to take her apron off before dashing out of the house.

She gave Hannah a sour look. 'That girl, as you call her, is probably at death's door, considering they've sent the police out to find you.'

'They haven't given me much chance then, have they? I'm going there now.'

'You've had enough chance to get here, and it's further away.'

'Well, naturally, I came to thank Charles, and give him the news. In case you hadn't. But this one will be a boy,' she said, patting her bump. 'I'm sure of it. I'm carrying him different from the way I carried Jenny.' She put a caressing hand on Charles's shoulder and gave him a seductive smile.

'Bye for now, Charles. See you later, love.'

Marie watched her out of the ward, and then sat in the empty chair, still disgustingly warm from her. All the words of gratitude and thanks she'd meant to pour into Charles's ear were scorched to ashes by burning resentment.

'She was quick off the mark. I bet she was putting the lipstick on before Danny had finished telling her.'

Charles lifted his mask. 'She needn't have bothered on my account. I certainly didn't ask her to come, but I couldn't stop her. I haven't exchanged two words with her. I have got a headache, though, in case you're interested.'

'Well, I'm sorry about that, and I'm sorry I was so slow getting here, as well. I'm obviously not as fast as her, in any sense of the word. Trust her to be first on the scene to mop the fevered brow. Most mothers would have gone to their own child's bedside before anybody else's. What did she say?'

'What do you think she said? I'll give you three guesses.'

'Oh, yes. She told me, didn't she? She "came to thank Charles and give him the news". Would the thanks be for saving Jenny's life, or for putting her in the family way? I suppose she told you she's free to marry, as well, now her husband's conveniently dead. So why don't you get a move on and put up the banns? You might just manage to get the ring on her finger before she goes into labour, if you're quick enough.'

He looked at her as if she'd slapped him. 'You certainly know how to put the boot in when somebody's down, don't you? You're in a bigger rush than her. Don't we have to wait seven years before disposing of a man's wife and chattels when he's lost at sea? He might come back and claim them, after all.'

'In wartime? When his ship went down with all hands, after being torpedoed? When his name's going on the roll of honour of men who gave their lives for their country? I shouldn't think so,' Marie said acidly. 'Knowing her, I should think she could easily get a dispensation from any seven-year rule.'

Charles tore off his mask. 'All right, then. You look me in the face and tell me you definitely don't want me. Now. And I will, I'll marry her. Just to please you.'

Marie looked him in the face – and couldn't bring herself to tell him any such thing.

A staff nurse heard the argument, and came hurrying down the ward to her. 'I'm afraid you'll have to go,' she said. 'You're upsetting the patient.'

'If she's going, I'm going with her,' Charles announced.

'I wouldn't advise it,' the staff nurse told him, 'and neither would the doctor. He might report you to your commanding officer.'

'Bring me the discharge papers at once,' Charles insisted. 'I'll sign on the dotted line.'

Marie was appalled. What was she doing, picking a quarrel with the man who'd just saved her brother's life? 'No, you won't, unless you want your discharge papers from me as well,' she said. 'You stay here, and do as the doctor tells you. I'll come and see you tomorrow.'

309

'Marie! I love you! You're the only woman on earth I'm interested in,' he called after her as she left the ward with tears of anger and frustration in her eyes. She didn't even turn round. On her way to the hospital she'd imagined a touching scene of tenderness and reconciliation. On the walk back she berated herself for allowing Hannah to goad her into turning it into one of bitterness and recrimination. She felt wrong-footed and put in the wrong, when in reality it was he and Hannah who were in the wrong, not her. And what red-blooded woman could have held it all in? Really and truly, though, who could have? Charles might have saved Alfie's life, but he still had a lot to answer for. He couldn't expect to wipe everything else out because of that.

Marlborough Avenue was not much out of her way, and the temptation to see for herself the scene of so much injury to people close to her was too much to resist. The place was easy to find. It had been roped off and a couple of UXB notices marked the spot. Had it not been so late she would have gone on from there to see the Elsworths, but that would have to wait until tomorrow. Danny must have told them what had happened by now, in any case.

Although it was getting dark, before she returned to Aunt Edie's she knocked on the door of the woman who lived opposite Hannah, and whom she'd met before, and asked her to get a message to Trudie. She had a right to know what was happening to her granddaughter, and there was no guarantee she would find out from Hannah.

Chapter 27

George got home just before blackout at half-past eleven, looking dead on his feet, with the news that some kids playing in the debris of that bombed house on Marlborough Avenue had fallen into a camouflet, and were lucky to be alive.

'Those kids were my brother and Jenny,' Marie said, pouring two cups of weak and milkless tea.

'Alfie? He should have been back in Dunswell.'

She handed him a cup. 'Yeah, he should, but the little bugger decided he'd meet Danny Elsworth for a game of billiards before he went. There's a scone there your mother left for you before she gave in and went to bed.'

He took the scone and walked out of the kitchen and into the dining room.

Marie followed. 'What is a camouflet?'

'It's when a bomb goes off underground without enough of an explosion to break the surface, so that instead of a crater you get a hole filled with gas and smoke. Sometimes the crust will hold for weeks and stand walking on, sometimes it gives way at the first touch. I had an inkling it might have been Jenny, as soon as we got the news. I've warned her off what's left of your old house a few times. But I never reckoned on Alfie.'

'They're both in the Children's Hospital now.'

He gave a grim nod. 'Well, they're lucky. Fall into one of them and you stand a good chance of being gassed. They're generally full of carbon monoxide. The bomb disposal lads will be there tomorrow, then there'll be another job for the council, filling the hole in and making everything safe.'

'Did you know it was Charles Elsworth that got them out?'

'No, I didn't. I didn't even know he was at home.'

'He'd written to tell me, but Aunt Edie put the letter on the mantelpiece, and forgot to mention it.'

His eyebrows twitched upwards, and he gave a wry smile. 'Forgot? Aye, I'll believe that. There are fairies at the bottom of our garden, as well. It's pretty obvious our mothers are plotting to get us fixed up with each other.'

'It hadn't escaped me. No offence to you, George, but the snag is, I still love Charles. I only realized how much when I went to see him in the hospital, and told him he'd better marry Hannah. He said if I could look him in the eye and tell him I didn't want him, he would. So I just stood there with my mouth open, and I couldn't say a word.'

'He called your bluff, then. But don't you believe it. I'd bet everything I've got left that he wouldn't have gone through with marrying Hannah, even if you had given him the boot. Only a lunatic would pick her as a life partner and the mother of his children.'

'It looks as if she's going to be the mother of one of his children, at least.'

'Oh, yes, I should have remembered that before I opened my mouth. Trust me to put both my size nines in it.'

'I'm absolutely churned up about it all, George.'

He gave her a look of the purest sympathy. 'I pity you then, because I've got past that stage – well past it – and the proof is that we've tracked the actor down to Scarborough, and if Nancy won't prosecute him, I'll prosecute her. I'll show her up in court. I'll crush her, for what she did to me. How's that for a cure for what ailed me?'

'Pretty convincing,' she said, slightly repelled by his vindictiveness, and by his pride in it.

'Well, don't despair. I was once as smitten as you are, and Nancy cured me in the end, just by being her devious, self-centred, deceitful little self. Fair dos, though, Charles risked a whiff of gas to get your brother and Jenny out of a hole. He deserves credit for that. But he's an arrogant, selfish bugger at bottom, and when it finally dawns on you, the churning up will stop, and you'll realize what a lucky escape you've had.'

'Maybe,' she said. 'I hope to God the sirens don't go tonight. That would just put the tin lid on it all.'

'Wouldn't it just,' said George.

'Don't let yourself get carried away with gratitude, will you?' Charles said, as they walked together in Pearson Park the following afternoon, after a visit to the Children's Hospital to see Alfie. 'I've moved heaven and earth to get a few days' leave, and risked life and limb to rescue your delightful younger brother and his little pal, and you've hardly got a civil word for me.'

'I am grateful to you. If Alfie had died ... well, I

don't want to think about it. I've already said I'm grateful, and if that were all you'd been doing, I'd have a million civil words for you. But it's not.'

'Oh, her again. Well, I'm sorry, Marie. I'm really sorry. I've said I'm sorry a dozen times, and I mean it, but she absolutely threw herself at me. What man turns it down?'

Her eyes narrowed, and her lips pursed. 'We were courting,' she reminded him.

'We weren't engaged.'

'No, we certainly weren't engaged. My friends were beginning to think I'd die an old maid. You were never keen to get engaged at all, as I remember.'

'I was keen. I just wasn't keen on rushing it,' he said. 'Because I knew once I was engaged, it would have to finish with her. And I did. I told her she'd have to find another husband substitute before I gave you the ring.'

'That must have been a wrench,' she said, with a sarcastic little toss of her head.

Charles's expression was wide-eyed, open and candid. 'It was, to be honest. It's a big hold over a man. If somebody's dishing it up on a plate for him, he can hardly help himself.'

'*You* can't, obviously,' she said, and a vision of their last parting on the station platform rose before her, when she'd thought him so tender and romantic. Now she knew him for the calculating, double-dealing swine he really was. He might have been grappling with Hannah that very morning, for all she knew. 'No wonder you waited till the last bloody minute, though, hey?' she said, and her disgust must have shown on her face.

'Don't look like that! I'd never have been able to keep up the good boy act with you otherwise. If it hadn't been for her dispensing her favours, you might have got ravished. Because you never let the brakes off. You've never let yourself go yet.'

And no wonder, Marie thought. She'd always had her father's warnings ringing in her ears: *Don't you dare bring any trouble home. We've enough to do without that, thank you very much.* And judging by Hannah and Nancy and the mess they'd caused, her father had been right, as well. 'What I can't understand,' she said, coldly, 'is why you ever started it in the first place. She's at least ten years older than you, and she was your mother's cleaner, for heaven's sake. Talk about fouling your own nest. Not to mention the fact that she's married.'

'For the umpteenth time, Marie, I didn't start it; I'd never have thought of it. I was a good little boy, till I met her.'

'Oh, pull the other one.'

'It's God's honest truth. Look, I'll come clean. I'll tell you absolutely everything, make a good confession like they taught us when we were in infants' school, then you might stop going on about it. I was in bed late because I'd been a bit merry the night before. Mum was out with the WVS, Danny was at school and Dad was down at the repair shop, and she came into my bedroom and simply got in beside me. I wasn't even awake at the start; it was like some sort of fevered dream. You've seen her, how she walks, how strong she is. She's an Amazon. She was like some sort of wild animal. If I'd been wide awake, I'd have been terrified.'

315

It was the first time Marie had heard the details, and the thought of poor Chas cowering under his sheets sent a tiny smile flickering across her face. 'Why terrified?' she asked.

'Why? Because it's not what you expect. It's not the accepted way of going about things. It was scary at first because she made all the advances. It makes you feel like prey. I certainly understood what women feel like after the first time or two with her.'

'But you carried on.'

'It was exciting. And then later on, having her, at will, whenever I wanted, made me feel ten feet tall. In the end I didn't feel as if I could do without it. Not without *her*,' he hastened to add, looking her full in the face, 'without *it*.'

That was rather too much detail for Marie. 'Don't then,' she flared. 'Don't let *me* stand in your way. If she's so wild and exciting and animal that she makes you feel ten feet tall, you'd better get after her while you've got the chance.'

'I don't want the chance. Because I don't love her. And I don't want to spend the rest of my life with a bloody wild animal.' He tried to put his arm round her shoulder, but she shook him off. 'Come on, Marie,' he coaxed. 'Have a heart. It's over and done with.'

'How is it over and done with, when she's carrying your child?' she blazed. 'It goes on for ever!' She threw up her hands in a gesture of anger and frustration. 'And how you expected to carry on like that and not get her pregnant is beyond me.'

'The same way a lot of chaps do, by being careful. By getting off at Dunswell rather than going on to Hull. So to speak.'

'You missed your stop, then.'

He muttered something she couldn't hear.

'What did you say?' she demanded.

'I said I'd like to miss my stop with you. Several of them. You might like it as well. It might improve your temper. Look, I've still got that special licence in my pocket. We could get down to the registrar and tie the knot tomorrow before I have to pack up and go back to base. Rents are astronomical in the safer areas, but I've made a few enquiries and, with the married man's allowance, we could just afford it. Somewhere for you and your mother to live until the end of the war, I mean.'

Exhausted by everything, and especially by her efforts to get through to the morally defective, overgrown child beside her, Marie slumped wearily down onto a park bench and gazed unseeing at the still water of the pond. 'Oh, Chas,' she sighed, 'what a shambles. I couldn't move my mother anywhere, she's far too ill. Aunt Edie helps me with her, and keeps her fairly cheerful. I wouldn't like to have to manage without her now. My mother's better off where she is. And George is good to her as well. He even offered to pay for the doctor.'

Charles flung himself down beside her, scowling. 'I don't want George paying for the doctor; I don't want George paying for anything to do with you. I'll pay for it.'

'You know, Chas, this might be hard for you to grasp, but what you want is not the only consideration. You sometimes come up against what

317

other people want.'

'Well, what do you want? Just tell me.'

'I knew exactly what I wanted once, and now I'm not so sure. Everything seemed so simple and straightforward before, and now it's complicated and, well ... dirtied, somehow.'

He was silent. She turned to look at him, and saw that his hazel eyes were clouded, and his face drawn with anxiety. 'That's why you don't want to get married. It's nothing to do with your mother.'

'Maybe. There's a lot to think about.'

'They tell you that confession's good for the soul,' he said. 'Well, it ought to be, because it's no bloody good for anything else.'

She softened a little. 'I wouldn't say that. I'm glad you've been honest.'

He looked a bit more hopeful. 'I've been a reckless, irresponsible fool,' he said, 'and I'm sorry.'

'Just try to get it through your skull that a baby is no trivial matter, will you? It's serious, and you've got to face it.'

'I will,' he said, 'I will, if it's mine – but it might not be. Have you thought about that?'

She gave up.

Quite a quantity of Mrs Elsworth's flowers seemed to have survived the digging for victory campaign. Glorious yellow rambling roses covered the pergola, honeysuckle climbed the garden walls alongside beans and purple clematis. The red rose bushes had also escaped. California poppies, marigolds and nasturtiums blazed among the vegetables, and fat bees burrowed deep into the snapdragons, mining for nectar. It was all a feast for the eyes, and balm to Marie's spirit. But for the sturdy Anderson shelter, she could almost have forgotten there was a war on. The family were sitting round the cast-iron garden table, and Mrs Elsworth had the bone-china teapot poised to pour the tea. She looked up and smiled, but seemed very subdued, as did Mr Elsworth and Danny.

'How's Alfie?' she asked, when Charles had disappeared into the house for two extra cups and saucers.

'He's getting well enough to be a nuisance. They'll probably discharge him when the doctor's had a look at him. Tomorrow morning, at the latest. We couldn't find anything out about Jenny, though,' Marie said.

Danny suddenly got up and walked off down the garden.

'What's the matter with him?' she asked.

Mr Elsworth put a finger to his lips, and nobody spoke until Charles came back with the cups, then Mrs Elsworth broke the silence.

'Jenny's died,' she said, in hushed tones. 'We just had it from the people in Newland Park. Hannah told them. Danny's taken it rather badly, I'm afraid. He says he should have been first down that hole, and if he had been, he'd have been able to lift her, and she'd still be alive.'

It was strange, but for all the times she'd warned Jenny away from dangerous places, Marie had never really expected her to come to any serious harm. She'd thought of the little street Arab as having as many lives as a cat. The shock hit her hard. 'Knowing Alfie, he'd have been like greased

319

lightning,' she said. 'Danny wouldn't have had the chance to be first.'

Charles looked upset, and surprised. 'He can't blame himself,' he protested. 'He did everything he could for her. It was just one of those freaky accidents. It was nobody's fault, especially not Danny's.'

'Well, that's not what he thinks.'

'Silly boy,' Charles said. He put down his cup and went down the garden in search of Danny.

Marie knew whose fault the whole episode was, but she kept her own counsel. Openly blaming a grieving mother for her child's death would be bad form, and what good could it do anyway? Nothing could bring Jenny back to life. Her thoughts flew to Alfie, and Trudie. Neither of them was likely to take the news of Jenny's death very well, either.

'They're burying her on Monday. There'll be a service at that church at the end of the street, and then the cortège will go to Northern Cemetery,' the neighbour from the house opposite Hannah's said, when Marie opened the door to her at Aunt Edie's house. 'Trudie told me to let you know. How's your Alfie?'

'It's knocked him for six. He still feels washed out. I'm just getting a meal for us all, and then I'm taking him back to Dunswell where he'll be safe.'

'Your fiancé turned out to be quite a hero, didn't he? How is he?'

A slight stress on the words 'your fiancé', and the all-too-innocent expression on the woman's face, made Marie suspect that her curiosity was not entirely confined to Charles's heroism. 'He's made a full recovery. He went back to the army this morning,' she said, giving nothing else away. If this woman was expecting some verdict on their courtship she was going to be disappointed. Marie hardly knew herself what she would do.

Alfie came to the door. 'What time is it? What time is the funeral?'

'Oh, I forgot to say. Two o'clock. He does look peaky, doesn't he?'

Alfie disappeared back into the house, while the neighbour extolled his bravery and presence of mind, and lamented the fact that his efforts had not been better rewarded, or *her fiancé's* either, for that matter.

Marie cut her short. 'Did Hannah tell Trudie about the funeral?'

'Aye. I don't know whether she would have, but Trudie went to the hospital late last night. She was with Jenny when she died, and if Hannah had tried to get rid of her I think she'd have swung for her. Hannah's crying poverty now because Larry's pay stopped the minute his ship went down, so Trudie's paying for the funeral.'

'Well, she loved her granddaughter,' Marie said, 'and it was obvious that Jenny loved her.'

'She did. I could hardly look her in the face when she told me, I feel that bad about it all. I used to have Jenny in my house for hours on end while Hannah was gadding off here and there —and then my husband got fed up with it, and put a stop to her coming.'

'Are we going then?' Alfie demanded, when she got back to the dining room, which doubled as a sitting room when her mother was asleep, or needing peace and quiet.

'To Jenny's funeral? I wouldn't be welcome, Alfie.'

'You'd be welcomed by her grandmother, or she wouldn't have sent to tell you when it was. And I want to go.'

Aunt Edie backed Marie up. 'Funerals are no place for bairns. Besides, you'll be back in Dunswell.'

'What's the point?' Alfie demanded. 'There's only one day of school left, and then we break up for the summer. And if Danny can stay in Hull, I can't see why I shouldn't. I could live at his house. Mrs Elsworth would let me.'

'You're going to Uncle Alf and Auntie Dot, and that's all there is to it,' Marie insisted. 'But I'll tell you what. I can't take you to the funeral, but if Uncle Alfred will bring you down on Monday, we'll make two nice bunches of flowers. We'll go and lay one on Dad's grave at about three o'clock. Then when the funeral party's gone, we'll put the other one on Jenny's, and say a prayer for her.'

Not trusting Alfie's state of health enough to send him back to Dunswell on his bike, Marie took him on the bus, and spent an hour with her aunt and uncle before the long walk back to Aunt Edie's – with the customary and always welcome gift of half a dozen eggs.

She went to bed that night and slept the sleep of the just – until twenty past one. Then the sirens went.

Mass had just started at St Vincent's when she sneaked in at the back of the church that Sunday. The unchanging ritual, the lilt of Gregorian chant, the familiar responses, were reassuringly the same in a world that had changed. The incense intensified the effect. For Marie, it seemed the very smell of sanctity. It calmed and soothed her. The church was packed, and she spotted Mr Elsworth in the congregation. When Mass was over and people were filing out she stayed behind and lit a candle, thanking Heaven for Alfie's deliverance. Mr Elsworth came and stood beside her, dropped his money in the box, and put his candle beside hers.

'It's quite a conundrum, isn't it?'

'Devastating, I'd say, except for Alfie. With him, I feel as if I was waiting for the drop with the noose around my neck, and got the reprieve just before the trap door opened. Now I can breathe again.'

They went out of the church together.

'We haven't seen you since the day before Charles left. How is Alfie?'

'Much better. I took him back to Dunswell the day he was discharged.'

He looked a mite wounded. 'I thought you might have asked me for a lift. I wouldn't have minded a visit there; there's always something to learn from your uncle and aunt. But maybe you think I'd have been *persona non grata*.'

She smiled. 'Not at all. I was thinking of your petrol ration.'

'And your mother?'

'Her breathing's a bit better. George helps me

323

get her out of bed before he goes to work, and we put her back as soon as he gets home. She's weary by that time, so if he's late, Aunt Edie helps. Careful nursing, that's what the doctor ordered. And thanks for ringing him, and paying his bill. I'll pay you back.'

'It's not necessary.'

They walked in silence for a while, then Charles's father said: 'He does love you, you know.'

Marie gave a little laugh, and shook her head. 'Oh, I don't know.'

'He's been a complete idiot, and he regrets it. Bitterly.'

'"A man can hardly help himself" he told me. Well then, there's not much hope, is there?'

Mr Elsworth hesitated for a moment, then he said, 'You sometimes hear people say: the spirit's willing but the flesh is weak. But with most men of his age, the flesh is strong, very strong. If it weren't there'd be a lot less trouble in the world. But he has given her up, Marie, and honourable marriage to the woman he loves will keep him on the straight and narrow. I'm sure of it.'

She stopped, and looked him frankly in the face. 'There's a child.'

'I know,' he said, with a heavy sigh. 'I know. Come back with me for a cup of coffee. Marjorie would like to see you.'

'I was coming anyway. I wanted to beg some flowers from the garden, if you've any to spare? You've probably heard they're burying Jenny tomorrow. I won't be going to the funeral, but I'm taking Alfie to the grave afterwards.'

Mr Elsworth laced his coffee with condensed milk. 'I'm getting quite used to this stuff now. It's not bad.'

Danny followed suit. 'It's all right on a slice of toast, as well.'

Mrs Elsworth gave a grimace of disgust, but made no comment. They took their coffee into the garden, peaceful and with only the buzzing of insects and the chirrup of small birds to break the silence. A seagull soared overhead in a clear blue sky.

'They must have had a lively time of it in Central Fire Station, the night after Charles left,' Mr Elsworth remarked when they were seated. 'It sounds as if the whole of East Hull and Victoria Docks were demolished. They got Reckitts again, and Ranks flour mill, and Spillers...'

'And another air-raid shelter on Holderness Road got a direct hit,' Marie said. 'Poor people! I haven't seen Terry, but George says quite a number of bombs fell round the fire station as well. One of them didn't go off, so the station had to be evacuated except for the control room staff. I didn't sleep a wink after the sirens went, even though we got none of it, and East Hull got the lot. I'm just glad Alfie's back in Dunswell, out of the way of it,' she said, and then blushed. The Elsworths were keeping Danny at home, and she hoped they didn't think her last words a criticism.

Mrs Elsworth got to her feet. 'If any of us go, I hope we all go together,' she said, 'so there'll be nobody left to grieve, or struggle on alone. I'll fill a bucket of water, and then you can come and help me pick some flowers, Marie. Most of them are going to seed, but some of the roses are still good.'

They almost stripped the garden and then took flowers into the kitchen to wrap in newspaper.

'I suspected there was something going on,' Mrs Elsworth said, when they were alone. 'I wish I'd confronted them, but I was so afraid I might be imagining things, like some dirty-minded old woman. It's so difficult to accuse people of something like that. All my time was taken up with the WVS work, and the last thing I wanted was to have to do the housework myself, or even to look for another cleaner. And I suppose I didn't want to believe it. Other matters kept putting it out of my head, as well. I let it slide, I'm afraid.'

'By the time you suspected, it was probably too late anyway,' Marie consoled her.

'Rosemary for remembrance,' Mrs Elsworth sighed, adding several sprigs to the three bunches of flowers she was making. 'That poor little waif. Oh, Marie, she's having Charles's baby! My first grandchild! My grandchild, and what you said about the way she treated Jenny! I can't bear to imagine what sort of a life he'll have. And the most terrible thing is we're so helpless. What am I going to do?'

What made her so sure the child would be a he, Marie wondered. Maybe the fact that both her own children were boys made her think of babies that way. She racked her brains to find a glimmer of hope. 'Well,' she said, 'he'll be clean. She's a good cleaner.'

Mrs Elsworth turned back to her task. 'That's a great comfort. He'll be half starved, and half dressed, and left to roam the streets all night while she's out with God knows who, but really, compared to being clean, what does any of that matter?'

Marie started wrapping the flowers, the red roses against the newsprint impressed vividly on her eyes as a wave of anger rose within her. 'It's funny,' she said, 'Hannah's sure the baby will be a boy as well. No reason why Charles shouldn't marry her, now her husband's dead. Then the baby would at least have one good parent, as well as decent grandparents.'

At that suggestion, Mrs Elsworth's whole body seemed to slump. 'There's every reason why he shouldn't. He'd be miserable for the rest of his life. He doesn't love her at all, and he'd probably end up hating her. But the most important thing of all is: he loves you.'

'If he does, it doesn't seem to have got through to Hannah,' Marie said, starting on the second bunch. 'If you'd seen her at the hospital, you'd have thought he was already her property. She'll soon be presenting him with his firstborn son, and she's absolutely crowing about it. Judging by her hefty childbearing hips, I should think she's capable of bearing him a whole tribe.' Sheer anger made Marie's wrapping swift and deft.

'God forbid,' Mrs Elsworth shuddered. 'One's more than enough to worry about.'

Danny came into the kitchen as Marie started on the third bunch.

'Let me know when you're going, and I'll walk

with you. I'm going to call on a friend on Sunny-bank.'

She discovered Danny's ulterior motive as they neared Clumber Street, and the Maltbys' house, when he stopped and turned to her.

'You'll have to marry Charles now,' he said. 'It doesn't matter about Hannah. He saved Alfie's life.'

Marie took a moment or two to consider this piece of reasoning. 'I'm very grateful to Charles, but think about it for a minute, Danny. If an eighty-year-old hunchback had saved Alfie's life, would I have to marry him?'

Danny flushed. 'Of course not. That's silly.'

'And George saved my life. Does that mean I ought to marry him?'

'No, but you were never engaged to him in the first place.'

'Well, it just goes to show that the fact that anyone saved your life, or anybody's life, is not a good reason to marry them. The only reason to marry anybody is because you love them so much you couldn't think of marrying anybody else.'

'And do you love him so much?'

She turned, and walked away. 'It doesn't matter about Hannah,' Danny had said, but nothing could be further from the truth. Chas had carried on his affair with Hannah right up to their engagement. He'd two-timed her for months, and although she still loved him, Marie was sure of one thing. She meant to have a one-woman man, or none at all.

The sun was scorching her skin and a warm and

gentle breeze lifted her hair as she walked with Alfie under a clear blue sky down the pathway of Northern Cemetery to her father's grave. Wood pigeons cooed and a seagull soared silently overhead.

'It's really peaceful, isn't it, Marie? A nice place for them among the trees and flowers. I thought that when we came to see Dad's grave.'

Marie nodded. In the distance they saw the covering being dragged back from the grave as the funeral party arrived: not a great many people, just Hannah and a few of her relatives, Trudie and a few of her family, the vicar, and the bearers with their little burden.

Marie stooped and pulled dead flowers out of the holder on her father's grave. 'Take these to the bin, Alfie, and fetch me some water. Try not to stare, there's a good lad.' She pulled a trowel out of her bag, and occupied herself in digging out a few weeds.

When the graveside ritual was over, and the people were going, Trudie came over to speak to them. 'I thought I recognized you. You're Alfie. Yes, I saw you in the hospital, and the ward sister told me all about you. You're a brave lad.'

Alfie gave her a wan smile, but didn't speak.

'I'm so sorry,' Marie said. 'I couldn't come to the funeral. I don't know if you know the full story, but it would have been very awkward.'

'Oh, yes, I know the full story,' Trudie said, 'and I didn't really expect you. But you tried to help our poor Jenny, and I just wanted you to know, it's broken my heart, losing her.'

Marie squeezed her hand. 'We've brought a few flowers.'

'Come on, then.'

They followed her to the graveside. Alfie gazed down at the little coffin deep in the gloom of the earth, cut off from the drenching sunlight. After a minute or so he looked at Trudie, and thrust the flowers into her hand.

'She was running to me,' he said. Tears welled into his eyes and he sniffed hard, fighting desperately to hold them back. 'She was running – to *me*.'

Trudie pulled him towards her, and held him close, murmuring: 'Don't cry, don't cry,' while tears streamed down her own face.

Marie felt choked. Trudie dabbed her eyes and then left them to catch up with her own party. Marie tried to lead Alfie away, but he stood his ground. 'You said we were going to say a prayer.'

She thought for a moment, then recited: 'Grant unto her eternal rest, O Lord, and let perpetual light shine upon her. May she rest in peace.'

'Amen,' Alfie said, then added: 'She didn't want eternal rest, she wanted love, and sunshine. It'll be our mam next, you watch. Then that'll be the end of our family altogether.'

'No it won't,' Marie protested. 'She'll probably get better, and anyhow, you've still got me.'

'I don't think she wants to get better, and I won't have you, because you'll be married to Chas.'

'I doubt it. There's a lot that you don't know, Alfie.'

'If you mean about Chas and Hannah, I do

know,' he said.

'Who told you?'

'What does it matter? People talk, and if you keep quiet they don't even realize you're there.'

'Danny told you.'

'What does it matter, anyway? You'll still marry Chas. I know you will.'

'You mean you think I'll marry him because he saved your life.'

He looked surprised. 'That's got nothing to do with it.'

Marie frowned and shook her head, utterly perplexed. 'What on earth makes you think I'll marry him, then?'

He shrugged. 'Everybody knows. It's obvious you're dead keen on each other.'

She laughed aloud. 'How?'

'It's a way you try not to look at each other when other people arc there,' Alfie said, with another shrug. 'And then you steal a glance at him, and he catches your eye, and then you smile and look away, and he smiles and looks away. And he does the same thing.'

Marie smiled again, but briefly, at the memory of the first few months of their courtship. 'That was before you were evacuated.' It was also before she got to know about Hannah, but she didn't mention that.

'You'll marry him,' Alfie repeated.

'Even if I did, you could still come and live with us.'

He shook his head. 'I'll stop with Auntie Dot and Uncle Alf. Pam'll stop in Bourne, and she'll never come to see us. You'll be married, and that'll be the end of our family.'

Again she protested, but she had a horrible feeling he might be right. Alfie was facing it better than she could face it herself. This 11-year-old lad in his short trousers had suddenly become a man.

She went upstairs to bed that night feeling heartsick – and sick of feeling heartsick. She was wearied with all this grief and misery and pain. What was the point of living if there was no pleasure in life? She tossed and turned for hours, dreading the wail of a siren that never came. At daybreak, suspended between sleep and wakefulness, she dreamed of going home. The door was locked and barred against her, and try as she might at every door and window, she couldn't get in. She could see the battered brown leather suite, the small table and the lamp that stood on it in the shape of a wooden helm with a parchment sail, both made by her father while in hospital after the Great War. A fire burned merrily in the grate, and she could smell the lavender polish on the lino surrounding the carpet square. Alfie's train set was laid out on the carpet, and his aircraft recognition weeklies were piled on the settee, beside his cigarette card album, his shrapnel collection and his bag of marbles. It was vitally important to get them back, and Marie hammered desperately on the window. Jenny stood inside with her hands on her skinny hips, mouthing: 'It's my house now.'

'Wanna play battleships?' she heard Alfie's voice, but faint, and followed by an awful silence. Her heart stopped. She awoke with an empty, hollow feeling inside her, a hunger, a desperate craving for home and everything home had meant.

Terry knocked on the door the following afternoon, quite jaunty, despite the inferno of Thursday night. 'Fancy going for a jig before they drop the next lot of bombs?' he asked. 'There's sure to be a dance on somewhere.'

'Well, I'm glad to see you all in one piece. It took me hours to stop shaking after the last raid, even though it was all East Hull, and we got none of it.'

He gave a sardonic little chuckle. 'It certainly kept us jumping. Eighty-nine fires we had to tackle, and the biggest was at Spillers grain merchants in Cleveland Street. A silo with thirty-odd thousand tons of grain – we could have lost the lot. We daren't risk dousing it, because if it had swollen and burst the walls of the silo it might have ended up in the river. Imagine it – it could easily have stopped the traffic altogether. So we had to let it burn, just damp it a bit and get it away from the bottom of the silo.'

'Haven't you got any nerves at all, Terry?'

'Enough to keep me awake. To make matters better, a bomb had burst a water main, so we had to run the hoses to the river. But we managed to save most of it,' he added with a self-satisfied little smile, 'just so you can have your bread and jam.'

'Spillers would have been well named, then, if it had all spilled,' she said. 'I think ours is the only city that's had such terrific raids since the

Germans goose-stepped into Russia. They can't leave us alone. Is there some strategic benefit in killing us, or are we just the handiest target?'

'A bit of both, I think. What about it, then? Are your ribs better? I fancy going out for a dance before the next onslaught.'

'My ribs are all right, but – on a Tuesday? You find a dance anywhere, and I'll come. I could do with a change of scene.'

'He's here again!' George teased, when Terry called for her that evening, brushed, polished and clean shaven. 'Well, don't think you're going to hog her all to yourself, it's my turn next. I'm claiming the next outing.'

'What about Nancy?' Terry said, slightly taken aback.

'Oh, that's finished. I've transferred my affections to Marie, to use solicitor language. So watch out, you're not the only one in the running.'

'I didn't know I was in the running,' Terry said. 'I thought she was engaged.'

'I am,' Marie cut in, carefully made up and wearing a dress she'd tactfully borrowed from Nancy, rather than wear Margaret's again.

'Well, all's fair in love and war,' George grinned. 'Seems to be, now, anyway. So I'm playing by the new rules.'

'Not with me. Strictly as pals, George,' Marie repeated. 'Got it?'

'Anything you say, sweetheart. Have a good time.'

Terry offered Marie his arm. 'We will.'

She picked up her handbag and the drawstring

bag containing her dancing shoes and took it.

'Is that the same man we saw at the dance the other night? He's changed his tune. Seems quite chipper for a bloke who's just lost his fiancée,' Terry commented, as they walked away.

'Not so much lost, as dropped. That actor that she ran off to London with – he's discovered where he is, and he thinks he's going to get them both into court. He's obsessed with it.'

'Do you think he'll succeed?'

'I don't know. Nancy's not keen at all, but even if he does, I don't think he stands much chance of getting any of his money back. He'll just end up even further out of pocket, as far as I can see.'

'He's throwing good money after bad, then,' Terry said. 'Anyway, he's braver than me. I think I'd rather face another fire like Spillers than a court case. Good places to keep away from, courts. I've never heard of anybody coming off best in any court battle. I think I'd rather settle my differences man to man, and leave the law alone.'

'Pistols at dawn?' she laughed.

'Probably not pistols,' Terry said. 'Probably not at dawn, either. Maybe when he's on his way back to his digs, after the evening performance.'

There were a couple of other firemen out with their partners. They all did as much chatting together as dancing, about various incidents they'd dealt with, the people injured and damage done, especially at Reckitts. Listening to them, Marie yearned to get back into the thick of things.

'I've got to get back into nursing; I'm sick of standing on the sidelines, kicking around in the

335

house all the time,' she told Terry, when they took the floor for a quickstep. 'I wish my mother had gone to stay in Dunswell when I asked her to. If she had, she wouldn't have been blasted the second time, and maybe I wouldn't either. And our Alfie would never have come down here to get gassed – and maybe Jenny would still be alive, as well.'

He leaned back from her with a wry expression on his face and shook his head, his blue eyes looking directly into hers. 'Listen here, Marie, you can't think like that. You might just as easily have been injured somewhere else, so might Alfie. So might Jenny, and there are worse ways to go than carbon monoxide. Never dwell on what might have been. Never look back, unless you want to drive yourself mad. Just take life as it comes; it's the only way to survive. Besides, you're not on the sidelines. You are nursing – your own mother, and nobody needs you more.'

She was quiet for the rest of that dance. He was right, of course; she was nursing, but what she missed was the companionship of the hospital, the busyness, the being in the middle of the action, and the inspiration that came from knowing they were all working together towards the same end. Still, he was also right that it was pointless to dwell on things that couldn't be altered.

'My mother is ill,' she said, when the music stopped, and the master of ceremonies went to put another record on. 'Really ill. The doctor said she might recover, but she's not making much progress. I suppose I'd better telephone our Pam again, and tell her she might not have a mother much longer. It's up to her what she does about it. She can never say she wasn't told.'

'She's gone out,' Mrs Harding said, when Marie called round the following day to see Nancy.

'Will she be long? I've only nipped out for an hour while my mother's dozing. Aunt Edie's there, but still, I don't want to leave her too long.'

'Well, I'm not sure.' Mrs Harding hesitated, then glanced up the stairs before pulling Marie into the front room and closing the door in such a cloak-and-dagger fashion that Marie knew what was coming next. 'The lodgers are in, so we'll have to keep mum,' she said. 'Don't tell anybody else – especially George; she'd hate me if she knew I'd let on – but she's gone to the chemist. For some pills.'

'What sort of pills?'

'Pennyroyal. She's missed twice. She's hoping they'll make her come on. That's what they're supposed to do.'

Marie's eyes widened in alarm. 'I know what they're *supposed* to do, and I know what that stuff actually does. Don't let her take them. All they'll succeed in doing is poisoning her, and they won't get rid of the baby when she's done. I nursed a girl who'd taken that stuff as a tea, day after day, until she'd done herself so much damage she'd had it. She hung on for two months, and then she died of liver failure. And the doctor said that's what happens. It never gets rid of a baby – unless the mother takes enough to kill herself along with it. Nancy ought to know better.'

Mrs Harding put a finger to her lips, looking

pointedly upwards, indicating the lodgers. 'Ssh, don't talk so loud; they might hear. She's desperate. Desperate enough to risk it.'

'Don't let her do it, Mrs Harding. Just don't. Take them off her, and throw them on the fire.'

'Oh, Marie,' said Mrs Harding, wringing her hands in distress. 'If you only knew what she's going through, the tears she's cried. She's lost everything. Her nursing, George, that rotten actor and everything he promised her ... and George is pushing her into going to court, and she can't face it, the shame of it. She says it'll be all over the papers, and no bloke worth having will look at her again.'

Marie remembered George's eyes when he'd told her he had the actor's address, how they'd fairly glittered, like Shylock gloating over his pound of flesh. He'd turned so much against Nancy that he wouldn't care if he destroyed her. And here was Nancy, already desperate enough to kill herself. In Marie's book, her friend had been punished enough. Sheer pity overcame all her scruples about spoiling George's revenge.

'She hasn't lost everything,' she said. 'She's still got you, and she's got me. Maybe she'll have that actor, as well, if she goes to see him and gives him a chance to redeem himself. If it was a joint account, and Nancy had a right to draw the money, I don't see how there can be a case if she refuses to prosecute him, so she could give him a choice: make an honest woman of her, or she'll have no option but to do what George wants, and bounce him into court.'

'How can she? She doesn't know where he lives.

And George says he's definitely got a case against her and he'll do her, if she doesn't do Monty – and he'll do it, Marie. He will.'

'What would be the point, if she hasn't got a bean?' Marie said, and paused for thought. 'And Monty won't know that, will he? She could bluff him, turn the tables on him, take him in, just like he took her in. George has tracked him down to Scarborough; I'll give you his address. You and Nance could go together; you could be back before the end of his evening performance. You might tell him you'll do him for your rent, as well, if he doesn't do the right thing. Just don't tell a soul I suggested it. Don't tell on me, and I won't tell on you.'

Mrs Harding hesitated for a moment, then: 'It's worth a try, I suppose,' she said. 'If she can get him to the altar, the baby will have a name, at least, and she'll be able to hold her head up as Mrs Shite-hawk, even if he buggers off the day after. Although I'm not guaranteeing I won't kill him, if I lay eyes on him.'

Marie nodded, and pulled the lace curtains aside, to look down the street. 'I can't see George taking her to court; she's got nothing. It wouldn't be worth it. Well, she's nowhere in sight, so I'll be off. I want to telephone our Pam, and then I'll have to get back. Just don't let Nancy take those bloody pills, that's all.'

In the phone box she could hear the piano in the background when Mrs Stewart lifted the receiver. When the music stopped, and Pam came to the telephone, their conversation was short and to the point, just a few words from Marie telling her that if she wanted to see her mother alive again, she'd better make it soon, because later would probably be too late.

Lucky Pam, Marie thought, when she put the phone down. No bombs disturbed her pleasant, country mansion carry-on. She never had to puzzle over ration books, wondering how to make two ounces of butter and four ounces of bacon stretch a whole week, and then have to listen to some government spokesman on the wireless adding insult to injury by telling her how much healthier people were, for having so much less to eat. No sick, dependent relatives for Pam to worry about. Pam's lot was a safe and comfortable home, plenty to eat – without even having to queue for it herself – doting guardians, no respon- sibilities, and all obstacles to her hours of piano playing removed, so that her passion for music could be totally indulged. And a passion for music must be a better proposition than a passion for a man, Marie thought, especially a man like Charles Elsworth. Yes, the war was the best thing that had ever happened to Pamela Larsen.

The next onslaught, as Terry had called it, came that night. Again, East Hull was the target. As she sat at her mother's bedside thanking her stars that the bombs were not falling on her, Marie thought that the chances of Pam letting herself in for any more of this sort of terror were practically nil, mother or no mother.

In the evenings, as Marie washed her weary mother's grey, drawn face, and combed her lank and lifeless hair, she sometimes thought she was too ill to last the night, and then thought how sad it was that she should die so young, not yet fifty. Every night, her mother hung on, and woke the next morning not much better, but no worse. Alfie cycled down from Dunswell every other day to see them, and had ceased to protest at having to go back. The 'little rotter' seemed to have grown sad, and old beyond his years.

Saturday was the day that Nancy and Mrs Harding were going to Scarborough. Marie thought of them while working in the house, and later, while weeding and watering on the allotment, wondering whether she'd done right in suggesting they went to confront Monty. She'd been blasé at the time but, now it was too late, she began to dread the outcome, imagining a hundred snags and horrible developments. It served her right. Her anxiety was just punishment for her persistent meddling in other people's business. She gave a wry smile at the sudden thought that that was precisely what Chas would have said.

Chapter 28

On Sunday morning, as she walked towards the cemetery carrying two little posies, Marie saw Hannah coming towards her, dressed up and made up, but not looking very happy. No feral child to follow in her wake now, or watch her from a doorway. She went by without a sign of recognition, and Marie gave none either. Wherever she was trotting off to, it wouldn't be to see Charles, at any rate. When Marie arrived at Jenny's last resting place, the little grave was covered with flowers, and Danny stood there, alone.

'I was coming to see you,' he said. 'Pam telephoned, and asked us to tell you she's coming over on the ferry, tomorrow.'

'Well, you were wrong, Alfie,' Marie told him out of earshot of her mother, when he joined them for a meatless Sunday dinner. 'Pam's coming to see us – or she's coming to see our mam, at any rate. She's coming over on the ferry tomorrow.'

He pulled a face. 'I shouldn't think she'll be staying long. Next air raid, and she'll be off. Sooner, if anything.'

'I can't say I blame her for that,' Marie said.

Alfie's eyes narrowed, and his brows twitched together slightly. Dark suspicions had evidently sprung into his mind. 'Where's she stopping?' he demanded. 'Not with us, I hope.'

'Come on, Alfie. She's your sister.'

'I know she is. And I don't want her looking down her toffee nose at Uncle Alf and Auntie Dot.'

Marie laughed. 'Just tell 'em she's coming as soon as you get back, will you?'

After the meal was finished and the washing up done, Marie decided she had to know the worst about the Hardings' trip to Scarborough, rather than sit worrying about it. She left George reading his paper, and Alfie and Auntie Edie keeping her mother company, and went to see Nancy.

Mrs Harding answered the door, and gave her

a reproachful look. 'It was a disaster,' she said. 'An absolute disaster. She cried buckets on the way home. Honestly and truthfully, I know you meant well, but I wish we'd never gone.'

Marie's heart sank. 'What happened?'

'Go and ask her, she might talk to you. She hasn't said two words to me since we got back. She's upstairs, in the bedroom.'

Marie climbed the stairs to the bedroom that Nancy shared with her mother. She was sitting on a stool in front of the dressing table, brushing her fair hair and staring at her reflection. Their eyes met in the glass.

Nancy did not turn round. 'I heard you come in.'

'Nancy, I'm sorry. I'm sorry I ever suggested it.'

Nancy's chin jutted forward slightly. 'Have you got any money?'

'Not much,' Marie said, cautiously. 'Why?

'Oh, not for some backstreet abortionist, don't worry about that; I know what a moralist you are. I fancy getting out of the house for a bit, that's all. I fancy going to the matinée at the pictures.'

'I suppose I could go,' Marie said. 'George is in, and Aunt Edie. If they send Alfie for me, your mother will tell him where we are.'

They went to see Gloria Jean in *A Little Bit of Heaven* at the Carlton on Anlaby Road. Marie sat through the film with her mind only half on it, not daring to ask what had actually happened in Scarborough. Nancy said nothing about it until they left the cinema, then the floodgates opened.

'It turns out he couldn't marry me even if he wanted to,' she burst out. 'He's got a wife and three children living in Brighton, and he's got no intention of leaving them for me, he says – although I doubt very much that he ever goes to see them, either. The liar! The liar! When I think of the lies he told, Marie, deliberate lies: he knew why he'd never married, he was waiting for me, and all the rest of the shit he gave me while he was robbing me blind. And then, when I tell him I'm having his child, he calls me a silly tart! "Prove it," he says, "prove it's mine!" Well, he's shown himself in his true colours now, and if he thinks he's getting away with it, he's one off! I'll go to court – I'll tell them everything. You just tell George when you get back, he can get his solicitor pal to fix it up as soon as possible, just let me know the time and date. I want it over and done with before I start showing too much.'

'Well, he deserves it,' said Marie, at a loss for anything else to say.

'Hell, aye, he deserves it, and he's going to bloody get it. My mother wants her rent, as well. Montgomery Holmes! You know what his real name is? Bill Pratt!'

Although she'd already heard so from George, Marie nearly burst out laughing. What did I tell you? were the words that sprang to her lips, and it was as much as she could do to bite them back. 'I wish I'd never suggested you going to see him, though,' she said.

Nancy's cheeks flamed, and her eyes darkened with fury. 'I don't! I'm glad I went to see him. Yeah, I was upset yesterday – really upset – but this is today, and today I'm out for blood, because I know him for the rat he is. It's finally sunk in,' she said, and tapped the side of her head three times to emphasize the point. 'Clever, smarmy Billy Boy Pratt is going to see all his chickens coming home to roost before very much longer. He'll be laughing on the other side of his face soon. I'd get him hung if I could, for the way he's treated me.'

Marie was waiting on the quay when Pam walked down the gangway of the Hull ferry. The day was hot, but Pam looked as cool as a cucumber in an up-to-the-minute short-sleeved dress, the blue of which brought out the blue of her eyes. With the white hat, shoes, gloves and handbag she might have stepped straight off the cover of Vogue – except that she was far too young. It looked as if the Stewarts had ploughed every single ten and six they'd ever received into Pam's wardrobe, and a lot more besides. One of the ferrymen followed her, honoured to be carrying Pam's best suitcase, in toning grey. He put it down by Marie.

'How is she?' Pam asked.

'Not very well, or I wouldn't have phoned you.' Marie glanced at the suitcase. 'How long are you planning to stay?'

Pam gave her a quizzical look. 'I don't know, it depends how ill she is. You said she was dying.'

'I often think so, especially at night. I never expected you to come, though.'

Pam's face resembled chiselled marble. 'I love my mum,' she said coldly, 'in spite of the way you try to make me feel. I was lucky when I was evacuated, that's all, and I don't see why I should apologize for it to you. Auntie Morag – I mean

Mr and Mrs Stewart – didn't want me to come at all. They said it's not safe. And it isn't safe. The Germans are bombing Hull as much as ever they did, in spite of being in Russia. They thought I should just write a nice long letter every day, that someone could read to her. But I'm not very good at writing letters.'

'Well, we'd better go and get the bus, then,' Marie said, setting off in that direction.

Pam hesitated for a moment, and then picked up her suitcase, and followed.

When they boarded the bus, Marie made for a seat on the lower deck, but in spite of her suitcase, Pam started up the stairs.

'Why are you lugging it up there?' Marie asked.

'You can see more from the top deck,' Pam said. 'I want to see everything.'

They travelled through the town centre and along Spring Bank with a good view of all the devastation, but apart from occasional murmurs of 'it's terrible', and 'it's awful', from Pam, little was said. Later, as they walked towards the pile of rubble that had been their childhood home, Pam's pale face blanched further. They came to a stop, and surveyed the wreckage.

'I don't know how you got out of it alive,' Pam said.

'We nearly didn't. And your mam's gone into a decline since, that's for sure.'

Pam shivered. Marie glanced at her face, and guessed at the unspoken thought: *If I'd stopped here, I'd have been under all that.*

'Mrs Elsworth invited me to stay with them,' Pam said, 'but I'm not going to. It'll be a nuisance having to travel every day, but I'm going to stay with Auntie Dot and Uncle Alfred.'

Their mother's eyes lit up at the sight of Pam. She smiled, and came to life.

Pam returned the smile. 'How are you, Mam?'

'All the better for seeing you, my bairn,' she said, her smile broadening, as she gazed fondly at her younger daughter. 'Doesn't she look a picture, Marie?'

'She does,' Marie agreed. 'I've done soused herrings for tea, Pam, just like Dad used to do them. And a bit of lettuce and stuff from the allotment.'

Marie made a tray up for her mother and Pam so that they could eat together in the front room, and spend as much time as possible together before they got the bus to Dunswell. She herself ate with George and Auntie Edie in the kitchen.

'Hello! Somebody at the door,' George said, when tea was nearly over. He scraped back his chair and got up to answer the knock.

Danny Elsworth followed him back into the dining room, and sat on the empty chair, gazing around. 'Did Pam come? I came to ask if she'd be staying at our house.'

'Well, she's here, but she's decided to go to Dunswell, out of the way of the raids,' Marie said.

'We thought she might. Dad told me to tell you he'll take you up there, if you like.'

'He'd better be careful,' George said. 'I know a bloke who's been prosecuted for improper use of the petrol ration. They're getting as hot on that as breaching the blackout, now.'

'Tell your dad thanks, but I don't want to get

him into trouble,' Marie said. 'He's been had up once already; they might come down hard on him, if taking us to Dunswell lands him in court again. We can go on the bus.'

Pam walked through the dining room with two dirty plates. Danny watched her go into the kitchen, and stared at the door until she returned.

'I think you know Danny, don't you, Pam?' Marie said.

Pam stopped and gave him the sweetest smile. 'I think I remember you from school, although you were a bit older than me. You go to Hymers now, don't you, Danny?'

He nodded slowly, eyes riveted on her, a wide smile spreading over his face.

'Do you play a musical instrument? Have you got a piano?'

'Well, we used to have a piano,' Danny said. 'Mother tried to get Charles and me to play, but neither of us was interested and nobody else could play, so she got rid of it.'

The spark of interest died in Pam's eyes. 'Oh, well, I'll get back to Mother, I think. I want to spend as much time with her as I can before I have to go to Dunswell.'

She left the room, and Danny took a moment or two to come out of his trance. 'I'd better be going – to let Mum and Dad know what the arrangements are.'

George saw him out. As soon as she heard the door close Aunt Edie gave a roguish laugh. 'Ooh, your Pam's made a conquest there,' she said. 'Did you see his face? He couldn't take his eyes off her. Properly smitten.'

'You should have seen him look at the door to the front room when we went through the passage,' George said. 'I think he was trying to see through it.'

'Well, she's fit to look at,' Marie said. 'No denying that.'

'Like her big sister, then. Although I think you pip her to the post in the beauty stakes.'

'Don't be daft,' Marie protested.

'I'll carry the suitcase to the bus stop for you, if you like.'

'You've been at work all day. You stay here and put your feet up. Read the paper. We'll manage it all right between us, if we take turns.'

'Tell you what, then,' George said. 'You get yourself there with her and that suitcase, and don't worry about getting out in time for the last bus. I'll come and fetch you back on the motorbike just before it gets dark. That should give you a couple of hours, with double summer time. Your mam will be all right. I'll come straight for you, if not.'

'What about improper use of the petrol ration?'

'Ach!' George exclaimed, loading that one syllable with as much derision as it could hold. 'Improper use of the petrol ration my foot! I'll come for you.'

'I hope Alfie warned you we were coming,' said Marie.

'He did, and she's welcome,' Auntie Dot said.

Uncle Alf smiled a welcome and took the suitcase from Pam, his eyebrows rising slightly at its quality, and that of Pam's outfit. 'What did you

349

think to your mam, then?' he asked.

'I thought she's aged terribly, and she seems very tired. And I thought that awful scar might have faded,' Pam shuddered, 'but it hasn't, not at all.'

Marie was amused to see the reaction of her uncle and aunt to Pam's BBC tones. They looked completely thrown.

The extent of their attachment to Alfie showed itself when the conversation turned to his attempt to rescue Jenny. They quickly realized that Pam knew nothing about it.

'Why didn't you tell her, Marie?' Auntie Dot asked.

'I just never got around to it, I suppose,' Marie said, her face impassive. She knew that both Pam and Alfie would have a very good idea why she hadn't. Pam had displayed no interest in Alfie's welfare when he'd lived in Bourne, and Marie had seen no point in troubling her with any further news of him.

Uncle Alf made up the deficiency. Pam got the full story, every detail of Alfie's heroism and presence of mind, and his admission to hospital.

'So, there you are, Pam,' Marie said, pointedly. 'A different version of your brother from the one you got from the Mortons.'

Alfie sat reading his *Spotter*, with nothing to say.

Pam had the grace to look abashed for a moment or two, and that was all. Then she turned to Marie with resentment in her tone: 'How was I expected to know, if nobody told me?'

The wireless was on in the background, with Forces radio playing. Marie pricked up her ears at the name Lieutenant Elsworth, as another message from Chas came drifting over the airways. Auntie Dot heard too, but kept silent.

'Isn't that Charles, Marie?' Pam asked. 'Turn it up, Auntie Dot.'

Uncle Alf obliged, and the strains of 'It Had to Be You' filled the room.

'Huh! Never be cross or try to be boss?' Pam repeated, when the song had finished. 'So you're cross and bossy with him as well as me. I don't know why he puts up with you.'

Uncle Alf turned the wireless off, and Pam's remark was left hanging in the air like a bad smell, until Auntie Dot muttered: 'I don't know why *she* puts up with *him*.' Nothing else was said, although Marie knew she'd have had to stand a lot of leg-pulling had they not known about Charles's affair with Hannah. She was just glad she hadn't been at the Maltbys' when the song was played, considering some of the remarks that would have greeted it there. Aunt Edie had already accused Chas of keeping a harem.

Pam's pale complexion slowly turned pink. 'I don't know why you're all looking at me like that,' she said, with a toss of her head. 'She *is* bossy. But if Charles Elsworth enjoys being bossed about, well, that's his lookout.'

Chapter 29

Pam came down to see her mother with Alfie every day that week, on Auntie Dot's old bike. Their visits were a tonic to their mother. She began eating better and took more interest in things, and had started talking a bit more hopefully about keeping the family together after the war.

'You could probably come back now, love,' she told Pam a couple of days later, when Pam returned from a walk round the town centre, where she'd been taking snaps with her Brownie box camera, like a regular bomb-site tourist, with Danny Elsworth as her guide.

Pam's reaction to the devastation was the same as Marie's had been. 'All the beautiful buildings I grew up with have been destroyed,' she said. 'Nearly everything I remember from my childhood, gone. Some terrible things have happened here.'

Again Marie read her thoughts by the expression on her face. *They might have happened to me.*

'We haven't had a raid all the time you've been here,' their mother went on. 'You'd be all right at Dunswell. You could live with Uncle Alf and Auntie Dot, like Alfie. It would be nice for you to be together again.'

'I can't, Mum. I'll have to go back to Bourne on Monday,' Pam said. 'I've got a music exam, and there's no piano here for me to practise on. I really ought to practise for at least two hours every day. I'll have to go back.'

Her mother's disappointment showed on her face.

'I thought there might be a piano at Uncle Alf and Auntie Dot's, but there isn't,' Pam said, giving the impression that a piano might have kept her in Dunswell.

Their mother's scarred brow creased in perplexity. 'Oh,' she repeated. 'I don't know where we could get one from.'

'Come and give me a hand with the washing-up, Pam,' Marie said. When they were out of her mother's hearing, she asked: 'Can't you stay a bit longer? It's bucked her up no end, having you here every day. Another week, and she might have turned the corner.'

'Well, I might if there was anywhere I could practise, but there isn't. And it's not only that,' Pam said, with a certain disdain in her eyes. 'They're very rough, aren't they, Uncle Alf and Auntie Dot? We might have been poor, but Mother was always so particular. And there's nothing to do there.'

'No, they're not rough. They have to work hard on the smallholding, that's all. And there's a million and one things to do. You could help them.'

'I don't know anything about working on a smallholding, and I don't want to. I've got my music exam coming up, and I don't want to fail. I have to practise, and there's no piano here. I only came because you made it sound as if Mother was on her deathbed, and she's not.' Pam's expression seemed to indicate that she thought she'd been dragged to Hull on false pretences.

'People can't die to order, you know,' Marie said. 'I genuinely did think she wouldn't be here long. In fact, she probably wouldn't be, if you hadn't come. What's bucked her up so much is having you here.'

'I'm going back to Bourne on Monday,' Pam said.

On the bus journey back from Corporation Pier, Marie unburdened herself of her irritation with Pam by scribbling her first unrestrained letter to Charles since her shock at his continued involvement with Hannah. She was still uncertain how much she wanted to speak to him, but she so desperately wanted to have someone to confide in about her sister's behaviour.

Pam patiently waited a whole week for her mother to die, which is a lot more than I expected, but when she didn't oblige, she hopped it back to the Stewarts, and beautiful unbombed Bourne, and her piano, with a camera full of snaps of bombed-out Hull to show them, including one of our old house. That should convince them that sending her back here would be tantamount to murder. She was pining for them, or their way of life, rather – the piano most of all, I think. There's nothing to do here, she says, while she stands watching everybody else work their fingers to the bone. For two pins, I could have left her to go back on her own. She managed it after the raid, so why not? But years of being told to look after the younger ones got the better of me, so I helped her to lug her suitcase and saw her safely onto the ferry. She's promised to come back after she's taken her music exam, but I don't believe she will. I'll be surprised if my mother sees her again this side of the grave...

Marie's hand became still, as she thought of their goodbye. Pam had looked distant – not quite sad, but as if she were bringing a chapter of her life firmly to a close, with just a little regret. Alfie had seen further than she had herself, Marie reflected. Because of the war, their once close and loving family had been shattered, and scattered, and finished. Nothing would ever be the same.

'It's funny,' she wrote, her attention back on her letter, 'we didn't have a single air raid while she was here. But I expect we'll have another one before long...'.

She spilled her feelings onto the page and felt considerable relief, then, wondering whether she was really doing the wisest thing in sending it, she finally dropped it into the post box.

She was wrong about the raids. August turned out to be comparatively uneventful – with only one air raid in the middle of the month, which demolished three shelters, killing twenty people and badly injuring fifteen, and a rather more successful one at the month's end, which managed to kill and injure more than twice as many people, and to damage sixteen shelters.

With Pam gone, Marie was back in the old routine of housework, allotment gardening, and caring for her mother – which exempted her from war work. Alfie visited a couple of times a week,

Terry called nearly as often to take her dancing for an hour or two, and when he was on duty George occasionally stepped into the breach, although he had started walking out with a girl from the Guildhall, called Eva. A trip to the pictures with Nancy, Mass at St Vincent's and a visit to the graves on Sunday completed the weekly round.

Chapter 30

'When did Pam say she was taking her music exam?' her mother asked fretfully one morning, as Marie and George lifted her out of bed. 'I'm sure it was before the schools go back.'

Marie knew it was before the schools went back. The exam was the eighteenth, to be precise, and today was the twenty-eighth. 'I don't know, Mam,' she lied, picking up the comb to tidy her mother's fair hair.

The letter box rattled, George went into the passage to pick up the post and returned with a letter from Pam.

Marie opened it, and read it aloud. Mr and Mrs Stewart were taking her for a holiday to Cromer while they had the good weather, and she would come to Hull and spend the half-term holiday with her mother, instead. She passed her music exam with distinction, and what a relief that was, after missing all that practice while she'd been in Hull.

'Mr and Mrs Stewart are taking her to Cromer for a holiday,' her mother repeated, her voice sounding hollow. 'Mr and Mrs Stewart don't bother asking for *my* permission to take my daughter on holiday to Cromer, and she doesn't ask, either. It looks as if I've been cancelled altogether.'

George slid quietly out of the room, and Marie heard the front door close after him as he escaped to work.

Aunt Edie flushed with indignation. 'Bloody shame, that's what I call it!'

'Oh, come on, Mam,' Marie urged. 'Just concentrate on getting better, and we'll get a house. We can have them both back then.'

'Where's the money coming from?' her mother demanded, tearing down Marie's shaky castle in the air. 'Anyway, I don't think I'll ever be able to manage a house, again. I'm no use to anybody now. I've outlived my usefulness, and that's the truth,' she said, putting a final stop to that well-meant but impossible suggestion.

She ignored Marie's protests and said very little else, but sat in silence all day, until Marie and George were lifting her back into bed that evening.

'She must know how ill I am,' she said. 'She's not a child. She must know I might not last until October.'

'You will last until October, Mam, and a long time beyond it. If she'd thought you wouldn't, I'm sure she'd have come.'

Her mother said no more, and Marie left Aunt Edie sitting with her, while she got on with the housework.

Much later, George and Marie shared a last cup of tea in the dining room.

'How's the court case going?' Marie asked, for a change of subject.

'Oh, it's all going through,' George waved a hand, airily. 'Going through the motions, you might say. Monty's days are numbered.'

'Or Billy Boy Pratt, as Nancy calls him. She's done a complete turnaround. She's as keen on "doing" him as you are, now.'

George seemed not to relish the mention of Nancy. 'It's in her best interests, isn't it?' he said, and lapsed into silence for a while. Then: 'If we got married,' he said, 'me and you, I mean – we could live here until we got a house nearby, and then we could keep an eye on both our mothers, make sure they're all right. I've got a decent salary; I could just about manage it.'

'What about Eva?'

'Eva's all right. Nothing serious, yet, though. It's not gone far enough to break any hearts.'

'Do you think my mam'll be here long enough for that?' Marie asked.

'Well, you were telling her so. I was just going on what you said. And if she does get better, they'll both need a bit of help.'

She didn't ask: what about Charles? And neither did George. But he didn't push his offer. He went to bed, and left her with the thought.

Chapter 31

From the day she got Pam's letter, Marie's mother seemed to lose all interest in everything. She hardly ate a thing, drank enough to swallow her pills, and not much more, and sat gazing into space for hours at a stretch. Aunt Edie persisted in trying to cheer her with pleasant reminiscences, with no success. Terry took Marie dancing for an hour on the Sunday, but when he came again a week later she shook her head.

'Sorry, Terry, she's too ill to be left.'

'Surely she'll be all right for an hour,' he coaxed.

'No, I'm not leaving her.' Marie was adamant. With the loss of her home and her two younger children, her mother had lost the will to live, but she wasn't going to die without at least her eldest with her.

Terry hesitated, the caressing glances in his blue eyes telling her what his own 'strictly as pals' had forbidden him to say. 'All right, then. I'll call again, in a week, just to see. Hope she'll be a lot better by then.'

Then gradually, day after day, her mother slackened her hold on life. George took on the little there was to do at the allotment, now that most of the produce had been harvested. Other than for trips to the post office and local shops, Marie was completely housebound, seeing nothing of anybody except Alfie, who came down at the weekend and a couple of times during the week.

When her mother's breathing became difficult, Marie sent for Dr Thackeray. 'How long can it go on?' she asked, when he'd completed his examination.

'Not much longer, I think. She might be better in hospital, in a cardiac bed. It might make her breathing easier.'

'She wants to stay here, and what difference will it make, really? Will it save her life?'

'No.'

'She stays here, then,' Edie said.

Her mother, sweating and struggling for breath, managed a smile for her friend.

Marie spent the night in the armchair.

'It's a pity ... you can't like George,' her mother gasped, at about three o'clock in the morning.

'I do like George,' Marie said, taking a cloth to wipe away the sweat that stood on her mother's face and neck.

'Marry him, then ... and look after Alfie, and Edie.'

It was the last time she spoke. She died at five o'clock.

Dressed in slacks and a blouse, Marie was ready to go to Dunswell before George came downstairs at seven. 'My mam's gone. Tell your mother, will you? I'll phone the doctor on my way. Can I borrow your pushbike? I want to get there well before Alfie goes to school.'

Alfie was just at the gate, school cap in hand, when he saw her approaching on the bike. 'She's dead, isn't she?' he said, when she was within earshot.

Marie nodded, and drew to a halt beside him.

'I blame our Pam,' he said. 'If she'd come when she said she was coming, Mam wouldn't have gone downhill so quick.'

'You don't, really. You told me she didn't want to get better before ever Pam came – and you were right.'

'I do, though. She started to pick up while Pam was here, and if she'd stayed, she might have got better, instead of just giving up.'

'Come on,' Marie said, wheeling the bike through the gate. 'Let's go in and ask Auntie Dot to put the kettle on. I don't think there's much point in you going to school today.'

When Marie got back from Dunswell she found Aunt Edie smoothing her mother's fair hair back from her face with one hand, and holding one lifeless hand with the other. 'Oh, dear me,' she kept sighing, 'oh, dear me, I've lost my last good friend. Poor Lillian. She always had so much life in her, she used to run rings round me. I can hardly believe she's dead, but she must be – she feels so cold. She had a rough time of it at the end, poor lass, but I really believed she'd get better.'

'I can never thank you enough for everything you've done for her,' Marie said. 'You were the best friend she could have had. And George – I think he's done more than any other man on this earth would have done.'

'We used to have some grand times together, when my husband was alive,' Aunt Edie said, a faint smile lifting the corners of her mouth at the remembrance. 'Those parties your mam and dad used to have, every New Year's Eve; the pranks your dad got up to, he'd have us laughing till our sides were sore. And now there's only me left.' Aunt Edie's face lost its animation, and her eyes their light. She turned and gave Marie's hand a squeeze. 'You did right by her, anyhow. She couldn't have had a better daughter, and don't feel as if you've got to move, because your mam's gone. You're welcome to stay here as long as you like. For ever, if you want.'

'Thanks.' Marie returned the squeeze, then stood looking at her mother with her arms hugging her own waist, holding the void that had taken the place of her stomach. 'And now I've nothing to do but wait for the doctor to come and sign the death certificate, so I can set about arranging another funeral,' she said. 'Oh, I'm so weary of it all, Aunt Edie. I sometimes think there'll be no end to it.'

They heard someone in the passage, and then George popped his head round the door, grinning from ear to ear. 'Can't stop,' he said. 'We're on our way up to North Hull. I just wanted to tell you that that bugger's in court next week! He tried to get the hearing moved to Brighton, but the police checked the address he gave. His wife and her parents live there all right, but he doesn't! And he's not likely to be living there again, by the sound of it. So he's been bailed to appear at the Guildhall!' He burst into guffaws of laughter and left, whistling a snatch of 'The Spaniard that Blighted My Life', his face alive with unholy glee at the thought of getting square with Bill Pratt and Nancy.

'Well, fancy!' Aunt Edie exclaimed, in tones of outrage. 'Whistling and carrying on, and your poor mother just gone.'

'He did the best he could for her while she was alive, Aunt Edie,' Marie said. 'That's all that matters.' And in spite of the circumstances, Marie felt the corners of her mouth lift. It was good to see George so cheerful, for a change.

'How is she?' Terry asked, when he stood at the door that evening.

Marie shook her head. 'I was at the undertaker's this afternoon. That'll tell you how she is.'

'You won't be feeling much like dancing, then.'

'No. I wouldn't mind a walk, though. I should be dead on my feet after being awake all night, and racing about all day, up to Dunswell, and then to the registrar's and the undertaker's, but I can't keep still. I feel like a cat on hot bricks.'

He offered her his arm. 'Come on then, let's be off.'

She called a goodbye to Aunt Edie and George, and took it. She felt drawn to Terry. He'd had his young wife torn away from him; he had suffered that massive blow and survived it, and she looked to him for some hidden knowledge, some deep wisdom to help her through her own grief. They walked rapidly up to the park and along its pathways, saying little, and then Marie flung herself down on the same bench she'd last shared with Chas, and wept.

Terry sat beside her, saying nothing at first.

When the tears abated, he said, 'Your mother's troubles are over, Marie. Nothing can touch her now.'

'I'm not crying for my mother. I'm crying for myself.'

He gave a short laugh. 'Well, isn't that the truth! We all cry for ourselves; first time I've ever heard anybody come straight out with it, though.'

She pulled a handkerchief from her cardigan sleeve, and blew her nose. 'Isn't it stupid to think of yourself as an orphan at the age of twenty-three? But that's just how I feel.'

He put his arm round her and she rested her head on his broad shoulder.

'It's not stupid,' he said. 'Get your crying over, and then – don't look back. It'll break your heart.'

Was that the best he could do? That wasn't what she'd hoped for from him. She wanted to look back. The future seemed to hold nothing but pain, and fear, and uncertainty. Back was where happiness and comfort and love and laughter were, and she wanted to hold on to it. She wanted to keep what was past, to regain all the wonder and hope and beauty of her young years, to retrieve all the loving and all the caring and the security of those times, and the people who'd provided it all. But the mother and father who had nurtured and protected her from her birth, the custodians of her life and her history, were gone. She wanted not only to look back, but to go back, to everything that had slipped away from her, and stay there, safe for ever in her cosy little home, in her beloved and unspoiled city.

Chapter 32

Pam's face looked white and pinched, and apprehensive. She looked into the coffin, saw her
mother's scarred face and burst into angry floods
of tears. 'I hate them. I hate Auntie Morag and
Uncle Alec for doing this. Oh, my poor mam! I'll
never forgive them. I never asked to go to Cromer.
It was all their idea. I'd have come back to see my
mam if it hadn't been for them, interfering and
arranging it all behind my back. I'm never going
back there.' The anguished face that looked
towards Marie was the face of a child, admittedly
a spoiled child, but a child, for all that.

Aunt Edie's eyebrows went up slightly. George
gave Marie a grim smile over Pam's head. Alfie
gave a contemptuous snort, and stared out of the
window.

Marie looked at Pam in her new and flattering
mourning clothes and thought how well the
Stewarts had cared for her. They obviously had
plenty of money, and few other demands on it.
Pamela had been treated like a fragile piece of
Dresden china, since she'd been with them, and
she'd loved it. Now there was nobody who
needed Pam's help, nobody who could be hurt by
her defection, and it was pointless for her to cut
herself off from them and their cultured way of
life, and all the good that they could do her and
her family could not.

'It's too late, Pam. There's nothing to keep you here now,' Marie said. 'Nothing! I can't help you; I can barely help myself, and I've got no home to offer you. Alfie can't do anything. Uncle Alf and Auntie Dot would do their best, but there'd be no piano, and no music, and no music college, and you'd have to get a job.'

'I don't care,' she said, between sobs. 'I don't care about it any more.'

'You say that now, because you're upset. But stay with Uncle Alf and Auntie Dot for a while, until you make your mind up, and when you get there don't mope about saying there's nothing to do. There's plenty, so do your share, and think about things.'

Alfie whipped round to face her, eyes wide and expression horrified, probably at the thought of having his sister billeted with him. Uncle Alf and Auntie Dot's eyebrows also rose slightly at her presuming on their good nature, but Marie had no qualms of conscience about being so liberal with their charity. They wouldn't be troubled for long. Now that her pangs of remorse and sentiment had had a proper airing and the blame for her sorry showing as a daughter had been placed firmly elsewhere, Pam's hard-headed self-interest wouldn't be long in reasserting itself. If she stayed with her rough relatives in Dunswell for even half a week it would be a miracle.

'You know what somebody said to me, not very long ago?' Marie continued. 'He said, "Get your crying over, and then don't look back." So if you decide to go back to Bourne go with a goodwill, and bear no grudges – they're poison, and they'll poison you. The Stewarts have treated you like a daughter, so be a good daughter to them. You've got no other parents, now.'

Pamela was already drying her eyes. 'You're right,' she sniffed. 'They have been good to me. I think it would break their hearts if I didn't go back.'

The sun was low beyond the Humber, gilding the ripples on its muddy waters. 'I think we've seen the last of her. I don't think she'll ever come back, now,' Alfie said, as they stood together on Corporation Pier after the funeral, waving Pam off on the ferry that very same evening. The Stewarts had bought her a return ticket, and as Pam had said, it would have been a pity to waste it. And she didn't know anything about working on a smallholding, so she would just have got in everybody's way. Would Marie and Alfie give her apologies to Uncle Alf and Auntie Dot? Besides, Uncle Alec would be waiting for her in Lincoln, and missing the ferry would have meant having to telephone him.

Unlike Marie, Pam had no need to look backwards for a sense of comfort and security, and with the Stewarts her future looked rosy. The past had few charms now for Pam. Marie had no illusions about her sister's self-centredness, but she had given her a fierce hug before she boarded the ferry, and felt a terrible sadness at parting with her.

Just you and me then, Alfie,' Marie said. 'Out of a family of five, just a brother and a sister, still together.'

'If you can call it together, with you in Hull and

me at Dunswell. I think we should still get to-gether every Sunday, though, and go and put some flowers on the graves.'

'So do I. But I might not always be able to manage it. I'll have to go back to work.'

'Where? The infirmary's been bombed.'

'They're still using it as a first-aid post. I'll have to go and see Matron. There's sure to be some-where they can put me to use.'

Chapter 33

'You ought to go and spend a morning in the police court sometime when you've got nothing better to do,' Nancy said, as they were walking to the pictures on Anlaby Road the afternoon after the court case. 'Some of the people you get in there, well, it's an eye-opener. I was terrified when I first went in, but when you've sat through hearings about somebody pinching two bottles of milk off somebody else's doorstep, and people up on child neglect charges for not feeding kids when they'd no food in the house, and no money to buy any, and then – hark at this – they get *fined* for it – well, it just puts things into perspective. I think Billy Pratt was the only real criminal they had in there all day. Probably all week.'

'I've already been to the police court,' Marie said, as soon as she could get a word in edgeways. 'They had me up for breaching the blackout, remember?'

'Oh. Was that when I was in London? Anyway, I'd forgotten.'

'Probably because you were too busy planning your elopement and worrying about Monty, as we knew him then.'

'Don't remind me. The judge more or less called me an absolute fool in front of everybody in the court, and George was sitting there looking like a terrier at a rat-hole. I was really upset, until my mam said: "Well, that should make it easier for you to get maintenance money off him when he gets out of gaol," and it will, so I felt a bit better about it, then. I'm not going to wait until he gets out of gaol, either. I'm going to see about it as soon as the baby's born. He pleaded guilty, so that made it a lot easier. Oh, yes, he's going to pay me, whether George ever gets a penny back or not, and frankly, I've stopped caring. Has he said anything about it – the court case, I mean?'

'Not to me. I haven't seen him. He was out with a woman called Eva last night, and he didn't get in until after I'd gone to bed, and he was off to work just as I was getting up this morning.'

Nancy seemed slightly taken aback. 'Oh! He's gadding about a bit lately, isn't he?' she said. 'I suspected him of being after you at one time. I wouldn't have put it past him, just for one in the eye for me. But I'd have thought you'd have gone back to the Elsworths, now your mother's gone.'

'Well, Aunt Edie says I can stay with them as long as I like, so there's no rush, and I'm still thinking about the Elsworths. If I went there, it would look as if it were a definite thing between me and Chas, and I'm still not a hundred per cent

369

sure. Anyway, I'll be going back to work soon, so I'll probably be living in a nurses' home, depending where they put me. But I expect George will be bringing Eva home to meet his mother before long, so it might be just as well if I'm somewhere else.'

'Huh. Bloody good luck to Eva, then,' Nancy said. 'She can expect a good prying-into from his mother's blind eyes.' After a short pause she dismissed thoughts of George with a shrug of her shoulders, and was back on the subject of Bill Pratt. 'I'd love to see "Monty" in his new stage costume, trimmed with arrows! I hope he's breaking rocks by now.'

'You said you wanted him sewing mailbags.'

Nancy's eyes narrowed, and her mouth contracted into a grim little smirk. 'No,' she said. 'Mailbags are too good for him. Oh, I'm glad it's over and done with, Marie. It wasn't as bad as I thought it would be, but I'm glad it's over with. I'm sorry about your mam, by the way. Sorry I couldn't come to the funeral, but it wouldn't have done, would it? Not with George and his mother being as spiteful as they are. Did you give her a good send-off?'

'Not as good as the one we gave you,' Marie said. 'There was no expense spared on that one. We just had a few close friends and relatives. Not the whole neighbourhood, this time.'

'You're a sarky bugger, aren't you? You do like to have a dig, now and then,' Nancy said.

Marie and George walked home from the allotment on Saturday carrying two heavy bags of potatoes each. The days were shorter and cooler with the approach of October, and she had wanted to get most of the potatoes up before she went back to nursing. When George nipped into the newsagents on Newland Avenue to buy a paper, she wasn't sorry to put her burdens down and rub her hands back into life while waiting for him.

Back at Aunt Edie's, they deposited their bags on the kitchen floor, Marie feeling very pleased at being the giver, for a change, rather than the one accepting help. 'There's enough to fill two more bags still in the ground, and cabbages, parsnips and turnips, as well, and Brussels later on. You should hardly have to buy any veg all winter. You'll have to ask George to get the rest up, once I'm back to work – if I have to live in, that is.'

'Don't live in, then,' Aunt Edie said.

'I might have to.'

'Well, go and sit down, and I'll make you a cuppa.'

The settee and the wireless were back in place in the front room. Although still crammed with furniture, it had a horribly empty feel now that her mother was gone, and her sickbed had been taken back upstairs. Poor Mother. Marie switched the wireless on, for a bit of the cheerful music or banter from the comedy shows to banish the cloud of despondency descending on her.

George sat on the settee, and began avidly scanning his newspaper. 'Here it is,' he said, folding the paper at the page and jumping to his feet again to call his mother from the passageway. 'Hey, Mam! Come in here and listen to this.'

Auntie Edie came in, looking puzzled. 'What's up? What's the matter?'

'Sit down and just listen to this.'

She sat in one of the armchairs.

'"Defrauded Credulous Girl,"' George read.

'An actor with a repertory company that recently played in Hull is stated to have posed as a single man and persuaded a young woman to break off her engagement and go to London with him. Bill Pratt, a married man of thirty-five, of no fixed abode, was sent to prison for six months after he pleaded guilty to charges of making off without paying rent to his landlady, stealing an engagement ring, and obtaining two hundred pounds by false pretences from Miss Nancy Harding, a 23-year-old nurse of Duesbury Street, Hull. After Miss Harding had given her evidence, the magistrate remarked, "It is utterly amazing, in this day and age, to find that there are still such credulous young women about!"'

'Six months!' he exclaimed. 'When I heard the judge say that, I thought all my birthdays had come at once! Six months!' and tossing the paper towards his mother, he roared with laughter, rocking to and fro on the settee, and slapping his knee, relishing the memory of his victory. Aunt Edie read the column with a broad grin on her face, then throwing herself back in the armchair she joined in the laugh, and soon had to pull a handkerchief out of her apron pocket to wipe her streaming eyes. Out of loyalty to Nancy, Marie restrained herself, but it was impossible to suppress a chuckle.

'Well,' George gasped, as soon as he recovered the power of speech, 'I caught the man that blighted my life, and I dislocated *his* bally life! I'd threatened it for long enough, but I was never really sure it would come off. So now it has. I've got him! And I might still dislocate his jaw when he gets out of gaol.'

'Pity you've not got your money, though,' his mother said, suddenly serious. 'The years it took your dad to save that eighty pounds he left you.'

'Aye, poor old fellow, I think I've seen the last of that. She's seen that off, and everything else with it.'

'Huh!' Aunt Edie snorted, 'She'll get what she deserves, don't you worry about that. Pride goeth before a fall, it says in the Bible. She didn't know when she was well off, and now she's having a bairn, and no man beside her. She'll soon know what that's all about. She'll never be able to hold her head up round here again.'

A look of anguish flitted across George's face, and was gone.

Terry crooned words of love and romance in her ear as they glided across the waxed dance floor of Beverley Baths to the throbbing music of the band. It was Saturday night, and the place was full of young people out to enjoy themselves: couples; girls out with their friends, dressed to the nines and confident of getting partners among the influx of foreign servicemen.

'It really bucks me up, coming out with you, Terry,' Marie told him. 'You never seem to let anything get you down. Not for long, anyway.'

'I'll give you a tip,' he said. 'If you're feeling low, don't sit on your own feeling sorry for yourself. Get washed and brushed and get your glad rags on. Get out among people – your friends, me, for example – and put a bright face on it. Laugh and joke as if you hadn't a care in the world. In the end, the act will stop being an act.'

'Is that what I do? Feel sorry for myself?'

'No, you get your glad rags on and get out with your friend. Now let's see you laughing and joking.'

'That might take a bit of practice.'

'Start now. This should cheer you up: it's nearly the end of September, and we've only had one air raid this month, and we only had two last month. Things are getting boring in Hull, now that Hitler's keeping the Russians entertained.'

'No ill feeling, but rather them than us,' she said. 'Hitler's sort of entertainment gives me the screaming abdabs. I've had enough to last me a lifetime.'

'Aye, well, joking apart, there might not be much more of it. He might have bitten off a bit more than he can chew, with the Russian winter coming on. It beat Napoleon, and I reckon it'll beat Adolf.'

They danced in silence for a while, then Terry asked: 'How's it going with your young man? Is he behaving himself?'

'As far as I know he is. He writes nearly every day, and I've had a couple of requests played on the wireless. He can't do much more, being miles away, can he?'

'What about her? Has she had it, yet?'

'Her' and 'it' needed no explanation. Marie stiffened and frowned, not thanking him for dredging that Hannah business up, just as she was beginning to enjoy herself. 'Not as far as I know,' she said.

He gave her a wicked smile, and a squeeze. 'Well, if you decide you want somebody closer to home, you won't have to look far. I'll step into his shoes as soon as you say the word. Am I taking you out next week?'

'I'm not sure when I'll be free. I'll be working at the dressing station on Endike Lane by next week. Still living at Aunt Edie's, though.'

'Oh, well, I'll call sometime next week, and find out.'

Marie arrived back at Aunt Edie's with dance music still playing in her head. Feeling much too lively for sleep, she spent an hour writing to Chas, giving him all the news.

Chapter 34

There was a blustery wind and it looked like rain when Marie and Alfie reached the grave that now held both their father and their mother. Alfie squatted to push chrysanthemums through the holes of the thick glass top of the vase.

'At least they're together again now,' he said, standing back the better to see his handiwork.

'I miss them,' she said, and put an arm round his shoulder.

A flash, and a crack of lightning interrupted their moment of silent remembrance. 'We'd better get a move on,' she said. 'It's going to belt it down.'

They hurried away, to Jenny's grave. The flowers on that little mound were dying. 'Shall I put them in the bin?' Alfie asked.

'Better not. It'll start throwing it down in a minute. Just lay ours on top,' Marie said.

Alfie obeyed. 'Poor little Jenny,' he said.

'Yes,' Marie agreed. 'Our mam and dad died too young, but who would have thought a 6-year-old would be gone before them?'

The heavens opened as they said a hurried prayer. Marie unfurled her umbrella, one damaged spoke flapping like a broken wing as they dashed towards the cemetery gate. Alfie took her arm, and huddled into her for shelter.

'Well, boiled eggs for tea, again, thanks to Auntie Dot,' Marie said.

'Yeah. Better than dregs,' he said.

'What are dregs?'

'It's a riddle for you, Marie. If spiced ham is Spam, what are dregs?' he grinned.

'Dried eggs!' she laughed. 'You daft ha'porth. But they taste like dregs, I'll give you that.'

A man was walking towards them, maybe in his late thirties, with the gait of a sailor. He hunched his shoulders and pulled up his jacket against the rain as he strode along, a gaunt but handsome man with rain dripping off his fair hair. As he passed Marie they glanced at each other.

He nodded. 'Hello.'

'Hello,' she said, and turned her head to watch

him walk down the path. When he stopped beside Jenny's grave she felt the hairs rise on the back of her neck, and chills tingling from her ears to her knees. A couple of lines of doggerel ran through her head:

As I was walking up the stair
I met a man who wasn't there.

She stopped, rooted to the spot. Alfie gave her a curious look. 'Do you know him, Marie?'

She shivered. 'He's somebody I've seen once or twice, but I never knew him,' she said.

She was tired enough, after the unaccustomed exercise involved in a busy day caring for patients, but Marie had something on her mind that she could not set aside. She itched to know for sure, and so she changed quickly into slacks and jumper, and took the first trolley bus into town. From there she took a bus to Hessle Road. When she turned down Scarborough Street, she saw him again, that man who had so disturbed her, walking away from her this time, down towards the docks.

Trudie answered her knock. Marie pulled her out into the street and pointed to his fast disappearing back. 'Who's that man?' she demanded, just before he turned the corner.

Their eyes met. 'He's my son,' Trudie said.

'Larry?'

She nodded. 'Come in.'

The sailor had returned from his watery grave then, only to find his daughter sunk into hers. Marie shuddered and sank down onto a hard-backed chair beside the Welsh dresser in Trudie's front room. 'I was right, then.'

Trudie sat on a chair arm opposite her. 'It's a miracle. I would never have thought it possible. He was as near to death as any man could be. He can just remember the torpedo hitting the side of the ship, and the scramble for lifeboats, and after that he can't remember another thing, until he woke up in a hospital bed in Newfoundland with a broken arm and a broken jaw. It turned out he'd been picked up with a couple of others by an American vessel. He can't even remember how it happened. He couldn't eat properly for weeks – he says it's a wonder he didn't starve to death. He was skin and bone, and he's not much more now. He'd lost his boots, and everything but the clothes on his back had gone down with the ship. He hadn't a bean, no money to pay anybody, and nothing to come off the shipping company, either. They reckon if you're floating about in the Atlantic, or lying in a hospital bed, you're taking an unofficial holiday.'

'I know,' Marie said. 'It's unbelievable. The whole thing's unbelievable.'

'Well, believe it. You're paid until the ship goes down, and not a minute after, and now he's in debt to people from Newfoundland to Hull, and everywhere in between. And you already know what greeted him when he got back. Her, out to here,' Trudie said, holding the palm of her hand a foot from her stomach, 'all his money spent, and ready to drop, so he knew it wasn't his. So he said, "What's this, then?" And she said, "You can see what it is, and I don't suppose you've been without a woman all this time." Cheeky bitch, as if he'd had any time or money to get with any women. So he just walked out and came down here. I nearly collapsed. He didn't even know about our Jenny. I got the job of telling him that – and after he'd trusted me to watch out for her.'

'How terrible,' Marie said.

'Oh, I felt so awful, I was nearly wishing he hadn't come back, so he wouldn't have to hear it. But she made it so hard. If they'd still been living nearby, I might have stood a chance, but she rented that house on Clumber Street as soon as he was on the convoys. Handier for the dance halls, I think, and well out of my reach. The poor bairn couldn't run to me from there, could she?'

'Didn't he write to you?'

'He was unconscious for days, and when he came round he couldn't even remember who he was or where he lived. He couldn't talk properly, and his right arm was broken. He eventually got somebody to write to her, though, and let her know he was alive, and he asked her to tell us, but she never.'

'When was that?' Marie asked. 'How long has she known...?'

Marie had another visit planned for the following afternoon, to Park Avenue. She found Mrs Elsworth dressed in an old skirt and jumper in the rear garden, sitting on her heels, busy storing potatoes in boxes for the winter.

Marie got straight to the point. 'Have you seen Hannah lately?'

Mrs Elsworth stood up. She hesitated for a

379

moment, then admitted: 'We went to see her the Sunday before last, before the last air raid, and offered to pay for her to have the baby in Poperinge Nursing Home in Cottingham. I had both my boys there, and we knew she'd get good care.'

'Oh. I see,' Marie said, sharply enough to show her aversion to the idea of their having anything to do with Hannah.

'She's having my first grandchild, Marie. What can I do?' Mrs Elsworth asked, with a helpless shrug. 'I don't see how I can cut her off altogether. Anyway, her answer was that she didn't want to be in there, having all those snobby women looking down on her. So we suggested the nursing home on Cranbrook Avenue, but no, she'd rather have the money it would cost, and go to Hedon Road. She's very short, now that she's alone in the world. We weren't offering money, but when she turned the nursing home down, she seemed to expect it in lieu, so we gave it to her. And there's another thing that makes us feel we ought to do something: her husband having died in the attempt to keep us all fed. We haven't seen her since, but she must be very near her time. She's left our friends on Newland Park, so we don't hear anything now.'

'Well then, you can cross the killed husband off the list of things she's holding over you. Her husband's very much alive, and stopping with his mother off Hessle Road. And Hannah's known he was alive since around the beginning of August.'

Mrs Elsworth froze, looking intently into her eyes. 'Are you sure? Absolutely sure?'

'I've seen him. I've spoken to his mother. There's no mistake.'

Mrs Elsworth slowly shook her head. 'My God,' she said, after a pause. 'To come back to that! His child dead, and his wife pregnant by another man. But that removes all danger of Charles marrying her, I'm glad to say, at least until her husband decides what he wants to do.'

'I don't think there was ever any real danger of Charles marrying her,' Marie said drily.

There was that intent look in Mrs Elsworth's eyes again, as she gazed into Marie's. 'There's none,' she said, 'unless you throw him over. I hope you won't, but I can't say I'd blame you. Which reminds me, there's a letter for you. He's coming home on leave, and Mrs Maltby forgot to give you the letter he sent last time he was coming home, apparently. He says it's particularly important that you get this one. I'd have sent Danny to find you, if you hadn't come today. And I ought to tell you: Leonard and I, we've offered to have the baby if she can't look after it. I can't bear to think of him having the same sort of life that Jenny had.'

Marie said nothing, but the shock must have shown on her face. She walked back to Aunt Edie's turning that prospect over in her mind. Leonard and Marjorie, with Hannah's baby, a constant reminder of Charles's betrayal, and an everlasting excuse for Hannah to intrude in their lives, perhaps causing as much trouble in the future as she had in the past. What were the Elsworths thinking of? Marie's dearest wish was to chase Hannah right out of her life. She wished they had never suggested it.

She read the letter as soon as she got back to her room. It was long, and affectionate, and avoided all mention of Hannah. He would be home on Friday the tenth, and he would guarantee to be the most faithful and devoted husband who ever lived. He was genuine, she was sure of it, and she was filled with optimism. She wrote a short letter back, telling him that she was looking forward to seeing him.

Chapter 35

Marie went round to see Nancy later that week, and arrived in time to see her come home, still wearing her auxiliary nurse's uniform. To anyone who didn't know her, Nancy's pregnancy wasn't obvious yet, but it was bound to cause some comments within another month or so. For Marie, the uniform and the slightly swelling tummy under it underlined the end of all Nancy's hopes of getting her nursing finals, and all her prospects of a good marriage.

'You'll have heard about Hannah, I suppose?' Nancy said.

'What about her?'

'She's had it. Eight pounds two ounces.'

'A boy?'

'A girl. Big enough then, wasn't it?'

'How do you know?'

'One of the nurses at the union infirmary has a sister who's working as an orderly at Hedon Road.'

'Small world, isn't it?'

Nancy grimaced. 'A lot too bloody small some-times,' she said. 'It'll be my turn before long, to set all the old fishwives' tongues on fire.'

Marie said nothing, thinking back to the day she'd come to visit Charles in the hospital, and found Hannah with him, patting her bump, and proclaiming that the child would be a boy, be-cause she was 'carrying this one different'. So much for that. And what did Charles think to his parents' offer to bring up his baby as their own, Marie wondered. There was nothing about it in the letter. Perhaps they hadn't told him.

'Yes, we've seen the baby,' Mrs Elsworth said, when Marie went to see her the following day. 'Hannah brought her last night, after taking her own discharge from the hospital. I just hope she hasn't done either of them any harm by it. I didn't step out of bed for seven days, after I'd had my babies, but that woman – she's a law unto herself.' Her eyes lit up with sudden amusement, she chuckled, and added: 'She seemed quite sur-prised we knew her husband was back in Hull.'

'I'll bet,' Marie said.

'I really think she might have gone on playing the tragic widow, had we not told her.'

'I shouldn't wonder. I hear the baby was a good weight,' Marie said, burning with curiosity about it, in spite of herself.

'About eight pounds, I think. Mine were both around that weight, but it's quite big, for a girl. She's a beautiful baby, but...' Mrs Elsworth hesi-tated.

'But?'

'Well, I can't see any resemblance to either of my boys, that's all, or anybody else, on either side of the family, but I suppose that's not unusual. And it's early days yet.'

Marie gave a sardonic smile. Much as she would have liked to believe that Hannah's baby was anybody's rather that Charles's, she couldn't pin her hopes on Mrs Elsworth's failure to see an obvious likeness to him in a baby of a few days old. By his own admission, Chas's encounters with Hannah had been a lot too regular and a lot too enthusiastic for there to be much chance of her being anyone else's, and those hairgrips had been found in his bed at exactly the right time. If his mother was now trying to make out that baby wasn't his, she was kidding herself, and if she hadn't seriously believed the baby was his, she would never have made that insane offer to bring it up. Maybe she was attempting to back-pedal about that now, Marie guessed. 'Newborns are queer-looking little creatures anyway, I always think,' she said. 'The ones I've seen have never looked like anything but each other.'

Mrs Elsworth bristled slightly. 'Quite,' she said. 'Anyway, we told her Charles will shoulder his responsibilities.'

Charles was shouldering his responsibilities now, then, Marie thought, and wondered whether the offer to bring the baby up had been withdrawn. She didn't like to ask.

Chapter 36

'I shouldn't be in a pub really,' Marie said, as she walked into the Queens Hotel on Charles's arm on the first evening of his leave. 'Nurses have been sacked for less.'

They had come out to set a date for the wedding and make plans for the future, including finding a house – and there were a few other matters to be discussed.

He squeezed her close and dropped a kiss on her forehead. 'You're not in uniform, and it's in your own time. You can do what you like in your own time. It's a free country, or what are we fighting for?'

'It doesn't matter whether I'm in uniform or not. Nurses are not to be seen in pubs, and if Matron hears I've been in one I'll be on the carpet.'

'We're here to talk, somewhere warm and congenial, and out of the way of my parents,' he said. 'It's too dark and too cool to be tramping round the park, and it's probably going to chuck it down with rain. Anyway, you'll be leaving soon, so what does it matter? You'll be married before she can sack you, and after you're married, she'll sack you anyway.'

'You're absolutely right. But I still can't get over it, so let's sit in that far corner, where we won't be noticed.'

He went to the bar and came back with a pint

and a bitter shandy, and sat facing her, hiding her from view with his back to the room. 'Well, I've been to see Hannah,' he said. 'I got that job over with before I came to meet you. I told her I'm glad that her poor bloody husband's come back, and I'm sorry for the trouble I've given him. I gave her a substantial contribution to the baby's upkeep, and I said we'd be getting married before my leave's ended. So that's it.'

'Did she say anything about your mother and dad offering to bring the baby up?'

'She did.'

'What do you think to it?'

'I think it's a terrible idea, but I don't know what would be a good one, under the circumstances. Hannah says her husband's adamant he won't take her back with the baby.'

Marie sipped her shandy in silence, turning that information over in her mind while watching the people huddled in the quiet corner on the opposite side of the pub. They had evidently wanted to escape too much notice as well, since they were doing a brisk trade in black market goods, probably looted from shops whose owners had been unlucky enough to have had windows blown out and walls blasted off during the raids. The landlord and the barmaids were studiously turning blind eyes.

'What do you think to her, then?' she asked. 'The baby, I mean?'

'She's a pretty little thing. It's funny what a difference seeing her makes. Everything's suddenly become hideously real. It really brings it home. What a shitty situation, and there's no way out of it without hurting somebody. I feel sick to my stomach.'

Marie was quiet again for a minute, deep in thought, wondering whether she herself was capable of making the heroic sacrifice it would take for her to bring up Hannah's baby: a baby that his mother was insinuating might not even be Charles's. 'Your mother said she couldn't see any likeness to anybody in your family,' she said.

'Neither can I, but I seem to be the most likely candidate, and although I'm bloody sure there are others I don't know them personally. And the timing's right, so it would be pointless to argue, as well as beneath my dignity. There's a child, somebody's got to feed and clothe her, and it looks as if I've been elected. I'm only sorry it involves you. It makes a dent in your housekeeping money before we're even married.'

'That doesn't worry me unduly,' Marie said drily. 'We've got living on next to nothing off to a fine art in our family, so I'm well equipped for making a little money go a very long way.' She grimaced and, despite his letter, full of solemn promises that he would stick to his marriage vows, she couldn't help adding: 'Just make sure you don't get any more babies where you shouldn't.'

He frowned. 'You do like to rub it in, don't you? I've given you my word I won't.'

'Speak of the devil,' Marie breathed, and pressed hard on his foot, her eyes wide as she glanced meaningfully to where Hannah stood, and then looked back to Charles. 'Don't turn round yet. In fact, don't turn round at all. She's just walked in, and she's got the baby!'

Hannah was not quite her old self she had that bit of extra fat round her middle that Marie had often noticed on women just after they'd given birth. But her hair was carefully arranged, and she was made up. The widow's weeds were gone. She was well dressed, but the baby in her arms was wrapped in a matted, yellowed, old knitted shawl. She approached a quiet couple who were sitting with friends in the centre of the room. 'I've just been round to the local, looking for you,' Marie heard her say. 'Somebody said you'd be here.'

'Yes, better beer,' the man said. 'Better class of customer, as well.'

Hannah put the baby in the woman's arms. 'You have her,' she said. 'I've listened to you harping on about wanting a baby often enough, so now you've got one. I can't keep her. Larry's home and he wants me back, but he won't have her.'

The man gave a sardonic smile, and shook his head. 'He wants you back? He must be puddled. He's swallowed too much seawater; it's affected his brain. But then, it's probably not his brain doing his thinking for him.'

Hannah ignored him, focusing solely on his wife. 'You have her. Here, there's a bag of nappies and things, and there's the bottles and the National Dried. She should make something, she's from clever enough people.' With that, Hannah dumped two carrier bags on the chair beside the woman and walked away.

'Hey, hold on a minute! Haven't you forgotten something?' the man protested, scraping back his chair, and getting to his feet.

Hannah turned to him, but didn't move a step. The bargaining in the opposite corner had ceased, as every eye turned towards the momentous trade being conducted in the middle of the room. Completely unabashed, Hannah continued as if she and the woman she was dealing with were the only people present. 'If you'll have her, I promise I'll never take her away from you, no matter what. She's yours for good.'

The sight took Marie's breath away. She had an impulse to spring to her feet, to drag Chas to Hannah and knock their heads together, and order them to love and to cherish this infant they'd so carelessly brought into the world. Had she been certain that Hannah would make a half-decent mother, had she not had a tiny, niggling doubt planted in her mind about Chas being the father, she might have done it. As it was, she froze.

'Oh, aye, she's ours till you change your mind, knowing you,' the man said.

'She is a beautiful little lass, Bert. She's beautiful,' the woman said, looking intently into the baby's face and holding her tighter. 'I'm for keeping her.'

Hannah went and sat close to her. 'She's good, as well,' she said. 'She never cries, and she's nearly sleeping through the night already. She's no trouble at all.'

Bert looked at the baby, and then his wife, and then at Hannah. His eyes narrowed and his mouth contracted into a hard line. 'If we take her, it's going to be done legal. You sign her over to us. I'm not having you coming round to stake any claims, once she's settled with Molly.'

Hannah's face was unreadable. 'I won't,' she said. 'I'll be with Larry. I'm giving her up for good. Just look after her, that's all.'

Marie jumped up and swept past them all, out of the Queen's Hotel and into the dark, wet October evening. She unfurled her umbrella with its flapping spoke and sped across the road and down Princes Avenue, feeling as if she'd swallowed a brick. A baby – she'd just witnessed a baby being given away with about as much ceremony as if she'd been a stray animal, or one of those black market tins of corned beef or packets of cigarettes the corner party had been selling.

'Marie! Marie!' Chas was running after her. He caught her elbow.

'That's the most awful thing I've ever seen in my life,' she gasped. 'She gave her own baby away, and she acted as if it was nothing!'

'What can you expect?' he demanded. 'A woman like that, who'll betray her husband and let other men do anything they like with her. If she'll do that, well, what won't she do?'

'A woman like that?' she echoed, breaking free from him and walking rapidly away. 'What about a man like that,' she called over her shoulder. 'What about a man who'll romp around with somebody else's wife until he gets her pregnant, and then sit and watch their baby being given away in a public house!'

'What could I do?' he asked, catching up with her. 'What could I do to stop it? I've no say in it. Should I have jumped up and said: "She's mine! Give her to me!" What would you have felt about that? Would you have wanted her in the middle of our marriage?'

A surge of anger made Marie irrational. 'I'd have wanted it never to have happened! I'd have wanted you not to meddle with anybody else's bloody stocking tops, and promised lands!'

'You're just being childish! It's too late for that. It all started before we even started courting!'

'Then it should have stopped.'

'You know what I sometimes think?' he exploded. 'You don't want a flesh-and-blood man at all. You want a bloody eunuch!'

She ran until she could run no longer, then slowed to a walk to get her breath back. Chas had stopped following her by then. She walked on, thinking about what he'd said, and wondered – could she? Could she have brought that baby up, a baby whose mother she so heartily detested? She doubted it very much, and she tormented herself with that thought until she got back to Aunt Edie's and fell, weeping, into George's arms.

Chapter 37

'Leave him, then,' George said, when she'd spilled it all out to him and the storm had passed. 'Leave him to look after his own illegitimate children. Why should you have to be bothered with it?'

She drank the remains of the watery cocoa he'd made for her. 'I'm on an early tomorrow,' she said, picking up both empty beakers. 'I'll just rinse these, and then I'll have to get some sleep, or I'll be fit for nothing.'

'No, think about it, Marie,' he said. 'When this war's over, there'll be plenty of work in reconstruction. I'm a civil engineer, there'll be openings for me everywhere, at decent pay. We could travel England, the world even, me taking work on contract, save up, and then go to America, maybe settle there, where they're more interested in what a chap can do than in his accent, or whether he went to a bloody council school.'

'You'd leave England?' she said.

'Not half,' he assured her. 'New start, new system. America's the best.'

'I never knew you felt like that.'

'No. There's a lot people don't know about me. Anyway, think about it. We could get married, and travel the world.'

'You couldn't leave your mother.'

'Think about it,' he said, ignoring her last comment.

She went to wash the beakers, thinking about it. Perhaps George had forgotten his mother's existence in his flights of fancy, or envisaged taking her along with him. Or putting her in cold storage somewhere until his return.

The kitchen door opened. 'Marie,' George said. 'It's Chas. He's at the door.'

'Tell him I've gone to bed,' she said.

'He'll know you haven't. He saw me come through to the kitchen.'

'Never mind. Just tell him.'

George was back in the kitchen within a minute, carrying a huge tin of jam.

'He's gone. He left you this. He says he'll see

you after work tomorrow.'

Marie shook her head. After everything that had happened who but Chas would have thought of going back into the Queen's for a tin of black market jam? The answer came to her almost at once. Alfie. Another one with a strong practical streak in his make-up – Alfie might have done something like that, she thought, and it suddenly struck her how alike they were, at bottom.

George was looking expectantly at her, still holding the jam.

'You have it, George,' she said.

'Well,' he said, eyeing the tin with evident long-ing, 'it'll liven the rations up, won't it? I won't say no to a scrape of it, now and then.'

'Open it now, if you like,' she said. 'I'm going to bed. I feel drained, as if somebody's pulled the plug, and all my energy's gone down the sink hole.'

'Think about what I've said, Marie,' George repeated, already rummaging in a drawer for the tin-opener. He stopped, and turned to her, quite serious. 'About us getting married, I mean.'

'All right, George,' she said, too sickened by the sins and sorrows of the world to be capable of adding to them by turning him down just at that moment. And her mother's dying wish had been that she should marry George. So what was to stop her? He was kind, capable, hard-working, and good-looking, in his quiet way. He'd never had any entanglements with any married women, and he had no children to complicate matters. They had similar backgrounds, and to any im-partial observer it would look like a perfect

393

match. It might even *be* a perfect match.

She went to bed, and awoke the following morning reliving her parting from Chas at Hull station, when she'd watched him go, certain that they'd marry, and visualizing herself presenting him with his firstborn child. But his firstborn child had gone astray, and was not hers.

Chapter 38

Charles was waiting for her outside Endike Lane Council School at the end of her shift at the dressing station there, wearing his army uniform, and on foot.

'I say, I'd have liked it better if you'd come to the door yourself yesterday, instead of sending that twerp George to lie to me about your being in bed,' he said.

'Oh, well,' she shrugged.

Seeing that no apology was forthcoming he said, 'Come on. I'll walk you back to your aunt Edie's, and as soon as you're out of your uniform, I'll take you into Hull for your wedding outfit. We should just catch the shops before they close.'

'You can't do that, Chas. It's bad luck for you to see it before the day.'

'I'll give you the money, and you can get Nancy to help you choose it, then.'

'You're so sensitive, Chas. Asking Nancy to help choose a wedding outfit might not be the most tactful thing to do, at the moment.'

'Oh, well. Somebody else, then.'

They walked on in silence until they got to the crossroads.

'Did you tell your mother her granddaughter was auctioned off, with the tins of jam?' she asked, as they turned down Cranbrook Avenue.

'I did not. I didn't tell her anything about it. I gave Hannah a pile of money for her upkeep, though, and I didn't see her pass it on to the couple who took her.'

'Bert and Molly, do you mean?'

'All right, Bert and Molly. I think they've a better right to it than Hannah. I've a good mind to go and demand it back.'

'Well, why not? You can probably take it in kind, if she's already spent it.'

She'd hit a nerve. Charles stopped, grasped her shoulders, and shook her. 'You talk about being sensitive. I can't listen to any more of this. I'm beginning to think you enjoy sticking the knife in. You're driving me mad!' He walked swiftly away from her, then started to run, without a backward glance, his army boots clattering on the pavement.

She smiled as she watched him go, not the least bit sorry. Charles Elsworth had done wrong, and he deserved to feel it. She walked alone to the end of the avenue, then along Cottingham Road. When she turned down Newland Avenue Charles was out of sight, not waiting for her, as she had anticipated. She felt a twinge of apprehension, and speedily dismissed it. Surely he wouldn't let one caustic little comment drive him off for good. He'd loved her too much and too long for that. But the twinge became an ache, as the stark fact that no other man would do for her struck Marie with the blinding light of revelation.

At the end of Newland Avenue, rather than turn down Princes Avenue she walked along Queens Road. Then, regardless of rules and uniform, she boldly entered the forbidden portals of the Queens Hotel and asked a woman who was doing some cleaning to fetch the landlord.

'That couple who took that baby the other night,' she said. 'Bert and Molly. Do you know where they live?'

He gave her short shrift. 'No. And I wouldn't tell you, even if I did.'

The woman who was doing the cleaning followed Marie to the door. 'I know a Bert and Molly,' she said. 'They live on Park Grove, opposite the entrance to Pearson Park.'

'Did George tell you? He brought Eva here for her tea while you were out at Charles Elsworth's yesterday,' Aunt Edie said, when Marie got back.

Marie's eyes widened in surprise, and her eyebrows lifted slightly. 'No, he never said a word, and we were talking for a long time.'

Aunt Edie gave her a very knowing look. 'I know. I heard you come in. They're getting on like a house on fire, him and Eva. In fact, we both like her.'

Marie's eyebrows lifted further. 'What's she like?'

'A bit taller than you. Brown hair, brown eyes, rosy cheeks. She looks real healthy, but then she would. She comes from a farming family in Holderness; they don't go short of much.'

'No, I don't suppose they do,' Marie said, remembering the milky coffee and buttered scones in Bourne.

'Me and your mam, we'd have liked to see you and George make a go of it at one time. But I don't think that's on the cards, is it?'

Aunt Edie seemed to be determined to get all those cards on the table. Marie took a deep breath, and chose her words carefully. 'George has been a good friend to me, Aunt Edie, and I love him for it – as a friend. As a brother, even.'

'You're too hooked up with that Charles Elsworth–' Aunt Edie spat his name – 'even after everything he's done.'

Marie didn't dispute it.

Aunt Edie fixed her large blue eyes on Marie's face. 'Well, George needs a woman who's all for him. He's just about got over that Nancy,' she stressed, 'but Eva's a different kettle of fish altogether. A straightforward, honest young lass. If you see them together, you can tell she thinks the world of him. He's lucky to have found her. I think she'll make him a good wife. In fact, I'm sure she will. And I'm sorry to say this, thinking about your mam, but he doesn't want to be kept dangling by somebody who doesn't know whether she wants him or not.'

Those big, supposedly half-blind eyes saw plenty, and Aunt Edie was warning her off. She wasn't having anybody mucking her boy around again, and she couldn't be blamed for that. Marie wondered if she'd got wind of George's yearning to emigrate, but to hear that conversation she would have had to get out of bed and creep halfway down the stairs. Marie wouldn't have put it past her. Her lips twitched into a tiny smile at the thought. And a girl from a farming family might be the very thing to keep her George near his mammy – especially if she had no brothers.

So, whether Chas came back or not, Aunt Edie was telling her she'd better pass up her chance of travelling the world as the wife of a civil engineer. It was a pity, in some ways, but she was right. Maybe it was to do with being an only child, with a father who'd died when he was young and a mother who had no other interest in life but him, but George seemed to have been born old. He fitted with his parents' generation better than with his own, and they'd been creeping into middle age when they'd had him. As his mother was so fond of saying, George was a good lad, but Marie lacked that feeling for him that a woman ought to have for the man she marries. There was no spark there. None at all.

'Don't worry, Aunt Edie. Everything will work out for the best,' she said, certain of the truth of her words in their case, and trusting to fate in her own.

Marie and George strolled together in the park after tea, reminiscing about their childhoods, the kindness between their two families, and the feeling, at that time, of total security in their peaceful little homes. George would always be a part of her happiest memories of childhood, Marie thought, more precious to her now than ever.

'I sometimes think,' she said, 'that they must have had a struggle to survive at times, but we knew nothing about it. At least, I didn't. All I saw was that they were always busy, busy, busy, always doing, never idle, making the most of everything. But I never felt any of the strain.'

'That's the thing that sticks in my mind,' George said, 'how peaceful it was, and how safe I always felt before my dad died. That's what shattered it for me. That's when I realized what a cold, hard place the world can be.'

'It shattered the whist playing as well,' Marie said, 'You remember them trying to teach us, months later? But neither of us was much good at it, and they went on to play brag after that. Your mother was dead keen, I remember that. Her eyesight must have been a lot better then than it is now.'

George gave a sceptical little laugh. 'My mother's eyesight seems to come and go, a bit. There was nothing wrong with it before my dad died. I sometimes think it's a way of clinging on to me, or maybe making me feel indispensable. She'll survive, if we go on our travels.'

There was an expectant silence, as George waited for her answer.

'I don't know how it'll work out between me and Charles,' she said hesitantly. 'I only know I can't marry anybody else.'

He paused for a moment, then sighed. 'Well, I can't say I'm not disappointed, but you've never been dishonest. And I'd no real hopes that you would marry me. I've always known you were too gone on him. But bloody good luck to you; I hope you'll be all right. And Eva's the best consolation prize going. We'll be all right together.'

'I've no doubt she'll have a better dowry than mine. All I've got to offer is a set of garden tools, and the cobbler's last you rescued from the ruins.' She grinned, as a thought hit her. 'Eva might giveth what Nancy tooketh away,' she said.

He lifted his chin, and grinned back. 'Well, there is that,' he nodded.

Terry arrived an hour or so after they got back to the house, to take her dancing. For a split second Marie hesitated, toying with the thought of going, and then decided not to risk it. If Charles arrived while she was gone, it might be the final straw. Taking a leap of faith, she said: 'I'm expecting Charles any minute. We're getting married next week, by special licence.'

Terry put on a face of mock devastation. 'Oh, no, you can't be! Not when I've been pulling all the stops out to get you into my clutches all the time he's been away.'

''Fraid so.'

'You're throwing yourself away! I'm the one you should be marrying! Black armbands on for me, then,' he grimaced.

She laughed as she closed the door on him, thinking what easy company he was, never too many demands, never any awkwardness. But the black armbands summed Terry up for her. She could never see him or think of him without thinking of Margaret, and Margaret's death.

She returned to the front room to listen to the radio with George and Auntie Edie, their companionable silence interspersed with laughter at the jokes. After half an hour she started surreptitiously twitching the curtains, looking for Charles. The street was empty. She went to get her coat.

'I'm just going for a quick walk. I won't be more than half an hour,' she said.

She walked to the end of the street, and crossed Princes Avenue to Park Grove. At the entrance to the park she stood and looked at a well-kept house. She was tempted to knock on the door, but there was no excuse she could have given. She walked away, hoping to bump into Charles on her way back to Aunt Edie's. There was neither sight nor sound of him, and no mention of his calling when she got back to Clumber Street. Marie couldn't bring herself to ask whether he'd been. Aunt Edie would have told her if he had, since she no longer had a motive for keeping it from her.

Chapter 39

There was no Charles waiting for her when she finished work on Sunday, either. She felt an awful pang, but pride forbade her to go to Park Avenue to find out what was happening. Charles had run off, and Charles would have to come back, with no prompting from her. She lifted her chin, stiffened her back, and walked swiftly down to Clumber Street, stubbornly fighting back the tears that were pricking her eyes.

Alfie was waiting for her with a few chrysanthemums he'd brought for them to take to the graves, and the usual half a dozen eggs for Aunt Edie. Marie hugged him with the pent-up fervour she would have loosed on Charles, had he come to meet her.

Alfie's eyes widened at this effusive display of affection. 'You all right, Marie?'

''Course I'm all right,' she said. 'Why shouldn't I be all right?'

'I don't know. You just seem a bit ... keyed up, somehow. I don't know.'

'I'm all right,' she repeated. 'I'll just get changed, and then we'll be off.'

The day was bright but cold, and she was glad of her slacks, thick jumper and jacket on the bike ride up to the cemetery. After laying the flowers on their parents' grave, they went to Jenny's.

'They've got her a nice headstone,' Alfie commented as he reverently laid his flowers on her little grave.

Marie read the inscription: 'Beloved daughter of Hannah and Lawrence Reynolds'. 'Hmm,' she said. Maybe that was true in Larry's case, but she doubted it very much in Hannah's. Divorce could never be an option for Marie, but she wouldn't have blamed Larry for ending his marriage to Hannah. She didn't deserve him.

'We ought to get a headstone for our mam and dad.'

'Well, we will, as soon as we've got some money,' Marie promised.

'It's getting real cold. It's Hull Fair weather,' Alfie said, when they left their bikes in the yard at

Aunt Edie's, and went into the house. 'I used to love going after dark, with everything lit up.'

'Well, Hitler's put paid to that. He's put paid to a lot of things,' she said, 'including our family.'

She rode with him half the way to Dunswell, then turned back to Aunt Edie's, hoping to see Charles on the way, but there was no sign of him. It was beginning to get dark, and the last thing she wanted was to go back to Clumber Street, to sit in the house with George and Aunt Edie listening to the wireless with minutes dragging by as if they were hours, while she waited for a knock on the door that never came.

Instead, she turned into Pearson Park. Quite a few people were out, making the most of the fresh air and what remained of the daylight. The grass and roads were strewn with leaves of red, gold and brown, and the bare branches looked like filigree against the sky. The park was lovely, peaceful and still, but it couldn't calm the fret arising deep within her. She rode through the whole of it, and then saw a woman pushing a spanking new pram, looking at her and walking in her direction, as if to speak to her. But Marie was mistaken. As she got nearer the woman showed no sign of recognition, and walked past. Marie turned the bike and dismounted beside her.

'Can I have a look?' she asked, looking straight into Molly's eyes.

There was still no sign of recognition. Molly beamed at her, and stopped the pram. The white, beribboned bonnet just visible above the muffling blankets would have given the baby's sex away, if

403

Marie hadn't already known it.

'What's her name?' she asked.

'Lucy.'

'A lovely name for a lovely baby. I like her bonnet. Who did the knitting?'

'Me,' Molly laughed. 'I've got piles of it. She'll probably have grown out of most of it before she even has it on.'

'Lucky girl. I can see you're going to spoil her.' Marie looked intently at the child's face. The curve of the lips reminded her of Hannah, but that was all.

'You can't spoil babies,' Molly said. 'The more you love them, the better they are.'

'You're out a bit late with her.'

'It gets her to sleep. Coming for a walk gets her to sleep better than anything.'

Marie pulled two half-crowns out of her pocket and put them in the pram. 'For Lucy's money box.'

Molly's eyebrows shot up. 'I can't take that. It's half a week's rent, for some people.'

Again, Marie looked her straight in the eyes. 'You can't refuse it. It's bad luck.'

Odd, after that awful scene in the Queens, that Molly had failed to recognize her. But she'd had eyes only for Lucy, then as now.

Perhaps Charles had been right when he'd said the child might not be his, Marie thought, as she cycled back to Aunt Edie's. Whatever the truth was, she was relieved the little girl was well cared for and, to her shame, very, very glad that she was not with the Elsworths. Even so, she couldn't shake off the feeling that there was something not quite right about a child's not knowing her own parents, or even her own grandparents. Not only not quite right, but altogether wrong. Still, this imperfect arrangement was undoubtedly the best thing that could have happened to Lucy, things being what they were. And if she was honest, it was certainly the best thing that could have happened to Marie and Chas – if there was going to be any Marie and Chas. Serious doubts that there would ever be a wedding began to gnaw at her, and when she got back to Aunt Edie's she couldn't resist asking: 'Has Charles been?'

Chapter 40

Marie couldn't sit still. The moon was three-quarter's full, easily enough light to see by, so she left the bike and walked across to Duesbury Street. A very dishevelled Nancy answered the door, obviously the worse for drink.

Marie followed her into the house. 'Have you been at the home-made wine, Nance?' she asked, although the question was unnecessary. She could smell it on her breath.

'Well, if I have, it's nobody's business but mine,' Nancy said.

'All right, then. Keep your hair on. Is your mam in?'

'No, she's not. What's up? I didn't expect to see you on a Sunday night. I'd have thought you'd be out with Chas, or one of your other blokes –

George, or Terry.'

Marie would have loved to unburden herself, but Nancy's antagonism put her off. 'Well, I'm not,' she said. 'I'm here. I thought I'd have an hour with you.'

Nancy flopped down onto the settee. 'Huh! He's let you down, then, has he, your Chas? Do you want a drink?'

Marie shook her head.

Nancy took another gulp from her glass. 'All the more for them that do, then.'

'You should lay off that stuff, Nance. It never makes anything any better.'

Nancy ignored the comment. 'Yes, you've fallen out with Chas, so you've remembered I exist. Well, you've done right. Come and tell your old pal Nancy what a swine he is. They're all swine. The lot of them. I hate them all.'

She was obviously looking forward to a maudlin session of self-pity and blaming everyone else for their troubles, but Marie had no sympathy. Nancy was getting a dose of her own medicine, but she was so blind to her own faults that she couldn't see the justice of it. Marie listened to her with scorn, wondering that such a blind, selfish, self-pitying creature could ever have attracted anybody. She'd never had any patience with drunks, wallowing in their misfortunes and slobbering over people, and she had none with Nancy. It disgusted her, but she bit her tongue and heard her out.

'...and now I'm going to be lumbered with his bloody kid!' Nancy finished.

At that attitude towards the unborn baby, Marie

saw red. Red danced and swam before her eyes. 'You know what, Nance?' she said. 'You've caused a packet of trouble for people who thought the world of you. You ditched a good lad without a second thought and gave a con man all his savings because he kidded you he was going to get you on the silver screen. You asked for it, Nance, but George didn't, or your mother either. Your mother's said she'll help you. Many a mother would have chucked you out.' Marie looked pointedly at Nancy's swelling abdomen. 'And in case you've forgotten, that bloody kid's yours, as well as his, so if you don't want to be lumbered do it a big favour, Nance. Once it's born, get it on the bottle as fast as you can and then nip up to the Queens Hotel and give it away to the first couple you see.'

It took Nancy a minute to absorb Marie's unexpectedly brutal home truths, but when she did, her face turned to whey. 'You're a cold fish, Marie,' she gasped. 'You've never let your heart rule your head yet.'

Marie gave her a penetrating look. 'Was it your heart that ruled you, Nance? Really? Or was it your vanity? And maybe your greed? You mistook a plausible con man for somebody who could make you rich and famous, so you chucked George and crushed his hopes of a bright future with you in his little dream bungalow – without even a goodbye. You left him to trudge round the mortuaries, looking for your corpse. Not much heart in that, was there?'

Nancy rallied enough to hit back. 'I'm sorry. I'm sorry I wasn't dead. It sounds as if you and

George would be happier if I had been.'

'There's no heart in that lie, either. Or in the way you're talking about your baby. That's going to get a warm and loving welcome into the world, I don't think. You could do with letting your heart rule you there, but I doubt if you will. So seriously, why not do the same as I watched Hannah do, and give it away? Then you'll be rid of your lumber, and free to go on your merry way.'

'You say some nasty things sometimes, Marie. Really nasty.'

'I know,' she said. 'I can't keep my mouth shut, at times. It does me no good at all, but I can't seem to help it.'

You managed that well, Marie, she thought, on the short walk back. Margaret dead, her friendship with Nancy probably destroyed for ever, George and Terry signed off for good, and Chas driven out of her life. She might even lose her job, if Matron heard about her expedition to the Queens Hotel. The last remaining props of her existence, bar Alfie, and she'd kicked them all away. Deep down, none of it really mattered, except Chas.

And out of those two babies, Hannah's might have the best chance, all told. She was out of the hellhole altogether, with somebody who had a heart and plenty of love to give. Funny, Marie couldn't bear to call her Chas's baby, even in her thoughts, but although she tried to shield herself from it and in spite of all the nonsense about who she didn't resemble that was exactly what she was – Chas's firstborn child. 'So face it,' she said out loud.

George guessed where she'd been. 'How is she, then?' he asked, when she got back.

'Feeling very sorry for herself.'

Marie saw by the look on George and Aunt Edie's faces that Charles still hadn't been for her. Aunt Edie would certainly have sent him round to Nancy's, if he had. Neither commented.

She went to bed. Instead of fretting herself into her grave she would blank her mind and blot the whole world out, at least until the morning.

Chapter 41

When morning came, she was up and dressed early, on the horns of an agonizing dilemma: whether to swallow her pride and go to Park Street to see Chas, or whether to stick it out and wait until he came to her, and risk losing him altogether. She lit the gas ring and put the kettle on, and then turned it off again. She hadn't the patience to wait for it to boil. She would go.

She ran upstairs for her jacket, and as she descended she heard a familiar knock. Through the stained-glass leaded light in the door she could see a distorted but recognizable shape. Charles Elsworth. She checked her hurry, and sauntered along the passageway to open it.

'Hello, stranger.'

'Stranger nothing. It's your day off, isn't it?'

She nodded.

'Come on, then. Time for us to go and get your

wedding clothes,' Chas said.

Tingles raced up Marie's spine. The sky took on a more vivid blue, and the colours of the houses opposite were suddenly brighter. She took care not to smile too broadly.

'What wedding clothes?'

'*Your* wedding clothes. You're going to marry me before my leave ends, and get the best, most faithful and devoted husband who ever lived.' His wide hazel eyes searched hers. 'What do you say?'

'I can't.'

'Why not?' he demanded. 'Come on, Marie, have a heart. I'm a reformed character. I mended my ways completely on the day we got engaged.'

'I mean...' she said, dragging out the suspense, 'I can't go with you to get wedding clothes. It would be bad luck for you to see them.'

He laughed, and relaxed. 'I won't have to see them. Just take plenty of clothes into the changing rooms, and I won't know which you've chosen. They can put them in a bag for you. All I'll have to do is hand the money over.'

'All right, then,' she said, and then heaved a heavy sigh. 'Oh, Thornton-Varley's! All the beautiful clothes they sold, everything of the best. Why did they have to go and get flattened?'

His shrugged. 'Search me, but there must be somewhere still standing. What does it matter, anyway? I'd marry you with dirty feet, in your gardening gear.'

'I wouldn't, though,' she said, and might have added that she would settle for nothing less than the sheerest nylons held up by the very laciest suspenders. She'd soon show him what stocking tops were all about, she thought, and her stomach was suddenly full of nervous flutterings.

'You won't have enough coupons to get a boat-load of stuff. Clothes this morning, and married this afternoon,' he said. 'It's all arranged. My parents and the people at Dunswell are going to be our witnesses.'

She ran upstairs to get her coupons, and left the bedroom with the thought that she would never spend another night under Aunt Edie's safe and kindly roof. George was just coming out of his room, ready for work.

'I'll be married by the time you see me again, George,' she told him.

'Good heavens! That's sudden,' he said as she dashed down the stairs. She heard his 'Good luck!' as she shot through the door.

She stopped, after closing it. 'If we go now, we'll be over an hour too early for the shops!'

'We could misuse half a gallon of petrol to go out for a drive, and consummate the marriage,' he said.

'Get lost. We'll go and have a cup of tea in the British Restaurant,' she said.

'It's not as good as my suggestion.'

'It's the only one on offer,' she assured him. She'd held out this far, and she could hold out a bit longer. Their wedding night was going to be a proper wedding night, something Charles Elsworth would remember to his dying day.

There was no music, no choir, and the flowers in the church were what were left after yesterday's Mass. The bride carried a small bouquet and wore a simple blue costume, which brought out the startling blue of her eyes, and which she intended to wear for years afterwards, or until she got too fat from having too many babies. The brief ceremony was performed by the priest of St Vincent's before Uncle Alf and Auntie Dot, Leonard, and Marjorie, who had broken her vow never to set foot in a Catholic Church just for this occasion. The pestilential younger brothers of both bride and groom were also present, and behaving themselves pretty well, for younger brothers.

They walked the short distance back to Park Street after the wedding, and opened the door to the aroma of two roast chickens sizzling in the Rayburn, courtesy of Uncle Alf, who had wrung their necks that morning – rather reluctantly, as they had been good layers. The substantial dinner was followed by an unusual wedding cake, hastily made from eggs from the smallholding at Dunswell, the last of Marjorie and Dot's sugar and cocoa hoards, and butter traded for Dot's eggs.

While the older women were doing the washing up and the men were arguing about the progress of the war, Marie and Alfie sneaked out of the house together and walked to Northern Cemetery. Marie pulled three flowers from her bouquet, and then laid it on her parents' grave. 'Don't worry about me and Chas, Mam,' the young Mrs Elsworth prayed. 'I can manage him all right. And I'll see Alfie all right, and our Pam, if needs be.'

'Don't worry about me, either,' Alfie said. 'I'm all right with Auntie Dot and Uncle Alf.'

Alfie laid the other three flowers on Jenny's grave and then, leaving the dead to the peaceful twilight, they walked out of the cemetery, hand in hand.

As soon as Uncle Alf and Auntie Dot had left with Alfie, and the three superfluous Elsworths had gone for the bus to Hedon to spend the night there, Marie and Chas took up where they'd left off before that devastating air raid, with the addition, this time, of silk underwear, lacy suspenders and sheer nylon stockings. When he had manfully transformed her into Mrs Elsworth in fact as well as in name, Marie laughed up at him, her triumph complete.

'I never thought we'd get together again,' she said. 'You never came to see me for two full days. I thought you'd gone for good.'

'Don't think I didn't try to be gone for good, either,' he grinned. 'But seeing it was hopeless I just had to bind my wounds, ready for the next battle.'

'Does it have to be a battle?'

'Only as long as you make it one.'

'Truce, then?'

He wavered, and gave her a suspicious look out of the corner of his eye, his brows drawn together and lips compressed and turned up in a half-smile. 'How long will it last?' he demanded.

'For the rest of our lives, I hope. Unless you–'

He pressed his forefinger against her lips. 'If you're going to say what I think you're going to say – unless nothing!'

She looked at him and laughed.

'You bloody were, weren't you?'

'My lips are sealed,' she said.

413

The publishers hope that this book has given you enjoyable reading. Large Print Books are especially designed to be as easy to see and hold as possible. If you wish a complete list of our books please ask at your local library or write directly to:

Magna Large Print Books
Magna House, Long Preston,
Skipton, North Yorkshire.
BD23 4ND

This Large Print Book for the partially sighted, who cannot read normal print, is published under the auspices of

THE ULVERSCROFT FOUNDATION